MUSIC AND SILENCE

Also by Anne Redmon

EMILY STONE

MUSIC AND SILENCE

A novel by

ANNE REDMON

HOLT, RINEHART AND WINSTON   NEW YORK

Published by Holt, Rinehart and Winston, 383 Madison Avenue,
New York, New York 10017.

First published in England in 1979 by
Martin Secker & Warburg Limited.

Library of Congress Cataloging in Publication Data
Redmon, Anne.
Music and silence.
I. Title.
PZ4.R319Mu [PS3568.E362] 813'.5'4 78-14172
ISBN 0-03-047176-1

First U.S. Edition

DESIGNER: Joy Chu

Printed in the United States of America
1 3 5 7 9 10 8 6 4 2

Grateful acknowledgment is made for the use of the following:
Ezra Pound, Personae. Copyright 1926 by Ezra Pound.
Reprinted by permission of New Directions.

The author would like to thank Amanda Medina-Breden
for help with the technicalities of the cello.

To Benedict,
Christopher,
and J.A.C.

MUSIC AND SILENCE

CHAPTER I

The houses around Theodoric Square were built, originally, for gentle people. Who but the gently bred could have withstood their high gloom, their porticoes sustained by Doric columns? The cold, steep hall stairs could have been managed only by strapping maids, who would have answered bells from distant drawing rooms, pulled by ladies, ladies not precisely exalted, but well-enough-off to cultivate a lack of energy; to assume an air of mandarin unconcern in the eyes of the world.

How could even they have supported such vastness? How, even then, in the days of the dear, dead queen, when the houses came into being? How did—even ladies—endure the idleness identity offered them, enforced upon them in dark, draughty, varnished, high-ceilinged rooms? It could be said that they caught a vision of the river, which completes the fourth side of the square, and liked it; allowed the lapping of it and its rising fog; were faintly stirred, perhaps perturbed by the deep notes from barges which slipped hidden under Vauxhall Bridge, down past Westminster and the Tower, into the wider reaches (not visited by ladies, except, of course, in charity) of Bermondsey, the Isle of Dogs, Essex, and the sea.

It is more probable, however, that ladies, and their husbands too, were fortified more solidly by an ambition that Theodoric Square, being in Victoria and not so very far from the Palace, would in time assert itself as a new Belgravia. If sacrifice of comfort were to be made; if cosiness were to be forgone, then wasn't it in the hope of exaltation to come? It must have been.

As it happened, upper-middle-class society had expected in vain. The houses, which are ranged round a garden once only accessible by private key, a garden once exclusive to residents of the square, were broken up into flats years ago. Now, in the autumn of 1968, the nannies feel the existing park doesn't count so much as it did. A few of them still huddle under dripping trees, but their charges are no longer scions of families with aspirations to social success; they are children of divorced women, career women, or of rich, itinerant foreigners. Not many families live in the square now. A great number of single people occupy the flats. They tend to work at unconventional hours, although by no means all of them do. They are, as a rule, too well paid to be overtly sordid, but a few elderly ladies, who have stuck it out in the square, who would like to maintain its original ethos, even on eked-out trust funds, think the whole moral tone of the place has declined. They suspect licence behind their neighbours' doors, but cannot prove it. The square has a raffish handsomeness which evokes tolerance for other people's habits . . . a tolerance which does depend on leaving alone, on being left alone.

Dr Pazzi was particularly fond of late autumn. She was not one to glut herself on nostalgia or on anything else for that matter, but the season, with its high sky and wetly falling leaves, never failed to attack her with sweet pain. Generally, she found counterattack—even solace—in having a good deal to do, but on this particular October day as she walked with shopping trolley and little purchases along the north side of the square, she permitted beauty to have its way with her. Her somewhat angular walk slowed into a stroll. A leaf or two rose and sailed— her eyes sailed too with leaves and beyond to the logical architecture of the square where she had elected to live out a life of solitude. Dr Pazzi was in the habit of giving thanks for what befell her, for what she liked and for what she didn't like. She gave thanks for having found the square, the fifth-floor flat, even the climb she had to make in order to achieve it.

It was nice to have moved near the river; nicer still to get away from Mama—no, here she checked herself . . . it was nicer still to see Mama comfortably settled back in Rome with Tatty and Giuseppe and the children. Mama had never liked nor understood the English, and although her money had enabled her to be quite as Italian as she'd liked in Eaton Square, the whole attendant light and atmosphere, the perfume from the Spanish steps at dusk, the cruising priests, the reverence for old age and motherhood were not to be bought in London like a pound of Parma ham.

Beatrice was forty now and alone, at last. No more luxuries, no more bills. No more Eaton Square. No more drinks with aristocratic neighbours. Letters from Mama extolled a new-found bliss in Rome.

Beatrice was careful of commandments and felt it risked a lot to call them burdens. Still, it was relief to find honourable release from the one about mother and father.

Her life in Theodoric Square was simple to the point of being stark: it seemed to carry with it omens of the profound. Today there was this charismatic autumn wind; then there was the peace of earthenware after so much porcelain; white paint and hours spent in meditation; then, like a sign, there was the cello.

Dr Pazzi had found herself, quite unwittingly, above a gold mine—how else could she describe it? Her flat was directly above the flat of a musician. At first she'd thought the music came from a gramophone and had tried not to feel sticky about people who played gramophones loud and late; besides, she had chosen comparative poverty as a context for her solitude, but quite early on, it became clear to her that the music was live and for some reason this made all the difference. *Eccola!* The Lord provides. And He had provided no second-hand Bach, nothing one could take home in a plastic bag and whirl round on a machine, but a working out of Bach late, late into the night. Beatrice would lie on her white, clean bed, her eyes half-closed and follow the cellist's train of thought—the music's train of thought. She liked the stops and starts of it, the practising of it, even more than the entire work which now and then the cellist put together.

She was more than intrigued by the sound. It was a deep, beautiful, liberating sound.

She turned her mind to the cellist now, precisely because several weeks had gone by without a sound from her. At first,

Beatrice thought she'd gone away on tour, perhaps; she was good enough. Beatrice wondered if she'd heard her give a recital some time ago at the Wigmore Hall, but then decided she hadn't. Other noises, however, had come from the flat which were not consistent with the idea of the young woman's being away. Now and then she heard a stifled cry, and once the slamming of a door which frightened her. Last night, she had been tempted to go down to see if anything was the matter; she'd woken to the sound of shattering glass.

Should she have gone down last night to see what was the matter? One could not exclude a motive of idle curiosity or some lack of respect for the woman's privacy. Beatrice had become furiously English in order to counteract the floridity of her background. It was for that very reason she had said a prayer and left it. Her interest in the cellist and her music was extreme; she felt engagement in the work—hints in it—an effort in it beyond normal effort to . . . she reached for her key.

Beatrice had barely seen the young woman herself. On the stair and in the hall what had she seen? Her name was Miss Eustace—maybe Mrs; she felt Miss. Miss Eustace, at any rate, had quickness and fluidity of movement. Her hair was long and trailing, her clothes, which seemed to partake of the hair, took on where the hair left off and flowed to the ground. Her appearance was not consonant with the sound she made. Beatrice hoped she wasn't a hippy. The casualty ward was spilling over with these: they filled her with pity and revulsion. What they had made of opiates she used for the relief of pain!

Miss Eustace looked almost young enough to be one, but there was something too unusual about the face to suggest quite that. She'd hardly seen the face anyway. The hall was much too dark. She wished she had gone down after all; it teased her conscience that she hadn't. Of course there was always the possible accusation that Beatrice might want to be getting to know her. Beatrice felt that artists didn't like that; that they were accustomed to—well—flatterers, and despised them.

She threw up her hand, then, with the key, entered. Beatrice had become with age a little precise. Her gloves and shoes were neat. She wore a soft tweed coat which hung from her shoulders like a bell. It suited her extremely well. She took a scrupulous care of little things. She stood in the vestibule and brushed imaginary specks from her tweed sleeve, returned the key to the special compartment in her purse, then propped the bun on the back of her neck into shape. Her hair was still deep black and her face, a perfect oval, held a shape of youth and even beauty; but her toilette consisted of getting things straight rather than enhancing natural charm. She'd stifled vanity long, long ago— no, pressed it. She'd pressed and pressed her body into service until it really did—hardly did—no longer hurt.

The stairs she had to trudge were long and very steep. The hall, for all the flats that had been made around it, excluded light entirely; it was absolutely dark. The system of lighting was primitive: it was necessary to press a large button on the wall which lit the stairwell up to about the fourth landing where it would snap out and leave the climber to feel the rest of the way in the dark. Beatrice often did not bother with the button. To go in the dark seemed a relief from Eaton Square where everything was lifts and electric candelabra and a doomy, liveried porter who drank. Nevertheless, whether she pressed the light or not, she ascended quickly. There was always a grope at the top. She wondered how Miss Eustace was today. She really did.

By the time Beatrice reached the third landing, she was a little out of breath. This was no real comment on her fitness; she lived an abstemious and energetic life. If she was not one to admit or allow emotion, she was one to let an involved kind of thought get her down. Anxiety? Pain? Bewilderment maybe, at where she was and what she ought and ought not to do in-formed her body so that its nerves and muscles resisted effort. It was hardly surprising, then, preoccupied as she was, as wrapped in the dark of the hall as she was, that she didn't hear the noise until she was well on the way to the fourth landing where Miss Eustace lived. The scream seemed so much an expression of where her own mind was tending that it appeared to be inly heard.

There was another scream of female rage and fear; the hoarse sound of a male voice raised past mere hysteria. Beatrice stopped, three quarters up with her clumsy cart, and fumbled for the banister. Should she? She ought. Well, should she? Lovers had quarrels. Beatrice, perhaps because of her work, had an idea of the ferocity of nature—when all at once it was decided for her. The door of Miss Eustace's flat burst open. The light from her room illuminated the figure of a man who, slow and coiled, stepped on to the landing, stood and heaved with deep trembling breaths which hissed between his clenched teeth. He was shabby, middle-sized, and middle-aged. Nothing in his appearance prepared Dr Pazzi for his eyes. They were set deep in his skull. Why did she think of them afterwards as mustard-coloured? She'd hardly seen their colour in the shadow. They were possessed of an intensity far, far beyond the most extreme emotion. They were dreadful, dreadful and extreme. He stood, for a moment, as if hung in suspended animation above her. In a reflex beyond her control she crossed herself as the faithful in last moments do, letting the shopping cart tumble from her hand. At this gesture, he gave a snarl. As he lunged down the stairs, she thought, "This can't be so, this can't be so, he's going to kill me," but he hurtled right past her down and down, kicking her trolley with violence to the landing below. She heard it bouncing down, wicker and wheels bouncing, and the sound of running footsteps blurring into each other. The front door banged and he was gone.

She sat upon the stair to catch her breath and regulate her heart. "Oh, my goodness, Miss Eustace!" She'd hardly composed herself; she pounded on the door which, in the confusion, had been slammed.

"Miss Eustace! Miss Eustace! Are you all right?"

For a long time, she heard nothing. She gripped her imagination and made it still. Years of practise had made her learn to swallow panic down. She knocked again, and again, quietly, insistently.

At last, the door opened a crack, then another. Beatrice was more unnerved by her relief than she had been by her fear. The door now opened wide and she was face to face with—Miss Eustace? Oh, my God, Miss Eustace!

Miss Eustace, at the sight of her, breathed open-mouthed,

eyes closed, then sagged, hand still clenched around the door-knob. Dr Pazzi's imagination, no longer under discipline, searched wildly around for stab wounds. Her arm shot out, she braced the falling woman (girl?). Girl occurred because she fell into her like a child and sobbed.

"Are you all right? You're all right, aren't you? He hasn't hurt you, has he?"

Miss Eustace pulled away instinctively. "He didn't touch me." It was hard for her to articulate the words and she was certainly unable to stand alone.

Beatrice took her arm and supported her. "I thought he'd attacked you. I certainly thought he'd attack me—he ran down the stairs—what a terrible face . . ."

Miss Eustace was now still and queer as if she were about to be sick. She gave Beatrice a look which communicated a fundamental inner trouble. "You saw it. You saw it too."

It was an odd, odd look. It really was odd. It made Dr Pazzi feel very queasy. The shock, of course, the shock to both of them.

"Miss Eustace," she said, "you must sit down. I believe you are suffering from shock." Dr Pazzi put her foot over the threshold.

Miss Eustace shook her head from side to side quite violently. "Thanks very much. I'll manage. Very kind of you. I will manage." She backed off clumsily into the little partition wall that divided the passage from her main room, knocked a Bentwood hatstand into the convex mirror that hung above a hall table, and put her hands over her mouth. "Have I cracked it? Have I cracked it?" She did not look, but asked Beatrice. The hatstand was hung with heavy coats; it slid to the ground.

"The mirror's not cracked. It's all right . . ." (She almost said "dear," she often said "dear" to her patients. She forebore to do it this time. She could not voice it.)

She stepped back on to the landing. "Miss Eustace, please . . ." She was almost dumb. Why couldn't she say? She just shook her head and couldn't say. "Please let me help you." This was all she finally managed.

"Everyone wants to help. That's what that man said. Wanted

to *help!*" Miss Eustace hardly suppressed fury and bitterness. She
was panicked and feral. "Who are you anyway?"

Dr Pazzi was accustomed to offering help in a place where
people knew who she was. Still, she couldn't say. It was the
shock—the shock to them both. "I—"

"I know you live upstairs. I've seen you." Miss Eustace put a
peculiar emphasis on "seen."

"I'm a doctor. That's why—"

"A psychiatrist, I suppose," she said bitterly.

"No, I'm not a psychiatrist—not in the least bit. I wouldn't
know where to begin." Beatrice gave a nervous laugh she
thought sounded a little silly.

"Then you'll be a gynaecologist, won't you?" Miss Eustace
was nothing short of ferocious.

For some odd reason, Beatrice's eyes pricked with tears. It was
the shock. It must be. "Not at all. I specialize in cancer—the
treatment of cancer." She felt quite disoriented. Psychiatry?
Gynaecology?

"Well, I haven't *got* cancer. If I have I don't care!"

The more they argued, the more Dr Pazzi realized that it was
impossible to leave. Her commonsense began to reassert itself,
not without a struggle, and she spoke evenly. "Miss Eustace, I
never thought you had cancer"—and gently—"I'm only a neighbour."

The whole temperature of Miss Eustace's panic seemed to
drop to a level of almost malevolent cold. "You're probably
religious then. It's the way you said 'neighbour'—it's the way
you said 'help.' "

Miss Eustace looked at Beatrice. Beatrice knew that it was also
the way she looked and not just the way she spoke. There was
no point in denying it, however, in the face of anger. Wasn't
there a point in suppressing it in the face of pain? She couldn't
deny it, though. "Yes, I am."

"You do believe in God?"

"Yes."

"Well, have a look at this then." At this apparent non sequi-
tur she pulled Dr Pazzi through the door by the arm. They

stumbled over the fallen hatstand. Miss Eustace led her into the living room. They stood a while in silence. The scene of devastation absolutely fixed Dr Pazzi to the spot. A lingering chill was in the air as if the heating had been off for weeks: the room itself had been violated. Pictures hung askew; the curtains were wrenched off the rails; ashtrays spilled over with the stabbed-out butts of days. An antique table leaned against the wall on three legs—the fourth leg had been used as a bludgeon. A vase lay smashed on the floor and a few coffee cups were also broken—their dregs flung wide had seeped into the good, pale carpet. Beatrice felt sickened, as if she'd walked into a desecrated tomb. Why tomb? Was it the chill? She looked at her neighbour. Miss Eustace's eyes followed every movement of muscle on her face with great urgency.

"Did he do this? Did that man do all of this?"

The hostility of Miss Eustace suddenly failed her. She shook her head again from side to side; it was a wider gesture than before—of puzzlement and not of self-defence. "I did," she said. "I did it all myself last night."

They stood again in silence. Beatrice reconstructed the room with the eye she had for order. There was nothing in its former intactness that had anything to do with what she herself had sensed of the woman who stood next to her. She was all too familiar with the system of décor: old wood, new chintz, a tasteful coffee table; mediocre oils in gilt frames; a tarnished silver ornament or two. She had not done Miss Eustace social justice. The mantle of what was ladylike and well-to-do had fallen on them both, although she doubted it had been in the same way. Without intending to, Beatrice walked over to the window and twitched the sagging velvet drapery. It shocked her to feel pleased as the curtain fell.

The light in the room became high and icy. Miss Eustace looked small and completely out of place. Beatrice saw that she wore a red dressing-gown, even though it was nearing dusk. She communicated that she did not belong to the room, although it might belong to her. She was fairer than Beatrice had supposed and her face had more intellect in it than her behaviour up to now had allowed for. She realized that Miss Eustace had been intently watching her.

"I thought you'd be appalled." She made a nervous movement with her hands. Beatrice could not help noticing the hands which were unnaturally strong for a woman, particularly the left hand. Both hands had callouses on them and stumpy, peeling, jagged nails.

"Appalled?" She shook her head which now rattled with branches of medicine, broken furniture, and an inquisition on her religious beliefs. Why that? Why her religious beliefs? Why had she taken such questions for granted? Submitted to them as if it were perfectly normal for Miss Eustace to ask about them as a kind of prerequisite to admittance to this extraordinary room?

"I know what you think—you think I'm mad."

Beatrice did not know why it had not occurred to her before that Miss Eustace might be mad. She looked at her closely. "Are you?" She saw once she'd said it that it was an absurd question. One could hardly ask a lunatic if she were mad and expect an accurate answer. She'd wanted to know.

"I think I must be—to have done all this." The girl started to cry.

"Miss Eustace, it is clearly ridiculous for us to stand here and talk about whether you are sane or mad when you are so very upset and shocked. Have you any brandy?" Beatrice was very careful with words in case she slipped up and sounded Italian. This made her seem stiff, but she was unaware of giving such an impression. Even after thirty years in England she was still anxious to get it right.

"Then I'm bad." She crumpled up into a wasted armchair she appeared to have slashed. She cried some more.

"Brandy," Beatrice said. Tears did not leave her cold. The tears of Miss Eustace particularly moved her, but she didn't know why. She wanted to touch her arm and comfort her, but could not. She could only ask again for brandy and this made her feel failed.

"There's some in the chest," the girl at last managed to say and waved a hand towards the other end of the room.

The chest was carved and interestingly painted. Beatrice

poured some brandy into a dusty glass. She noticed that an expensive gramophone on top of the chest had been left untouched in Miss Eustace's little episode of the night before. She held the glass up and squinted at its contents as if it held so many cc's of saline solution. She took the glass to Miss Eustace and sat down in the chair across from her. She watched her drink the brandy.

"Aren't you having any?"

Beatrice shrank from having any.

"You've had a shock too." The crying had stopped. The girl seemed almost languid with the alcohol.

"Oh, no—I—"

"Don't drink with patients?" There was something both perceptive and destructive about the question. Beatrice suddenly felt herself pinned by a sharp eye.

"I don't drink much," Beatrice said. This was true, but she was shamed because it wasn't the truth. She didn't know what to do.

"Have some of mine. The spirits will kill the germs."

Beatrice hesitated.

"Cancer isn't catching."

Because the glass was offered as it was, Beatrice determined that meekness was the only course. She gave Miss Eustace, however, her own sharp look; then smiled. She took a sip. The brandy did, of course, make her feel better. "Thank you," she said. "Thank you, Miss Eustace. That is—a help."

Miss Eustace suddenly put her hands over her eyes, then let her fingers drag down her face. "I'm sorry," she said. "You didn't really want it."

"It's all right." It was all right. She took another sip of brandy and felt still.

"What's your name?"

"Pazzi—Beatrice Pazzi."

"Where have I heard that name before?"

Beatrice hated her name and did not want people to have heard of it before.

"It's the name of a chapel—in Florence. I saw it once. Is it your family who built it?"

"Brunelleschi built it," Beatrice said miserably. "We're a cadet branch. At least my father said so." The memory of the burden of names and names, of Guelphs and Ghibellines, of names and names—Beatrice found her eye trailing out the window. It was getting dark.

"My name is Maud. Don't go on calling me Miss Eustace. No one calls me that unless I owe them money."

"Maud," Beatrice said and looked back. It was good that they were talking about names, not traumas. She forced herself to consider discussing the Pazzi Chapel prophylactically. It then occurred to her that Miss Eustace—Maud—was trying to make friends. Either she should or shouldn't have had the brandy. Having had the brandy with Maud, she could not call her Maud, she felt.

But Maud was no longer with her. She had drifted or ebbed back into herself. Her eyes were abstracted and she bit her thumbnail with teeth only, drawing back her lips from them. There was a gap between them and they were yellow from smoking.

Beatrice herself withdrew. "Are you better now, Miss Eustace?"

She did not answer. She seemed to look deeper and deeper into a pool of self. Beatrice closed her eyes and saw. What pain did she see? Feel? "I mean Maud."

At the sound of her name, Maud looked up. "I'm sorry," she said.

Beatrice cleared her throat. "I should have come down last night," she said. "I heard the sound of glass breaking."

"Why did I do it?" It was almost a cry of despair. "I don't understand."

Beatrice thought Maud ought to understand. She cast an earnest look around the whole perplexity of the flat and Miss Eustace. It hurt her eyes somehow to do this and she felt a fraud.

"Why do you ask *me?*" Beatrice asked this because it was of some personal importance to her to know whether Maud had asked the question at random or whether she wanted to know from Beatrice in particular why she couldn't understand why she'd done what she'd done. She was shocked by the mess, but in an inward way, however, she was utterly at home with the nature of Maud's question and the intensity with which it was asked. Her own eyes hunted Maud's. Like meeting animals they engaged upon a circling round possible contact, fight, or truth.

"I was going to say," Maud said after a pause in which she became increasingly lucid, "that I let you in—just as I let that man in—because you both believe in God. That has come to seem to me like a place to begin rather than any other place I've begun from. It frightens me and I'm only driven to it. I just don't understand, you see. I just don't understand what's happened to me!"

Beatrice became slowly aware that Maud had said she'd let in the man who had hung above her on the stair because of his belief in God. Her hand unconsciously sought the brandy glass, then fortified as she was by her success at self-control—with past successes too at self-control—the hand returned itself into her lap. "The man?" Her voice sounded distant and calm.

"I'd thought he was someone else at first, you see. I've been expecting someone to come—for months—no, it must be only a few weeks. Someone so important to me—do you understand? Someone I loved so much. I've been living here in silence for weeks and weeks, do you see? It's so quiet. It's terrible. Oh, I've watched you come and go. Frankly, I thought you'd be the last person here to—I'm sorry."

Beatrice reminded herself that sufferers and children had a right to offend. It was a kind of privilege that couldn't be taken advantage of by the recipient's hurt feelings. "It doesn't matter. Go on about the man." All the same, her mouth tasted stale.

"Weeks and weeks. There hasn't been another human face or voice or creature. I can't tell you—even a moth or a spider would have done—and I can't see anyone I know. Really. I can't. I've broken with everybody.

"They live—my friends live—these friends. Well, *she* isn't a friend, but *he* lives in Chelsea, only in Chelsea. You see, I thought they'd come after me. *She* won't let him, of course, but that's beside the point. I've been waiting and waiting: you can't imagine what I felt when I heard the buzzer. I pressed it and opened the front door without even *asking* who it was. I was so sure, so sure he'd come. And then it was that man."

Their eyes met over the man.

Maud looked into her hands. "I know it was a risk letting him in." She looked up at Beatrice now sharply. "But what have I to lose?"

"I don't know yet," said Beatrice with a sudden humour she now and then had.

Maud didn't like this, but was not to be deflected by it. "I can tell you, I thought I had nothing to lose when I saw he wasn't Alba. He said he had important business with me. I thought maybe he had come *from* Alba."

"Not Alba the cellist!" Beatrice was truly impressed.

Maud's eyes seemed to raze some thought she had projected into the middle distance. The look was so powerful that Beatrice was forced to follow its path over her shoulder to a photographic portrait in a silver frame of a man she barely recognized, but did recognize as Thomas Alba whom she'd seen as a young man perform at the Albert Hall. She drew in her breath and decided it was better to say nothing. Maud forged on past the silence this interlude had created. "It became clear—" she cleared her throat. Her words seemed to be chosen with a care to their businesslike use. This gave them a stilted effect, as if they walked out on stilts over the strong emotion which eddied round her. "It became clear that he was not from Alba, but from God. So he said. Instead, as it were." She dropped a cracked little giggle. "So I let him in."

They were pitched into a deeper silence. It was getting quite dark and the wind smacked the windows with rain. Beatrice reached out and turned on a light; she was somehow surprised that the light worked. The yellow lamplight drew them together. Beatrice hesitated. "Did you ask him the same question you asked me?"

"You mean, why I wrecked things?"

Beatrice struggled with a nod. She felt oddly moved.

"No, I didn't ask him that. I'm not quite sure what went on. All I know is that it very quickly got out of hand." Her statement was so rational in contrast to her shaking body that Be-

atrice was at a loss to know quite what to do, to know on what
level to approach her. "What do you mean?"

"Where is the foot of the Cross?" It was as if all the brandy and
soothing had been for nothing. Maud's eyes seized an inward
vision and fixed themselves upon it. Oh, not shock. Beatrice
apprised longer, deeper shock. Something that had shocked and
shocked and shocked again the girl's mind to this pitch. There
was something so raucous about the voice, so hoarse.

Gently, she said, "Have you been thinking about that for the
last few weeks—that sort of thing?"

"No! No, that's what's so odd. I haven't. I don't understand
why it upset me so. I've thought about God—as I said to you
earlier. I've even prayed once or twice. He just went on and on
about it. 'Are you saved?' 'Well, if you don't know you are, you
aren't—I don't know—then over and over again, he got wilder
and wilder, 'Come to the foot of the Cross.' I kept asking him
where it was. It made him angrier and angrier."

"That was because he couldn't explain it." Beatrice felt a funny sympathy for the man.

"No, that wasn't it. It was demands with menaces—he was full
of threats. I can't explain it. His face was terrible. I was never so
terrified in all my life. He kept going on about my crime, some
crime I had committed. You saw him. If you hadn't seen him I
wouldn't believe it had happened."

"How did you get him to leave?"

"I screamed. Or at least I think I did. I think I screamed. Yes,
of course I did. He's going to kill me."

Beatrice was at once alert. "Did he say so?"

She shook her head. "I just feel it. You have no idea what he
was like."

Beatrice had an idea what he was like.

The man's fanaticism touched the lip of an inner wound and
she winced. To Beatrice, religion was not a pastime; it was an
absorbing hole in her centre which she fell into nightly, daily: it
permeated the veins in her hands and occupied her temples as a
whole way of life. With her, it had got beyond an idea which
made her happy or unhappy; it was not a duty but a reality she

plumbed without finding its depths and aspired to without discovering its height. In her work she was accustomed to death daily, and although she had bent herself in some respects away from a too-close inspection of it, it was familiar to her and not a particular outrage. She had had to distance herself from death in order to cope with it and she had come to assume it into the pattern of her religious beliefs, which coped with the awesome and the gruesome adequately for her. Her ulterior life, however, was not so resolved or connected.

Her fear of the man was at once made clear to her. A deeper death than a mortal one insisted itself on her mind as the true threat she had sensed on the stair. Fanaticism filled her with a revulsion most people have at physical cruelty. The excesses of Savonarola had been for centuries a family grudge (not that she in any conscious way took things seriously: she had, however, been brought up with the awareness of them). It was really more for her own self she feared the libertine quality in religion: that it could be a form of emotional self-indulgence obscurely horrified her as it would horrify a true lover to see a photograph of a beloved used for pornographic purposes. To have seen God shoved down Maud's throat in the way which had clearly happened was as odious to her as a rape. This is what she had seen and sensed. That Maud—this puzzling and unnerving girl with whom she had the barest external contact—should also see and sense the attack upon her soul in such a way filled Beatrice with a shudder of discovery that bordered on a communion. Any violation of any soul disturbed her, and it was this that she felt bound to battle.

Her mind, of course, had not been entirely precise in these reflections, but she did have a habit of withdrawing from what actually went on under her nose into educated reverie. When she finally looked at Maud, she found herself suddenly too close to the eyes to swerve in time from an engagement.

"It's appalling," she said. "Appalling. God loves you . . . He doesn't want . . ." She simply couldn't express herself.

"But what have I *done*? What have I *done*?" Maud looked round the room and Beatrice could not avoid in her heart the piteousness in the tone.

She dumbly shook her head. "I don't know," she finally said, "what you've done." Beatrice wished she hadn't had the brandy. In itself it had not affected her judgment, but because she'd shared it she could think of no answer that would have served—that often did serve—her patients' questions adequately when "Why me?" "Why now?" were levelled against her. "You must work it out for yourself," she mumbled.

"I'm so frightened. I'm so lonely. I don't understand."

"The cello," she said. She was unable to substantiate this curious offer of a solution, so she waved her hands about in an Italianate way she instantly repressed. She was ashamed of the national characteristic of gesturing.

"What about it!" She had only driven Maud into deeper terror.

Beatrice swallowed. "It, well—I've heard you play—it, well—it seems a means of—to you of—looking for. I don't know. Whatever. I suppose you can't find salvation in it. It's only—"

"That it'll keep me out of mischief," Maud said quite maliciously.

Beatrice shook her head and was ashamed. "I didn't mean that" (though in some respects she had meant that), "I meant I found it very beautiful—like a meditation." She blushed deeply and her olive face lit.

Beatrice had clearly struck. Maud instantly softened. She closed her eyes. "I'm glad you heard it that way," she said. They were silent.

Maud had obviously decided that Beatrice might be conditionally trusted for her perception. She spoke rather stiffly. "I am no longer able to play," she said. "I have been so upset over the last few weeks that my hands shake too much and I can't—so much as play the C-major scale."

Beatrice looked at Maud's hands which had indeed been shaking since she had arrived. The colourless and null tone in her voice, the flat and unemotional statement of her disability at once demonstrated to Beatrice emotional disease in a way that Maud's flailing, her gasping, had not been able to do.

"What I played—the way I played—brought me to where I am now," Maud continued. "If I were able to play, I would not care—I would not need to ask for any assistance from religion or from anything else." She looked coldly at Beatrice, but somehow Beatrice was not eclipsed by the look.

"Why don't you write it down—your problem? If you can't play, why don't you write?" Beatrice was dimly aware, as she said this, that she might be avoiding Maud's need for a listener. If she, in effect, sentenced Maud to a life story, would she then have some control over the raking look, the punitive stare; over the demolishing affection for herself she felt—why did she suddenly feel this?—peeping through, unconsciously, seeping through like a gas under a door—seeping through the structured hostility, the mannered defences of Miss Eustace?

They both retracted slightly.

"I'll try anything," Maud said. Having got the sense of distance Beatrice had imposed, she smiled with a tinge of cynicism the wounded often have and herself made greater distance still through that.

Perhaps to make up the distance, Beatrice said, "I'll give you dinner tonight. You must come to dinner. You won't be able to cook for yourself."

Maud did not say she'd rather starve, but this pride was inherent in her refusal. A courtliness in it reminded Beatrice that they were both ladies.

"You're right. I'll write it out. It's a very good idea. I don't know why I hadn't thought of it. Thanks awfully for helping. You've been wonderful." Beatrice knew that she hadn't been wonderful.

She rose. "If there's anything at all I can do to help, do come upstairs and ask me," she said.

"Thanks. Yes. Thanks a lot. I will."

"I mean it," Beatrice said. She had not, in quite a time, been reduced to the misery of self-justification.

As she turned to leave, Maud smiled and at once Beatrice was seized, lit and warmed: it was involuntary, electric and alive and held within it the anticipation of a contact she sought—oh, sought.

CHAPTER II

What can Dr Pazzi do that Dr Bender couldn't? Now Dr Bender, he thought childhood important. It was clear to him from the start that I never had a chance. He had a couch which I had to lie on so that I couldn't see his face.

Isn't that trust? To tell your secrets to someone who won't let you discern how you are getting on with him? Actually, I never let him into that much about me, perhaps because I was never talking to him but to his theories.

All the same, I had the sneaking impression that I was getting a kind of starred first in mental contusions. The very little I told him was enough to awe him. At least I hoped it awed him. Awe is something to leave a person with, especially if they, like Dr Bender, couldn't care less whether you live or die.

I'm twenty-six now, and I left his consulting rooms many years ago with the distinct impression that my end was completely predetermined by my beginning. In fact, I've always had a belief in destiny, have always felt helpless in its control, and I am not at all surprised that I let that dreadful man with his probing nose and his plastic Bible into my flat. I am not at all surprised that he spoke as he did of *God's* predisposition against me.

Dr Bender once tried to make a distinction to me between the condition of being unloved and the condition of being bad. I don't think that any of this would worry me if I could play the cello again. Being able to do that certainly gave me the comfortable illusion that I could help myself, that I had some defence; but since Alba I can't. I can't. I can't.

It's a little bit like being struck down, when you *can't* do something you want to do. Doesn't it have hints of punishment? Doesn't it have hints of a plan in the mind of God?

Oh, God; that man! That dirty, squirming, revolting little lunatic, putting his fingers all over my flat! Insinuating hell at me! All the things he said! Surely I am intelligent enough to dismiss them! But they stick in my mind almost as if they were alive, his words, and eat away what little confidence I have left like acid.

I almost told Dr Pazzi . . . did I tell her? It's the image of the Cross that violates me most of all. Now why does it do that? Why? I'm not religious except that in funny little ways I've felt from time to time that religion might help? Explain? Control? That it might tell me why I suffer; that it might heal me.

But not this! Not this image of the Cross. It accuses me. It torments me. I don't know where it bloody *is!*

Is it pain? Is it sin? Is it death? Is it outrage?

Am I being offered it? Am I offending it? Will it go away? Does it make excuses for me? Does it forgive me?

If so, for *what?* I don't understand what I've *done!*

All I know is that I'm going to end on the end of that man's knife. The tread of my character is so insistent, so unstoppable. I can see myself letting him in again and again and again, knowing I shouldn't, not even wanting to! The dice are loaded before I even roll them. Didn't they roll Alba? Didn't they roll Ilse?

Maybe they rolled Beatrice Pazzi.

"Write it all down," she says! It makes me bloody laugh. If she could see the look on her face!

But you can say to her credit that my very act of sitting here, letting one word flow after another prises me at least from *willed* hopelessness. If, in writing, I say I have no hope, I cannot be telling the truth. The mere attempt to sort things out is an investment in the future.

You see, I could never tell another human soul about Alba. Not Dr Bender, not Dr Pazzi, not anyone at all. The experience of my flight from him was one of such profound evil that I feel the advice of no one could matter, the comfort of no one could comfort, the explanations of no one could explain at all what happened to me.

Was I perpetrator, victim, or both? He was my sun and now he has gone out.

Dr Pazzi didn't want to get involved with me: I could see that. You can hardly blame her. I hated the way she seemed to see into me. She kept on touching me with her eyes where it hurts me and I wish I could bury myself away from what I thought she saw, yet at the time, I felt I *wanted* her, longed for her to stay. I wanted to love her like I wanted to love Alba—purely, without physical sensation. It brings an impulse to do myself violence to think about how nobody understands this. Why can't anyone understand this? This is what I wanted to tell them with the cello. I told *her* that on the cello. I mean, that is what she understood from it. She said.

Oh, I've watched her coming and going. I am intimate with her movements. Her correct head and awkward walk have always been imbued with a kind of romance for me. Her name would be Beatrice!

It was such a terrible shock to discover that she was a doctor. What an irony! What a turn up for the books.

Oh, my Papa, oh, Sir Giles Eustace, doctor of a high degree with your medical nose! You treated the gynaecological uproar in women through rubber gloves and at one remove. Aborting, tying off, searching through a speculum what you didn't understand in a way which refuted all mystery so that even Amy, Mummy, and I were reduced in your mind to specimens!

He fed his own profession with three unstable women: my mother, needless to say; Amy, who drinks; and me.

Dr Bender had his crack at me just after I left the Royal College and just before I went to America to study with Janorsky. I had been ill with love that time too. Love seems to be my disease. I can remember it without pain now, but at the time it was like a death sentence, when Martin Horowitz, with whom I was doing the Beethoven sonata in C, played a theme from it casually along the piano, and not daring or able to meet my gaze, my passionate regard, said, "Maudie, you need a psychiatrist."

I still don't know what I *did*. What did I do to make him say that? I'd even thought we might marry. We ate together, slept together, loved each other's sound. Why did he leave me like that? Was it my look? My intensity? Dr Bender thought I was paranoid. Dr Bender sucked a pipe and I might as well have told him he was orally fixated. The man was a tone-deaf slab. Minds to him were what wombs were to my father. Both men treated what frightened them the most. Put it in hospital and remove it; brainwash it. Spray goblins with Flit and deny the existence of angels.

How silly.

Dr Bender would have said that Beatrice's attraction for me stemmed from a neurotic desire to find a mother-figure in older women, which stemmed in turn from a subconscious wish to destroy my mother who destroyed herself anyway which makes the whole impulse arise from guilt for which I could not possibly be responsible being, as it were, under the age of consent when my mother died.

My love of Alba can be seen as a fundamental urge to repeat the experience of rejection by my father, and so on and so on and so on.

What did he make of Martin? That foursquare, heterosexual relationship was seen by Dr Bender as a *compensation* I was trying to make for rejection in my early childhood.

Dr Bender, good-bye.

Dr Pazzi, now. She's a different kettle of fish. She is *not* tone-deaf, or blind. When we've passed on the landing as the light flashes out, we see each other. I know she's listening, listening for me now. How wonderfully odd it was that it should be *she* who mounted the stairs as the man tore down! How straight she sits, how frightened of intoxication. How much her arm, which keeps at arm's length, longs to drop. Oh, how she yearns to fold, to smile, to be less angular! Oh, how she longs to die!

Why did I say that? Never mind.

Shall I talk again about the man on the stairs? The man in the duffle coat? His hair is thinning and his cheeks emaciated; his eyes globular. He left his Bible here. Written crudely in it is his name: "Arthur Marsdan"—no address. He slipped it from his plastic briefcase with sensuous delight, and anger, sensual and controlled. It is his instrument, that Bible. I understand the need for instruments. No, I shan't talk about him.

Keep your eye on the notes. Attend to the phrasing. Polish up the fingering. Let the ear hear. Do not rhapsodize about the composer's intentions, but learn them intellectually. Listen, listen, listen and work, work, work.

My earliest conviction as a child had to do (not oddly) with the brain: with thinking straight and with survival. It was the mandate from music which absolutely cleared the air.

We lived in Suffolk where Daddy had retired when Mother lost her mind. He'd had a rich practise up in London where I was born. My aunt told me (and no one but my aunt ever told me anything) that women flocked to his consulting rooms, and I can quite see why—he was a handsome devil. My mother was a social cut above him—not a cut maybe, but a slice. She'd done the season and I have a tattered cutting still which recommended her as beautiful. There is a photograph of her with bobbed hair and a bunch of flowers modestly clutched to a beaded shift: her eyes mild, her smile a little wild and odd even then.

We *will* talk about music. My mother was a very accomplished woman. Until her poor mind was gnawed away altogether, she did crewel embroidery with a large tapestry needle— a kind of peaceful absorption on her face—and she played the piano in our dusky drawing room. We had an old Broadwood grand; a rose bowl full of dried flowers and rushes and bird plumes always stood on it whatever the season. And when my father would drag himself off to Bury St Edmunds for the day, she, like someone out of earshot of the guard in some peculiar house-arrest, would—nerves pitched up hard and flat—make for the piano. She was a terrible musician—terrible—no discipline at all: she played like a clockwork toy wound right up— Chopin, Beethoven, Tchaikovsky—until after a while her muscles would relax and a lyricism emerged.

My terror of my mother was out of this world and that is why I know that music was never with me a habit or a taste or even a vocation, but an absolute demand on me. I clutched the skirts of one nanny after another against her except, except—when she played the music.

I can see it now, as riveting as any conversion envisioned by the man in the duffle coat, my standing on the kitchen table being dressed by some hired-hand or other, when quite suddenly I heard. Ours was a house of emanations. I heard a tune my mother often played, and her mediocre voice singing. The song came through the swinging kitchen door—*"Röslein, Röslein, Röslein rot, Röslein auf der Heide"*—at least that is what I now know it was, Schubert.

The tune came clear to me and suddenly was mine. The sound was neither beautiful nor ugly—I simply caught it as a baby catches words and speaks them, and music for me was ever after real. I must have been three or four.

Everything else seemed imaginary. I soon worked out when Mother wanted to play. She was more ritualistic than a clock. She timed her pleasures and her pains with manic exactitude. When her face darkened over in its musical mode, I'd dash into the drawing room and hide in the shadow of the china cabinet by the wall. I'd close my eyes and wait, torn between terror of discovery and longing for the music, until she came and played. She never saw me once, but then she never saw me ever. I'd watch her blind eyes unscramble notes—her fingers play them sometimes coarsely, sometimes well. From time to time she gave a hoarse laugh like a tart in a roadhouse. I became so accustomed to her repertoire that I'd wait for the right notes to come. Perfect pitch is the only perfect thing I've ever had. I'd know when her face came over delicate and calm that she had got it right and that my pleasure wouldn't be denied me.

When finally she left the room, I'd steal up to the instrument and look at it, ashamed to touch the glossy keys. I was in awe of the piano; it seemed like a strange god to me that it could tranquilize my mother so and give such passionate desire to me, I felt it should not be abused by error or ineptitude. I longed for the perfection of its song even then.

I never got the courage up to play it until the day I realized that Mother always slept after each performance. It was a deep narcotic sleep; it took a while for me to understand that nothing, but nothing woke her out of that—not thunderstorms, nor my baby sister crying. She'd play and she was out.

I think I was afraid that the piano wouldn't love me. What an odd thing to say. I became convinced that when I touched the notes, it wouldn't respond: that it would withdraw the favours that it granted to my mother. For a long time that first time, I sat on the stool before it, wondering if it would animate itself and play without my having to touch it. At last, consumed with fear, I stroked a key and sound leapt up and kissed my ear, and then another key, and others still, until a whole alphabet of keys spilled out spelling nothing but giving hope of meaning. The only things that acknowledged me when I was young were that piano and my sister Amy. When I touched the instrument, it played, and when I pinched my sister, she screamed.

Weeks went by of Mother making music, conking out, and my experiments with C, D, E—E flat, C sharp—B, F, G sharp. At last I discovered a little tune, "Three Blind Mice," that Nanny'd taught me.

My hands shake too much to go on: fever, excitement, hope.

All night long I've been thinking about Daddy, not a moment's peace, God knows, but endless thrashing.

When I broke up my flat I thought I'd killed the cello. Maybe I should have killed the cello in the fray. No, I'm not insane—only picturesque. No one can know how I've coddled that instrument; how I have fed it with linseed oil and bedded it in scarlet velvet, loved it, exercised it, spun out such music from it to make the gods ache. It used to speak for me like an oracle. I hardly needed to touch it before sound leapt out. I was its sibyl. I gave it form and gave the breath to what was already in it.

Beatrice didn't see my music room. No one has ever looked at it but Alba. I knew only he would never mar its chastity. (Mark that Dr Bender. Mark that Dr Pazzi.)

Daddy. Now why should I have been obsessed with a memory of Daddy? The very word "Daddy" invokes the establishment of law and order—the law of dread and the order of silence. I saw clips from his life and times all last night. Daddy with his egg and paper and his "Isn't that woman (Mother) coming down for breakfast?" Daddy polishing the Daimler with a duster as if the bodywork were wilfully dull. Daddy throwing

Amy from one end of the room to the other. The absolute scorn of Daddy for us all.

Daddy came most of all to life in his consulting rooms in Bury; that is what I remembered last night. One day I had to make a special journey to take him a message from the school, a form I think it was he had to sign allowing me to go to music camp (this was long, long after Aunt Aileen had bullied him into letting me have lessons—at that time I was quite adept).

For some reason I see this clearly: various middle-aged ladies were seated in fine, straight-backed Georgian chairs around a Turkey carpet. There was a faint odour of perfume mixed with methylated spirits. Nurse Nancy showed me in. Nurse Nancy trembled and bridled and looked scared of the door behind which he was, and scared of me. At the same time she made up to me while I stood still, so scared of the door was I. Amy and I always called her Nurse Nancy and we still do when we have occasion to refer to her at all. I don't know why we called her that, her name is Margaret. She was my father's mistress and after Mother's death she married him. I suppose we should speak of her as our stepmother or call her Margaret as she wished us to but I am too weary of the situation to try, too weary and too pitiless. We never see her.

Father at last entered the waiting room in his white coat. You could see his foulard tie welling up beneath it. He had a heavy neck and drawn brows underneath a high-domed head. He walked with a slight limp from a wound he had sustained during the war. He was very tall.

What made me and the seated women rise when he came into the room? They did not rise, but I remember it that way. The impression of their rising came from the way they vibrated to his presence. They vibrated expectantly to his exacting eyes, his fine, disdainful nose, the curious brutality round his mouth. They quivered and they loved him; they ate him up with their eyes. Nurse Nancy nearly whimpered with it. He looked all around at them like a bleary old ram. He deeply hated women as I said and liked to subjugate them—us.

I had been certain of his anger at being interrupted by a minion from his home, which he so despised. He was always angry—all the time, although he very rarely showed it. Every movement of his hands and every word he uttered was an expression of contempt. I was astonished when, in front of all the ladies, he put his arm around my shoulders in a showman's effort to communicate some natural affection. He did not debase himself further with honeyed words, but he went far enough. His voice came out like velvety soup—of course I could go, whyever did I think I mightn't be able to? How could he reasonably object to my coming in if the form had to be signed right away? He did want to show his patients what-a-brilliant-daughter-even-the-great-Thomas-Alba-has-his-eyes-on-her.

They murmured "the darling" as if I had been three. How I wished I had been three. I simpered and did the imitation of myself that was expected, hating Father concomitantly with loving Father, and hoping that this meant at long last love. Needless to say, nothing of the kind was so.

Is that the reason that I tried to kill my cello? I *didn't* try to kill it, I tried to break it.

Or is it Alba whom I at last have had the courage to mention in context of my life story which I'm so thoroughgoing on? Now we're back to reason. I met him at a very early age through the offices of my good Aunt Aileen.

My Aunt Aileen was responsible for everything in my early life which made any sense; it was she who is responsible for Alba. If it were not for her, and for him, I would never have played the cello at all.

Aileen now lives in a mews house near Harrods. It is where she should have lived all along and where she is content to stay now. Her little sitting room is filled with mementos of what she calls "the Past." After Mother's death Aileen took Amy and me into a much bigger place she had then behind the Brompton Oratory. I used to sit on a little petit-point footstool and hug my knees to myself as she talked with almost mystical vision of this period in her life—the Past. Images of Berlin, Paris, and New York emanated from her mouth in curls of scented smoke. She had a taste for Russian cigarettes before her doctor made her stop. Our Uncle George was a diplomat. He died young and, I believe, happy. No one could have failed to be happy with Aileen. Uncle George's old friends from the Foreign Office emerge from time to time in Aileen's salon; they seem to be cunningly fashioned out of blocks of ice; I cannot imagine they were her Past, particularly not Horace, who is her boyfriend. Aileen lightly suggested lovers in dancing pumps and scandals at the Embassy Ball; Bohemian painters and assignations in Montmartre; Prussian officers who drank champagne from her shoes . . . tiny sips from a tiny shoe.

I cannot think she had all that rip-roaring a time. She toddles out in a ratty mink down the Brompton Road to a place where they blend fine teas. She has a relationship with the young shop assistant. They exchange little notes and queries about the weather. She toddles home again with Lapsang Souchong and perhaps a few crumpets from Harrods's Food Halls. She isn't all that old; it's just that she has run out of imagination.

When young, Aileen was full of razzle-dazzle. At least she was to me. Aileen with her vain, peripatetic, spontaneous heart! She swanned into Castle Gloom and lit us up. It was she who discovered my talent for music, partly because she was loving and astute, but I think it more likely that she had music on the brain because she was at that time in love with Alba.

As far as I can make out, everyone was always in love with Alba.

The music that I stole from Mother was never heard by anyone until Aileen came down one day from London, perhaps to stem the flow of Mother's craziness, perhaps to keep an eye on us—she did a lot of that. The magic of Aileen was never highpowered, but it was most effectual. I regarded her then as a reliable fairy godmother, incapable of making pumpkins into coaches, but quite able to see that things went right.

It must have been Aileen who heard me play. I do not know for sure because I never saw her listening. All I do know is that Daddy called me into his study one evening and announced to me that I was going to learn to play the piano and properly. Great pains had been gone to—some expense had been incurred—to secure for me a teacher, Mr Young, who would absolutely make sure a note never slipped from my grasp. I was to work hard or the lessons would be stopped. My father never descended to childish diction when addressing us, but his meaning was always easy to decipher. How Aileen had swung it I will never understand, and really I don't want to.

At any rate, I never let my father down. I have only the vaguest recollection of Mr Young, who was an old, grey-faced gentleman with dry and crispy hair. He seemed a ghost in comparison to the substance that he taught me. I was starved for every bit of information he could give. I crammed my mind, stuffed, swallowed, gorged on scales and staves, crochets and semi-breves, great wedges of Czerny fed me washed down with gulps and gulps of watered-down Bach.

I was careful not to let my obsession with the piano show. I could not wait to practise; I felt that I would die if I did not. I'd choose the most discreet and empty times of day and only then would nervously approach the instrument. I'd fall upon it and attack it for its nourishment—never getting enough, never getting enough. Sometimes I would creep down at night just to look at the piano (I never dared to play it then). I'd look upon the keys and sound them in my mind, insatiable for more than they could give me.

It was not until I heard the cello for the first time that I remember having that complete sense of drunken ease that came from being finally satisfied.

It's such a shame that Aileen wasn't a fairy. In her youth she looked like one. Perhaps she is—as things for me have always happened round her—the Sugar Plum Fairy from the Christmas tree.

The day I first heard the cello she and Uncle George had come down for the weekend. Amy and I sat starched on the drawing-room sofa trying not to scuff our shoes on the carpet. Normally, we were inwardly inebriated by Aileen's visits, but this time something had happened, something had gone on that we did not know about, and no one would explain why Mother sagged by the fire biting her nails, why Uncle George looked pained and mystified, why Aunt Aileen looked bitterly at her hands as if she blamed them for being helpless. No one said a thing.

Suddenly, Father leapt up and switched on the wireless in the manner of one who attempts, by pressing a button, to drum the whole human race from his consciousness.

It must have been Bach. I am quite sure it was. It entertains me to think that it was Alba playing, but it was probably Casals. At any rate, it fell all round my ears, my mind as pure as shook-out snow, shaken snow softly pure. Whatever I had heard on the piano was as nothing to it. The cello transfigured that element of music that I lived in and so transfigured me. The sound of it overrode everything: my mother's crying, my father's anger, my uncle's embarrassment, my aunt's tight consternation. They were cancelled out, swaddled and hidden in the rush of . . . what I was . . . not what I heard, but what I was.

Such feelings are too complex for a child to articulate, but I must have communicated them at least to Aileen. After tea and before she went, she huddled me in her mink in the cloakroom amid the muddy gumboots. "You liked that sound, didn't you, darling—the sound on the wireless—that cello music?" I pressed my face to her neat waist and nodded my head into it. I could not speak for the brilliance of the memory.

"Would you like to meet a famous man who plays a cello most beautifully? I'm sure he would like to meet you." I never trusted luck, much less enthusiasm. I merely nodded, expecting that any joy I might express at the idea of such a treat might make it vanish. Aileen hugged my hard little head; she bristled like a soft fir tree. I could not understand why she looked as if she were about to cry. Even then, I found her vaguely sentimental. If I had ever allowed myself to cry, my God, where would I be?

A month after my seventh birthday, my father put me on the train to London. I wore darned black lisle stockings, a Harris tweed coat cut one size too big for me, and a brown felt hat. Father told me it would be my own fault if I got lost. If I couldn't hang on to my own ticket and read the words "Liverpool Street Station," then what use was I? He said I was to meet a "virtuoso" called Thomas Alba, that I was an extremely lucky child, and that I'd better behave. I had no idea what a virtuoso was; I had some notion it had something to do with the dentist and I was very much afraid.

I never saw so much that was curious in my life. From the moment my foot touched the platform, the whole of my universe seemed to become deeply altered. I had thought somehow that I was expected to get to Aunt Aileen's flat by myself and this had terrified me the whole way up to London because I did not know her address and I had not asked Father for it. I was not very much worried about getting lost among strangers; I was much more upset by the idea that I would be found by Father and punished for my mistake. So when Aileen and Uncle George appeared behind the clearing steam, and when they waved, smiled vibrantly, engulfed with kisses my form which had been so diminished by fear, I felt as if a whole brass band had marched into the station for my sole benefit. They took me, whirled me up into themselves. I might have come into a fortune. I was stunned.

I was given a pink satin bed in a deep lacy room. It had a little bedside lamp, I remember, which fascinated me, a thing made of shells and a sort of corrugated shade, no, pleated shade decked with pink ribbon. I was sure I had never seen a thing so beautiful. Aileen took me shopping. We seemed to be assumed up in Harrods's lift to a sugared place full of fluffy petticoats, lawn nightdresses, everything in cases as if in a museum, all too wonderful to touch. When my father died a few years ago, Amy and I found ourselves more than comfortably well-off from the fortune he left us. As children, we had always supposed that we were poor. No one in our household ever spent money unless it was well spent. Aileen sprinkled money like fairy dust. The assistant even put her money into a tube which, at the press of a button, flew round the shop on a wire. I went in threadbare and came out bearing everything in white and smocking and patent leather and tissue paper.

That night I remember thinking that I must have stolen it all or that it did not belong to me after all but was on loan, or worst of all that I was being given it as a consolation for being sent to this dentist Thomas Alba. For some reason, I had the idea that he was going to kill me in the interest of science, perhaps . . . I don't know why.

Over an enlightened breakfast of bacon, toast, tea, porridge, marmalade even (I am sure that was rationed, perhaps there wasn't marmalade, but it felt as if there was), Uncle George said from behind the *Times* that it was preposterous a little girl should be brought up as I was being brought up (he was inclined to speak of me as if I were not there) and that it was absurd for a seven-year-old to come up to London for the sole purpose of being grilled by Alba. I looked down at my bacon—my grilled bacon—and imagined with fainting mind an ordeal by fire. "Well, it's certainly for her own good, George. It's the only way she'll get out of that ghastly situation. I must say I worry more about Amy who hasn't any gifts . . . What's the matter, darling, aren't you hungry any more?" Later, in my school days, I had to read *Iphigenia in Tauris*. The same sick, lurching feeling came back to me—I saw myself all gussied up in sugar pink and white—a sacrificial victim to the gods who so potently ruled my young life.

"Well, *I'm* going to take her to see Donald Duck," said George. And he did; he moved portly and important down the cinema aisle, and glutted me on Disney. I crammed a whole childhood into that one weekend. Even now, the animated, talking duck skids around my brain, a creature capable of anything, who could be flattened but not killed, struck by lightning, but not electrocuted. He somehow held out hope.

At tea-time on Sunday, I was groomed for the kill—that is how I felt. It is curious, when I think about it now, that I made no resistance; that I never told kind Aileen my fears; that I was so passive to my fate. I was taken in a taxi by her to a huge, heavy Victorian mansion where we went up and up and up in a lift. At the door, she said: "And *now* the greatest treat of all—Alba!"

Finally, I spoke. "Is it going to hurt?"

"Hurt? Hurt? Why how extraordinary you should say that. Of course not!" The door opened wide and there he stood—Alba.

I shall never, I can see, shake the notion of magic from my mind. Everything to do with that afternoon spelt out for me reprieve, safety, warmth, depth, and even love.

Although he was (and is) very tall, he never loomed. He was dressed in green—at least that is how I remember it—and he wore a floppy tie loose round a creamy open-necked shirt. He had a beard and a moustache, black and so soft that you wanted to lace your fingers through it; his eyes were black and luminous and large. He looked strong and solidly built. His face, when he saw us, broke out into such a vivid and spontaneous smile that my heart shook.

"Aileen!" he cried. He pumped her by the hand. She kissed him. "And this is your niece?" He had no foreign accent, but his intonation was foreign.

I'm sure of it, I know it—I communicated to him my fear. He took one look at my up-turned face and his face changed and softened. He slowly crouched down and took my hand. "So you're Maud," he said, "and you want to be a musician, just like me." His voice was supple and indulgent, as if he were already proud of me for no reason I could think of at all.

Without thinking, I said, "You're a musician? I thought you were going to be the dentist."

Aileen said, "Really, Maud." Alba laughed quietly, his breath smelt of cigars. "Oh, no. I hate the dentist," he said. "Now come in, won't you both, and we will talk."

Oh, the pleasant maleness of his flat! I shall never forget it, such an aura there was of smoke and leather, whisky and slippers and hard work. Piles of things lay around the place. Everything I saw there I wanted to reach out and touch softly for the blessing it might give me. He seated me with tea. I felt suddenly a lady; I also felt a child for the first time in my life. My heart enlarged.

"Now," he said, "your aunt tells me that not so long ago you heard someone play a cello and that it was to you somehow like the circus to hear it."

"What's a circus?" I asked.

Aileen and he exchanged looks.

"It's a little hard to explain," he said. I instinctively knew and loved it that he wished somehow to spare my feelings. "But you did particularly like that noise."

I cocked my head and thought. "Well, I liked the piano until I heard that on the wireless. I keep trying to make that sound again—on the piano, I mean—but I can't so I don't like the piano any more, much." He smiled like someone diagnosing the symptoms of being in love.

"Have you ever seen a cello?"

I shook my head. Aileen in a low hiss said, "My dear, they haven't given her a clue about *anything.*" Alba looked at her with a trace of annoyance.

"I'll show you mine." He rose and brought forth the instrument. Oh, that pitiless instrument that lies locked up in my airless room. If only I had been repelled by it. As it was, I looked at and fell in love at first sight with the shape, the sheen, the whole arrangement of it. He plucked at it a bit, tuning it. "Is this the sound you mean?" And he played and I sat on the edge of my seat and I watched and I listened and he played some more and more and more and as my appetite was not filled he played still more again until the vibrations must have warmed the walls: they sank to the pit of my ear and the seat of my mind. The last thing it was was like being in love. It was like watching someone spell out to you a message from an angel; it was like losing yourself and finding it; it was an experience of almost scientific engrossment. When he saw I was satisfied, he stopped.

I have a vague recollection of Aileen twittering on the sidelines. "*How* lovely/what a genius/darling Thomas/*what* a marvel . . ." All I said I whispered and breathed. "How do you do it?" He looked at me and I looked at him. Our faces matched and met in a curious area where his adulthood and my childhood did not obtrude. It was an experience of uncontaminated, intellectual joy.

His eyes did not waver from mine, but he spoke to Aileen. "I've never taught children," he said, "and for various reasons, I am unable to teach even this child. But I do think it is clear she must start." He turned to Aileen full face. His bow dangled from his fingertips as if he were lightly unconcerned with the beauty he had just created. "From what you have told me about the background, it may be difficult to get lessons for her."

"Not if I have anything to do with it," Aileen said grimly. The glamour of Aileen was always only skin deep.

He jumped up. "I tell you what—we'll have a game," he said.

"I'll play a few notes. I'll tell you what the first one is and then you tell me the names of the others. Do you think you can do that?"

"I'll try." I knew it wasn't a game but a test, but I didn't mind, nor was I nervous at all. His eyes gave me every assurance that I had already passed somehow without trying.

He achieved the distance between himself and a great black piano in two lolloping strides. "Now, don't look," he said. "This one is middle C."

Up and down and round the scale, we swung. The noise he chose was the noise I knew every time . . . G, B flat, A, F, E flat. That in itself was not curious or interesting; what I do remember, and perhaps wrongly, was that I seemed to know before he chose what note it was going to be. There was nothing so precise as premonition about it; it was more that I anticipated his will in the discovery I had made of him.

"Remarkable," he said when he was through. "Remarkable." And the word has marked me from that time onwards, a word not from a parent or a teacher—remarkable—but somehow from one adult to another the way he spoke it.

"Can I play something now?" I was neither showing off nor spellbound. If I look back on it now, I can remember an almost physical relief I felt which I could not then interpret. But I can see that the relief lay in this: that the private, wordless language of my inner ear was actually spoken by someone else.

"You couldn't play my cello," he said. "You're too small."

I looked from him to the cello, then back again and I got a funny feeling that he wasn't being quite truthful. I would have touched his face, his hands, his chair, his books—would have, could have, and wanted to—but never that great glowing instrument he had laid so casually on its side. As large as it was and as much as he made of it, I knew it was a secret. And secrets I had of my own.

"I *meant* the piano," I said at last with a lift to my chin. He started slightly, then smiled. Aileen, who had all but disappeared into the couch, said, "Maud!"

Accustomed as I was to cringing, I didn't. Alba swooped upon me laughing. In one great lift I was on the piano stool. I was beside myself with his charm, that Prince Charming charm he had. I played him everything I knew; he crouched beside me nodding to the rhythm. In a way, he danced. "That's good—she's good," he said to Aileen. He scooped up his cello. "Here—play that Schumann again!" he cried. That little duet of ours had all the feeling of a jamboree. I have never before or since had so much fun.

Is that all that happened? I feel there was much, much more to it than that—the afternoon which became the central legend of my life! Now I am so utterly finished by him and his wife and his bloody cello! Why did he see me in the first place? If I had already shown promise on the cello itself, I could understand it. Was he courting Aileen in her incarnation as courtesan? I felt no adult signals passing over my head, no ugly half-hints of sensuality between them. And why wasn't Ilse there even in shadow form? There was not a snail's trace of her arch, padded, sinuous femininity anywhere in the room or in the blurred conversation of my two benefactors.

Beatrice has just come and gone with a bowl of home-made soup, a carton of expensive cigarettes, and a tube of strong glue. She wondered if she could—would I mind awfully if she did—mend my table leg. She is so hesitant. She mended my table leg. I sat and watched her from my chair. She mended Mother's Staffordshire dog too. She said she'd get me something at the shops. I said I didn't want anything from the shops. I said I had enough to eat in here, but the soup has only made me ravenous.

She saw my manuscript with half an eye. Her little smile made me want to tear it up and stuff it in the fire.

Does she know what I nearly did with that table leg?

It happened without warning. I've been so dazed, felt so unreal this month since I left Alba. I don't remember anything but sitting at the window and looking at the river flow. And on that night, before the visitation of that evangelist (Evangelist, evangelist—if that is an evangelist then I am tone-deaf. Am I tone-deaf?) the tears began to slide. I went to make myself a cup of tea, when suddenly—I did not know I'd do it—suddenly, I hurled the boiling kettle, wrenched it from the socket and hurled it out of the door. Lucky it didn't hit the wall. Lucky I wasn't scalded. Did I carefully avoid the wall?

With systematic thoroughness, I then proceeded to the living room and pulled from the mantelpiece every little gimcrack stupid thing and pictures from the walls. The wonky leg from off the dinner table I took for a cudgel and I smashed the china dog, the vase, the furniture, old coffee cups.

And then that funny little voice hissed inside my brain—coming roughly from the lower-left-hand portion of my brain—that I must kill the cello and everything would be all right. All would be well. It seemed like the voice of conscience speaking low and firmly to me that the cello was the fundamental root and cause of all my evil.

The music room was locked; it's always locked. I took the key. I felt already soaked in blood. I stealthily unlocked the door, the table leg in hand. If I hadn't switched on the light, perhaps I would have done it. Who knows? But I wasn't about to be surreptitious on such a matter—not on a matter of conscience or consciousness—oh, no.

I approached the case and sprung the clasps. I could not open it for a moment. I looked around the clutter of the music. The piano was thick with dust. The windows seemed to terrify me most of all. They were huge and black as coffin lids, the curtains dripped with the notion of murder. I threw open the case. The cello lay there pleading and helpless, naked and helpless. I cannot say what I saw because I ceased to see the instrument at all. Only, I remembered deep beyond time as I know it a face above my face which crooned, a white face above mine and fingers laced through bars—must have been the bars of my cot, must have been—as I lay paralysed and pleading with the face: a nightmare surely—surely a nightmare.

Meek with dread, I closed the cello case and ran crouching from the music room. I sealed it up behind me and I'll not go into it again.

CHAPTER III

Beatrice restored the glue to its rightful place in the kitchen drawer. She drew the curtains over the sink as it was getting dark. "So early now," she said aloud. The window faced a blank wall, but she drew the curtains anyway every evening out of habit and out of the sense of self-containment that it gave to hear the rain spitting against the window behind starchy folds. Her hands felt empty. She turned the tap and rinsed them, peeling scraps of glue from them under the cold water. She was not sure how much more she should become involved with Maud.

She questioned soup and glue. She so rarely obeyed impulse that impulse itself had practically deserted her: that she had given in to its rare whim that evening troubled her, obscurely shamed her.

All day at work she'd seen subtle tones of Maud—indeed, of her own self reflected in everything she'd done. She saw herself as part of the perpetually administering body of the hospital. Oh, more than soup and cigarettes had come from her and those under her: Brompton mixtures, tests, tests, tests; a crisis called for running nurses and hanging, swinging plasma. Mr Shepard died. Mrs Shepard tried to cry so that Beatrice would not be scandalized when all along she'd known that after twenty-seven years of conscientious nursing in a basement flat the woman was emotionally gaga and spent except for waves of rage at a self she saw was wasted.

It had been an average day.

It had not been an average day because she had not before experienced this curious shame of hands. Every time she reached to touch even her pen to write out orders—but mostly

. . . to touch heads of clutching patients—she felt a strange revulsion at herself. Could she have spent twenty years worming her way into the heart of a false position?

"Forty is an age," she said knowingly to the cat—she said with knowing balance of mind to the cat. She deliberately made herself a cup of tea, but she dunked the bag absently with the spoon until the cup was black with bitter liquid.

It was her white coat she'd noticed most, that and the squealing, running, rubber shoes of nurses. It would have little to do with Maud, of course, her day of spiritual indigestion. If serious, if more than indigestion, it would have been coming for some time: incubating, so to speak.

She tasted the tea, her mouth drew up reflexively. Her mind from the unexpected nastiness of black tea was jogged down one more notch to the day's real point and trouble: that she had felt from early morning this sudden wizening of the heart towards them, the patients. Never before had they been so much them and she so much us. Never!

She refused to make a drama of it. She was too staunch to rely on mood.

All the same. All the same, as if a negative electric current had been passed into her body where a positive one had flowed for years and years, she had recoiled physically from them. She had felt dragged by their asking, their demands. They had lost personality and become a collective body merely open-mouthed. The feeling that they were malingering—all of them—had quietly insisted itself on her. Mr Shepard? Malingering? Why he was dead!

Why did the image of Maud hang in their eyes?

All day Maud had hung bleakly in the west of her consciousness like a winter sun. A descending phrase of music that the girl had practised weeks ago kept coming to her inner ear: a definite descent in a major key (she supposed), and then a climb. It was something of Bach's she thought. An image of spiders came to her as if the girl had been throwing up threads of music and throwing them down to catch something in the dark. That abstract bit of Maud she liked. As she now sat, spiders presented themselves to her even more emphatically, many-jointed and enveloping with webs. She shunned such judgments utterly.

Still. She remembered with a shudder her own smugness at the zoo some years ago when she and her nephew Giovanni had found themselves in the insect house and Giovanni shrank into her skirt at an aquarium full of bird-eating spiders. She'd held him up to the glass and said, "Look how wonderfully God has made them!"

"Why does she repel me?" she asked the cat in a plaintive tone. The cat swayed gently to and fro. Beatrice knew as soon as she had spoken that Maud did not repel; but that she odiously attracted. "Why odiously? Why?"

It had been all that she could do to restrain herself from running in with soup when she had come home tired. Instead, she had walked discreetly . . . but had grabbed up the glue as an excuse to stay there usefully employed. All these favours in response to what? Her favour-giving nerve was very highly trained: on the just and the unjust alike she'd rained good down ignoring gratitude or lack of it. Why this emotion now? This shaming wish for contact?

Maud had practically glared her down that evening, and the previous one when they had met. It had been pointless to attempt to engineer the girl round to some hospital or other. She shouldn't have tried. But she had, over her shoulder, while gluing.

"The smile!" she said. She spoke so loudly that the cat jacked up its ears, widened its eyes, and jumped off the table and wandered to the white living room where everything was quieter. "It was her smile," she said again softly. Not the ironical one—no, no—the other one when she'd lain on the sofa the day they'd met. Beatrice had no frame of reference for such a look. She'd been so confused by everything else that had gone on that she'd quite forgotten it.

She hadn't quite forgotten it at all. She had been seduced by it to an altogether different picture of Maud she'd formed.

She was careful with words like "seduced."

Sexual seduction was not implied, not in any way that made a scrap of difference to the main thrust of the smile. It had been a beautiful smile, a radiant smile, a grateful smile—but something more; it had as its element a voltage which when applied to her own heart had given floods and waves and torrents of emotion which pressed to be acknowledged by her brain. It had happened out of context to the gist of their conversation.

Why was that?

Beatrice was carefully disposed not to sneak away from such a question. She thought and drew blank after blank. Too soon to tell of course—why—she simply must accept what was.

Shame of hands. Did she have feelings of shame or was it real shame?

What she thought, suddenly, not felt, was that she hadn't felt, hadn't been feeling, since God knows when. She inspected shame for a moment but with an ironical little twitch of mouth, placed it gently to one side for future inspection. What else did she feel? No, correction, when had she last felt?

Jonathan? Oh, yes, Jonathan. As far back as *medical school.* Surely not. Hearts and flowers, oh, God, at medical school. Whilst sewing up cadavers her own hot, wet eyes for the hair at the back of his neck, those inexpressible shoulders, swam with the heavy presence of him.

She knew very well she'd been a beautiful girl. "Never hold yourself cheap, *cara mia"* (that was Mama). All right then, she'd been a beautiful and expensive girl. With Beatrice there had been no carrying on. She'd cringed at dancing parties with odious drunken students. Had that been pride? No, not when her feelings (feelings again) had been so enraptured by purity. All grinding, sifting, and weighing in chemistry had pleased her, absorbed her, and all the elements of the human body in its abstract form had given her delight—passages and channels, veins and capillaries, networks of nerves, follicles of hair—she had been only a little sickened at first by the gruesomeness of corpses. After that, the beauty of how they had been created gave her wonder.

That body had not been made for debauchery, nor affliction either. She was clear about debauchery anyway.

Occasionally, she took herself to the Tate Gallery on an afternoon off. She liked the apparent limitlessness of marble floors to

stand on. She'd always felt small before art as she did before
nature. Blake was a frame of reference for her, particularly the
one engraving of God creating Adam with the serpent coiled
and twined round Adam's leg. The serpent always put her in
mind of disease. She'd stand there quietly absorbing, clutching
her handbag—poor, poor Adam. Now and then she'd go home
rested by the thought of mystery incalculable.

She drank the tea, determined not to waste it.

Was she afflicted? And anaesthetized? Had she lost the capacity for pain?

Why was memory so disjointed? She and Jonathan sipped
orange squash through straws on the steps of the Albert Memo-
rial after Beethoven one evening. How she had confided to him
all her precious aims and goals of service, and all the time she
had been drunk with the dark in his hair. Then a car crash. Why
did she say that? There had been no car crash, just the back seat
of a car where he had said with final cruelty from the shadows,
"You're too much of an angel for me, Beatrice."

Always and forever being too much of an angel for everybody! She'd been the family saint, all right.

There was an emotion, if you liked. A sensation of profound
loathing quaked in her. It is, she thought, the easiest thing in the
world not to love a saint. "Kitty," she cried in the direction of
the other room. "Kitty, do you think we ought to start a Saints'
Lib?"

Darling Beatrice won't mind if we:

All go to Rome and leave her in charge of the house.
Ask her for money.
Get her to fetch the trunk from the boxroom.
Make her cook the dinner on Cook's night off.
Allow her to tidy up.
Don't love her.

Carissima Beatrice, we beseech you, oh, elder and most invisible daughter, to help us in this day of trouble, strife, and trial!
She'd submitted to it all.

You could rely on Beatrice.

Beatrice followed her father's coffin in her mind's eye to the grave. The lurching catafalque jerked her mind and incense permeated her clothes. She had been very small. They'd buried him in Rome. She'd had the impression of the vastness of death, the vaulty church, the imposing bier, the looming, coal-black hearse; and then, a mere descent into earth and the shattering of the Pazzi.

Mama and family had wafted up to control the atmosphere. Beatrice barely remembered her father, but she had reconstructed him. (You take after your father.) His family had unbelievably not been quite up to Mama who was a little scornful of the Caesars, Brunelleschi notwithstanding. In retrospect, it warmed a forgotten element in Beatrice that Maud had known, remembered, the Pazzi Chapel. Had her eyes lit with the absolute, geometrical, chaste, serene perfection of the place? It was to Beatrice the cool light of the Annunciation; it had a shuttered peace. She could not escape the image of wings, a rush of clarity and the ambivalent face of a sheltering Virgin, half-knelt in a balletic stance, her crushed-velvet clothes frozen round her, half like a queen perpetually rapt.

To Mama such Tuscan vision was merely and incredibly an expression of the rise of the middle class. The Pazzis were, for all their antiquity, not so antique as the Orsinis. Beatrice's branch, at any rate her father, had been unforgivably addicted to hard work and enterprise. While perambulating through Museo this or that, Mama greeted Etruscan antiquities with a jocular familiarity. Her Romanness, Beatrice had come to understand, was a simple and stupid and subtle way of getting at her father who had escaped the empurpled virago into his study where he had contemplated Dante (another Florentine). In another way, Mama's Romanness (or rather her assertion of it) had more to do with a difference the Pazzis had on the matter of appetite. Beatrice's father had tended towards a secular kind of asceticism, whereas Mama tended to excess. This appetite must have seemed to be one for life when Mama was young and beautiful. As she got older, she had tended to too much, and not too discreetly consumed Strega (the smell of anise disgusted Beatrice) and food. Well, whatever it was, their lineage wasn't much use these days. Had ceased to matter really before the First World War.

Beatrice found these memories irksome. She shrugged, got up, and cast the dregs of tea into the sink. She felt as little real connection with her family as she could manage without having to reject them. Duty had served and she had done it cheerfully to profit her soul. And, *eccola!* Tatty had married a count whose lineage had utterly replenished the soul of Signora Pazzi: now, balmed in tisane, sustained with ruddy frescoes and the sound of trickling fountains of her son-in-law's villa outside Rome, Mama was wrapped away from pain.

Beatrice rubbed her tightened forehead with her thumb and forefinger. Tatty had been good, after all, in taking Mama on, but this did not explain away to Beatrice her own spent youth. She clawed the air with her other hand as if to drive away self-pity.

She had always wanted a flat of her own. She had always wanted simplicity. She was aware that she could have achieved these goals at many stations of her lifetime. Had she really wanted them? Had she not dared?

She could not endure the sight of pain, could not endure it.

Every time she'd tried to move away, one of her family had wrenched her afresh with pity. There had been poor little Tatty (Her real name was Immacolata. Beatrice gave an uncharacteristic snigger.) rabid with the boys to the point of nymphomania. There had been Giorgio fleecing Mama out of a small fortune. There had been agonizing rows, which Beatrice calmed. Mama was simply incapable of coping with the least practicality, and even a feather of one of these burdens would have killed her. So Beatrice covered for Tatty and Giorgio.

Often she'd been tempted to abandon Mama to shift for herself in the cold douche of reality, but it was inescapably true that such a shower would have destroyed her. She *had* to be nurtured in her illusions—had to. One could see the truth, but did this give one the right to inflict it? What good would it have done to have pointed out that Mama's blood was only mauve, not blue as all that? What good would it have done to have pointed the grim finger at Giorgio? What good at all would it have done to have announced to Mama the travesty of Tatty's white wedding dress? Her own frustration? But now, oh now her protectorate was at an end! Mama had said her rosary every night and she would go *on* saying it every night, swathed in a welter of black lace until the day she died. And she *would* die in peace if it killed Beatrice.

Beatrice wondered if she were wasting time in such reflections. Her life had schooled her to be frugal with anything that absorbed her in herself.

What kept her going—rather what *had* kept her going (now she was not so sure)—was silence. She was chiefly good at silence; in fact, she was quite remarkable at it.

She'd had a room of her own in Eaton Square, as spare and bare as she could make it without drawing attention to herself; and what she'd done in it was to practise silence. Every day could stretch her to inhuman limits—twelve hours of total hospital added on to five of utter family—but when she'd shut the door she greeted and was greeted by what became to her more and more incomprehensible: a soundless sound, a dark light, something in the area of the bass vibration a whale might make while cruising in the fathoms.

At first, she'd merely thanked God for sweet relief, for a recharging of her overspent heart. She'd slipped into it all, assumed it with her dressing-gown and sat at the window tranquilly.

She'd clean teeth, sleep, forget, only to find this solitude redoubled in her next engagement with it. She wondered if she wasn't becoming a little unbelievable to want, as she seemed more and more urgently to want, a relationship with thin air, but then the air wasn't so thin at all, but thick with presence, almost gravid with possibilities which had hitherto occurred only to a kind of intellectual faith she'd had.

She seemed called to the heart of it: it quickened in her. She had no language to deal with what it was. She was a thirsty beast at a night water-hole—slaking defied the question of source. All she knew was that her days' activities became a chorus punctuating sharply the burden of her nights' song.

She came abruptly up against Maud. She squeezed her eyes

tight and paced into the living room. With an irritable gesture, she turned on the light and in doing so stumbled on the rush matting. "Damn!" she said, then covered her mouth.

Never in her life had she ever stepped out of character like this. Oh, there'd been ups and downs—wars of nerves, little scars sustained in fights with Matron (she was forced to call Matron Pam, but she never thought of her as anything else but Matron). But all this bitterness she'd gone in for in the kitchen, that was not what she'd come out into the wilderness of Victoria to see. She stiffly walked in rhythm; not what she had come out to see. "Saint, indeed," she said aloud. "Saint, indeed," she said as she sat down on the sofa and ploughed her hands through her hair.

"What did I come out to see?" she said, not without effort. She looked a little wildly (for her) around—the white walls, the varnished floor, the hessian curtains, and the absolute furniture she'd chosen for herself at Peter Jones—tables expressing what it was to be a table and chairs expressing what it was to be a chair and nothing in excess of that and that is that and that. "A convent waiting room?" (She teetered on the edge of horrifying herself.) "A final demand?" she said altogether more softly.

"How silly," she said after a long pause.

After another pause, she said, "It was the cello in the silence that got to me—the cello and that funny man. That's all." She went to the window and peered out on to the square but, in the dark, saw nothing.

CHAPTER IV

Never before was there a silence like this one. I look from one window to another window. I wander from one room to another room. If I talk aloud, my voice vanishes into it, dies in my throat;

I turn the radio on, then off, on, then off. I do not trust the gramophone and am afraid to touch it. All sound does is to measure the vastness, to describe the limitless quality of death. I am afraid of death. I am crying.

You must understand how I came to this. Who is "you"? There has got to be a you that is not me. Got to be, got to got to. Where was I? You. Alba used to be you. Oh my God I think I'm going to be sick. No. It's all right.

He was too good to be true. Sometimes I couldn't believe my eyes about him. Do you know he gave me my first cello? After our first meeting he gave me a half-size cello. It arrived in a special van and when it came out of its crate, it was wrapped in pink tissue paper rather clumsily, stuck with raggy bits of Sellotape and tied round the fingerboard with a vast red ribbon. The card attached said, "With love from Thomas Alba."

What could anyone do? I had to have lessons after that. Every week I went to Bury to Miss Berg. Her house smelt like a cellar. She hung up mushrooms and onions and herbs to dry. She'd taught cello at Dartington and had a taste for dirndls. She was not flabbergasted by my talent nor by my tenuous asssociation with Alba. She seemed to be more interested in the state of my nerves because I had a dreadful tic. She made me rosemary-leaf tea and held my hand quietly before each lesson. No one could have been more disappointed than I at the sound the instrument first made, but she, snowing rosin dust everywhere and dandruff (if it must be known) would say: "We battle on, Maud, we must battle on!"

I battled. What else was there to do? I battled through my hatred of the ugly sounds I made. I battled with my fingers and my sagging right arm and the sinister bass clef and as many notes to the scales as I could cram into one bowing. Fought the desire to let mind wander, conquered the desire to slip into pale thought (as Mother became more and more bizarre) through denser and denser thickets of feeling till . . . it caught light and my playing became denser and denser to the point of real release for me from pain. I was, from childhood, a calligrapher of music with those thick black strokes of tone describing formal profundities of sound to the one who listened . . . Alba.

I tunnelled the music through to him. He was the imaginary audience for whom I played. I always half-saw him over Miss Berg's shoulder. When I practised in my room, he was there, sitting in the window-seat that looked out to the sea wall. Smiling and relaxed, he stroked his soft beard. When I made a mistake, it was for me more of a blotch on his honour than on my own. He never winced but gave a troubled frown until I got it right—then he was clear and his face understood.

I talked to him in my bed at night. He'd sit and listen and smoke his cigar and stroke my hair and close my eyes and leave the room with the door half-open because I was afraid of the dark.

I didn't talk only to him; I talked to my doll as well. She had a dirty face and fuzzy spikes of hair and I would describe Alba to her often, telling her that when I got good enough at playing the cello, I would take it and her to London, run away from home to him. I was always going to appear on his doorstep immaculate in my success. I never, in these fantasies, wore anything less than white. He would catch his breath and I would enter. We would not need to talk. He would take up his great cello, tune it, and present it to me. I would play it, opening up all heaven before him.

Are stars only rocks close to? I am of those few living persons whose dreams have all come true—to the last detail, each one. Am I so mad as the lady with the lamp up there—whatshername—Beatrice, seems to think when I say the man out there is going to kill me? He *is* going to kill me.

I know about death because I saw my mother die. Nobody knows that, not even Dr Bender.

No, no . . . it is much the safest course to remember Alba.

My Aunt Aileen fed me snippets of fuel for my passion. Do the insensitive *know what they are doing?* Her visits to us became more frequent as Mother's health declined. She'd rattle her baubles at me and declare that she and Alba had dined in Bucharest.

"How is your charming niece? Is she making progress? Do send her my love." In Paris they'd embraced after the most astonishing Dvořák. Barely had he drawn a breath before he asked for Maud. She gave me lush descriptions of his villa in Rome. I mentally walked about the gardens and leaned upon the balustrade, breathing the evening air.

I realize now I think of it she told me about Ilse. How Alba had married a beautiful soprano. What puzzles me is that I simply assumed Ilse into my whole fiction about him without a qualm. I thought about her, of course. I imagined her somehow as being graceful, queenly, and full of repose. Aileen said she'd done the "definitive Countess Almaviva." I wasn't sure what "definitive" meant, nor did I know about Countess Almaviva, but I got from Aileen's description the powerful impression of an exalted lady in a high wig and tiny shoes and silken clothes. Prince Charming and the fairy princess lived for me under fluttering pennants near the clouds.

I followed their fortune in the *Times* and on the Third Programme. I hoarded cuttings of Ilse at Salzburg or of Alba in Vienna. The *Times* sent people out to hear them. Words failed them to describe the brilliance of Mr Alba's sound. I'd catch a snatch on the radio—mostly of him, hardly of her—but in their sound I knew them utterly. What did he express when he played to me but a magic innocence? His music had the quality of incantation. The only cellists who could touch him for what he had were Casals, Rostropovich, and Piatigorsky. Fournier and Tortelier aren't a patch on him. Ilse too had magic—her voice soared and dived and trembled on the brink of purity. While I lay bound in ice, they came to me over the air like a warm breeze. That they knew me and I knew them made me a companion in their freedom.

They were howlingly famous for a while and . . . then . . . they . . . stopped. . . . I am confused.

I shall battle on. I shall!

I did not notice their eclipse for various reasons. The first of these is scarcely credible: I grew up.

Shortly before my mother's death, I was given a choice. Miss Berg decided that I was so far advanced with my music that I should put in for a place at the Royal College. This would mean my going up to London every Saturday. There was no question of my going up to London every Saturday, let alone for the audition.

I really was going to talk about Aileen and uncover Mother only it is so dark and quiet and I'm so hungry.

Aileen came down the week before Mother died to apply her energy to our situation. Who had told her but Father that she was needed? I could have told him what was needed, even at the tender age of thirteen. A nice hospital for Mother . . . of course, of course, and boarding school for Amy and me. He wasn't bound by economic need: the will proved that. I reach and fail to touch the wisdom of his decisions. The worst effort is to stretch at why he never told us she was mad. *Maybe he loved her.* It occurs, but how?

Aileen junketed down in her motor, a silver Daimler. She wore grey gloves, grey pearls, and a grey hat in which to view her messy sister. Mother was all bone—hollow eyes and hollow cheeks and hollow temples—and she piddled in her bed. Sheets smelt on the line, even after washing, of rubber and urine. Tufts of brittle hair stuck up half dark, half blonde (she'd been a naughty girl and poured a whole bottle of peroxide on her head before anyone could get to her). Yes, indeed. She was so shaky and passive to death. We never saw her except fleetingly when Miss Russell let her out for air. She'd scratch at the door and whimper.

Aileen heralded the triumph of Fortinbras. Something was in the air; Amy and I sniffed it like animals. She mumbled with Mother behind the locked door of her room. There were sibilant whispers with Father in the hall, the sound of the decanter opening, discreet drinking in crystal glasses was going on. She went to and fro in grey all the while looking *divine* and in control. Effortlessly, she joined us in the schoolroom, or nursery, really. (We never had a governess and went to grammar school, actually. Nonetheless it was called the schoolroom out of respect for Mother's past. A concession to learning was a map of the world on the wall.)

This is what's so trivial. All along while I sat numb as a corpse I wanted only one thing and that was to be able to go to the

Royal College after Christmas. Amy was all over Aileen like an insane puppy: craving, sucking nearly at her clothes, while I had it in mind only to become the most famous person in the world if only, if only something would happen to let me get up to London once a week. I think I would have chopped my whole family down in order to attain this end.

The house was so alive with secrets that we moved automatically on tiptoe. It was quite paranormal how the walls seemed to buckle and sway and mouth predictions of the future. Omens dripped from the chandeliers. Now and then there was the foreign slamming of doors and Father didn't go to his consulting rooms at all. Once, in passing the dressing room where he slept, I half-caught the sight of Aileen's pretty silken nightdress sagged on to the floor. I do not know what crisis had been reached nor can I judge nor will I.

When I say I'd grown up, this is what I mean: Aileen had a crocodile handbag Uncle George had bought from *Cartier* (Aileen still talks in italic when it comes to brand names: *Fortnum* and *Cartier*, *Gucci* and *Pucci* and *Yves Saint Laurent*—yay yay). This handbag contained goodies all the time. She was sweet, you know, she was kind. I think. Little dolls in national dress appeared from the bag. Plastic make-up sets from Woolworths emerged, rings with phony rubies heart-shaped, scarves depicting Napoli in sunshine. Amy forgave her everything for these. I've never forgiven her bloody failure.

I remember the day she left us, we had tea in the drawing room. Father sat like a waxwork Fu Man Chu in the wing-backed chair that I (oh, Christ forgive) am sitting on right now and no one spoke. Aileen poured tea as if nothing at all was going on. At last, Father rose and put on his sombre Homburg and black coat to take his daily constitutional along the cold sea wall. As soon as he was gone, Aileen, with conspiratorial giggle, hooked us into her cashmere arms and opened up the handbag. She had brought a ceramic rose for Amy, the outright favourite, Swiss chocolate for both of us, and "Something rather special, darling" for me. It was a programme from—let me see—Zurich, of a cello recital. Amy created a one-child ovation for Aileen while she stuffed her mouth with chocolate. I stolidly stared at the snapping fire. "Aren't you going to open it?" How could she have been wounded when we were so oppressed? But she was. I never give gifts myself so how could I know what it feels like? All I know is that I didn't want to open up the programme. I was irritated by the programme, but I did and there was Alba's face—the only photograph I had—caught in dramatic chiaroscuro. He leaned across the fingerboard rather like a shepherd over his crook. His face, somewhat aged, was still youthful, he seemed to brood gently over his flock: the whole world which praised him.

There's no business like showbusiness. Aileen has always said the photograph is the perfect portrait of him, which just goes to show something about Aileen. Somehow I was urged to throw the thing on the fire and let it burn. The picture seemed to mock my own sticky romance with him and I hated it.

Underneath the picture, there was a tidy scrawl which looked more like a caption than handwriting. He writes tiny characters in black ink very straight and clear as if he were guarding against excess. "My dear Maud," the legend ran. "Your aunt tells me of your progress on the cello. How fortunate for me it was to see the beginning of what I know will be an interesting career. I hear there is no need to tell you to work hard. Perhaps we will meet again when I next come to London. Yours sincerely, Thomas Alba."

His signature broke through the bounds of restraint; it was somewhat florid.

Aileen beamed at me over her cup. She was knocking back tea that day with more than usual abandon. I myself went cold at the blow that message gave to my imagination. Now I know Alba well, I do not think it necessarily imagination which went cold. It is odd, isn't it? Here I was dreaming of a glorious future during my mother's last agony, and there was Alba's promissory note of it, at which only weeks before I would have rejoiced. One would have thought that the dream parent/lover/rescuer he was to me galloping in such fashion to my aid at such a time might easily have enslaved me deeper in gratitude; when all I felt indeed and still do about that signed portrait is a flat grudge against the vulgarity of my own aspirations and the lowness that he stooped to by affecting them himself. Next to the goings-on at Castle Gloom, all else that day seemed trash, powerless to stop the inevitable.

All the same, I simpered at Aileen and thanked her. I remember. Amy, who was ten that year, stood at the door of the drawing room holding her half-eaten bar of chocolate as if all appetite for it had suddenly died. We stopped and listened. Again, the sound which had hung around the house for days started.

"I think I'd better go up and see her," Aileen said quietly as she replaced her cup on its saucer. She left us then to ascend to our barking mother who strained and hounded for her above.

It is very late but I suppose I will have to tell about Mother otherwise I won't tomorrow morning. Well here it is. I was in the garden about noon on Friday after she left—Aileen that is—the garden, that is, that faces the sea. I had my doll—I was too old for her, her name was Mary—but then I mentioned her before. There was a stone bench covered with spiky yellow moss where I went daily to commune with my doll Mary. On the day, that day, I heard a tap on the glass of the window where Mother was incarcerated, but I didn't look. Then I heard a low whistle and still I didn't look. Another low whistle. Then I looked and there she was; there she hung like a piece of jacked-up meat on a hook. She was there, strangling on the cord of the curtain, her hands tore up at her throat, her feet jerked, her eyes bulged, her tongue stuck out—her tongue stuck out which never spoke an unfragmented word to me of love stuck broadly out or licked away my tears and she was naked and then she jerked and she was dead. It really didn't take long at all.

There, I have never told that to a human soul, let alone my own. I am swimming with relief. She hung there swinging. I stood there and watched her swinging. I should have gone in and told; but it didn't seem right to go in and tell, it seemed wrong. It seemed right to go on watching, not telling. He would have hurt Mother if I told and annihilated me. Should I have told? Do you think I should have told? I did the oddest thing and I was quite conscious of doing it and calm with doing it. I took the head of Mary in my hands and I pulled it off her body and I walked down to the sea and I threw the head in and the body of the doll in. And what I really do regret is that. I should have told, you know. Should I have told? She might have been alive after all—why did I judge her dead? How could I judge such a thing at thirteen? Would she have been all right? Oh, God she would, wouldn't she have, if I'd gone up and undone her? It just seemed right that's all to stand there and watch her swinging. What could I do?

When at last I went inside Father and Miss Russell were crying. I thought he'd be angry at her, really I did, but he was crying and they said to me she'd died of a heart attack and they put abroad that she'd died of a heart attack when all the time she swung with her purple tongue. It was my fault, surely it was my fault, it's never stopped being my fault for one moment not once—not ever—for the last thirteen years. What do I do when it's my fault, where do I go when *that* is true—to what? I see gaping forever underneath. Who said tell the truth and shame the devil, who said? I am shamed. I.

Is that man out there the vengeance and the righteous wrath of God on me for never having told? Why, I saw her dying! Didn't it flit through my head to tell, I couldn't move yet I should have should have ought and ought to have moved and done something about it. Where do you go with faults? Should. Where do you go? Ought. Is there legal reason for my lapse? Why I don't know and cannot know what to do about this.

CHAPTER V

Arthur Marsdan lived in lodgings near Hammersmith Bridge. His landlady was a Mrs Abbott whose astral name, she said, was Zora. She kept twelve cats, all of them black for luck, but luck was an experience which had by-passed Khyber Road entirely.

In their separate ways, the rules of chance governed, even dominated, the inner lives of Arthur and Mrs Abbott, but neither of them knew they shared such a principle. In the first place, they barely communicated with each other; in the second place, they had both jettisoned free will to such a degree—had flung the idea so far from their lives—that any reflection on themselves being the agents of principle would have been absolutely foreign. Things happened to them, they never happened to things (this was not the truth but what they saw); consequently, from very different points of view, they had arrived at the conclusion (which was never even consciously seen as a conclusion) that threatening forces, inimical to them, operated all around them.

The expression Mrs Abbott gave to this was a vague sort of interest in spiritualism. When overtaken by the deathly hush that lack of fortune gives, she would totter out of the house and find herself some séance to attend. Mostly she sat in the sitting room, a place cast in a perpetual state of twilight, a place where heavy oak furniture stood thick with dust, where the carpet lay stuck to the floorboards with the urine of cats. There was a framed photograph of Mr Abbott wearing moustaches and a soldier's uniform; there was a more recent photograph unframed, its edges curled, of Mr Abbott in his coffin. There were many tinted pictures of past cats. The efforts she made nightly at cabalistic contact with the fading shreds of her reality would make one weep. She had been no good, no good at all at reaching Mr Abbott or the cats when they were living.

The air in the room was stifling and rancid. Mrs Abbott forbade the opening of doors or windows: she guarded her cats' virtue with the starchiness of a Victorian chaperone. Nothing distressed her half so much as the randy yowl of toms. Her cats were all female; she consigned them to a life of perpetual virginity. She also guarded a rubber plant from death. Her theory was that such a tropical sort of plant—a plant which came from such a very hot country—would perish if exposed to normal British weather. The thing stood on a plastic lace mat rigid with filth. It emitted a kind of humidity.

It was really rather surprising that she had allowed Arthur Marsdan to occupy the top of her house. Respectability was the code of the neighbourhood; it was the code she had been brought up on. When she had taken Arthur in nearly fifteen years ago, she knew in the front of her mind that widowed women committed suttee on the settee, avoiding maleness in the house on pain of social death. The back of her mind was never so conventional. The odd-ball, stifled, vulnerable look of Arthur—a younger man so nervous and so quiet—had touched a quality in herself she was at home with. She took him in as a lodger with hopes, hopes that were dashed in silence on the stairwell as they passed one another, hopes that longed out of the window after him as he left the house without a word or a sign, hopes that expired as nightly she dressed archly teasing her hair into a wild bouffant, and waited in the parlour for his ardour.

Arthur Marsdan paid his rent, kept his room monastically clean, but although he never communicated in any depth with anyone, he was not lonely. He had his thoughts. The history of these thoughts was most complex. It was never very clear where they left off and where he began.

Ostensibly (and for twenty years in actual fact), Arthur worked for the Gas Board. He had worked there for the last twenty years but had not noticed the passage of time in any particular respect. His work had been neat, his sums, accurate; if he was not bound by the overall drift of time, he was certainly bound very tightly to a precise reading of it. Until lately, he had never once clocked in late; punctuality had been his pride. The meters, too, with their rigid little hands marching along, had filled him with an obsessive and slightly anxious fascination. From house to house to house he would go unwearily inspecting and collecting from the consuming machines. He liked the feel of shillings; he liked the bags of money. He liked the entering into people's homes and taking dues—the dues, just dues and just deserts. He never, ever smiled or spoke or took a cup of tea. His expectation always was that people were, in one way or another, attempting to rob the meters. With this conspiracy afoot, he had thought it wisest not to compromise himself with any sign of friendliness, no matter how trivial that might be.

He had no notion either of how long it was he'd spent at Mrs

Abbott's, nor did he know why he had chosen Mrs Abbott's house to live in. She disgusted him. Even from the first day when he'd seen the rooms in that lean month after his mother's death, she had nauseated him. Her flesh was damp; her upper lip was downy and damp, the dampness soaked up by face powder only superficially; she had a way of thrusting her hips first out of a doorway, of hanging on the landing and hungrily watching, of forgetting to close the door when she was half-dressed, of lurking near the toilet when he went in. She had, above all, a smell which overrode the stench of cats, not of sweat, nor of soap; it was an attractive-repellent scent, a female smell: there was always the half-expectation that she would rub against him damp, damp and sensual. How he loved to hate the faint remorse which sprang from his paralysing desire for her! How he loved to hide from her on the landing, snub her nervous passes. How he loved to hear her hear him urinate; how he loved the powerlessness of her lonely, lonely, gaping, obvious hunger for response. No, he never even thought of moving from the only place he'd ever found where he was in control.

The regular tick-tock of Arthur's life had been punctuated on a Sunday by his goings-on at church. It was there, at this sombre, red-brick, evangelical place that the pendulum stopped, then radically swung in quite another direction over the pit of his less-obvious life.

Oh, for years and years now it had been a most virtuous practise of his. Nobody could fault the respectability of the place: the dour decency of oak pews, the solemn adjurations to good behaviour in the style from which Arthur himself had hardly varied. Passing the plate was an enjoyed busman's holiday for him from the meters. Passing out in the vestry with revelation was something else again; but it was what he found (after a series of inner circumstances) he got up to.

It was a question of his thoughts getting out of hand. He had always, always handled his thoughts, handled them and touched them since childhood secretly; they were what he'd never been supposed to have—not his own thoughts, not thoughts to himself, not solitary ones. Mother had been against them. How did he know that? How did he know she'd been against them? She had not been merely a harmless old lady, but a model of maternal rectitude. Look at what she'd sacrificed, bringing a boy like him up without a father. (What had she sacrificed? It had never been too clear—never clear.) She and he had done everything together—his best friend ("A boy's best friend is his mother," she had often said). There was no chance of being out of her sight for a moment. She resented school. No, not fair, he had disliked school. She had kept him home so often to protect his delicate dislike—the harm, the criticism he felt of looming older boys, of giggling sexy little girls. She was always most marvellously, most monstrously careful of his diet. Oranges (she said) made him loose. He was a growing boy. She stuffed him like a Strasbourg goose with buns. He lolloped about in fat, straggling after her to market, wandering to her bedroom in the night where she made him lie on the end of her bed always inviting him closer into it, always denying him access with her jumpy moods. All men were vicious (she said) but Arthur. Arthur was perfect. Now and then she'd get him to massage her neck and shoulders. Her head fell back, with permed and frazzled hair back, brushing his fingers ("Your fingers are so strong, Arthur"). Now and then a desperate social worker came, fidgeting, sitting on the edge of the uncut-moquette settee avoiding Mother's—fidgeting because of trying to avoid Mother's—X-ray eyes. She had X-ray eyes. When he thought thoughts to himself, she knew. She was not only perfect, but omniscient, omnipresent, and omnipotent. She even knew things he didn't think he thought. She was always telling him what he thought. She made up long quarrels with what she thought he thought. And then she would cry.

His own room was the fortress of thought. Not dirty thoughts, oh no, never them—with them lightning would strike, but you didn't know exactly where or when; yet lightning was always there at the ready. He didn't believe in God so much as Thor. He did not think, so much as sleep, in the torpid paralysis of will.

It was all right to think about God. Mother allowed that. They talked about religion often. Mother had wanted him to be a clergyman but he didn't have the "O"-levels. How could he have the "O"-levels; he never went to school except long enough to read and write and do his sums. So that is what he thought about: letting God down by not being a clergyman, and after a while God assumed a shape to him, a shape of horror unprecedented in the history of religion—surely, surely, no one but a Toltec or Aztec or Inca could have conceived such a god. Perhaps Kali had such an aspect.

In one way, this god of his subtracted from him every single human wish or thought or hunger and left him quivering like a whipped hound. In another way, his idol gratified the inexhaustible need he began to have for destruction. When Mother criticized him (as she often did) for just being there—sitting and in some way failing to respond to her—he trembled with the terror of the lightning. But when they sat together listening to the wireless and some dreadful disaster was reported on the news— a hurricane or flood, a plane crash or an earthquake—Arthur began to feel slaked for the sake, for the sake of . . . whom? It must be God.

It was shortly after Mother's fatal heart attack that his thoughts found form and meaning.

The trade Arthur had got into first of all was house painting. Mother had thought it *infra dig.* and ululated over the washing it made, but a promise from the head of the firm that Arthur, if he did well, might get advancement soothed her. It soothed him to paint. More than anything he loved to go into a room with fresh brushes and new, fresh, fresh white paint (the incalculable smell of it), a brown, dirty room, preferably, like the ones at home, and little by little eat up with white, lick with white the walls. Often he wanted to lick the paint on with his tongue. He found a kind of peace in this. He also liked the coloured houses of the middle class; he loved their brassy furniture, their framed clean pictures; he loved their silver gleaming and their crystal ashtrays. His eyes were starved for art—any art however humble was his food. Beauty at home was forbidden almost as much as truth.

What he didn't do to enjoy himself then! It was the only reprieve he ever got. The head of his firm was a kindly, fatherly man who rather took to him. Arthur lost a lot of weight. He went on sallies to the pub. He learned to make a little joke or two, and, even though he never went near a woman, he began to think that one day he might like to try. His boss even went so far as to suggest that Arthur might be good at drawing, but when he got home, his mother was so sagged to her knees in loneliness that the feeling drained away, and the thoughts that had nearly vanished during the day crept back and haunted night. Her tears and her "Oh, Arthur, you've been drinking" when he'd only had a half pint at lunchtime pulled his fragile mind into a curious shape.

Life waited with shiny ribbons to be untied; life waited to devour its own contents; but, whatever life was, it had to do with insatiable desire.

Arthur was just on the point of going for the ribbons when his mother died. His boss had persuaded him to have a pint after work; they'd done a good job of a house in Pimlico, had been given tea by the cheery mother of five who occupied it, and sauntered to the tube in the spring air. "C'mon Art," Fred had said. "But my mother will be worried." "Hang your mother, boy," Fred had said, swaying from the strap. He had looked almost grave.

Arthur had swaggered (almost) back to Baron's Court where he then lived. For the first time in his life, he adopted an attitude towards her. "H'llo Mum!" he cried (jauntily). No answer. Of course. She lay, her skirt rucked up by the fall, drunkenly by the hearth. It was all a question of timing; Mother had had perfect timing. She was dead. The tea she had prepared for him was cold, long cold, stone dead like Mother. The pot, the red-checked tablecloth seemed to crawl with cold and half-curled, cold, old kippers and yellow, cold scrambled eggs. She'd been that sure of him clocking in on time that she had scrambled eggs. Her own half-eaten meal testified to her grievances against him. Without thinking, he looked round for a note. It seemed only natural that she would leave a note. How dead she was was evident in her curled-up lip and open fish-eyed stare; her dentures had been jarred from her mouth by the fall, a little blood seeped from her nose on the hearth-rug and had been smeared casually on the bloodless grey-brown tiles.

Arthur was never sure of what he had done then; he could not remember. There was something disagreeable, something about days having gone by before he and the corpse were discovered. There was a drifting memory of a certain kind of smell. Once he had singed his hands with the gas poker in order to get rid of it.

For months after her death, Arthur had wandered around in a woolly state of non-explicit pain. For one thing, the painting job was over, gone and dead. He burnt his overall in the garden; when Fred had come to call, he had hidden trembling in the parlour. Bit by bit, he walled up everything. Sometimes in the night he woke with terror that his blood had turned to water and his bones to ashes. He kept an open razor by his bed to prove, with sometimes more than a nick, that he was really there. Once he hit an artery and before he fainted, he watched with weird happiness the pumping of the deep brown blood.

If it hadn't been for the Newsons he might have shaved himself away altogether. Mr Newson, the clergyman who had buried Mother, had a little something more than grim determination. It started (when Arthur wouldn't answer the door) with the tracts. A tract a day keeps the doctor away. He would see a shadow in the frosted glass, then the little pamphlet struggling through the letter box, then lying on the mat as if almost animate. He was afraid of them; they piled up one by one as an accusation from the angels with whom he held a nightly concourse and who hissed and spat into his inner ear a curious, tuneless threnody—a funny, gabbled, garbled noise— Obey (they said—it was the only word he could make out). Obey. Bey-O-Obadiah-bey, boy, boo hoo hoo, Ob-dob, dob, blob—Ob-i i i i-bey boy. It went something like that. God didn't like him, was so angry that—sometimes he saw himself riven in half by lightning, riven exactly in half, and each half hermaphroditically reproducing, until a whole army of Arthurs marched like robots round the parlour up and down the stairs, cruising like ghosts and as ineffectual.

What was left of his mind pulled against what came through the letter box, then pulled towards it as though he were part of a gigantic machine which stretched elastic. At last his terror became so great that he read them, sat down at the kitchen table and read every last one of them, shakily like one who visits a palmist. They spoke of SIN. Of the fundamental wickedness of MAN. Of the DEVIL and his clutch, clutch, clutches. Come to the foot of the Cross and be saved (said they). Only the elect was saved (said they). If you weren't elect that was just too bad (said they). Abandon all hope all ye who haven't got what it takes (they said). Oh, the way they talked about damnation, it made one wriggle, it made the news in the *Daily Mirror* look like Mickey Mouse. *Blam!* Off the face of the earth tens and tens and thousands of lives would struggle (and so what) in the everlasting fire.

Arthur fed on this and this fed upon Arthur. His mind, his knees, his neck were turned to jelly. He crawled around on his hands and knees begging not to be obliterated, begging to be obliterated. He would mean "God make me live" and would say "God strike me dead." He kept wishing to be blinded. At one point he nearly put out his eyes with the carving fork. The shadow persisted outside the door. At last, Arthur let Mr Newson in.

Mr Newson was as foursquare as anyone you might wish to imagine. He had a jutting jaw and had been a rugger blue at Cambridge, which was astonishing given the way he carried on ... but not really if one thought about it in any depth. When he had scragged Arthur and brought him down, he sat on his head and told his own story. He himself (he said as he sipped PG Tips in the parlour) had been one helluva guy and now he was one heavenuva guy. *See?* Arthur saw, but Mr Newson didn't because he wasn't looking, blinded as perhaps he'd been on the road to Grantchester. Arthur must come to the foot of the Cross, then all of that anxiety would subside. In fact, Mr Newson was more threesquare than four—he had a shadowy side. Perhaps Arthur had a devil, he said. (He was indulgent about this.) That might be why he'd shown such resistance to the tracts. Arthur talked about Mother until he was blue in the face. Mr Newson talked about the grip of the devil until he was blue in his. What was Christ like? Arthur wanted to know. Mr Newson smiled mysteriously that he hoped Arthur would find out. What, Arthur wanted to know, would happen if he didn't find out? Well, that was too bad, Mr Newson allowed.

As their interviews continued, things became so dire for Arthur that he nearly jumped the gun with the razor. The voices got a lot louder. They rather sang in chorus with Mr Newson. What Arthur couldn't establish was where the foot of the Cross was. Mr Newson wouldn't tell him. Mrs Newson, who came in on the act because she was even more justified than Mr Newson (it seemed to both of them), wouldn't tell him either. She reassured him, though, that the prayer circle was giving him a lot of attention (poor soul).

At long last, they took him in a charabanc to Billy Graham. With bated breath, everybody waited for Arthur to be saved. They were not disappointed. The results were spectacular. Arthur hardly knew what he was doing.

On one side he was flanked by Mrs Newson dressed in the stern mufti she adopted. Her hats never fitted—they were not vain hats but justified hats which gave her the appearance of a barrister in wigs—her hair was that grey and smoothly crimped. On the other side, he was flanked by Mr Newson. Behind and in front of him the rows of the just contained him: those already too righteous for the tears they prepared for him to shed. His eye wandered over the vastness of Earls Court, the lights, the dazzling whites of flanked, banked, massed choirs of boyish girls and girlish boys. He began to entertain the strange impression that he was in the dock of a courtroom. Yes, the very courtroom of the Lord. What was the accusation against him and why had this been rigged up specially for him? He was as a man who had spent aeons starved in dungeons, pasted, nearly carved into the walls, accustomed only to the darkness and to the company of spiders, suddenly pulled up into the light. He was nearly blinded and very confused—all too logical for him to be so—how could anyone not be so, depraved as he was beyond the barest shadow of a doubt. The Newsons settled comfortably down as the evangelist began to warm up. Somewhere in the giddiness of Arthur's inner sight he got the feeling they were eating peanuts as at a cinema. And then the centrifugal spin began. He hardly saw the figure who spoke, he caught the barest minimum of words, what pumped into his mind was tone, the genius of inflection on and on working round his skull. *Come* to the foot of the buzz buzz, *Wash* in the blood of the buzz buzz, *Clean* for the buzz. Saved by the . . . and on, he was drawn, the feeling drew out of his—where was the—confusion—lights spun about him and words whirled and he was weightless surged up with the heat of the air—heat beat his mind—his body began to struggle—were there electrodes? His tongue slobbered out, teeth gnashing against . . . He felt hands holding down his arms, then COME propelled him down down down he was down the aisle and fell at the feet exhausted and declared his loathsomeness. In his mind, there was the tearing of everything apart, he rent and tore . . . things thudded like stones of the temple of the Philistines and to all intents and purposes he was dead.

When he revived to the sight of the satisfied, the slaked faces round him, he was calm—calm and much, much better. He was saved. Was he saved? He certainly was beyond a shadow of a doubt. The Newsons couldn't get over it. All the way home in the charabanc, they wanted him to sing songs. He was encroached upon by an unreasonable drowsiness.

There was really not much to do after that. That was that.

For some time Arthur was shaky, but he was better. He got his job with the Gas Board; he moved to Mrs Abbott; he passed the plate at church and things settled down. The Newsons were not slow to lend him a helping hand; in fact, he became rather a star which was very nice for him. He recounted his experience in the way he began to see it at Bible-study meetings and at fork suppers in the Newsons' home. He eschewed tobacco and drink; he never thought of women. He was only too pleased to be in one piece.

In actual fact, he was in two distinct pieces. What the lightning bolt had dislodged only buried itself not quite six feet underground.

The Newsons' house was narrow. There was absolutely no room in it for dissolution and they themselves were so in love with the escape they'd made from worldliness, from sex, from materialism that it never crossed their minds how Arthur really was. Arthur really wasn't very well. The more he put his shoulder to their wheel, the more he confirmed the belief they had in his spiritual health. His zeal for doing their errands was enormous; his fascination for their Bible appeared endless. Everything he did for twenty years fortified the element in Arthur which was truly dangerous. His justification had put him well and truly and irrevocably on the other side of the tracks to the human race. That he forebore to drink put drinkers in disgrace; that he had nothing to do with women put women in the position of being dirty; that he never gambled made cards the devil's pasteboards; that he never smoked made tobacco evil; that he had had one admired and effective experience, which everyone told him was the experience of being saved, made every single stranger whom he met a suspect: he quietly accused humanity of being the archenemy of God.

Whole areas of life closed increasingly to his mind. He could not pass a library without condemning everyone who read a book other than the Bible. He could not see a cinema or theatre without knowing what evil went on there. He could not hear a fellow worker curse without a judgment coming to his mind. He could not bear the touch of a human hand on his arm. He always expected rape. The more he hated others, the more he truly hated his own self which groaned beneath the burden of having been reclaimed. The part which was still swampy loathed and longed.

In January of 1968 (it was something of a New Year's resolution), the Newsons started a campaign against the Permissive Society. They launched it with a fête in the garden Arthur had dug for them. It had started when Mrs Newson, passing the newsagent's window, had seen a large and glossy picture of a nude in boots. Mr Newson had been dragged along. He (being a chap and also having once been such a helluva guy) was able to pad on in and have a better look. The shop was run by a whistling, bobbing middle-aged man whose irritating smile and whose deep devotion to the flesh were left undiminished by Mr Newson's vain expostulations. "We've all got to make a living somehow, guv," he said, zinging his cash register for a little boy who wrapped his mouth round a lolly.

A crusade in Hammersmith was now in order. Mr Newson never shirked, nor Mrs ever, either.

"We live in a time when Satan rules the land. I challenge you to stand up for Christ today. Have courage today. Tell your newsagent today, the strip-club owner today, the immodestly dressed girl today—the error of their ways. I challenge you to join the great crusade.

"Ask them now, today, the question, 'Are you saved?' Oh, they will hate you and reject you, but what care you when Jesus is your friend? The more they hate you, the more you can be sure that you have struck home."

Mr Newson said this from the pulpit. Arthur, on hearing this guidance, was curiously paralysed inside; he groped his way round the half-empty church with his green baize plate. He made no note (as he usually did) of the stinginess of his fellows' contributions.

The Newsons were too busy shaking hands at the church door to notice that he'd fainted in the vestry. When he came to, he thought he'd had a vision. Fainting he associated with vision. He could not remember clearly what he had seen; he saw the house on fire and Mrs Abbott and the cats on fire and all of them including himself walking around in agony but unconsumed by fire. The most appalling aspect of the swoon was the incandescent glow of flame which like a fluoroscope revealed the bones and sexual organs of himself and Mrs Abbott.

His first waking moment he associated with self-loathing—with the horrible truth of what he really felt; but hastily the safety curtain dropped on the awful danger warning he'd been given. He was assisted by the logical scrambler that the Newsons had provided on the day of his experience at Earls Court and had sophisticated in his mind ever since. If he was saved, then it was impossible for him to think bad thoughts, therefore the bad thoughts must come from another source; that other source could hardly be Satanic as Satan he well knew had no hold over the elect. It must be (as this was irrefutably true so far) that he had heard the beginning of a call from God in response to Mr Newson's sermon. That he and Mrs Abbott had been shown together in his swoon left her utterly off the hook.

Damned as she was (theologically speaking), she did not live the kind of immoral life that Mr Newson had described. It could therefore be nothing other than the women of the sermon who themselves by their impurity, by their impiety, had caused his mind thus to fail or rather to see.

All that he had seen and lusted for—women that his mind had refused to register—seared up from the inferno of his tormented brain and brightly danced in what was conscious.

He staggered to his feet now firm of purpose. He'd tell them what for. He'd bring to them salvation and never count the cost.

He wrung the Newsons by the hand at the church door. "Your sermon was really inspiring," he said (he'd never dared to call them by their Christian names although they'd asked him once, so he called them "you").

"Thank you, Arthur," Mr Newson said indulgently.

Arthur hesitated. "Do you think you could give me a little something from the Scripture Union—some pamphlets I could put through letter boxes? I'd like to help with your campaign."

"We knew we could count on you, Arthur," Mrs Newson said. Her own contribution to the crusade had been to station herself every Saturday night outside the Hammersmith Palais accosting girls with Tyrian-purple lips (oh, their villainy was of the deepest dye no doubt). The momentary ruin of their evening's enjoyment had given her more gratification than their insults had given her pain.

They heaped Arthur up with ammunition. He staggered home in a daze.

On Monday, Arthur bought a duffle coat to protect his Sunday suit from the elements (he wasn't going to go about this thing in workman's clothes). There was something about the coat which particularly appealed to him. Was it the cowl? He did not know. It seemed to jump on his back from the rack in the shop in Shepherd's Bush.

He was plagued with dreams of fire—so much so that he became afraid to sleep. Instead, he read the Bible until nature shut his eyes. He pieced together bits of Scripture (he liked hell best) until he'd sewn a monster in his mind which needed only activation. He'd never cared for Jesus very much. He looked at justice and saw justification; he looked at mercy and saw only a grudging and tight-fitted invisible hand, happier with smiting than with help. It was impossible for him to ask for grace or, for that matter, anything else. He himself became all he needed. He began to wonder if he wasn't an angel, but he became more deeply convinced (although he did not recognize it) that he was God.

The pitiful impossibility of this subtle conviction tore his mind to shreds. The last little core of self he had began to fry. Memories of childhood came disjointed back. His mother had shattered with a word the little drawing he had once done of a naked woman. She must have been right. She was right. She had the gift of infallibility. He himself had seen the nakedness as something to be wondered at, but never mind and she was right. She was.

The cold ham and salad of his youth rose up to choke him. Burn baby burn (he had touched himself in the park when he wanted to urinate). Cauldrons of shame poured over him for the secret sin he had performed amid white tiles. The unacceptable face of Arthur leered at him through an eerie and inflamed light. A torrent of clichés rained down on his head: handsome is as handsome early to bed and penny wise curiosity killed the mutton dressed up as lamb. Oh, lamb, Arthur lamb, *don't* kiss me, Arthur, you'll muss me. Men only wanted one thing. But you're different, Arthur, different from your father (ugh). Give me a kiss. Give your not-so-old mum a kiss.

Interspersed with these, great stabs of glory shot through fire . . . blue, they were, like flames from gas, a flame so hot it lit a cold path for him down its own light. Mrs Newson and Mary Whitehouse became the handmaidens of the Lord. Not women they, not of this . . . Grossly, Grossly, Grossly immoral society of ours . . . the pill, the prick, the pounds and pounds of naked flesh, the jiggling, tasselled whores raked claws at him from newsagents' stands. Mini, maxi, name it—it goes down. The devil wears white tiles and sex, the monster from the deep lagoon, crawled up a primal drain.

The tide of fire receded every morning leaving a trace of something like charred cork in its place. He started his campaign two Tuesdays following the Sunday when he'd heard the call.

Arthur's release from twenty years' strapped-in emotions both exhilarated and exhausted him. He was like a Chinese woman whose feet have been unbound; it was like walking on knives to live. Oddly enough, pain was the least of what he felt; in one sense he had ceased to feel altogether. He certainly had stopped thinking; he shunned and forswore rationality as he had done house painting so many years ago. He became insensitive to the normal course of grief, happiness, surprise at a spring day, or fear, because he had become pure emotion himself, thus far had the checks and balances of will and understanding been gutted in his fiery mind. He became fearless and invulnerable, yet paradoxically he was all fear and vulnerability. He stuffed letter boxes full of home-made signs: "Repent—this may be your last chance!" The letter boxes babbled back damnation at him. He became a party to the secret knowledge of who was who in the spiritual hierarchy that his being now apprised. The pure emotion that he was spurted here, flared up there. He began to choose at random passers-by whom he knew to be damned. He never approached a woman without in some way burning her.

In the watches of the night, under the bare bulb of his ascetic's room, he evolved himself into a theory; he came to be an abstraction. He raked the Bible more and more for coals to his flame. Although famished for Spirit, he did not know to ask for it. Words were his reality now—something to be wrenched away from flesh. He studied how to be the wrath of God.

He lost his job at the Gas Board because he failed to clock in; he failed to turn up altogether. He forgot about the Gas Board. He actually did not notice when he'd been dismissed. He had gone so far beyond the convention of explaining himself to himself or to others that he never even shrugged.

When he stopped paying Mrs Abbott, she was tempted to ask for the money, but somehow she didn't dare try. She'd hear him moaning and thrashing in his room; she was afraid to pass him in the hall. The flesh stretched around his cheekbones and his eyes burnt with a claustral fire.

As for the Newsons, he quite forgot them too. He no more

went to church and when they came looking for him, he was never in. "He's perfectly well, thank you," Mrs Abbott told them—she had no truck with clergymen. She thought they didn't see the deeper things. Their mystification knew no bounds. Arthur had entirely disappeared.

What no one knew, to do them all some kind of justice, was just how far he'd gone in every kind of way. The women of Hammersmith had ceased to interest him; his method of approaching them frustrated him. Somehow they never really filled the bill. Oh, they feared his stealthy voice, all right; they feared the vacuum quality in him which sucked them in like undertow, but something was missing in them. They splashed him all over with nervous giggles or withdrew into a hardened, arms-akimbo look. The little fear they gave him jingled like loose change around his mind; it didn't buy him what he wanted. Perhaps it had to do with their looking so familiar, this kind of woman that he'd lived with all his life. Amid the vegetable barrows on the North End Road, he could hardly get a purchase on his mission. Somehow Mother trailed invisibly behind; her death had made her grow like anything, had made her eight feet tall to his five foot six. Oh, she had grown in direct proportion to his growth; just as she had loomed three feet above him when he was a boy, so she did now. He lifted up the hammer of God to smite, yet he could only bring it down with a dull thud. When he approached a girl, he thought he saw it smash. "The wages of sin is death, sister." He saw, before he said this, the pink, brown, or black flesh split under the blow and, drool, not blood, but something colourless like sweet and sticky juice. Under this vision was another vision which harrowed him: himself he saw on hands and knees, licking like a dog the juicy ruins . . . sniffing, licking, slobbering now with love, gobbling the peachy flesh. But when he'd spoken, how flat and patting came out the words; they didn't do a thing.

An incident he saw on the Fulham Palace Road decided everybody's fate. It would have been so trivial to anybody else; to Arthur it was much more than enough to point the way he had to go. He stood, ears ringing, near the bus stop over from the cemetery one fine autumn day having quite run out of fire.

What he might have done (if the bus had come first) would have been to have gone on home. Had he done so, he would have found Mr Newson waiting for the fifteenth time on Mrs Abbott's doorstep. As Arthur's absence from the fold drew out, Mr Newson had started curiously to prickle underneath his scalp. He had never liked Arthur from the very start and as this dislike had had in it the elements of being unkind, he had overlooked and overlooked again with stalwart will the qualities in Arthur that repelled him. Now that he was gone, Mr Newson's instinct (which he rarely listened to because it frightened him) began to toll like a submerged bell. It wasn't apostasy he feared; he queerly thought of something else—what else, he could not tell.

At any rate, Arthur, as he waited, suddenly became aware of a highly polished silver Jaguar parked a little way from where he stood. An elegant, assured young gentleman sat at the wheel; next to him, speaking urgently, there sat a beautiful young lady. They appeared to have been awkwardly transplanted from Bond Street. Somehow they cast a spell; having seen them, Arthur could not look anywhere else. All at once, for no apparent reason, they lunged at one another and embraced—no, much more than that—they devoured each other open-mouthed, they thrashed and tore like a pair of mating sharks. What were they after and why were they like this in the Fulham Palace Road in broad daylight? They seemed to want to be consumed, to be gutted by each other. They did not appear to care what anyone saw.

Endless guesses could be made over why they had lost all self-control. Had they, perhaps, buried in the nearby cemetery their only child? Were they, in fact, escaping the stifling clutches of an unjust parent? Had they just reconciled a seemingly irreconcilable quarrel? Or was it simply a common case of lust; a little flutter of adultery in a part of London where nobody knew them, away from that bastard of a husband and my wife who doesn't understand me.

Arthur knew all right, all right. His Jaguar, her Hermes scarf, his suit, her crocodile handbag told him what to know. It wasn't their impurity which stank so much as what was sleek and beautiful and rich that they had to back it up. "It will be better for Sodom and Gomorrah than for you . . ." occurred to him, and having occurred to him, it became true, not only of the couple in the car whom he knew nothing about, but of everyone who might correspond to them in any detail of appearance, world without end, amen.

The bus came and went without him. He knew, he truly knew now where he had to go and what he had to do. Pure impulse that he was, he set out at once to conquer the West End.

He found his real milieu. If he had hesitated from some undisclosed pity he had for his own immediate neighbours in Hammersmith—some familiarity they had with whatever identity was left to him—he certainly had no such feeling for the rich. Absolutely all the stops were out now. The more impenetrable servants slammed the door in his face, the harder he became in the deep notion he had of sinfulness which lurked in the interiors forbidden him. He imagined all kinds of hell going on behind the insurmountable barriers of wealth and class and education. He broadened out now into an all-out war on everything that did not pertain to him. He dragged around the streets of Knightsbridge, Kensington, Westminster spitting fire at every well-heeled woman that he saw. They did burn better, they gave a better class of smoke; they physically recoiled from him from one end of Sloane Street to the other. Somehow he got a much better bite out of his insults to them; the revulsion they gave in return excited him.

The curl of a scented lip, the shrinking of a gloved hand, the gasp from a cultured throat—these things gave him a power he had never experienced before. He dazzled in the heights of being noticed, of being potent with women who, heretofore, would never so much as have given him a glass of water or the time of day. He shook up words like "God" and "Kingdom" and "Judgment" in corrosive acid and simply poured. He had little or no idea of what he was saying.

His retreat from the higher slopes of gentle breeding to the slightly lower ones of Theodoric Square came quite by accident. He had zig-zagged all the morning around Eaton Square accosting Lady this and attacking the Honourable that, when a dowager of stout proportions came upon him haranguing her daughter. Flanked by her two waddling terriers, she descended upon him like a Valkyrie and threatened him with the police. Arthur had been moved on often enough by police. He somehow never feared them: they seemed to have something in common with him. No, it was an expression in the dowager's eyes, it was the way in which she gripped her shopping bag, it was the frizzled, grizzled set of her hair, the firmness of her mouth that suddenly made the world spin round without him. What did she smell like? Whom did he remember? It was as if he had been mistakenly walking about on air; looking down, he proceeded to drop. Before he fell, he staggered off; he jumped on a passing bus and found himself at the top of Theodoric Square.

It took him a little while and a walk to the river to recover his former wildness. There was a fine rain, water descended into water. He loved the guzzling, sucking sound—the flow; it hypnotized, it drew out his terror. He hovered like a black and brooding bird above the flood. He was in union with the tide.

Maud. He hardly knew the meaning of reflection, but Maud—that he had found her was enough. How had it been possible to know that she was journey's end? He liked to use her name as a charm; it took on solidity in his mouth when he uttered it. He said it over and over again. She had become his mantra. Every detail of her was alive—the stained red skirt, the thin wool shirt, the high head, the strong hands—he could not get enough of her; her face was somehow valuable . . . there was the nacred pallor of pearl about her skin in which were set her jewelled eyes, bright as two naked filaments from shattered bulbs: her eyes, they burnt, they ate into his brain. He could hear the blood pumping round her veins; he heard, felt, and sensed the underground rhythms of her. He had found her that day he had gazed in the river. Who had given her to him? God? Had He given? God the giver was never Arthur's view of Him. In Arthur's view He mostly wanted mayhem. Never mind articulate thought; his intellect lay bleeding. How many times had he knifed it when it had jumped up and tried to tell him something?

Oh, the hard of heart, slippery past him on cold street corners; oh, the ladies! What were they to Maud? What were those one or two lukewarm reactions to his Maud. He spewed them out of his mouth for Maud, Maud, Maud.

He fed on his hot vision of her in his cold room in Hammersmith. Never, never, never, had anyone ever, ever, ever *heard* what he said. She had heard what he said. The fear in her eyes burnt out his mind and warmed in consequence his heart. Her afterimage on his closed lids burnt blue. His risen arm had smitten and she had reeled beneath his blow. His mind flicked over and over again the vision of her twisting hands.

In sleep, she came to him in a shower of blood. There was something all red and fiery about her—she danced across to his bedside like flames. It began to develop in his head that she wanted him . . . his soiled sheets proved to him how much she wanted him.

In his dreams of her, she would beg to be saved; beg to be beaten for her sins. He had her pulped and bleeding—blood and fire and pain—together they reached an ecstasy, merged as they were in pain.

She must be artistic, he thought, when he thought. With a face like that and hands like that and beauty like that (oh, that beauty he'd forgotten, that love of white paint, love of trees, a yearning came back like health). No wonder she wanted a beating. People like that wanted a beating. Hadn't he seen the devil in her heart while sitting in her very white painted room? Her breasts had parted to reveal a black-and-red confusion.

Signs and wonders came to him out of the air . . . noises to torment a Caliban. "Arthur, Arthur, Artie? Are you coming to beat the hell out of me Artie? To beat the devil out?" The voice was slithery and sugary pure. "You'd better come and get me, Arthur. You left your shadow here and you never know what I might do to it." A sniggering fat laugh followed. "Come and heal me, Arthur, come and save me." Now pleading, still mocking. The voice was at odds with the memory . . . the lifted head, proud back . . . oh, she racked him with longing, her Ariel voice seduced his ears with song. In his fragmented dreams, he buried his head in her lap deep and let out a long and shuddering sigh.

To save his love goddess from the pit became his fundamental deep desire.

There was one, oh, one, yes one thing in the way: an almost insurmountable odd thing he couldn't get the better of: the woman on the stair; yes, she.

Where had he seen her before? Did he recognize her? The face was associated in his mind with relief from pain. Or was it to do with the few and unsought-after times he'd realized that he was in pain? It was not the face he knew, but the expression in the eyes; the eyes charmed and comforted a vestige of himself which knew the gravity of his condition, that knowledge which he feared and shunned.

How did she communicate with him; how had she? There was presence in her. She had looked so horrified—not at him, but for him. She had crossed herself like one who sees a hearse—there but for the grace of God go I.

She did not put him in mind of women at all. Women with cold, insatiable mouths, women whose eyes turned you to stone; women who having sung their lyric song drowned you and ate you. This woman was no woman at all who did not do these things.

She was a spirit.

She haunted the landing.

He got the impression he had run straight through her, but her eyes had stuck to his head and were watching his thoughts about Maud.

She was Maud's devil, Maud's angel of pure light plummeted.

All he'd seen was eyes in the shadow of the stairs. What did she want with him? Why did the memory of her hunt him down? Arthur never asked questions he did not immediately answer—he chose an answer randomly from prefabricated phrases in his skull. "The whore of Babylon" occurred but was rejected. "The Angel of Death" came closer and lodged home. Death's angel mouthed doom in silence. More and more to him she wore a hood. More, she sang, pitched out to him a nocturne—something deep, obscure, and thick as night—thicker than death-cap mushrooms in the glare of moon. She was a gate made of pearl that mocked his enterprise; she was something with closed doors behind which—she wasn't like those bastions of the rich.

She'd found him out, but when he searched for her, she disappeared. Why should she be couched on the foot of his mountain where his darling's eyrie stood unless, unless she'd been *put* there. Was he equal to thrashing it out with her? He could not now envision meeting with her again. She fortified the stairs. The eyes already ate into his purpose, drained him of his intention to exorcise Maud. "If you think I have a devil cast it out" was sonorous to his inner ear—indeed fugal the way it fractured into myriad little tongues of flame that sang it.

He would get Maud—no fear.

He vanished from Mrs Abbott's house for good; his impulse drew him on to the garden that belonged to the house in Theodoric Square. Easily enough he jumped the fence; he found a covert in a rhododendron; from there with hardly interval for food or sleep, he watched Maud's door.

CHAPTER VI

I said my Aunt Aileen brought in the reign of Fortinbras and so she did: a reign of order, sense, and calm, a reign of sanity, a reign of not so good and not so bad, a reign of gels we'll muddle through. The death of Mother and the death of Uncle George within three months shook Aileen down from international heights to the limited and cosy plane she lives on to this day.

Such a lot of funerals. They burnt Mother. The flap went up then down; down, down she went into the burning, fiery furnace and Father flung her ashes in the sea. They played offensive music—piped Bach, dead Bach, I could have done it live.

Uncle George was buried from St James's, Piccadilly; his funeral was almost as chilly as my mother's. Perhaps the fact of death itself numbs the mind. At least he had friends who came to waffle on over Aileen's baked meats. Awfully (waffle-waffle) sorry (munch), darling (slurp). Oh, God.

Father took us to the Continent. He made that time his final effort with us. The trip was our last family exercise in unrelieved misery. From Cherbourg to the Bay of Naples he never smiled. He stood fully suited on pleasure boats, in market places blackly glaring at the sunshine, and Amy and I observed a rule of almost total silence except in hotel bedrooms where we burst with giggles in relief that at least he'd gone away for the night. He simply wished that we should cease to be. What we found out was that our lunatic mama had held us together. Her death had been a drastic mistake after all. We sat frigid and silent in the Piazza drinking *acqua minerale* around her dreadful absence.

When we returned, Father told us we were moving to Aileen's. "In my circumstances, I can hardly be expected to look after two growing girls. You will attend school in London and will return here for whatever part of the holidays your aunt sees fit to release you." *Fiat.*

As the train pulled out, Amy went berserk with delight. I, on the other hand, experienced a scalding pain. I don't know why I loved him.

As soon as we were established in London, Aileen whose secret grief was barrenness, spared nothing. Whereas before we'd had boiled mutton on Sunday, cold mutton on Monday, minced mutton on Tuesday and so on through the week (I still heave at the smell of caper sauce), we were now fed on every delicacy imaginable—trout, asparagus, strawberries, pastries. She sent us to a pukka day school; we had riding lessons, swimming lessons, parties. She gave us charm bracelets, brooches, rings, and pendants; heaps and heaps of clothes; hair-dos; bath salts. Our room was feet thick with ruffles and rugs; we nearly stifled in perfume. Amy and Aileen fell in love. They ceased to like or understand me. They became involved in vestal orgies of swapping skirts and shoes, of gossip and of Amy's crazes. Amy was fanatic for normality and she obliterated Suffolk with every kind of excess—horse frenzy, clothes frenzy, boy frenzy—and as Aileen had little occupation and less sense, she raised herself as high priestess of my sister's cults.

I became a cellist. A life not without its rigours. Let me see. I'll write a little blurb. Maud Eustace, best in her year at the Royal College. Compared to Jacqueline du Pré but thought a little more intense. Studied in America with Janorsky who said: "I theenk you are a lettle beet too nairfous, but nonetheless . . ." English Chamber Orchestra in chorus line, then Maurice Moore Quartet. Was told "too soloistic." Success followed by study with Thomas Alba until just the other day.

My personal history reads less well: I had love affairs with nearly anyone I could lay my hands on.

It wasn't as simple as that.

What I cannot understand is vision.

I seemed to be buried in my body, groping through ligaments of pain.

Why, what I wanted out of life was surely honourable. It is hardly a soft thing to break one's fingers eight hours daily over four lengths of catgut, to slave over minute relationships of note to note, to hammer all desire into a lust for perfection. As I suggest, my mind failed time and time again, fainted, failed, and weakened over the inhuman demands of my art.

I fell in love time and time again with personifications of sound—mostly Martin, chiefly Martin for the diabolical things he did to the piano. We were consumed with the Brahms we played together, the sweat poured off in rivulets while all the time the control was there. He harrowed me for my mistakes. I burst into tears. I sliced him down for his. He stormed. He almost kissed me in St James's Park where we took wine and sandwiches one day to clear the air. I would have died for him. Why did he have to go and say I needed a psychiatrist? I did die for him; I went to Dr Bender, that Freudian necromancer given to reading the dregs of the mind, given to gazing at the forehead and prognosticating. Oh, he had everybody fixed!

And where is Martin now? Oh, sweet Mozart! Winning the Leeds competition. I heard him once on Radio Three and how he has come on, spinning feather strokes up and out and leaping for joy like the morning stars. He is now immeasurably above me. Why, why do I love the unattainable?

I was dirty with the attainable—never Martin. I would not sully him with myself. I couldn't even catalogue the third-rate fiddlers that I slept with. I gnawed my hands with desire for the cheap and easy. I don't remember having a virginity to lose: just a scuffle and a cut and it was gone, then another and another, faceless, and every time I bit into the apple of it the worm poked out and mocked me, beckoning deeper and worse. Oh, I built up quite a reputation I was obscurely proud of.

All the time I was deeply ashamed.

Do they know the rack they turn on and the spit they roast on? These panders and minions of hell who pinch and tweeze the brain, engorging it out of all shape and sense and reason? Does the pursuit of pleasure kill pleasure? Perhaps the soul *does* die. Am I angry at that death, or at the death of desire which reached its inevitable base in Maurice Moore?

Maurice had a vulpine look. Why speak of him in the past tense? He has a vulpine look. His lips come out somehow prow-shaped and thick. He is the apostle of everybody-who-is-any-body. He and his wife Dulcie live in Belsize Park, but they say it's St John's Wood. Their lavatory (which they call "the bog") is painted in rust-red and on the walls hang the framed, auto-graphed portraits of Ormandy and Söderstrom, of Fischer-Dies-kau, Klemperer, Heifetz, Shostakovich, Rostropovich. He might as well have hung up Rameau or Beethoven for all the meaning that these people have to Maurice or that Maurice has to them. It made me feel a little sick when I perceived that Alba was among them too, in the same photograph he'd sent me through Aileen so many years before. Everybody knew that Alba had seceded from the rat-race many years before. He'd lost touch with Aileen and I confess I hadn't thought of him myself in any depth since Mother's death. When I saw the portrait hanging there, I felt both afraid and ashamed of it and so forgot it. But I used their other "bog" until our final parting of the ways.

Maurice plays the fiddle. He was a child prodigy and in that I do pity him having been touted round Europe in an Eton collar from the age of six without an education to sustain him (at least I can say for Father that he made me go to school). I do not think that Maurice ever had a burning genius—but burning parents he did have and a remarkable facility. All I do know is that he has stuffed his ears with applause against the real demands that music makes. He hears, in a muffled way, the currency that pitch and tone can represent, and with it he buys more applause.

This isn't to say that Maurice isn't competent at his job; he is both competent and confident. I never saw a man work harder for himself. He hardly sleeps, but when he does, I'm certain that his dreams work for him too (he wouldn't let the golden opportunity of any moment of the day or night slip from his grasp).

He's got lots of friends down at the Beeb. He broke through, not so very long ago, into the world of telly chat shows for which he has evolved a Pagliacci laugh, with which he seems to hide his furrowed brow weighted (and who cannot suppose it) with the high calling of art. He never smiles, but when he attempts to, he flashes capped teeth. He cannot stroke his cat without showing off to it.

What is base . . . ?

What *is* base?

Maurice had no answer to this question, neither did he admit the possibility that the question might be asked. What cross is there? I found him at the foot of my life.

He found me on the beach at Aldeburgh and I made sure he'd find me there too. I knew he was looking out for a new cellist and I'd caught him—throughout the festival—following me with eyes, breaking off conversations, submitting to the trails I'd left behind me of veiled and amorous regard. I'd developed, in those last days, a strong technique in the equivocal for men.

I had complicated my life unnecessarily with a horn player whose insistence on taking me seriously bored me somewhat. He wanted to leave his wife for me. He so accused me by his presence that I cut a rehearsal to avoid him. We were doing Brandenburg Four. Maurice was chatting up a big alto in the pub. I'd followed them there and stood so close, nursing a gin, that he, who couldn't take his eyes off me, included me in their conversation. I made it known where I was going, then went. I sat on the shingle for a while, the same strand which ten miles up the coast backed on to my family home. I gathered little stones into my skirt and tried to make shapes of them: owls and bears and hearts which I inscribed with chalk.

And then he came. He stood some yards off, energetically throwing pebbles into the sea. He waited for me to prise myself from my occupation, and then in quite a casual way he crunched up. "May I join you?" He did not wait for a reply but sat and lounged next to me. I felt very clever.

His hair had more than a few streaks of grey, but he was tall and fit as a fiddler of his prominence (not eminence) should be. I did not feel and never felt the most trivial desire for him. "I followed you here," he said. The catch of him excited me though.

I shook my hair around my face and peered through it at him. He was forced to shift in order to speak to me directly. I went on scratching owls.

"You're well thought of," he said.

I held out still. "That's nice."

"Of course you know my little group?" He referred to his quartet.

"Of course." I kept looking through my hair at his even teeth, that sensual, prow-shaped mouth I spoke of. I knew the works of his quartet all right—melodramatic, self-important Beethoven, tidy, wooden Haydn. I thought nothing of him, nothing of him at all and yet he gleamed with fame.

Critics never knew what to say about the Moore Quartet. It had such dazzle and such style. The man from the *Guardian* once used "insincerity" to effect, but it fell short of the mark. I think (and I do speak from experience) that Maurice never really liked music very much. What he lacked in liking he made up with powerful, electrifying sound—mere sound. Heigh-ho. And still you couldn't fault him bar for bar. He always stayed on the right side of the law. He's the only living man who could make chamber music vulgar. I ask you. Chamber music.

Maurice always made me think of a courtier, well-connected to some faceless emperor who held all of our careers in the palm of his hand. Maurice squeezed or opened the hand. He wasn't averse to making a king or queen or two and he had a wicked inclination to depose as well. A word or two to Deutsche Grammophon; a word or two against at Dulcie's lavish dinner parties (poor Dulcie, poor, poor Dulcie).

Still—stars shine.

"John Branston's leaving us in September, going to America," he said.

"Who's he?" I knew perfectly well who he was.

"Our cellist. Have you plans?"

"I'm not entirely sure." I was entirely sure. I hid my jumping wrists in my skirt. "When's the audition?"

He has his own way of dealing. As I wouldn't look round, he lay back on his elbows on the damp shingle. "Oh, I think we might waive that in your case. I like your sound."

"You can't know too much about it unless you can walk through walls," I said.

He laughed. I always hated the way he laughed. I hate the sea too. Hate it. But I looked out at it. "My dear I do walk through walls," he said. This was not, as it turned out, an idle boast. Everyone, I surmise, is psychic about something. Maurice was immune to the immaterial unless he gained by it. His second sight was wholly trained on the best in what was new. He had the feel of trends before they started.

"I think it would be more creative if we had a chat," he said.

We drove out to an inn for dinner after that evening's performance. I'd expected to go with the other members of the quartet but they didn't come. I seethed all the way there about this, and about the Mozart that they'd done. I like Mozart. I feel a loyalty to Mozart that Maurice wouldn't understand.

The inn bordered on a deep canal where black swans swam. We ate outside. A becalmed sailing boat floated without tide to bear it about a hundred yards from us in the channel. Two little children peeped over the bows into the still water. It was late for them to be up. They ate crisps and drank orange squash. Now and then they fed crisps to the swans which had no gratitude.

The children watched Maurice and me as we took our food in the evening air. I wore a little black thing with a deep décolletage. Maurice was invulnerable to the children's blinking.

"How did you like the Mozart?" He leaned upon the table with his elbows and looked down my dress. He played with crumbs of roll. His eyes were all heavy and he swarmed me. We were drinking a lot of wine. "Did you like it?"

"It was terrible," I said, thinking to hold on to some integrity. It was too late to hold on to any integrity. I'll never know where Maurice's was, if that's a comfort, and it isn't. Insults ran off him as if he had been waterproof, asbestos, or maybe even stone. He hadn't even the grace to blush; he only smiled more cosily with his seducer's charm. "Great!" he said. "That's great. I like criticism. Tell me where I—where we went wrong."

I told him. He neither defended his bridges nor stuck by his tempi. The more I raved the more he smiled saying all the time, "That is really good. That's great."

We kept on drinking and we kept on eating and I found it difficult to hold on to my mind. He took my hand and kneaded it. I felt sick and paralysed with weakness even though I knew with my good bowing arm I could have knocked him down. He kept on stroking and squeezing my horny hand.

"How do you see us shaping up if you took Branston's place?" He seemed all pointed mouth and tongue. Although it was chilly, his hand was slippery with sweat. I'm so weak. I pulled away, then felt ashamed at having put myself at a disadvantage.

"Deeper," I said. "Less shallow."

"That's good. That's great. We need more depth." I thought he was going to plunge into my shoulder, but he merely knocked off a midge, then settled again and sat, sumptuous in his control of me. If I can't control men, they frighten me. If I can control them, they bore me.

Maurice called for stronger wine even though I said I didn't want any more to drink. He, seeing his time was not quite right, launched into his new-frontiers-in-music line. He never lost his stride, not for a moment. He kept it up with eyes and lickerish mouth. He, of all people, started talking about cooperative music and committed music and committee music and how his committed musicians played community singsongs, ding-dong. I was too drunk to listen. He must have got all that from Dulcie, for when allowed to speak, she sometimes voiced the thoughts of Chairman Mao. At least she voiced thoughts. She also wore a large pectoral cross. She was a strange, strained woman.

I kept watching the children in the boat out of the corner of my eye. I started to reel into Steak Diane. "Do you think that lady's drunk?" one child said at last. Voices walk on water. I looked around and saw solemn eyes in the half-light of the boat lamp.

"Mummy's drunk," the other said. I knew the—tone. I knew the child's feelings. Maurice pumped away at my knee. I mouthed the steak, and then I suddenly got up and stumbled to the water.

I don't know what possessed me. What can have possessed me? "Mummy's going to throw herself in," I said.

Maurice was not too far behind me.

I threw myself in.

God, but the water was cold! It wasn't very deep, but it closed over my head. All I thought of before they hauled me out was the most ridiculous pair of words. "Contemporary music. Contemporary music. Contemporary music." Those words ran through my head as I became engulfed in duckweed.

When I was wrapped in blankets on the bank, Maurice told everyone I'd fallen in. I had fallen in. I'd no intention to die, just to immolate myself before the children's pain. I looked for them, but the boat was gone. I guess the drunken parents had moved the boat on with a motor, to be removed from the spectacle of me.

Maurice was very much impressed by what I'd done. Maurice enormously admired extremes. Somehow we came quite close, as if I had done something famous.

I lay in the room that Maurice had already rented secretly before the meal—hot-water bottles under my shivering, hurting body. He sat on the bedroom chair, one of those wicker ones, and swung his crossed leg from the knee. I can only say that I now know what it's like to be a fish in an aquarium watched by a cat. Mere lechery had now deserted him; he was on fire with greed.

When the chambermaid left, he slipped into bed. To *warm*

me—that's what he said. Oh, dear, oh, dear. And then he plundered and I clung. Who was I to struggle against men or water? No one wins quite like a victim and I got the job.

From that time on I really did do awfully well.

"The addition of Maud Eustace to the Moore Quartet has added considerably to their depth. She added an almost tragic dimension to the . . ." oh, hell what does it matter? Maurice was over the moon with me. He said I had improved the balance and Maurice thought day and night about balance, or so he said. He really couldn't get enough of me, and all the time, he harked back to the water, to that *profound* experience of me in the water. And all the time I made out to him that my feelings were so *deep* and I felt really nothing at all, not even pain, only ambition. There really isn't anything quite like applause or hushed recording studios or plush green rooms. But always collective. I didn't like that. Everybody I know who's any good loves to play with other people. I wanted to play alone.

I'm no good and I never was.

What's at base? What's at base?

It's true enough to say that I'm no good; that I used the quartet as a stepping stone to fame. I'm really not alone in doing that, but I think I am fairly isolated in my dishonesty. Because I had redeemed the quartet from the critics' mistrust of it, I knew I was secure. In consequence of this, I started taking liberties with long drawn-out *rubato*. I began to read *forte* louder than anyone else, *piano* with me became hushed, exciting *pianissimo*. All ears were drawn to me, and all eyes too: I invested in a wardrobe which, falling just short of bad taste, made me a kind of cheesecake of . . . *chamber music*.

In other and more personal ways I was forced to obey the conditions of sale. Maurice really loved to humiliate Dulcie. For years he'd done this with music, cramming her house with musicians who could talk of nothing else but music. The only way he'd ever point her out at parties was to claim loudly at some point in the evening that Dulcie was tone-deaf. "She couldn't play 'Twinkle, Twinkle Little Star' on the harmonica," he used to say, "but she's a good cook."

Dulcie always stood (it seemed to me) with her back to the

audience, shoving French loaves wrapped in foil into the oven, or taking French loaves wrapped in foil out of the oven. She drank white wine out of a glass that seemed perpetually full. The bottle and the glass stood on the stainless-steel hob—all the time. With my advent, Maurice's sadism knew no bounds. She always just missed his rummaging into my neck behind the cupboard door. He sometimes would refer to the geography of my flat—then—oops. He'd half-cover his mouth. Their two detestable adolescent boys despised her too. He made quite sure of that by dint of a continuous drip-drip of mocking sarcasm and disdain.

Could he turn me into Jacqueline du Pré or maybe yet Casals? He kept this possibility ever before my eyes. I never hated a man so much. He had a cold, reptilian touch. Everything he did tuned my nerves to screaming pitch. He always smelt of toothpaste, wine, and aftershave; he folded his clothes daintily on the chair; he was silky smooth and rude to waiters; he gorged his food but manicured his nails. He showed this all, all off to me because I was young.

I became older and older and colder and colder. I might have died of hypothermia if it hadn't been for Bach. I really have no idea at all why I took up the Bach.

My desolation was nearly complete. I'd come home late from a performance, let myself into the cold flat with the latchkey and just . . . sit in the dark for hours. I'd expel Maurice from my bed (Maurice had a kink or two) and send him home to Dulcie (who had not). I'd draw my bruised body up, hug my knees, and gnash my teeth and cry. My loneliness was like one cold long exhalation into space. I was more foreign to myself than the moon. I might have had a drunken dip into an East Anglican canal, but this time I thought of suicide in earnest. There was nothing profound about it all. Between me and the gas oven there was nothing at all but the vision of my mother dangling. I was stuck in a kind of sane madness: everything was as calm as the dead of night.

Love is king, even in the dead of night. Love is king. Love is King Kind. The choice came to me out of nowhere at four o'clock one morning that I could die, or yet again I could go into the music room. I got out of bed and stood in the cold and wondered whether I would sacrifice myself under the aegis of the North Thames Gas Board? I started to laugh. I laughed and laughed until the tears rolled down my face, and then with a kind of stateliness I proceeded to the music room and without really knowing what I was doing, rummaged around in the chest where I keep old music until I found the C-major suite, and I played it and I played it again and again.

Did I start up the suites that year as a kind of penance for my black sins? No, I didn't. I started them because they hang together so. No, I didn't know that till I started them. I just did them, that's all, spontaneously. Out of no reason at all, I went into the music room every morning about three in my night-dress, shivering cold with no dressing-gown and sat upon the stool and played the C-major—because I knew it—from start to finish. Then again. And again. I played till six or so, shivering and shuddering with the noise and the cold and the sun rising—shuddering at how bad I was, how good Bach was and why not try.

Was that grace? It seemed to come from absolutely nowhere, this curious, astringent urge to play. I'll have to ask good old Beatrice about grace or perhaps the man who waits in the garden.

The music room became my own night garden. I wished sometimes the night would never end for all the playing I did then in it. I closed my eyes and played to the scent of jasmine and oleander and the sound of birds. A shaft struck through of the lover I played to. All the time, my days were filled with hell. Who heard me then? No one. I felt devoutly blind.

On our Grand Tour after the death of Mama, Amy and I wore straw hats and white gloves. Worlds of children passed us staring, hurried on by mothers every bit as quaint as ourselves in antique rusty black. We were brought up to a standard of rigour which hurled us beyond the flesh, almost beyond the shame of being abnormal. My father desired to see Mont-Saint-Michel, that magic mountain which aspires to God. Italy had left what was Gothic in his soul untouched. We carried green Michelins (in French; no concession was made to our mother tongue) and were altogether starched in ribbons, Liberty bodices, and loath-some purple gingham.

We started from the vast, granite base, anchored beyond tides in the sea. We were slipshod pilgrims with no bleeding feet, no stomachs corroded by fasting, no penitential psalms at hand; yet, we had a Lenten look as we traipsed behind Sir Giles Eustace up and up and up the steep mound. We felt rather sick on *moules farcies* and *la fameuse omelette* de Mont-Saint-Michel which we had been forced to *déguster* at Mère Poulard below. Our father, with his prescribing pen, had written a postcard to Nurse Nancy (his then wife-to-be) at the table; the card was a lurid photograph of *crêpes suzette* accompanied by a recipe and the slogan *"Bon appetit"* inscribed in thick white script below.

We made our climb by a side road; our father's ears were flattened back when he saw the row of tourist shops which lined the main route. Amy had a cough, which she tried to muffle with her handkerchief. Father regarded illness in his children as a sort of betrayal. Her cheeks were pink from exertion. He stalked quickly on just as he strode on the Suffolk beaches. He never gave a sign of strain. He had always kept to a meagre diet and he took lots of regular exercise. *Mens sana in corpore sano* was his incredible dictum. We were made to think cholesterol was somehow subversive. To eat well in France, however, was the duty of a gentleman.

He never smoked; he drank only wine. I remember cringing before his ascetic excess; that he appeared to have no appetites awed me into submission more than his hangman's look or his wounding tongue. When, at last, it transpired that he was only saving himself for a last autumnal fling with gluttony and lust, something in me lay down and died.

I was detailed to read the guide book (in French) and to comment on it (in French) as we trod. The whole dizzying edifice, it appeared, had been erected by power-mad monks; the guide book had niggling, Frenchified things to say about corruption. Breathless, I still lifted up my eyes. Amy was bowed down; the more she tried to stop coughing, the more she coughed. The Archangel Michael pierced the sky; he had been vaulted up so high, he seemed to have descended from much higher still to rest upon the spire. How many angels, indeed, could have danced on the head of it? The dragon, thrust through, lay coiled below his feet. The ether round them was unbreathable and blue.

On reaching the top, my father drew Amy to one side with his thick grip. "You'll stop that noise," he said, "or you'll answer for it." Her face became scarlet with fright and held-back tears. We proceeded more solemnly (if that were possible) than before until our misery was mitigated by the tour guide, an attractive French girl who ogled my father's dangerous eyes.

Sometimes I think I am guilty of Amy, not so much for her downfall because she hasn't fallen down so much as picked herself up continually from the place she normally lies, but for herself. My aural senses are acute; I enjoyed pursing French *us* out through my lips—the feeling of guttural *rs* at the back of my throat. I enjoyed what I supposed was my father's admiration of me—the little signs that came while we ascended that I was passable whereas Amy was beneath the smallest consideration. I stood on the wide and ancient pavement in front of the church itself wondering at the vertiginous sea below; the sound of the wind blew all but the purest senses from me. Amy leaned over the edge and hawked out mucus; the girl was ready to be hospitalized with bronchitis. I was all in all given over to Ariel stone, to my spirit hovering over the Norman plain. Why did I not defend her? Was I not a sister to her? Why wasn't I a sister to her? She had nothing—not even music—she had nothing but a loving heart that was mangled and trampled and despised from the moment she was born.

My father shone like Lucifer on the French tart from the Sorbonne. She asked: "Votre sœur—elle est malade?" This she asked him, not me. The others on the tour stopped and watched Amy's dribbling mouth with horror. Her back was against the wall; our father on soft shoes approached; for the barest moment, I saw pride in her that would rather plunge from the height into the Atlantic to be pulped by stones than allow his hand even to stroke her cheek.

"Mais, Mademoiselle, elle n'est pas ma sœur," his French was workable, but his eyebrows were more expressive still than the sugary tone in which he gave the guide to understand just how chuffed he was at her mistake. "Elle est ma fille—ma jeune fille." He preened.

On his holy mountain, St Michael protects the innocent. Amy's moment had passed. "Mademoiselle, voulez-vous vous asseoir dans l'église?" The French girl ("votre sœur," indeed) was, after all, kind. Amy nodded, closing her spurting eyes. The small gathering drew back, as Father escorted Amy to a pew. A simple tribute to his youthful appearance and the respectful gaze of his audience had transformed him. Amy clung (there was no other place to cling) to his arm. Our father's height and handsomeness, his somewhat cynical charm, gave him the appearance of something more than a courtier—Richelieu, perhaps, or Torquemada on whose support depended a former heretic now purged by justifiable means.

He raised his hand in his consultant's manner. "Soyez calme, Mademoiselle," he said to the guide. "Je suis médecin. Ce n'est pas grave, cette maladie." The guide appeared relieved.

The doors of the church opened, we trooped silently behind. At once, my eye was seized—caught up the vaulted arches to a summit of pain and happiness. I gripped my sister's shoulder. She only wheezed and sank into herself. "I will stay with Amy," I announced. I never wanted to be anywhere but there, afloat above the nave. "If you think it's wise, Father," I added for safety's sake. Such beams of approval from the little party met my remark: had Father wanted to gainsay me, he would have refrained from doing so. He nodded shortly and the guide, suddenly sexless, launched into the mysteries of groins and flying buttresses with astonishing ease and mental assurance. They marched from pillar to post . . . "Regardez-ceci, regardez-cela," until quite forgetful of us, they were gone to dissect and digest yet another slice of history in the cloister. Amy shuddered with relief and I sat still as still beside her, daring her by my silence to utter a word. She coughed thickly into her handkerchief; she sniffled and sighed. "You all right, Amy?" I asked perfunctorily.

"I expect so," she replied. She turned her brown, dog's eyes to me. She was only eleven then and I thirteen ("votre sœur," "votre sœur," indeed). "What is he going to do to me, Maudie, when we get back to the hotel?"

I rose. We were high, so high up. Sun thin as onion skin shone through the watery windows; we basked in pools of demi-gold. My heart, my heart aspires. I saw myself somewhere around the altar with the cello—in union with the cello and sound drifting from me like the whitest storm of snow travelling up, up—filling the yearning vaults and never desecrating the silence. I said, "I don't know, Amy. I think it'll be all right now. He'll forget it because of the tour." My eye was counting stones to heaven.

"But I feel so ill. You don't think I'll die, Maudie?"

She clutched me, but I shrugged her off a little. "He wouldn't let us die," I said. My heart gained strength from granite simplicity. I was stunned by a sense of listening silence, which seemed to absorb Amy.

"He let Mother die." She murmured this because she hardly dared to think it. I had thought it and she voiced my thought. We stepped softly up past the high altar. We trod very softly for our subversive thoughts, our dangerous words. More and more branches of stone arched over us. We were led by our inner ear through this petrified forest to the heart of the silence where, encompassed by candles, we felt assured of safety. A flickering red light hung above a shrouded box. "Cette chapelle est réservée pour la prière privée."

"Do you think we ought to *talk* in here? They might chase us away." Amy had an inkling of rejection then—I think she even feared it. She couldn't believe that microbes would honour her with infection; thus, she put her cough down to weakness of will. God, too, was always suspect with her of having standards. Now, she positively courts rejection.

What she said jolted me and hurt. I saw her face leering from the window, heard her low whistle in my mind; but I made no reply to Amy.

"Why didn't he send her to a hospital where she would get better? Why didn't he do that?"

Our parents were like gods so high above us with their inscrutable motives. The silence of the chapel drifted round us

and expanded. Perhaps I eked out for Father a widow's mite.
"Maybe he felt he was doing his duty," I said, "keeping her at
home. Maybe she begged him not to send her away. I don't
think she would have got better anywhere."

We sat small on the little bench. Our hearts ached with cavernous need. "But I wanted her," Amy said. "I want her," and
she cried. Did she put her head in my lap, or was her wasted
heart at the feet of an unknowable God, Who, pierced afresh in
us, wept blood? I myself was always tight with tears. I held her
close and stroked her hair. "You will look after us, won't you?"
It was a risk to say that aloud to the listening air.

Our father never caught us at our prayers; everything forbid-
ding in his aspect suggested a mistrust of such weakness. But
who knows what he said to the night? At any rate, upon his
return with the guide, we had resumed starchiness and some
semblance of spine. We appeared to be reading our Michelin in
the long room near the postcards. Amy was white, but better.

Our father had been assuaged by history; his face was as
remote and as austere as a statue off the great west door of
somewhere. Amy was not sure her passover had been achieved:
she fiddled with a postcard she had bought for Aunt Aileen. He
motioned us on and we marched after him, marching down St
Michael's mountain to the sea. As we descended, my eye took
wing over the great bay. The sun shone hot from its height, but
here and there, dispersed over the water, isolated rainstorms
shook from low clouds and a spectacle of rainbows united sea to
sky. My mind ascended in a glory through the jewelled air.

The man with the Bible harangues my mind night and day.
What does he intend for me with his Are you saved and his
Come to the foot of the Cross? What does he mean by saved?
Saved for? Saved from? Saved at? Surely, we must be spent.
Musn't we? Musn't we?

I suppose Amy that day on Mount St Michael never came to
the foot of the Cross or did she? Perhaps never at the foot of it,
she was on it.

I have run out of eggs, bread, and energy. If I leave this flat
that man will see me.

I don't even know if he's there.

Perhaps I'm making this up—like Amy's bronchitis; or yet again, perhaps hereditary madness. There's always that.

I could face Beatrice if I hadn't been so horrid about her. Maybe it doesn't matter if I'm horrid. In that case, why does she make me so nervous? But I haven't been horrid. Why say I have?

I've either got to go out there alone or enlist her protection. The phone's gone dead—I haven't paid the bill—otherwise I could ring Aileen and she'd turn up with a Fortnum's hamper and fur tippets and letters from Alba and Christmas pressies and letters from Alba and everything would be OK.

As if he'd write. And would it matter if he did?

CHAPTER VII

Beatrice packed her suitcase with effort. It had taken her three days of solid will-power to stay on the planned course. She had planned her course with much self-denial out of a decision she had based on prudence.

She had accepted Celia Knight's invitation to Sussex rather as she might have accepted a blow on the face. It had come like a sign to her that her involvement with Maud, all the more one-sided (she thought) for the girl's withdrawal from her, was getting out of hand. It had become dreadful for Beatrice to pass Maud's door without going in. She had not gone in, knocked, or otherwise obtruded herself. Why was she so drawn to Maud's threshold? Why did she listen out for her with such intensity? What had made her care?

Beatrice was a detached reader of her own motives. She had versed herself in modern psychology and was not unaware that heavy emotion buried deep might sometimes surface and attach itself to inappropriate objects and that a psychic cut of jib might odiously reveal itself in middle age. Beatrice rarely gave herself the benefit of the doubt: it was hard for her to think herself clean if she did not scrupulously avoid contamination. She was not going to let her clean soul be tackled and felled by an hysterical cellist. She corrected herself. Felled by her *attachment* (sentimental in that it was based on nothing more than one traumatic conversation) to an hysterical cellist.

She'd go to Celia's for the weekend, and that would teach her.

The Knights were Beatrice's best married friends. Beatrice had quite a few friends, most of them almost as good as she was, some of them even better. None were so wholesome as the Knights. They grew their own everything and drove a Maxi always stuffed with children. Beatrice folded her shoes in tissue paper and removed her heavy jumper from its plastic bag. The Knights disdained amenities such as central heating, and although Beatrice admired their stance, she privately froze. She wondered whether or not to include a bag of sweets she'd absently bought for the children. She put them in her case, then took them out again, replacing them in her drawer. She was subtly frightened of the Knight children. They were helpful, keen, and kind. Their eyes were as bright as new-minted shillings; their breath smelt clean; their brains were clear; their clothes home-made (Celia was perpetually hitching up trousers, pins in her mouth. She spoke through a mouthful of pins). They all did chores, even the youngest, Mark, who could very nearly milk the cow. Not one of the six ever emitted a negative emotion. Beatrice felt that these, so purely removed from television and white sugar, might somehow be repelled by her small gift.

Beatrice wondered if she'd tell Celia about Maud. As she packed, she gave an involuntary shudder which obscurely shamed her.

She was sure she'd done the right thing to accept the invitation. She was not sure why it hurt her to do it, nor why her thoughts about Celia were not effortlessly positive.

Since Beatrice's family had departed for Italy, weekends had taken on new meaning for her. She was astonished at how she had filled her time before with Mama, Mama, Mama.

Mama, Mama, Mama. It made her throat ache. Mama always settled her gaze somewhere over Beatrice's shoulder.

The way Beatrice had spent her weekends since the move! Had it been in answer to a call? Alone. But not. Had she chosen it or had she been chosen for it? She quickened with excitement when she thought about it. It was as if she couldn't get the wraps off fast enough whatever it was. Yet the farther she went, the more she unwrapped, the darker it became. She trembled when she thought of it—prayer. With uncharacteristic irritability, she shrugged off the word "prayer." It was a contact. She trembled at unwrapping, or was she being unwrapped? She was deeply engaged in love. She bit her lip and sucked in her breath. Well, why did it torment her?

Oh, her soul, her soul! She had come to anguish over her good deeds. She wailed over her good deeds as a sinner might regret a misspent life. Somehow her deeds weren't good; but no deeds at all from Friday to Monday terrified her. She battled on in terror at not knowing what God wanted, but knowing He was in her want. Or was He? She sneered at herself. A lot of things she'd accepted without question made her sick. It made her chiefly sick to be so awfully good. Was this a temptation?

She would have liked to speak to a priest about it, but every time she tried her throat contracted. Once, on a retreat, where an expectant semi-circle of devout ladies volunteered information, swapped stories, and listened breathlessly to a talk on St Theresa, Beatrice had almost, afterwards, been able to ask, to say. She'd liked what the young man had said—she'd found him unconsciously sympathetic to her inward thoughts—but when she'd entered his confessional, all she could think of were her sins which she so clearly exaggerated that he ticked her off for having scruples. She went violet from shame at not having been able to speak. Why couldn't she speak about it to anyone who could help her? Convulsions of yearning struggled in her chest. Should she become a nun? A contemplative nun? Was she, in not being able to speak, *avoiding* a clear direction from the Holy Spirit that she should take the veil?

All of her friends, especially Celia, talked about prayer as if it were the easiest and most natural thing in the world. They'd abandoned the rosary, for instance. Beatrice sometimes crept through the rosary at the snail's pace of a bead a minute. She sweated with distractions. Even the bloody cat was a distraction. She'd find almost any excuse to keep her from her knees. Oh, I must tidy. Oh, I must phone. Oh, I must read the *Lancet*. Oh, I'd better find out about old Mrs So-and-so.

When she finally knelt, she found the difficulties astonishing. If her body had stopped wandering, her mind didn't. Surreptitiously, she watched the clock. She got pins and needles in her feet. Her mind went blank. Her soul went black. She urged her will to accept blankness and blackness. It was as difficult to open up to God as it is to prise open a tough old oyster. Her memory presented her with curious and inconsequential scenes from childhood so vivid that she couldn't repress them. She ignored all these things and grimly carried on. Where was the romantic vision of contemplation she'd had in Eaton Square? She had delved into the mystics and supposed that darkness and silence were mere habits of speech they used, being, as they were, on a much more exalted plane than she. She had discovered that darkness and silence were really dark and silent and that she herself hadn't a clue. That God did not necessarily open himself up to her because of all the nice kind things she'd done for Him was a blow to her self-esteem she simply had to fight on through.

Where the cello had come in, she didn't exactly know. All she knew was that once she'd heard it, she was channelled. It was like finding an underground river in the absolute black of a cave. Before she knew it, she was swept into it and her fear of loneliness had become a love of solitude.

Yes, of course, she was doing the right thing, going to Sussex. She had to get away. The cello had been one thing when faceless, but the cellist, that was another matter. The cellist with the face. What was the matter with Maud? What had happened to her? Why did the face pull her, accuse her? What did it tell her she was avoiding?

All she knew was that she really wanted to go to Sussex—today, now, this minute. She wanted to be in the bowels of a family, to be allowed to sit quietly in the corner of the Knights' living room amid the forest of toys and potties, inhaling fluff from the rug, sipping parsnip wine and calling it good. She never asked herself if the Knights really liked her; she was grateful enough to be tolerated. She was a poor conversationalist, she knew, and Celia, who was Irish, had the gift of the gab, was always talking interestingly and breathlessly over an atonal orchestration of children screaming, fighting, bellowing good news from school, puzzling aloud over arithmetic. The scrape of the paintwork as bikes fell and lurched into walls; steaming, sodden nappies plopping into chemical and disinfecting mixtures in buckets discreetly hidden; the howls that went up over injured knees and feelings delighted Beatrice as a symphony might. She sometimes shared a room with Carol, aged eight, whose window overlooked the downs the child took for granted. In very early morning, Beatrice would slip from bed, pad on bare feet over cold, old wooden floors and stand at the window barely breathing at the sight of the hills' exalted sweep—their emptiness. Once, she had caught sight of a rider. Had she? An early morning rider without a hard hat galloping across the brow of the hill. The urgent horse slightly frightened her, fascinated her before it disappeared.

She both did and did not want to go to Sussex.

"The cat," she said, "I mustn't forget the cat."

She spread the *Times* down for the cat and stroked its little ears. She was betrayed by a sudden nausea and sat down at the kitchen table. She sprinkled dried food in one bowl for the cat, wet food in another; she gave it both milk and water to drink. There was a temptation, she thought, in projecting human qualities on to the creature. It neither knew nor cared that she was going away for the night; it only blessed its luck at the unusual abundance of food, purred, and fell to, chewing the lumps of offal in its bowl daintily and out of the side of its mouth.

When the doorbell rang, Beatrice jumped out of her skin and stood trembling on the brink of indecision. Who was it? It was Maud, that's who it was. She felt caught out in a crime and was surprised to find her stomach leaden. Should she answer? Would she? Did she want to? Oh. She answered the bell which rang again.

It was indeed Maud, and once she had opened the door, Beatrice was overwhelmed to see her. The teeth of a trap sprung on her heart. "Oh, hello," she managed. "How are you?"

Maud uncovered her yellow teeth and smiled. Her wrists protruded thinly from wide sleeves of a dirty dress with Oriental design.

"Dr Pazzi, may I come in for a moment?" Maud's voice and eyes did not match her smile. Beatrice suspected that she had been constrained to come; it was not a friendly visit.

"Yes, do come in. I've wondered how you were." Although the sight of Maud nearly brought her to tears, it was a real effort to let the girl in.

"Thank you," Maud said. She entered. As she stepped into the light, Beatrice was shocked at how unwell she looked. She had the waxy appearance Beatrice associated with death. She was waxy, sunken, and still. She moved her head coldly round and looked at Beatrice. Only her hands moved; they worked convulsively together.

How *could* she have thought of going to Sussex! A throb of determination to go to Sussex passed through her.

"Would you like a cup of coffee? I'm just about to make one," Beatrice said, and headed for the kitchen rather as a bolt-hole.

Maud followed her. "It looks as if you're just about to go away."

Beatrice's conscience stuck her with such knives that she was unable to speak. She now felt she had obscured her real inclination (to go to Sussex) with a false conviction that Maud was a temptation to her.

"Or are you always so tidy? I expect you're always this tidy. Doctors often are. It's more hygienic."

Thank God she hasn't seen the suitcase! "Do sit down." When under attack, Beatrice always sounded like Mama.

Maud sat. "It's cold today, isn't it?" She kept on and on rubbing her hands. Beatrice had a little coffee grinder. All the time she ground the coffee she tried and tried to think what to say.

"May I smoke?" Beatrice associated the tone with very large casualty-ward waiting rooms.

"Of *course!*" She lunged forward with a Dresden saucer her West Indian nurse friend liked to use as an ashtray. She was ashamed and confused to see Maud retract.

"I'm afraid I can't offer you one—it's my last. Or *would* you like it?"

"I don't smoke."

"Oh," said Maud. "I just can't kick the habit. Weak, I guess. Still, I suppose you can't smoke, being a doctor. My father didn't smoke. He was a doctor."

"Oh, *really?*"

"Yes, he was a gynaecologist."

Beatrice remembered Maud saying something about gynaecologists. "He wasn't Sir Giles Eustace, by any chance."

"Yes. Yes. That was my father. He's dead now, you know. Did you know him?"

"He taught obstetrics at Guy's; I attended some of his lectures once. He was a very fine-looking man—he had a very keen mind. I'm sorry to hear he's dead." She found herself liking Maud better for being the daughter of Sir Giles Eustace.

"I'm not sorry. I hated him."

Beatrice was shocked. Parents had to her a sacred function. Any profanity always curled her edges up. She retreated into the coffee-making operation, pouring water from the steaming kettle into a fine if slightly cracked blue pot. She whisked the grounds round then skimmed the top.

"You needn't have bothered with real coffee," Maud said, when it would have been too late. "Instant would have done."

Beatrice had only an hour in which to get to Charing Cross. Still, she refused to hurry. As if the fate of the world depended on it, she put out cups and saucers and a plate of chocolate biscuits with a fine degree of ceremony. It had become hard to look Maud in the eyes; she cast side glances at her face. "I'm sorry—I'm afraid I don't have any instant," she said.

"Oh, I like real coffee *much* better. I was just sorry to put you to the trouble."

"No trouble," Beatrice said a little stiffly.

Maud had thought about Beatrice since the early morning. Beatrice preyed on her mind, but she admitted this only obscurely. The image of the woman upstairs occurred to her in varying degrees of intensity, but she was unable to glance at it directly.

It was important to her that Beatrice was there. She watched her comings and goings covertly from the window and every time she did, she was filled with dread. Beatrice's upright carriage, what seemed to Maud her godly and righteous demeanour offset in Maud the awe she'd felt at the coincidence of their first meeting. Had not Beatrice come in the nick of time? And why? Had not Beatrice directed her into the relatively constructive activity of writing her own story? The manuscript, which grew in piles by day and night, had caught her, absorbed her. As nightmares abolish waking terrors (or interpret them), so Maud's journal absorbed fears she never mentioned in it. When she looked up from her papers, or left them altogether, she was abandoned to the antagonistic silence around her. The colour of light weighed and oppressed her eyes. The sound of nothing except the occasional bump and scrape from neighbours gave her head the feeling of being under water, very deep. Sometimes she felt as if the capillaries in her skin would burst. She hardly slept for the odd colour of red behind her eyelids, and when she woke, she sometimes lay in agony at the thought that the ceiling might fall down on and bury her if she got up. She barricaded herself with words against loneliness—icy, black, and profound—which was what she really feared. It reached everywhere, permeated every inanimate object with its immanence. Tables and chairs had a grit-grey sheen and the noise of a far-off Hoover seemed to suck life away.

Why did the sight of Beatrice seem to strand her more? Beatrice had brought her soup and tried to mend things. Maud had sensed her hand hovering on the doorbell. Why did she want to push her away, reject little kindnesses? Would it not be nice to have a friend? Someone who'd listen? But judge.

Who could judge Maud? She was not capable of facing her own darkness; she could not trust the pit. She only floundered deeper in it, grabbing a snatch of melody or a man's coat as if those things could hear or save her. She did not understand that the best and most merciful gift of incapability had been given her, so she stood at the window without comprehending the root and source of her own violence.

Every look Beatrice gave her was a judgment. She was completely peeled and sore so that warm soup scalded and the cup of coffee she now held in her hands might have been cyanide for all she trusted it. Beatrice's neat flat was an accusation, her piety a mockery of the suffering Maud brought upon herself as retribution for what she hadn't done, while what she had done she whitewashed and coated with paint so that it would not add to what she hadn't—that great burden—committed at all.

Her decision to knock on Beatrice's door had come impulsively, or so she thought, but for days she had been in conflicting minds about it. Everything she had written, she had written for Beatrice, while all the time, she protested that she despised her. So she gulped the sweet, hot coffee and tried not to ravage the biscuit Beatrice had given her. Beatrice was forced to look at her. "Why she's starving, poor thing," she thought. She leaned deliberately on her elbows and made herself look harder still at Maud. "Tell me," she said with firm determination to be kind, "how have you been getting on?"

"I've written lots and lots of life story," Maud said between gulps. "If that's any use." She dashed the biscuit crumbs from her mouth with her sleeve.

"I'm sure it is." Beatrice felt her face go all bright with condescension. She wondered how much sicker she could make herself feel. "I'll read it—if you like."

"*No!*" Maud put her hand to her mouth. "I'm sorry—I didn't mean—"

Without trying to, Beatrice suddenly saw. "*I'm* sorry," she said. "I don't see people as having any right to intrude."

After a hesitation Maud said, "How do you get on—living up here all by yourself, I mean?"

"It varies," Beatrice said.

"I know," said Maud.

There was a pause. After a while, Maud spoke. "I've got one real problem . . . I didn't want to ask, but you offered so I . . ."

"What?"

"It's that I can't leave the—house."

"Agoraphobia," Beatrice thought. "Most interesting."

"Because of the *man*—that man you saw on the stair. I promise if you hadn't seen him too, I'd have thought I imagined him."

"Oh, I'm sure he's gone away by now." Beatrice spoke very gently.

Maud shook her head violently. "No I'm sure—I don't know why." She was agitated for lack of words. "It's just that I'm hungry and I haven't any food left. He's there. I know he's there—and even if he isn't, well—I can't go until I know he isn't. Do you see? I just wondered if you wouldn't mind popping down and having a look. Though I know it's a lot to ask." She stared and blinked at Beatrice. "Just a peep, you know."

The idea of going to Sussex ebbed from Beatrice's mind. She caught a brilliant glimpse of herself walking across the autumn downs. The vision of nature from high hills always spun her round, and her greatest exaltation was the wind. Maybe she could catch a later train and peace. Her mind, however, trudged up to what she had to do.

Trudging up to what she had to do never scared her. It was a certain way of climbing. Her will had grappling hooks and cleats. She followed clear directions about second miles and coats and cloaks. There was no question, if asked, she could not answer with texts to support. It was not possible to leave Maud alone in the house for the weekend whether she did or did not want to stay with her. Why, then, did her mind wrench itself in two directions? And why, then, did she suddenly feel pushed beyond endurance?

All week long she had stopped herself from seeing Maud. All week long she had faithfully denied herself what she had assumed would be a pleasure, an emotional indulgence. She had even felt noble in doing this; but now here Maud was of her own free will, or with what was left of her own free will, and Beatrice had the impulse to push her out the door and slam it. She longed for her white coat and the whole way of coping that went with it. Slam the door. She longed for the Knights and for

certainties; for the hospital where she knew she helped and for
Sussex where she knew she was being helped. Oh, order! She
wanted to make her feelings do what they were told, but she felt
engulfed by a need for love.

Maud inspected her face sharply. "Of course, if it's too much
trouble . . ." she said stiffly.

"It *isn't*. You mustn't think that." Beatrice struggled into her
coat. She loved her coat—the mingled tweeds, the softness of its
shoulders, the precision of its hem. Once buttoned up, it gave
her the correct distance from others and the elements. Maud
looked down. The coat had somehow made Beatrice inviolable.
She drew on her gloves, unconsciously holding her hands up
from a long habit of hospital régime. Her handbag lay exactly in
the crook of her arm.

"It's awfully good of you," Maud said.

As she closed the street door behind her, Beatrice became at
once alert to her mission. Oh, how she wished she was able to
talk to Maud! Just think of all the things she'd say! She had so
many radical solutions planned for her. If only she could talk!
What were words? Why couldn't she use them? How often she
had struggled out towards people she'd wanted to love and been
cut down, stopped still at the point of contact! Jonathan, Maud,
the priest, Celia—even Celia—were they afflicted by her pained
silence? Who'd stopped her tongue? Why was she dumb? Sometimes she wanted to embrace people out of sheer frustration.
Doing things for them was second best.

She stood on the scrubbed step and looked around. She
scanned the Embankment and then the street. There were only
milling shoppers and men in jumpers washing cars. There was
no sign of Arthur, but then she had not expected there to be a
sign of him. It was to indulge Maud that she'd gone down at all;
not only to indulge her but to prove that her fears were ground-
less. In her meditations on Maud in the last few days, she had
thought very little about him. She regarded him as nothing
more than the tiresome and pitiful flotsam all religions cast up
upon the shores. Westminster Cathedral was full of them,
shabby men with lurid eyes who stank and sometimes cried evil
lunacies at Mass. Beatrice always felt sorry for them and gave

them alms when they asked. She disliked those who officiously cleared them out of the church. They were a tax, she felt, that any system of thought had to pay for being too rigid. And they were humbling in that they sought the same God as she did, as instinctive towards Him in their craziness as she was in her awful sanity. It had never occurred to her that any of them would do anyone any harm.

Nevertheless, she stepped lightly down on to the pavement and crossed the road. If she were to reassure Maud, she would be thoroughgoing in her search. The traffic from the main road thundered by, overwhelming the sound of her footfalls. She camouflaged well, in her coat and her correctness, against the grey and dripping trees. Looking continually about her for a man she'd after all not really seen in the first place, she made for the iron palings around the garden and stood still, effaced by her own watchfulness. She searched the patchy, dog-torn ground methodically, and was about to give up when suddenly her eye rested upon what appeared to be a heap of leaves. Beatrice had a scientist's knack for never taking anything for granted. She tightened her grasp upon the gate. After a moment, the heap gave a shudder and Arthur Marsdan rose from the ground.

Beatrice stepped back quickly; her heart gave an acute thump. She retreated behind an outcropping of holly and looked again through the spiked leaves. A near collision on the dark stair, and yet she knew him! It was a hook sunk deep. She made the slightest mental movement towards flight and the rasp clutched deeper still. Beatrice was weighed down irrationally with a sudden ton of misery.

Arthur shook his head and pulled at the cowl on his duffle coat. He rubbed his eyes and sat on a bench. Even if Beatrice had not hidden, Arthur would not have seen her. He did not appear to notice the rain; he cast his head about on his neck as if head and neck had no real connection. He grasped the cowl to the coat, this time pulling it off. She saw his head was crowned with bone; it was a high, bony head. The muscles in his face worked involuntarily. Beatrice noticed things about him at random. He somehow wasn't uniform. He moved in a manner which suggested a pain he could be forgiven for not tolerating.

The only thing deliberate about him was the direction of his look; it was fixed upon Maud's window-ledge.

Beatrice put a gloved hand on the wire fence which continued from the gate. She did not hold it for support, but touched it for ballast. She was rooted to the sight of him; she felt physically sick.

What was she going to do? What should she do? For a moment, she couldn't move at all.

Surely he was harmless! It was ridiculous to be so jarred by him! Poor man! Surely harmless! Still, she didn't know why she couldn't move. She'd have to talk to Maud. She really would *have* to talk to her. She shook her head and forced herself away from the gate. In her confusion, she barely missed being bumped by a slow car crawling to turn right on to the Embankment. "Why don't you look where you're going, lady?" "I'm sorry. I'm so sorry." For the first time in years, she ran, into the house, and let the heavy door slam behind her. Oh, it was silly! She felt defiled by panic. She mustn't panic. She never panicked. She took deep breaths and went deliberately up.

She entered her little kitchen with a great show of composure. Maud had not moved from her place on the hard chair. Beatrice opened her mouth to speak, and then found she could not.

Maud stiffened and blenched. "He's there, isn't he? I can see it on your face."

Beatrice sat down hard but with some relief that Maud had noticed. "Yes, he's there. I'm afraid he is."

"You didn't think he would be, did you?"

"To tell the truth, I didn't."

They were silent. "I'm sure he's harmless," Beatrice said.

"Then why are you shaking?"

"Am I?"

"I told you. He's going to kill me!"

Beatrice sipped her cold coffee, "No he's not." Why did Maud fill her with such compassion? She could not bear to see anyone in pain. Could not bear it. "Please . . ." she said. She could not think of what to say or do. Maud sat on the edge of her chair, her eyes glued to the door. It was as if Arthur would walk through it, an invincible weapon in hand.

"Look, why don't we call the police?"

"It's useless! They're useless! I've thought of it. Don't you think I've thought of it? I can't bear the idea of their talking to me . . . rubbing their grimy fingers round my life! Can't bear it! I won't have it! They'll see! They'll see!"

"See what?" Beatrice asked gently.

Maud gave an exaggerated series of shrugs, one rapidly following the other. "Oh, never mind. Never mind. Just don't you mind about that."

"What don't you want them to see?" Beatrice actually held out her hand in pity at the misery.

"Don't *you* see it? *You* know. I know you know." The cat watched Maud warily.

"I don't see anything but you in a terrible state. Please, you must calm down. I won't call the police unless . . . Look, I expect you haven't eaten anything much in days. You must be famished, and really, you can't think about what to do until you've calmed down a bit and eaten something." Beatrice deliberated for a moment on what she had in mind. "I have a suggestion. Why don't you come shopping with me? Then you can have a look at that man *yourself* and decide what to do on the grounds of what you see. I'll be with you, so nothing can hurt you. Then we'll go to the market, get some food in for the weekend and when we get back, you'll have time to decide what to do—what you really feel."

Maud looked at her hands. "You don't want to, do you? It's charity."

"Please," said Beatrice. She felt as if she were calling someone down from a parapet.

"I'm sorry. I shouldn't have said that. It's a very good idea. I'm sorry."

"What are you sorry about?" Beatrice was intensely relieved. Maud was shaking her head as if to recover from where she'd been.

"I'll get my money and my bag. I'll meet you in the hall. Thanks." She got quickly up from the table and pushed her way out of the door. Beatrice put her tired face in her hands and mentally kissed Sussex good-bye.

Maud must see the police. She was determined to get her to see the police. She walked into her sitting room and stared for a while at the phone. She poised her hand over the receiver, then snatched it away again. It *must* be her choice. *Maud* must choose to do it. Had she been in trouble with the police? Beatrice was sure she hadn't. Was she subconsciously *wanting* Arthur to? Oh, surely, the poor madman wouldn't kill her. It was ludicrous— part of the delusion. Still, why was he there after several days?

She would soothe Maud down to the point of seeing reason. With something practical to do, Beatrice always felt foursquare. She must call Celia. She phoned Celia. "I'm afraid I won't be able to make it this weekend," she said. "A neighbour of mine is in desperate trouble, and I feel I can't leave her." Maud's terrible face was in her mind's eye.

"Oh, Bea, what a shame!" Beatrice didn't like being called "Bea," but allowed it. "Why don't you bring her down?"

Beatrice had the oddest desire to laugh. Maud amid all that emphatic zeal, that relentless good cheer! Smoky breath and cardinal sins. How did the Knights dream they could cope with that? They'd accept her. In the name of . . . It suddenly made her want to choke.

"No," she said. "I don't think so."

"Are *you* all right, Bea?"

"I can't *stand* Celia" came over her in an unexpected wave. She felt terribly guilty. "Oh, I'm *fine!*" By asking Beatrice if she were all right, Celia always made Beatrice feel that she was not all right. Celia always assumed that everybody was not all right but herself who was always all right.

"Well, I'm sure you're the best judge, dear. Still, you sound awfully worried." By "worried" Beatrice knew that Celia meant "hostile."

"I am worried. I'm worried sick about this girl. She's a wreck." She felt defensive anger prick her cheeks.

"Well, if there's one person in the world who'll set her straight, it's you, Bea."

"I don't want to set her straight. I want to like her." Oh, dear, had she really said that? To Celia? She'd apologize later. Yes, she would. Her ears were too hot to do it now.

"I see. I see." From the disembodied voice, Beatrice got the understanding nod of head. "Well, keep in touch. Maybe you'll come next weekend. We'll pray for you, of course, and for your little friend." How did Celia know she was little? Why not big? Why "little"? Beatrice tried to manage "thank you" but all she could say was "good-bye." When she put the phone down, she found her hands were shaking with the magnitude of her rebellion. She felt unstructured and frightened. She could hear word for word what Celia was saying to Colin now. "*Poor* Beatrice. Should have married. Had a family." Oh, she'd eaten homemade, old-maid bread at their house before.

"I *must* pull myself together," she said aloud.

She met Maud at the street door. Maud had wastefully switched on the light. She wore a long, dramatic, and expensive coat, clutched a little handbag, and carried an enormous, tattered shopping bag. Her face seemed to say, "What took you so long?"

How wrong, how really wrong of her it had been to be rude to Celia. And how could she be so self-involved when Maud's eyes seemed to pierce the front door with anxiety? "Don't worry," she said gently. "Look at how strong this door is. He couldn't possibly get in unless you answered the buzzer and let him in. You let him in before, but you won't let him in again."

Maud said nothing, but stared at the door still.

"Do you have a chain to the door of your flat?"

Maud shook her head.

"Well, let's get one. We'll buy one at the ironmonger."

Maud looked at Beatrice with a cynicism Beatrice did not understand. "Come along now. Let's go." Beatrice applied a gloved hand to the lock, opened the door, and again stepped out into the chilly day. Maud shrank behind her, then stepped out.

"Where was he hiding?"

"There. Next to that bench." They crossed the road. "He wasn't exactly hiding. I think he'd been asleep on the ground. I should think he's much too mad to hurt you, you know." All the same, it terrified Beatrice just to approach the gate again. Together they looked up and down the garden. Arthur was nowhere to be seen.

"But you said he was there. He's gone!"

"Oh, maybe he was just sleeping rough." Beatrice did not tell Maud that Arthur had been gazing at her window, but she remembered. It froze her blood to think the man was now at large, that she'd lost track of him.

"You see how pointless it would be to call the police," Maud said.

"I don't think it would be pointless. I think we ought to."

"Please don't. Please."

"The police wouldn't hurt you, Maud. They'd be on your side."

"Please."

"All right. All right. Come on. Let's go."

They walked towards the market.

Beatrice had never felt so useless in her life. Why, now walking out with Maud, did she feel more restless than ever before? What had she come out to see? What had she expected? Certainly to be useful. And there she was, flapping like an undone sail in the wind, feeling cheated and alone.

Why wasn't she being allowed to mend this broken thing who walked beside her? From an early age, she had kept custody of eyes. Her glance rarely left the pavement six feet in front of her. This rather rigorous habit, gleaned at the convent where she'd been to school, had the distinct advantage of giving her a sixth sense. She *sensed* Maud without looking at her. There was chaos in her walk, chaos in her dress which swished at Beatrice's neat heels. Indeed, the women appeared so dissimilar that they would have caused surprise to anyone observant who had met them coming down the long avenue of trees. Maud glanced nervously around, but no longer for Arthur. The light of day, the air fragrant with wind, grit, and petrol smells, the passers-by whose faces were adjusted in an expression of normal concern for normal concerns . . . all of these things challenged her and churned her up. She wished she had stayed alone in the flat.

Where was the romance of the music Maud had made in Beatrice's darkness? Was this it? The plain light of day showed only a stepping, shuffling neurotic who would not, could not be saved. Did it show that? Beatrice's whole life was governed by the administration of tests for disease. It was a good enough test to apply to Maud, asking her to ring the police, suggesting chains and bolts. How could she be saved against her own will? Saved, saved, saved. Are you saved? Saved? Saved? Beatrice did *not* presume to go any farther than trying to inject in Maud a simple will to live. She even smiled to herself when she remembered Maud's apparent fixation with religion. Just to get her walking in a straight line would be an achievement. Oh, she had prayed for her, and not just in words. Prayers for Maud had been pulled out of her with a forceful urgency she hadn't thought possible, and these, if anything, were the basis of Beatrice's confusion because there hadn't been anything dutiful about them; they had taken the form of an almost physical grief.

She really did not know what to say to her. Here was opportunity at last and she watched it fly away as they walked. It was the nightmare, so familiar to everyone that it hardly needs description, of missing trains by a quarter of a second; of going unprepared into final exams; of nameless terror chasing a self with suddenly paralysed legs. The muddy, ochre colour of such dreams edged Beatrice's peripheral vision as she tried to stride with professional self-confidence. She steered the shopping trolly, however, as if she knew where she was going. She was failing the one person she'd ever really wanted . . . to help? Know?

"I miss hearing you play your cello," she said at length. It was such a struggle to get it out that her words seemed patronizing. She cast a hasty glance at Maud, who remained icily dumb.

All right, here was her humble confession. "It helped me very much to hear you. It really did." Why did it make her sick with nerves to say it? Why did she blush to near tears into her shopping trolley? To have admitted . . . *what*, after all. Any artist would be pleased. It wasn't such an extraordinary thing to say. To have admitted something akin to love was different.

"I told you. I can't play any more."

Did a muffled voice mask pain? Anger? "*Why?*" Beatrice, carried on the dreadful emotion, could not stop herself asking this. "You were so good," she said, more evenly.

You open your mouth and you make mistakes. You speak

Italian when it should have been English. You apply a pressure when you never ever should have . . . made the poor girl halt and fumble her hands, worse than on the verge of tears. "I'm so sorry, Maud. Really I am. So sorry." She wanted to embrace her, hug it away. But only foreigners did that. She had experienced many rebuffs of touch as a child, but even Mama, at her worst, had held, kissed, touched without even meaning anything by it, even lovelessly had often touched: and brother and sister and even servants. Why, they'd all handled each other without thinking, without meaning. She'd never seen anyone so untouched as Maud—so unloved?—so without human availability . . . except, perhaps, herself. What had injected such starch in herself? You surely could not blame the English. You had to blame yourself. Oh, self.

"It's all right."

They walked on and reached the market, things going from bad to worse. They went deep in stifled feeling and apart. Beatrice had a headache. It began to assume proportions, growing from her neck and advancing its bulge upward to the inside of her skull.

All that food and no appetite! Fairy lights hung on stalls with cabbage and potatoes; oranges, grapefruit, and boiled, pink prawns. A smell of fresh bread hung about the air. People everywhere waited somewhat solemnly for food or dodged about calling to each other.

In Beatrice's early days of goodness, she had had to do with various old ladies whom she had trundled about the shops. She had worn them on her arm proudly, as a woman of fashion might have worn a fox-fur. She'd steered mumbling, passive old ladies; incontinent old ladies; old ladies dinned by oldness into an acute interest in getting from A to B and in whether a bit of fish for dinner would be nice. Beatrice had shunted them around, radiant with how boring they were. They all loved her and told her she was a saint.

Shunting Maud from butcher to fruit stand; from fruit stand to salad stall was not the radiant way to go about it. Her head pounded now with a truly awful headache. The streets were crowded to the point of making her despair, and a little boy of about five stepped on her toe deliberately and stuck out his tongue.

Beatrice wanted to ask Maud to dinner, but every time she looked at her, she was unable to speak.

Humiliation should be counted as precious. She knew; she'd read; she'd sometimes felt the distillation of its sweetness. It was not to her an absurd and masochistic piety. She saw the point of sermons on the subject, and she read them with genuine grief at how little she allowed herself to be abandoned to shame.

To be refused by Maud was a . . . no, she could not ask. Ah, what a creeping thing she was. She despised herself. What's ultimately more humiliating than love? Sermons! Oh, God! She checked herself, but still inwardly died.

She bought, however, too much food for one, and that almost unconsciously. Maud bought two hundred expensive cigarettes and spent a lot on tins in the little supermarket where she left Beatrice standing outside wondering if she were going mad. Wondering if she, Beatrice, were going mad. How stupid she was! She'd leave the poor girl alone. How she wished she'd gone to Sussex!

"Shall we go to the ironmonger and get a chain?" she asked when Maud came out. Didn't she hear? Or was she pretending not to hear? As they passed the ironmonger, Maud paused and looked in the window, but then moved on, giving Beatrice a sly glance out of the corner of her eye. One could not press it any more.

"Thank you for coming with me," Maud said at last, as they made their way home.

"It was nothing. I was glad to come."

It had started to rain hard. Beatrice had had the foresight to bring her umbrella. She opened it and covered the two of them. The shower's rich, tuneless staccato on stretched waterproof nylon soothed her. Her headache started to dissolve. Sussex would have been drowned anyway, and there would have been no walks on the downs.

Before she'd *met* her she'd loved. That sound. Whoever M. Eustace was who'd made it. It was quite infuriating to know one was in the grip of an obsession and not be able to stop oneself. Had *she* Messianic delusions? Oh, save me, save me! She, rescuer, and saint, saint, saint; which was all very well if nice and impersonal and it was all an obvious sacrifice: a sacrifice she felt every time she got up at a quarter to six, a sacrifice she felt when going without for others. This surely couldn't be a sacrifice, this degrading, despairing hope for someone else.

Just before they reached the gardens, Maud cleared her throat. "You asked me about the . . . instrument. About why I cannot play it."

Just when she was getting along nicely; just as her expertise in self seemed to sharpen and tremble on the edge of an idea! In a way, she did not want the digression Maud made by speaking; but she was instantly alert to the tone of voice dropping to a low register; it was not thick with intimacy, but it was going to confide. Beatrice understood that she must not look around; that she must not see Maud's face. She slowed her own pace, however, to hear what she had to say.

"You know about Alba. I showed you his picture."

Beatrice nodded slowly.

"What I played . . . what you heard . . . I didn't know it was possible to love another human being as much as that. I just didn't know it existed—that much love. I loved him so much that I played through to something beyond him. And now he is gone, I am completely left without it. I could go on if I knew where they had put—that . . . the thing in the music . . . when I lost him. Don't you see? They've taken him away and I don't know where they have put him?"

"Who is they?" Beatrice could barely whisper. Could barely breathe.

"Isn't there always a 'they'? It was a 'she' but I always think of it as 'they.' No, that's not true. I don't know why I said it. But if there was only something left, I could play. Please. Don't ask me again."

They walked on a little and Beatrice tried to speak. She thought she was going to cry. She beat her mind for words, but they wouldn't come. Suddenly, Maud clutched her shopping bag to her, picked up her skirts, and began to run. "I'm sorry.

I'm sorry. I'm sorry," she called over her shoulder. "Please don't call the police . . . please don't try to help. Please. I'm sorry." She stumbled a bit, then regained her balance and ran in the rain all the way home. Beatrice did not know what to do. She closed her eyes and sank, then straightened herself and walked on. As it had been in the beginning, it was going to go on and on and on. She was good at that and knew what to do with it.

Her *whole weekend*. She mustn't think like that.

As she put the key in the door that Maud had slammed behind her, she half-turned. From some way off, she saw Arthur Marsdan, scuttling along the pavement where she and Maud had walked. When he saw that she had seen him, he froze against the iron palings.

Beatrice let herself in the house. She really and truly did not know what to do.

CHAPTER VIII

Arthur Marsdan—that is the name written in that man's Bible—is waiting for his chance at me, but I am powerless to buck the purpose of his will. Why can't I move? Why can't I resist? I could go and stay with Aileen; I could even leave the country. It's not that I won't; I can't. I can't.

There, there, don't cry. There, there—a great girl like you. But what's to be done when you can't. Won't? Can't?

Surely Alba *must* have been my destiny. Aileen—destiny's tool.

She knew Alba and Ilse well. She was not innocent of them. What could have possessed her to think I could withstand them?

There he was; there he was—she brought him as my birthday surprise.

It started as a quiet evening, with Amy and Aileen and me, Amy's current beau—a pin-striped type called Guy who worked at Sotheby's—Horace, of course, and a glacial pair of swells called Candida and Nigel whose only lively interest appeared to be the opera. They lived and breathed the opera, so they told me over whisky and cashews. I could tell by my sister's eyes she'd been at it all day; she poached quietly in alcohol. When she'd reached such saturation, it was pointless to refuse her more. Horace and Guy stood by to prop her. She didn't need this as propriety itself propped her. I must say this for Amy; in company she's never less than a lady. Either Guy knew everything about my sister's drinking or nothing at all. He took her glazed appearance with unimpeachable sang-froid. Amy was always very pretty, very decorative. She dressed to advertise breeding rather than taste. That evening she wore grey-silk shantung and pearls; her manicured hands and manicured hair, sprayed into subtle bouffant, bestowed a merciful cover to her vacant eyes, her slightly wobbling stance; the correctness of Guy a merciful cover for failure.

She'd forgotten to get me a present. When she was little, she used to wet herself when startled, threatened, or ashamed. As she admitted her omission to me, that same look came over her face when she knew she couldn't hide the trickle and Nanny'd come and smack her. "Oh, Amy, don't be silly, of course it doesn't matter." I kept saying this and saying it: but we knew it mattered that she was drunk and it was of this we were both ashamed.

Nigel, Candida, and Guy launched into airy reaches of high taste—all Ming vase and *Così fan tutte,* they circled one another, crippling one another with boredom. Aileen flounced and swooped between us, dazzling here, trilling there while the Cordon Bleu cook swotted up a meal in the kitchen.

"Darling, I hope you don't think *I've* forgotten your birthday," she said. She too was angry at Amy being drunk, so Amy drank some more because she couldn't bear anybody's disapproval. Guy sidled a look at me out of the corner of his eye. I wore a well-made but bizarre Indian frock which set me apart. "My surprise is coming later." She had already given me a cashmere jumper. Aileen would have had us married to the likes of Guy.

"What do you *do?*" he asked.

"I'm a cellist," I said.

"How *interesting,*" he said, but didn't mean it. Maurice had given me an opal ring for my birthday. I fingered it and thought of him kindly; it was unconventionally set and suited both his and my opinion of me.

To be struck by lightning twice and live! What was the sensation when I saw Alba again? You see, I was reduced to ashes—made almost insane—by the sight of him. It's as I said, a destiny awaits me. Just as I'm in control of the likes of Guy, there is an epiphany—a blinding shock and I am incapacitated.

I heard the door. I distinctly remember that. Was it precognition? I looked up, knowing a fatality in the moment. Was he wearing a muffler? It seems that he was; at any rate, he was muffled in the dark of the hall—wrapped up as a present should be.

Did Aileen think people could be presents?

I didn't recognize him right away, not as he stood in the dark, but knew, remembered with shaking, something in the manner, the gait. But he wasn't walking. He was standing. Maybe it was the way Aileen greeted him, standing on tiptoe, glittering.

Slowly, even carefully, he unwrapped (he was always a performer) the scarf, the coat. I caught the shape of his face in the little hall. The high-bridged nose, the beard, all shed years from me; and then as he stepped into the light and looked around him, I knew it was Alba.

You see, I am a victim. Isn't it awful? Like Amy with her trickle and her drink, I stood intoxicated, oozing love.

I cannot emphasize enough how helpless I was, having caught sight of him. Even Amy reached out her arm as if to catch me falling. She gave a crooked, hurt little smile. "Maud Eustace, This is your life," she said, and I didn't understand what she meant, until I remembered it was a telly programme that she and Aileen had watched and hissed at in the past.

It was a cruel thing to do—not to have prepared me for him. Candida, Nigel, and Guy stiffened like pointers at the entrance of this star. Alba was in everybody's background as a household word. One doesn't precisely think of Vera Lynn or Charlie Chaplin, but there they are in one's mental furniture: a little dusting of the memory and no lustre is lost.

He was unconsciously conscious of his effect. His presence made others cluster round him out of a blind herd instinct. Everybody watched as he drew off a glove and smiled with engaging humility. Seeing him thus, it is not hard to understand how he had once become so famous. No matter how slight the cello's repertoire, a man like Alba could make the instrument dazzle in the open spaces of the Albert Hall so that each sonata, every concerto (heard time and time again by the audience) assumed a new sound because it was played under the fresh light of his eyes. He had had less earnestness than Casals and more command, more attack. He even had had humour—this I understood from his old recordings.

How his sound had sweetened and changed was hidden to everyone but me and Ilse. Of course, she knew.

Candida and Nigel didn't crane, but looked beyond Alba to the door. All performers are used to the Candidas and Nigels of this world. Alba slightly smiled. "I'm afraid my wife isn't coming tonight. She had a dreadful migraine at the last moment and sends her apologies." Ilse Hafner was still a name to conjure with. Candida and Nigel did not acknowledge their evening had been ruined until later on when they became apathetic.

I now think it possible that Ilse ruined their evening purposefully. A sense of the famous woman who wouldn't come to dinner and who hadn't rung beforehand to apologize hung about the air. Somehow he suggested in announcing, even feeling her absence himself, that he had come without his crown. She, his crown, both burden and adornment. Subtly, the company relaxed; and my birthday gift was left to me.

Couldn't he see it from that moment before we spoke? I searched his face, his hair, his eyelashes suffocated me with tenderness—pores, whorls on fingertips were alive and present to me. That his ears stood in such-and-such relationship to his neck gave me a certainty about proportion. His features proclaimed for me the genius of his Maker.

He'd aged; that didn't matter. It only gave him depth. His smile cut inches into me. He was my mother and my father and the only homecoming I've ever had.

Was he careful with me? Didn't he see I'd break? He treated me as if I'd break, at any rate, and, as in my childhood he'd crouched beside me, he now stooped to catch my rapid breathing, my full eyes, my breaking heart. How can an educated woman talk about a breaking heart? Yet how can an observant person of either sex look upon the phenomenon of aching chest, of anguish in the lungs, on that tortured sense of yearning, as anything else but a breaking heart? I shame and discredit myself with the idea of a breaking heart. Just to see him broke my heart. My heart could not contain the love I had for him. It seemed to spill all over the dinner table and into the aspic; it appeared to colour the wine and crammed my conversation with non sequiturs. My sister in her dove-grey habit became my better half, enunciating less squiffily than I, endless, dreary conversation I barely heard. I cracked up into the *boeuf-en-croûte*, and by the time the pudding came I was stranded and foreign, awash above the deluge of emotion I'd strained to check for so many years.

I watched my sister's carefully poised skull. Just how fragile it was, I alone knew. She held it still and at an angle as though internal bleeding might result from too sudden a movement. She showed me no affection, but she saw—Amy saw—what peril I was in.

I knew and she knew that it could happen any time, strike anywhere; that it had struck me. That she drank to avoid being stricken was at once completely clear to me.

It isn't safe, she seemed to say, for you and me to love anyone like that. There was a tinge of voices and visions around the experience: not that I saw, not that I heard. I simply understood the area of the consciousness from which our mother's voices and her visions came.

I cannot bear to think, as Alba sat and charmingly conversed, cracked nuts deftly, and honoured me with smiles and looks, that he didn't know and understand everything.

My simple assumption was that he understood everything.

He, the internal and constant companion of my childhood, seemed to sit quite still beside me so as not to frighten me. Ilse and Aileen would have thought my hands and stomach shook with desire; only Amy sensed and showed with bitter smiles how much I shook with fear. The terror of sitting next to him made me physically sick. The others kept up the clatter of silver and talk, but I said nothing. Alba and I seemed to communicate our awareness of each other by small movements of muscle and by hooded and averted glances.

Alba was the grand past-master at love and the violoncello. Aileen made this amply clear; there was a deep curtsey in her whole manner to him—a deep curtsey, yes, but with a trace of insouciance. She was behaving like Alice Keppel might have with the Prince of Wales—all loyal subject outwardly, and privately, who knows?

He evoked this behaviour in my aunt by means of a majestic, modest silence. The more she flattered, the more he appeared graciously honoured by her flattery. "No, no, too much," he appeared to say like someone staving off a superabundance of caviar. In fact, he did seem pleased to see her; spoke warmly to Amy and me about our dead uncle, and generally made himself agreeable.

He was both distant and responsive and there was nothing I could do about the hell I was going through.

Throughout the meal, I waited and waited for Alba to speak to me. Was I so clearly smitten? There are certain things you can't control. I waited while he amused my aunt and everyone saw my shame—nervous hands, bright spotted cheeks. I couldn't stop my eyes plundering his hair.

At last, with coffee, his damask napkin pushed aside, his crumbs of cheese—I would have licked his fruit parings—abandoned, he motioned me to him. He stood in a dusky alcove where my aunt kept her unread, bound books and a few badly chosen Wedgwood figurines.

"Do you play the cello still?" he asked.

I couldn't remove the crush in my voice. "Yes." (Didn't he know? I was wounded.) "It's my career."

"Oh, *really*."

"You started me off. Do you remember? And sent me my first instrument."

"I remember it well. I had hoped you would do something with your talent. I'm glad I was of use to you." He was courtly and detached but his eyes glittered with interest. "Where did you study? What are you doing now?"

"I was at the Royal College, then I spent a year in America with Janorsky."

"Ah, Janorsky! Wonderfully solid performer." I realized he thought Janorsky boring.

"I never made much contact with him. He was all involved with family and with Tanglewood."

"He was a good beginning," Alba said. "Such an emphasis on technique." He laid his cup and saucer down carefully on an occasional table—to hide, I felt, an obscure disappointment in me.

"When I came back to England, I got a desk with the English Chamber Orchestra."

"Oh, good. *Good.*"

"And now I'm with the Moore Quartet."

"Oh."

"Do you know them? Us?"

He frowned. "I've heard them on the radio. You did Beethoven—A minor—the other night. Is that correct?"

I nodded.

"Oh, dear. I wondered who the cellist was," he said. "I wouldn't have let you get away with that."

He reduced my pain with a low chuckle. "Have you done your Wigmore yet?"

I shook my head. I couldn't stop tears sliding down.

"Well, you ought to. You're clearly a soloist. I could tell that listening to you the other night. You shouldn't waste time on chamber music, unless, of course, you want to find a better lot than Moore and his friends. I don't blame you for trying to change his tempo. How can he play late Beethoven at that tempo?"

"He thinks it's stylish." My tears were checked. Alba smiled.

We smiled at each other at Maurice's idea of what was stylish. "You should do your Wigmore before you get much older," he said. "Perhaps you don't have enough money."

"My father left me very well off. I can easily afford Wig. I really needn't work at all. Actually, I hate working at the moment."

"No wonder."

"I play at night—for myself," I said. "I'm working on Bach. The C-major suite. It gives me a little satisfaction."

Why had he chosen such shadows to stand in? It is hard to define his expression. It was hard to read it. He looked at me so hard it gave me a shock. "I mean it is the deepest satisfaction I have. The only satisfaction. That's the truth."

"I know," he said. There was, what is called, the ghost of a smile. How could such a hackneyed phrase as "the ghost of a smile" be so accurate? So apt. Alba was gnostic. "I know, I know." Did he know? How could he know? Something uncanny like a nimbus always hung about his head. He was intuitive—an intuitive player. He reached beyond flesh and bones. He called out admissions of truth from me and rendered my pretensions silly. When he said he "knew" how important the suite was to me, he made the rest of my life seem a prevarication, if not an outright lie.

He hesitated for a moment. "Would you like me to hear what you have done? I do not take pupils as a rule. I mean to say I do not take pupils at all and I have retired from public life, but I feel very much that I could help you. I would regard such help as an act of friendship and not something for which I would expect remuneration."

Piatigorsky, Casals, Rostropovich, Alba. Even Dr Pazzi felt the power of the name Alba. But would she know what it meant for him to say that? Even if I had felt nothing for him, could she know what it meant? My sound had been so wretched in the Beethoven, yet he'd *heard*—no, "knew." Could I communicate to her his almost mythic power? He was like Cupid taking up Psyche, Jupiter regarding Io. It was is if he'd heard what I'd played in the night, as if he'd been in the room without my knowing it.

"When?"

"I'll ring you," he said, and stepped out of the shadow to join the others.

Amy was being sick in Aileen's bathroom, so I fled into her bedroom to cry. On the way home I threw Maurice's ring away.

The Albas' house was situated in a quiet street in Chelsea near the river. I had to drive round a considerable time to find it. My muscles and nerves that day were certainly never crushed, they were tuned to snapping. Vigour and agitation nearly screamed from my pores. When finally I arrived at their front door, having parked and disembarked my cello case from the car, I was hardly in the way of noticing much except the stillness of the street. I was struck too by the incongruity of the house with the image I carried of Alba. I had imagined him to live in a large house, dark and cavernous, filled with mothy Oriental rugs—somehow a wood fire and heavy chimney breast sprang to mind—wing chairs and muted reading lamps and shelves upon shelves of leather books discreetly tooled in gold.

Smart fresh paint had hardly set on his real threshold; the bright brass knocker—rather like a gargoyle—thrust its face at me. It had no function; there was a bell which I rang instead; it made an unmelodious buzz rather like my father's intercom.

The door was answered, much to my astonishment, by a magnificent middle-aged woman dressed to go out in a black Persian lamb coat. The coat hung open to reveal the great firmness and neatness of her figure. Her skin was slightly powdered, but its texture was supple and its colour had the quality of pearl; her throat was all but concealed with pearls themselves which glowed and responded to her skin and to the lustre of the November afternoon on which she'd chosen to step out. She wore a black hat stuck up at one side like a cockade. As she moved her hand forward, her clothes rustled and emitted heavy, soporific scent. Instead of taking my hand, she raised her glove to her knotted hair and touched it into place. She switched on the hall light, although it was hardly necessary, and as she did so, I realized that she was rather older than I had first thought. Yet the light too paid her compliments; her age took on the deep look of venereal experience, as if by being so long the instrument of men, she'd learned a depth of finished responses to them which not only pleased but inebriated them. She appeared to be terribly in control. She gave me a most charming smile which nearly sank me through the step.

She seemed to exact formality from me. "How do you do." I said. "I'm Maud Eustace. I've come for . . ." Mr? Maestro? Signor? Surely not plain Alba.

"Ah, yes. I know. I am Madame Alba." I do not know why I didn't at once understand that this was the Ilse that I'd heard of, thought of. She was so immediate and vivid, she did not seem to require a name or a reason to be anywhere.

"I hope I haven't come at an inconvenient time. I see you're going out."

She appeared to be charmed by such consideration. "Oh, not a bit. I'm just off shopping." (She looked prepared to sail down the Nile or more contemporarily to glide into some tango with a cad at a *thé dansant.*) She was not easily placed in the late twentieth century. Her smile fluctuated all over her face. It was difficult to tell what she meant by it. "You must be Aileen's niece," she continued. "How is good old Aileen?" She pronounced it "gute olt Aileen."

She did not wait long for me to answer; she turned and shouted casually and loudly up the steps like some less exalted altogether. "Maso! Thomas!" (she inflected the last syllable foreignly) "your visitor is here." The shout on the whole had a lilt to it—the whole thing came from her diaphragm; she gave the impression of having an operatic intimacy with him—Iseult at number seven calling Tristan to his tea. I felt like a cripple on the doorstep selling pins.

"We have no servants," she said as she turned back to me. "I can't abide their sloppiness." Her look of wifely pride flicked like a duster over the banisters. It was an extremely clean, plush hall lit by a miniature antique chandelier. It was that, I suppose, she had wanted to show when she turned on the light. She shouted again, then cocked her head. "You were the little girl whose half-size cello Thomas bought. And not so little any more, eh? We took great interest in you, and do now, of course." She shimmered a little, dispelling the gloom I had about her. As she heard him on the stair, she slipped out of the door past me. "I hope I will have the pleasure of meeting you again," she said, then vanished.

I craned after her. I almost had forgotten why I had come. She was always to everyone absolutely riveting. The luscious accoutrements of fame trailed after her wherever she went although she hadn't sung a note in years.

"I'm glad you came," he said. I turned my head. He was much less accomplished at smiling than she. His eyes picked out a grave tone in the air and reflected it.

"I met your wife," I said.

"Please come in."

"She's beautiful."

"Very," he said. He picked up my case. "That's a splendid case. Did you have it made by Hill's?"

I nodded.

"They've always made mine too."

I was a little hurt that Alba had such a beautiful wife, but somehow I was more hurt that she had left us standing in the hall. Something about Ilse made one want to possess her.

He seemed to sense my abstraction. He drew his breath in sharply. "Well, let's get going," he said.

I was nervous again. "Oh, dear."

"Never mind." And he was kindly. "I practise in the attic. My wife can't bear the mess and noise."

"Noise!"

He seemed careful not to scratch the paintwork with my case as we ascended. He laughed. "To her it is, after all these years. You've always done it, never lived with it."

"My sister felt like that," I said. "When I lived with her and Aileen, I had to practise at the College." No matter how many more auditions I might have, I'll always hate them. The dentist is—oh—nothing in comparison.

I wondered if Alba had lost his nerve—for audiences, I mean. People do. His music room was locked. Inside, there were little elements of surprise. It was, in fact, a separate entity from the rest of the house; it bore no relation to the thick, hygienic carpet just outside the door. Beatrice's flat reminds me of Alba's room; perhaps that's why I yearn so towards it. Minimal furniture stood about—each piece had a function. I looked around and saw that no effort had been made to adjust acoustics. A number of cases were stacked against the walls and a neat pile of blank manuscripts stood on an uncharacterful desk. I wondered if he'd taken to composing. I wondered if that was why he'd withdrawn. I thought of Moore's "*atelier*" and laughed. "You should see where Maurice works," I said. Nausea crept around the edges of my laugh.

That Alba didn't like me to be there suddenly struck me. He drew the door to and stood tense in front of it. "I hate to put you through this," he said. But I knew that wasn't all he hated.

"I don't like people coming into my music room at all," I said. "In fact, no one has ever entered it since they installed the piano."

He relaxed a little. "Oh, I've not really made it my own yet. We moved here only a few months ago." It was completely his. My stomach did a sort of convulsion.

"Well, let's unpack." His jaunty air had nothing to do with him and I hated it.

"I've left my rosin," I cried in strangled panic. He affected not to hear me.

"What a beautiful instrument!" He went down beside it. "May I?" I didn't like even Alba touching it. He lifted it anyway as a mother might lift a baby. "Gut strings!" he said admiringly.

"Janorsky made me get them."

"Quite right too."

"I couldn't live without them now."

"Know what you mean. The bridge is quite high."

"I like high bridges."

"So do I. *So* do I."

"I haven't any rosin," I repeated.

"Ah, yes, here."

"Do you like my bow?"

"It's superb."

I let him pet the cello while I applied the rosin. He caught my beady eye and gave it back to me. He modulated his look; he now gave every appearance of being a cosy old don. "What made you choose the C-major?" he asked. "It's not a show piece. If you want to demonstrate virtuosity at the Wigmore Hall, you'd be better off with D major or C minor for that matter."

He stung me out of nerves. I tuned and tuned. "I like it, that's why." Suddenly I plunged into the death-defying leap down to bottom C and let the open string resonate, then started the climb of the next few bars. "Nothing's better than that," I said, carrying circular climbs into the rocking consolation of the next figure. Before I knew it, I was on the open sea with the great expansion of it and had plunged magnificently into the Coda, breaking great chords of heart around me. Oh, I love those thick harmonies. I brought them off deep and satisfying, finished and brought my bow down to my side.

He sat very still, apparently bewitched. "*Allemande*," he said softly.

"Aren't you going to stop me?"

"Not just yet."

"I've always found the *Allemande* just plain difficult."

"I don't find it presents any particular problems. Go on."

"It's hard to sustain the idea of a slow dance through all that decoration." I stalled because I wanted him to tell me how good my *Prélude* had been.

"I want you to play the whole piece," he said firmly. "Then we'll talk about it. I've got to have some sense of where you are before I can give you any help."

I got on with it.

Playing for Alba was playing for no other. What was his will? As I leapt through *Allemande*, the basic rhythmic pattern occurred in such a way as I had never heard it. It kept on stating and insisting through octave jumps and arabesques and I was suddenly enchanted by the stately generosity of the baroque. Alba sat, stiller and stiller. He did not hint the rhythm with his body. I can only think mind called it out. I was so entranced with this that I splashed into the *Courante* and smudged the

precision of the bowing, but as if running for a train, I caught up
with my own interpretation which I rather insisted on his listening ear. All those bloody semi-quavers—I'm still too light and
girlish with them. But with the *Sarabande*. Oh, I think all my
heart for the suite is locked up in that *Sarabande*. Casals is too
restrained with it and Rostropovich too romantic. What is so sad
in it? The cello is a true instrument of tragedy. I did not know
then how to play what was unendurable, but as I searched his
eyes, I played the sadness and he with oblique look provided
something far, far more melancholy and at rest. When I had
finished this, I had to stop.

"You must play the *Bourrées* now ," he said.

I never had dried up before—where it mattered. Like a bur-
glar through drawers I ransacked my brain. It seemed to do
violence to me, having to remember. "I can't!" I looked to him
in bewildered panic. Sheer cliffs. I sometimes dream that I am
naked in the Albert Hall. "I can't remember how it goes."

"Da da da da da di dadadada."

My mouth was dry and my hands sweated. "Oh, yes." I
started to play the pretty little figure numbly. This time, Alba
sat back and well and truly listened. I cannot describe how he
did this—I only know that the effect was extraordinary. It was as
if his ear was firmly braced down under me; it was as if all my
life I had been a trapeze dancer without a net; he spread his
consciousness low to catch me. I stopped and started the dance
again. It wasn't until I'd changed key into the minor that I quite
got the drift of what I was playing. When I returned to the
major my playing was aglow with a *danse macabre;* I stabbed the
Gigue with fire, with all levels of bitter irony I knew—it was as if
for the space of a minute I'd leapt on to the bare back of a
demented gypsy horse and ridden. I finished defiantly, almost
with a curse. I didn't know how I'd played and I didn't care.

"I can see how you couldn't remember how to start," he said.
"It is what they call 'an immensely personal statement.' "

Alba's face was his second instrument. I look across now from
my encampment by the fire to his photograph that I nearly
destroyed in my dawn raid. There is nothing in it of that fluid

mobility of every minute muscle in his face. His joke was gracious; he intended with it to verify and mask at once my humiliation.

I mumbled in my lap. "I wouldn't have played it like that in public," I said.

"Let me tell you," he said after the hesitation of thought, "what you must do. You must play like that always in the back of your mind, but never in public. What I mean is that all of the suite must mean just that to you, you must recognize and know that ability to feel, but must get detachment. Do you see?"

"Dr Bender might have said that."

"Dr Bender?"

"He tried without success to psychoanalyse me."

"Perhaps you misunderstand me." He was a little cold. I really couldn't understand him. I felt rather weightless—he was so unlike Janorsky. Now Janorsky would have gone right into that *Courante* note for note and we'd have had two hours of almost unlimited mutual boredom, pain, argument, and final discipline. Janorsky never wanted heart and soul; he wanted music.

"Look." He started again. "Everything up to that first *Bourrée* was—just fine. I thought 'What an accomplished, lyrical player.' I enjoyed the little Janorsky derivatives—that very agile bowing in the *Courante* (I can tell you don't think too well of that, but it was fine). Nothing prepared me, though, for the *Bourrées* and *Gigue*. You don't know how good you really are, Maud, and how much you've got to learn. If only you could draw out that from the other movements— then focus. You would be good beyond your wildest dreams." He was unemotional but stirring. I was flattered and insulted to the brink of tears.

"Didn't you like the *Prélude?*"

"Ah, that was art," he said. I smiled. "But it didn't find your nature."

I laid my cello on its side and stood up. I went to the window and felt his eyes follow me there. The street below looked curiously like a row of dolls' houses. The trees had lost all their leaves but a few, and these looked painted on. I felt real. "I don't want to know too much about my nature," I said.

Alba's voice came as soft as true conscience. "You can't play from anything else," he said. "Your own nature, no matter how you hate it, is the fulcrum. Bach wrote music for people. People aren't meant to be jammed into Bach."

He might have given me a dissolved pearl which I drank. I descended into a sudden luminous calm. "Play for me," I said. "Play the *Sarabande.*"

"All right, I will."

It had grown so nearly dark outside that I could hardly see his face. No, it wasn't dark, but almost dark when the light from the afternoon fulminates before it finally goes. I watched him open his own case and take his own instrument to him—my heart exercised with the dumb privilege of watching. I was struck to the queasy pit with love. As he tuned, I caught a quiver of the promise of the thing's deep, jewelled tone. I was too rapt to judge the instrument's age or maker. Alba cast his eyes modestly down the fingerboard, finally plucked the strings, and then began. He started strongly, with a sense of meditation, a thought-out figure that was there to pin the mind to, that could be grasped; but in the repetition of the figure, he clasped closer around a kind of sorrow so distilled it was nearly abstract but not—because it had the pain of flesh; and with this purchase gained, he spun the rest aloft into an interior of song—infused, complex, both personal, impersonal and live—he gave, he opened up his mind, and when it closed with the last breathed note, I stood, rooted and watered by a sense of the compassionate so profound, so unemotional that I couldn't speak.

Neither could he. He wiped the cello down and rested it. He too was affected by his song. He looked as if he'd left a prison for a space and then returned. At last, he hesitantly spoke. "I haven't played for anyone for years."

In the light of what I had heard, I did not dare ask why.

"You're a good girl, Maud," he said. When he was thrown off-balance, he gave a quirky little smile learned, I suppose, in childhood and mostly forgotten.

"You demonstrated what you said. I've never heard anything more beautiful. I know I can never achieve that, but at least I know it's possible and that's important." I wish I hadn't spoken.

He got up, turned the light on, and broke the spell.

"I suppose with a busy concert schedule you can't come again for some time." He was now urbane.

It was vividly apparent to both of us that I must come again quite soon. How can I speak for him of my assumptions? Did he feel anything at all for me? Pity? He drew raw privacy from me.

I am overwrought. I am definitely overwrought.

I knew that Maurice was over forever. "I'll give the quartet up; if you think it's worth it."

I thought I'd gone too far. He raised his eyebrows. "How will you live?"

"I told you. I've got private means," I said. "My father left me a lot of money."

"I met your father once."

This quite surprised me as my father had never spoken of it. "Through Aileen?"

"Yes. Through Aileen."

"What did you think of him?"

He raised an eyebrow but said nothing. It was as if outrage silenced him.

Now I see how he meant to fob me off, distance me from himself. He was marking time. At last he said, "It's difficult for me to say. You see, I'm so out of the mainstream now that I might damage your career by taking you on. If you had a good agent, I'd feel better, because then you could work and study with me at the same time."

"But do you *want* me to study with you?" Alba was often exhausting.

"Oh, yes."

"Do you think Maurice has been bad for my playing?" Choosing a good teacher is like getting married in many, many respects.

Why that's an absurd thing to say. It is not generally so. Being chosen by Alba—choosing Alba—had for me the holy aspect of eternal commitment. He had no such sense of me. What were his motives then? Why, why, *why* did he snatch me up from nowhere and in mid-career? He was not an adulterer. And if I thought for some time it was my brilliance on the instrument that made him elect me, I was quickly disabused of that. He was lonely, growing older, had no children, no career, but that, like my *Prélude*, is only the artful shell of things where nothing of the nature of his goodness to me is described.

"You'll have to decide that for yourself," he said. "Our musical afternoons can continue in any way you choose. It is entirely up to you."

Oh, he covered himself all right. I have no one to blame but myself for what happened. He scribbled out his number on a scrap of paper. "Ring me when you find the time to come again," he said.

No one can know my sense of snow that night and all the next day. It wasn't snowing, but it surprised me that it wasn't. I practised Bach well into the night—I should have been marking the Mozart G-minor quintet that Maurice and his band and I were going to rehearse. The next day I awoke to a grey fine bright refraction of light and thought—surely snow—but no snow. I took a long walk along the river and wondered what to do.

At six, I knew the answer. I drove to Maurice's. Maurice and Alba were mutually exclusive and I knew this with absolute certainty.

As I parked by Maurice's bijou residence, certainty (moral or poetic) resounded through me like brass. To mount the steps was effort, to press the bell was more. Until two days before, I had supposed I'd go on forever with the quartet. I'd even looked forward (with some tired hope) to the Mozart as I'd convinced Maurice to import Jean Varley the violist. I'd admired her and thought she might help me to get Maurice to slow the tempo down a bit. He always took things at such a clip. I stood there appalled at the thought that I'd even cared.

Maurice had two teenaged sons, quite indistinguishable from one another. One was only slightly more surly and uncommunicative than the other. They both smoked pot, wore Afghan coats, and attended the Lycée Français. Their conversation was customarily loud and in French which neither of their parents fully understood. Bunny, I think it was, opened the door. He grunted a monosyllable in no recognizable tongue and let me in.

"Is your father at home?" I was brought up to toe the line to elders.

"Dad!" he bellowed up the stairs.

At length, Maurice, chafing hands together, came athletically down. "My God, Maud. Where have you been all my life?" I suddenly remembered that I'd cut a rehearsal. I never cut rehearsals and this shocked me. He rooted around with his nose somewhere near my ear. Repugnance deepened my purpose. He nibbled and mumbled. "But it's fantastic to see you!" In front of the shrugging Bunny who loped away to the Ping-Pong room. "You look far too marvellous to be ill."

I went rigid on him. The smell of him, eau de cologne and locker room! I saw with sweating disgust his face, my face, our face impersonal in my bed—it had been only Friday last.

He looked at his watch which was (he once told me) carved out of a solid piece of platinum. I think if I ever had a heart for him, it was for his pleasure in toys. The watch told the time in Bombay or Zurich at the flick of a switch. "Time for a drink. Let's see what Dulcie can rustle up. Hmn?" Poor Dulcie, cup-bearer to the gods. She'd bow her neck and take it. He jogged down a few steps to the kitchen. "Stop!" I said. "I've come to talk to you. I'm breaking with you and the quartet. Now. It's no use carrying on."

He turned and slowly came back. For a moment, I thought he flinched, but he recovered smoothness in an instant. "I think you'd better come to my studio," he said after a pause.

Maurice's studio was futuristic, a triumph of acoustical engineering and modern design. When he sat at the instrument panel governing tape decks, sound systems, head phones, winking lights, when he prowled from custom-made teak music racks to his eerily polished collection of violins, when he stood at his melamine desk on which there was an Epstein bust, he gave the impression of a highly evolved android whose business it was to transmit sounds from earth to some central computer on Mars.

"Now what's all this about?" he asked when I was seated. He had a monstrous canvas deckchair hung from steel struts; it caved me in—that and the missed rehearsal almost caved me in. He sat erect and made as if to sort letters on his desk.

I looked at him a while and thought, "This is life or death." "Art," I said at last, "is a blood sport, Maurice. If you will eat venison, you must be prepared to slit the throats of deer. I'm leaving. I'm leaving. And if you want to sue me for breach of contract, you can. I'll pay. It's that important to me."

He was silent for a moment. He made a mouth as if he'd sucked a lemon. At last he spoke: "Because I've never basically trusted you, Maud, I've made mental provisions for this eventuality."

I was astonishingly cut.

"You need not trouble yourself about wrecking my work; although it is quite clear to me that you haven't. As you've been on a pretty high horse for the last few months, I've been listening to others. I think David Brunstein will be delighted to join us . . . and as for law-suits, please don't let that thought distress you. Our agreement has always been based on something more subtle than money, hasn't it? From the start, I expected ruthlessness from you, Maud. You were always a bit of a wild animal—a lovely animal which makes a lovely noise—but voracious and incapable of human affection."

"And *you* had affection for *me?*"

He shrugged. "I remember watching you at Aldeburgh. You were so young and heartless. You reminded me of my own children . . . cruel, but not deliberately so. It gave you a strong romantic beauty. I remember that day you snubbed me on the shingle until the possibilities of what you might accrue from me sank in. And later—oh such a wounded bird, trying to die before my very eyes. Yes, I've had affection for you, Maud, but you wouldn't understand it."

"You never mentioned such insights to me."

He made an impatient gesture with his hand. "What would have been the point? You only presented a surface to me. You never loved me, just *allowed* me and I liked that. Underneath, I always suspected you of—what? how can I say it?—an aptitude for slavishness, a cess-pit of female vulnerability which I would have despised if I had unearthed it with home truths. We've both got problems, eh? Only yours are worse because you haven't learned to live with them."

I said nothing.

"Where are you going? Are you going to be a soloist? You're a soloist at heart. Ben and Frank agree. Quite frankly, we've all heard too much individuality from your sound. Mind you, you've been good for us, I guess. You've got more quality than any of us have."

"You were going to sack me?" My profession has been my honour. I shrank at the blot.

"My dear," he said with a wide sweep of his arm from his swivel chair, "I hadn't a clue what to do with you. By saying what I've said, I only meant to indicate where your strength lay. We all admire your musicianship. If I could be permitted to guess what has happened, I'd say that you had found someone whom you think will teach you the real art of performing. Even you wouldn't have the arrogance to go it alone. Especially you wouldn't have the strength."

"Alba." I slammed down an irrefutable ace.

"Alba?" Maurice laughed and looked wise. I had a strong impulse to crown him with his Epstein bust. "Alba was amazing, but he isn't any more. No one's heard of him for years. There's something distinctly funny about his retirement. Nobody knows why such a source dried up. He was going to be incomparably better than Casals, then—nothing. Of course, you're too young to remember."

"I knew him as a child," I said stiffly.

"Oh, well. I can't see him doing your career much good, that's all—he's too obscure."

"Janorsky too chose obscurity." I was vicious in the face of Maurice's adopted blandness. He shrugged again.

"I still can't see how he'll improve matters for you. If I remember his playing correctly, I can only think he'll make matters worse."

"He has a quality of soul!" I saw Alba's still and listening face and felt the way he'd pulled the music from me, leaving me weak.

"Maud, dear, what an extraordinary thing for a woman of your intellect to say. If you have a soul, which I very much doubt, it's in no end of trouble. My, my, the way you've carried on! Oh, you're quite right. Alba's got buckets of soul *and* technique, but he'll break you because . . . I find it hard to explain . . . he'll give you expectations, longings that you can't fulfill, lead you off the path where you can find a more than decent career based on hard work and good sense into an area where you will attempt to fly. You will attempt to rise from mortality to what is intuitive, ineffable (still working harder and harder) and you will fall because you haven't got the stamina. It is quite probable that Alba hasn't got the stamina either and that is why he's given up. His sound allowed a heaven, and, as there is no such place in my opinion, he went to pieces."

I tried to speak, but Maurice was well and truly launched. "I got that dig about obscurity. I know you despise me for chatting people up. You should *see* the nausea in your face sometimes— I wouldn't inflict such a look on a dog; but the practical truth is that one must survive. I know I'm not as good as you, but I've got to make a living and the best out of what I have." He paused then said abruptly, "Have you met Ilse Hafner, his wife—Alba's extraordinary wife?" I nodded and he shook his head. "She is Queen Neurosis. I like you well enough still to fear for you on that score."

I refused to speak.

"Oh, I give up on you," he said at last. "In a year's time, I expect to see you raving mad with straws in your hair."

No one talks like that to me and gets away with it. I flicked my ash into his heavy crystal ashtray. "You've got a mind like a piece of graph paper, Maurice, where you plot equations. Success is all you think of and it is a function of (a) hard work, (b) ambition, (c) meeting the right people—all neatly set out."

"Maud, there is no arrogance quite like your arrogance. You and Alba deserve each other."

"I slept with you, didn't I?" I said.

"I was hardly the first." We had indeed reached brass tacks.

"I think," I said slowly, "that you are possibly the last."

"I wonder," he said, "if Alba has taken that into account."

"Oh, Maurice," I cried, "what a relief it is to be free of you at last!" And jumping up out of the hammocky chair, I ran from the studio and down the stairs.

Dulcie, in a long wrap-around skirt, was flogging the cat in the hall. It had been scratching the newel post.

"What, are you going?" Sweet Dulcie, unmusical Dulcie, long-suffering Dulcie waits to die of boredom. I was struck by a queer impulse to embrace her and ask her forgiveness, but it would only have marked out in red the extent of her humiliation. Instead, I seized her hand and kissed it, "Dulcie," I said, "I think you're a brick." She gave me a bewildered smile. Somewhere under that cheesecloth shirt, there beat an English schoolgirl heart which responded to my words. I saw her with raised hockey stick defying bruised shins for the glory of the school. "I shan't be coming back, ever again," I said, "but I thank you for all your hospitality."

As I drove back to Victoria, I whistled a bar from the *Sarabande*. I felt as if I had turned a corner and found to my amazement that the streets were paved with gold.

CHAPTER IX

"Release D from the string—don't *make* D. Assume that Bach made an order for you to find. You needn't impose yourself on the music. Let go, let go. No, we'll do that phrase again. No, just those two notes. The relationship exists quite naturally. Don't strain after it so. Pah, *pah!* That's crisp and mannered. Of course that's how I play it, Maud, and it isn't mannered with me because I've arrived at it. It's consistent with my whole style. You have a more lush, romantic approach—so it jars.

"I wish you wouldn't clutch the fingerboard like that. It's

much much too intense. The cello's not a lover. There, don't cry. Look, I'll show you. If anyone's a lover it's your audience and the instrument is your communication—your means of giving. See?"

I saw and then I didn't see. I'd discover a phrase so vividly that my execution of it would be perfect—then I'd lose it when it came to playing it for Alba who taught like a zealot on fire for truth. "Casals again," he'd say. "Piatigorsky," he'd groan, intone these names. I wondered how I'd ever dreamed of playing Bach in public. The American adventure seemed deeply embarrassing. I did not see how Janorsky had let me loose.

Music to Alba was a law—like gravity—which existed previously to himself. It was never a series of throbs in relative tones. He loved music, but more importantly, he knew it. It emerged for him as a manifestation of the deep order of things as they really were. All his ardour was for finding, finding the central, heavy, pin-point force in what he played and deep within himself—so that not a common ground was reached but a fused whole.

My premise always was that chaos was the governing principle of life. Pockets of order were to be found in sonata form, moments of grace in the unscrambling of my bureau drawers. For Alba, the Spirit of God had moved upon the waters and nothing more was void.

So, I let go. And sound dawned with the clarity of light. I let C have its way with me and found C sharp, then D—even the scales—particularly scales sang through my blood noiselessly and gave me peace.

Maurice had predicted God. Maurice was no elementary fool. I became, as Alba and I progressed, tuned to a modality of being outside myself which was at the same time the ground of myself: the underground Jordan of myself. I put a toe in, but did not achieve baptism.

Aileen phoned several times. Nothing could have been clearer than what she wanted to discover about Alba and me. Against the immensity I imagined, I could only cradle the receiver in my palm well away from ear and laugh at the possibility of such lowness.

Ben from the quartet rang to sound me out about coming back. I was amused at Maurice's cowardice. Ben assured me that the new cellist (not, after all, David Brunstein) was *flat* half the time and *drunk* the other half. I let it all roll over me. The centre of my life was now the music room. No wonder I so greatly fear it now. Working was the way towards wholeness—I smiled a Mona Lisa smile.

In this clean, constructive life, I became less and less burdened by physical necessities. My appetites regressed and seemed remote. I ate randomly and slept little. Sex seemed a little perverse. I forgot I'd had it and I didn't miss it.

What ran dangerously past, unseen, was that great tributary to Jordan I cannot easily dismiss as evil. Everything seemed so heavenly pure and bright. The only clue I have to what I missed is embedded somewhere in a memory of my mother that in my period withdrawn from the coarser demands of the flesh recurred monotonously like a knell I didn't heed.

She was an ascetic if you like.

I can see her now, deeply engrossed in trees as she stood in our private Garden of Gethsemane in Suffolk. Food, clothing, even water were sources of phobia to her. She once became dehydrated from a fear she had of drinking. I can see her, can see her as motionless as an animal watching the trees in the garden as if they contained dryads. She wore old gumboots and a knitted hat pulled well down over her forehead. Miss Russell put her in woolly jumpers when wool didn't frighten her. She listened—or seemed to listen—to the growing of the trees.

When growing was all she heard, she would move cautiously towards one of them in particular—an old elm which stood in the centre of the copse. She would put her hand on it, and, like the blind, would feel the bark all the way from the roots, where she dug her fingers in the earth to as far up the trunk as she could reach, well below the lowest branch. The tree was curved and bent with age. She would feel the shape of the tree sensuously, then stand back with that perpetual, lifeless grin she had, and then, in one stylized shift of muscle, she would mimic the twisted tree. In this way, she would hobble contorted back to the house and stand for hours like the elm.

As someone said, the waters of the Jordan are muddy and cold.

Listening was not like that with Alba.

I listened a lot to Alba—not that he crowded me or spoke. He played. And when I didn't accompany him on the piano, I curled myself up in an old armchair he'd stuck in a corner and heard him. It was a far cry from making beautiful music together. What I heard I cannot divulge except to say that his music had the quality of human sacrifice. I did not know or want to ask what horns of what dilemma had goaded him; but I heard what had been dreadful for him worked out, resolved in something like a majesty of assertion that all—after all—was good. He was a great exponent of Brahms. My ear became curiously visual. When he played, I sometimes saw squalid memories weirdly fraught with gold, as if, even in the worst I had done, some awesome force had met me and there embraced me.

It was an extraordinary season of love, that winter was. So much of it now has been robbed and corrupted—called into doubt—what can I say about it? No furtive gropings behind veiled eyes occurred; no grand, Greek, Platonic affair emerged. What happened was no more, no less than mutual beholding. What I saw of him and what he saw of me fits into no paradigm that I know of. My mind can only be content with mystery. I heard, *heard* him although he did not speak and he was untranslatable.

I was simply not prepared for it.

I had no notion it existed.

I wonder if the starving feel simply weak and only hungry when they're fed. His hearing of me fed me, but it left me insatiable for more hearing of him and being heard.

It was an experience of contact in the dark. No words, avowals, kisses, shattered the embrace. He drew me most tenderly in and—never touching me—touched me.

Every week as I approached the Albas' house, I was filled with shaking dread of our time together in the music room; every day, I tried to categorize this dread. What was I afraid of? That this sense of union was delusion? Except in the deepening of his smile for me, he gave no sign of love. Was I afraid that I would destroy it? Or that he would? With one, stupid, irrevocable action? I yearned for a sentimental outpouring as a diabetic craves sugar yet knew such sweetness would produce coma.

But every week for months and months, it was the same. Sometimes Ilse let me in; sometimes she did not. When I saw her, she was always chic and deliberately kind, if wonderfully impersonal. Alba and I would go upstairs and he would work me out till the sweat poured and my mind and muscles gave him what he wanted.

If I'd thought Alba lacked Janorsky's rigour when I first met him, I couldn't have been more mistaken. That *Courante* I hadn't liked—I must have used two cakes of rosin up on the second bar alone until it skipped and flew from my bow. He worked me to a pitch of glittering energy; he sought out questions for every conceivable detail of the whole work. By the time he was finished with me, I could have justified the most minute intonation in essay form to a panel of unjust judges. In exhaustion and defeat, I was oddly at my best; having given up hope, I would suddenly find song. And when the cello sang, what did it tell me of my nature that he claimed I'd find?

My heart conceived a strange wish. What I sang told me more of this desire than of myself. At that time, it was never more concrete than a general fervour. To see the beloved I heard? To know more than was good for me? To be sure? To be sure, there was more in it than Alba and myself. I wanted to pierce with music what existed between us. I wanted to know. Oh, it was the merest shadow of a thought. But the idea of a veil presented itself behind which lay a face. Having presented itself, it would not go away. It described itself as the end towards which Alba played when, at the end of our lesson, he committed his sound to my ears. It defined itself as what I reached for in the short episodes of purity my own bow found.

There was no sense whatever of being admitted to the Albas' general life. To say I speculated on it is not quite true. As I ascended the stairs each week, I could not help but notice that all the doors surrounding each landing were closed, never ajar or giving hints of anything behind. There was an unvarying tidiness about the place which suggested a model home on show. Sometimes the subtle scent of food hung in the air, food and gloss paint recently dried. Now and then I smelt cabbage, or sausage, boiled and heavy and spicy. Occasionally, there was the odour of baking or an exotic smell of saffron. There were never noises such as occur in the running of daily life: radios, vacuum cleaners, footsteps, bumps, or jars. Only once, I thought I heard the sound of a bird's song coming from behind one of the doors. The telephone never rang, nor did the doorbell.

There was not the sense of emptiness, however, behind the silence or closed doors, nor a sense of lively domesticity concealed. There was rather the curious trace of pent-up feeling, as if each door might burst its catch with a pressure each room contained.

I know, Dr Bender, I know—pure projection.

It was not pure projection. Alba's eyes hesitated on doors as if he were prepared for them to spring open. The house never seemed congenial to him, nor did it seem to be his home.

Why did Ilse choose to act when she did? I started with Alba in November—it was March before she moved. Nothing had disturbed the smooth surface of routine. We trekked up the desolate stairs, worked, came down again, I left. Whatever Alba and I confided in each other was inherent in the music that we played. We never spoke of our private lives. He never mentioned her to me. He did not appear to abstain from mentioning her, there was no obvious holding back. I could understand her actions better if Alba and I had had a more social, more recognizable sort of rapport; then, it could have been said that she wished to include herself, naturally enough, in whatever bonhomie was going round. But there was no bonhomie, there were no jokes, loud laughs on the stairs, nor were there mutual wishes to make our friendship formal by meals and invitations. It may have been a quirk of loneliness or boredom, even curiosity, which made her suck me into their lives together—or jealousy of the sound we made. But I do not think so, I do not think so. There was no motive, no reason. No. Ilse was the most completely calculated woman: the calculation of her person was complete. But Ilse herself never calculated anything completely. Being motive herself, she was free of it. Her gift unchained her from the bleak necessity most people have to stop and think. Ilse had genius.

The day in question, the day of Ilse's move, shift, direction, taking of command, was in no sense different (I repeat) from others. The air was cold and tinged with spring. Our session had been difficult; we'd approached the attack on the *Prélude* yet again and Alba had been pleased with the way I'd hovered on the opening C before the scalic plunge. There's only the difference of a semi-quaver, there's only the quaver in which to catch the mind of the audience. He was pleased, he definitely was pleased, but not abnormally pleased. Not at all.

Yes, I do remember one thing different (but not very different): we ended early that day without his playing anything for me. He said that he was tired. I was disappointed, but from time to time he didn't play for me because of tiredness, so although it was different, it was not unheard of for him to stop short of, oh, I don't know, what I wanted, what I increasingly came for. I came to hear him, I mean.

At any rate, we descended the stairs as usual.

The drawing-room door was open. Ilse sat, directly in the line of vision, quite erect in a chair of the Empire style. It had no back but it had curved arms. It was black, but the seat was terra-cotta-coloured so that it looked like a Greek vase, a shallow one, a kylix from which Ilse emerged as if she had been the eerie result of a magic spell made over a potion that the dish had contained.

She was conspicuously knitting. There she was, so dark, so potent, and so beautiful in the perfect symmetry of the chair which set off to such advantage her immaculate firmness, knitting with all the concentration of a dear little homebody with nothing else to do. The incongruity of the image she presented was so bizarre that nothing was left to me but to stare. She seemed aware of being watched. She jabbed the needles upwards (more forcefully for audience) in the Continental fashion through pink, furry wool. After a moment, she slightly turned her head and spoke. "Will you not stop with me a while?" The affectation of her phrasing was oddly winning. At the same time, her voice—though light—was weighted with a subtle tone of accusation.

I turned to Alba. He stood very still for a moment, then, as if coming to a decision, he motioned me to go in and he followed. She contrived to continue knitting without a break in rhythm. She might have been an audio-typist for her businesslike absorption in the task.

My mind contracted on entering the room; it was a triumph of freezing aristocratic elegance, with something more, with something much, much more. At once, my eye was caught by a magnificent painting over the empty fireplace: every feature of the room fell gladly into place around it and the warmth of the room came from it. It was a nude—I thought by Ingres—an odalisque with turban who sat on yards and yards of casually crushed satin. Everything about her was oval and oblique. She was the more sensual for having her deep and moulded back turned to the painter. That she looked over her shoulder with her hard, sloe eyes; that the curve of her breast was only dimly visible; that her sheer skin seemed to burst almost like fruit; that she only half-suggested; that she seemed to weigh the possibilities; that she hovered over an invitation made her the triumph that she was of erotic love. And all the same, there was a weird innocence in her nakedness that moved me. Paintings like that should be in galleries just as music should be contained in concert halls. Art on the loose is dangerous.

"I see you admire the Ingres," said Ilse. She put her knitting in her lap.

"It's extraordinary. I thought things like that were only in museums."

"Oh, she'd only age in a museum," Ilse said. "I sit in front of her for hours—sometimes knitting, sometimes not. And do you know? the more I look at her, the more she glows. Do sit down, Miss Eustace." We sat, awkward.

The rest of the room was only an elaborate frame for the painting. There was a couch fit for Mme Récamier; there was a tall gilt mirror decorated with a swag of roses chastely executed and adorned at the sides with ribboned fascines. The windows were draped in velvet. Lyre-backed chairs with striped damask seats were posed in various areas of the space to give the impression that gifted conversationalists had just vacated them to go downstairs and dine. The only object which might have seemed at all out of place, had it been put there by lesser hands, was a large white wicker bird-cage—most ornate—which hung from the ceiling near the window. The canary in it was, of course, the bird I had heard singing. It hopped from perch to perch, giving, now and then, a mournful trill of recitative.

"What are you knitting?" I asked. There seemed nothing else to say.

"A bed jacket," she said.

"I wish I could knit that well." I had no wish to knit at all.

"I was taught at the convent when I was a child. No matter that we were gifted, they made us into women, ladies, I mean. One might sing lieder till blue in the face—still, sewing, knitting, even cooking took precedence. So, I sit here and knit in hopes that the devil will not find work for idle hands to do. I look at the Ingres and listen sometimes to your lessons. I ask myself, Thomas, has the child any progress more to make?"

Alba filled a stately chair well. The look of an abdicated king reasserted itself. Only leaning back, leg swinging from the knee, his hands pressed in an arch before his face, he looked more as if he saw the danger of being deposed and wished to avert it. He said nothing. I said hastily, "One always has progress to make." I felt uncomfortable.

Ilse picked up her knitting again. "You are lucky to have an instrument that doesn't wear out," she said. Her tone and carriage were somewhat severe. "The voice somehow loses its integrity after a while. I keep my little Melba here for vicarious pleasure." She nodded at the canary, never breaking purl and plain. There was something burnt out rather than worn out about Ilse. She was by no means too old to sing.

Alba watched Ilse intently. She seemed aware of this, although she never looked at him. "I wonder if you would do us the honour of staying to dinner tonight," she said. "It was in my mind all day to ask you and although I do not know if you can stay, I have supposed you might. I have made provision for it. It struck me that although you have entertained us—particularly Thomas with your music—we have not yet entertained you, a lapse which is entirely due to my own selfishness. I have retired so from the world we used to know that I rarely think of asking people."

I looked to Alba, but he had risen and gone to the window. He looked out into the street at what the March wind blew about. I could see his profile, but his expression was too subtle for me to divine. I did not know whether or not to stay. It felt wrong but it seemed right.

"Good," she said, as if I had assented. She put her knitting into a silk bag and seized the drawstrings together. "You must get a drink for Miss Eustace, Maso, while I go and cook the dinner."

When she had gone, he went to a rosewood cabinet and fetched from it a bottle of sherry and two crystal glasses. He did not seem at ease in the room. I realized that compared to Ilse, he lacked a kind of grace. He lacked at any rate a drawing-room grace. I disliked the drawing room and wanted to be out of it.

We sat, sipped sherry, and found nothing to say. Silences went well upstairs, but seemed awkward here. At length, I said, "Aileen used to tell me so much about you and Mme Alba when I was a child. I always imagined you to live in a place like this. Your villa in Rome. How I used to imagine your villa in Rome!"

That seemed to please him. He smiled and shook his head. "How did you imagine it, Maud?"

"Oh, quite out of this world! An illustration of a fairy-tale—with you the prince . . ." I blushed violently into my glass, "and your wife as the princess; long, sweeping staircases, gardens with balustrades where one could look out on to an endless view. It wasn't medieval, my dream, or Renaissance—it was more of a stage set to a Mozart opera. I used to see Mme Alba in a Watteau dress and powdered wig and with tiny, tiny shoes. You wore velvet breeches and carried a stick like a wand. There were no end of grand parties."

"And you were allowed to stay up?" He was so gentle he did not embarrass me.

"Oh, yes—a cherished child. A cherished *blonde* child, all silken curls and satin sashes who sat discreetly back and watched the dancing and smelt mimosa from the terrace."

"*Brava, archibrava!*" he said. "And where was the black fairy?"

"There wasn't a black fairy."

"There's got to be a black fairy."

"I had enough of those at home without letting them interfere with my daydreams."

"Ah yes, I know." He lit on a look of commiseration, then flew from it again. "Rome was rather like that," he said. "There were lots of parties and a good deal of Mozart. But as for cherished children, we had none." He paused. "We had one—a baby who died only a month after she was born. Ilse . . ." For an instant, I imagined he wanted to confide, but he checked himself firmly.

"I'm sorry."

He waved his hand aside. "It was a long time ago. I shouldn't have mentioned it. Please don't mention it to Ilse."

"Oh, I wouldn't dream of . . ."

"Of course you wouldn't."

There was a hint of a special plea for Ilse in all of this—a special excuse, a special past. It was clear to me from reading and observation that some people put enormous value on children and that the loss of a child was peculiarly hard to bear. At the same time, in that I myself had been lost, I obscurely blamed Ilse. The baby's death appeared to constitute some failure on her part to keep it alive. Alba apparently did not think so. He looked sad. I wondered if, in some measure, I had been elected by him to make up for this dead child. I felt I wanted to return to my fantasy.

"Did you like the house in Rome better than this one? Do you miss it?" I pictured a stone bench set in a row of yews, an antique faun behind. I pictured Alba sitting on the bench playing Vivaldi. He played Vivaldi awfully well.

"I've lived all over the world," he said slowly. "There is no place I miss, nor is there any place I like better than any other place."

That he was out of place in London came to me suddenly. "Your name is Spanish, isn't it? My aunt used to boast about your Spanish connections."

"I spent some of my childhood in Madrid; a lot of it here. My father was Spanish by birth, but a British subject. My mother was English. The name Alba conjures up castles, I know, but we were only distantly related—noble but impoverished. My grandmama thought it terrible my father had to work. He was a musician, like Casals's papa. His instrument was the harpsichord, but he gave piano lessons. 'Alba'—ah, he was like Don Quixote more—his name stuck out like a sore thumb everywhere he went to teach. It was a constant humiliation to him, his name, his nobility. After my grandmother died, we came here where work was not such a solecism and no one cared so much what 'Alba' meant. My mother was practical and middle-class. Papa died a much respected man here. He's buried in Highgate Cemetery—near Karl Marx—poor Papa. If he hadn't been so obsessed with family, he might have been a great musician, but owning land, houses, this was his vision of success. He lived in comfortable circumstances in Highgate (we had a pleasant Victorian house) and this seemed an unbearable limitation. It meant nothing to him that he taught at the Royal College. When I started to do well, he turned his face to the wall. He wanted me to be a gentleman, advised me often to marry well!" Alba laughed indulgently.

I didn't want Alba to have a past. I didn't want him to have had anything to do with necessities. I too wanted Alba to be a gentleman. Instinctively, I mistrusted his mother. "You freed yourself in fame," I said, without thinking. "Oh, Alba, won't you play again—please—people still talk about you, listen to the records that you made! What you've played for me is so extraordinary."

He looked at me for quite a time, not angrily. "I was afraid you'd start to say that," he said.

"I'm sorry. It just came out . . . but you're so *good*. If only for my sake . . .". I realized that I wanted him to do something for my sake—something brave. His face looked peculiar and worn. I felt a sudden deep, dragging fear coming from him. "It can't be right to hide what you've discovered."

"We won't talk about it, Maud, eh? We won't talk about it. Now it is you who are coming towards the career, the performance. Yes? It is you who have an aptitude for stardom. You who are going to play in public what you've heard in private."

I could not articulate what I wanted to say. What had I heard in private? What? If I imagined it, what was I imagining? Why should I imagine what I was imagining? Why wouldn't he play in public? Why was this place so private and cut off? Where were we going? Were we going anywhere? If we were going somewhere, when would we get there? How? Had we arrived already?

I'm not a fool. He sat back, said nothing, forbade nothing. I'm not a fool, really, but if he had paralysed my tongue with a spell, I could have spoken more readily than I could have violated his privacy at that moment. I began to be frightened. I remembered the Janorskys' house and Janorsky's choice of the simple life and relative obscurity. Still, something had moved there; there had been an influx and egress of other people. I lit a cigarette and smoked it nervously, then realized there wasn't an ashtray. "Do you ever have other pupils?" It was all I could manage and I did not know why I asked it because I knew the answer.

"No." I saw that I had asked for the tone of the answer. It was as flat as a command.

I opened my handbag and took out my matchbox, emptied the matches into my bag and stubbed out the cigarette. As I did so, Ilse entered the room. She was dressed to the nines in green *peau de soie* and pearls. "Ah, Miss Eustace, you smoke," she said. "How careless of me not to have provided an ashtray." I felt a little as if I had been caught at a petty crime. "Your dinner is now ready at long last."

When I was a child, I was set to read *Great Expectations* for "O"-level English. It's so long since I've read a book. Maybe I shall take to books in future; I say this because it is striking and odd to me that when I close my eyes and try to recall the Albas' dining room, all I can see is Miss Havisham and Miss Havisham's wedding cake and wedding dress. All I can see is a feast festooned with cobwebs, a fantastical room having no bearing on the real room and the real feast Ilse set. Still, I cannot shake the image from my mind.

What style, what ambience the room then had! What subtlety and what design! When I think of the heavy walnut and mahogany of my youth—ah, me. The walls were papered with thick apricot silk and candles burnt in dull gilt sconces. A Chinese screen depicting wading herons masked the hearth. The table was round. Ilse had laid it with exquisite care. A perfectly proportioned porcelain bowl, filled with overblown yellow roses, stood exactly in the centre. Roses were not in season and I cannot imagine how she procured such flowers, such effect, even from the best florist. They seemed to come directly from an early autumn garden. The folds of the damask tablecloth, the napkins stiff with sheen, were so pure and rich that I had an impulse to bury my face in them. The plates were of an Oriental design, red and gold.

It was almost like the boudoir of a courtesan, a room which suggested a whole antique world of confidence given and received, of revelations discerned only by an acute eye. It was a place where a gesture of the hand, a change of tone, would give away whole kingdoms of the personality. It mooted the intime liaison, but discouraged any depths of intimacy. Ilse watched me take it in as I was seated. She was too adult to give away—even, I think, to feel—any pride in her achievement. She wanted, more, to see if I would fit, artistically speaking, into her design. I did not. I felt ridiculously underdressed. Yet how much there was to her! In the same glance which humiliated me, there was a deeper shade her eyes gave of a real interest in me, which extended far beyond the appearance of my clothes and hair. She seemed to look straight at a level of personality even Alba didn't know I had. She communicated to me tentatively in the way Amy and Aileen used to do so many years ago, when they exchanged bottles of nail varnish and faintly scornful stories about men.

I looked at Alba, but found it difficult to make any contact with him. There was a tiny flash of something oafish about him. I wanted to shake my head in order to regain him, but could not because of the rigours that the delicate room imposed.

Ilse started to wait on us. Only in this did smoothness oddly desert her. She flapped in and out of the green baize door to the kitchen. "May I help her?" I asked Alba in an undertone. He squeezed his eyes shut and shook his head violently as if to silence me rather than to answer my question. Ilse appeared to halt in each step in order to avoid—avoid what? Her movements had the quality of ritual—step on a crack—her impassive face demanded silent attention to her actions. She brought delicacies of every kind: asparagus (again, out of season) embedded in hollandaise sauce; a glittering hock in tall glasses, the stems of which were as fragile as bird-bones. No one spoke a word. As she uncovered the silver dish containing the asparagus, Alba gave a formal gasp of surprise. Feeling that these were the rules, I too made a conventional noise. I flushed when I saw this put her off her stroke.

At last, she sat down; she picked up a stalk of asparagus, and, instructing us with her eyes to begin, she ate.

She consumed the asparagus half with her fork, half with her fingers in a careless, offhand manner. As if born to the purple, she downed it lightly. Asparagus might have been bread and cheese for all it seemed to matter to her. Alba, on the other hand, ate with a glance to either side of him now and then as if someone might take his food away.

"Have you seen darling Aileen recently?" Ilse asked from her glutted mouth. She began to eat voraciously now with bad manners which she carried off with upper-class assurance. She sucked the hard bits at the end for all they were worth. It took away my appetite to watch her but it made me want to smoke.

"Not for some time—I've been working too hard," I said.

"I have been meaning and meaning to invite her for tea or some other such collation." Ilse spoke English well, but with some disregard for its well-being. She cast out big words wastefully as she might have cast out a crocodile handbag which had somehow displeased her. "I would have had her to tea but I have not yet had the time. Aileen requires time."

I was surprised at such a strange and inaccurate reading of

character. "She has spoken with great relish of your past hospitality," I said. "Now, of course, I can see why."

Ilse smiled through a slight sheen of sauce around her mouth. She was pleased by gallantry in any form. "Did you know your Uncle George at all well?" she asked.

"I liked him. He once took me to see Donald Duck. But I don't remember him because he was usually abroad. My aunt was my mother's sister and so came down to see us more often. Uncle George died young, before Aunt Aileen took us in."

"Ah yes, poor George. He was—charming." She looked discreetly at her plate and let a moment pass in which more than charm was suggested by the word charming. Out of the corner of my eye, I saw Alba stop chewing; he looked hard at his wife across the table. I reluctantly pieced together what had lain between the Albas and my uncle and aunt. I remembered how particularly relieved Aileen had been to see Alba that day when I first met him. I had sensed they found a wistful solace in each other. It had seemed to be a bond deeper than mere friendship, but not as deep as love. It dawned on me that Uncle George and Ilse had betrayed them. It had given them a sad, ironic kinship. I wondered if I'd ask Aileen.

"You were close friends, the four of you," I said awkwardly.

"Very." She spoke abruptly. "They knew us in our hey-day. Has Thomas told you about our hey-day? I expect he has." She looked at Alba closely.

I felt as I had done when a child and my father and Aileen had talked about my mother over my head. "No, he hasn't told me anything. Except, just now he was saying how pretty your villa was in Rome." I was innocent, but I felt I had to sound more innocent than I was. I sounded guilty to myself. Was I guilty?

"Isn't it time for the meat?" Alba said.

She had succeeded in goading him to impatience a shade away from bad manners. She smiled. "Ah, he is a slave driver, my husband. All day long I wait on him. He's so helpless." She was winning rather than hostile. "Is he a Svengali with you too, Miss Eustace?"

"Please do call me Maud."

"Ilse is such a good cook, you cannot wonder." In saying this, I felt Alba had picked up a dropped stitch from several rows behind.

She laughed with quicksilver charm and rose. She flitted to the kitchen. Alba inspected me over the candles. He looked a little shy; then his face suddenly came alive with a private little smile for me. I was grateful for it and warmed by it. I wanted to reach out and touch his hand out of love. Then suddenly I wondered what he thought of me as a woman: I wondered if I attracted him. The thought made my hand contract around the other in my lap. I felt deeply ashamed and confused. As I heard Ilse clatter in the kitchen, I remembered Dulcie Moore. Shame for that episode caught me deeper. I don't know why I was sorry for it—I never had much of a conscience. I gave Alba a strained, worried little smile. I do not think I had underestimated the physical instinct Alba and I might have had for each other, nor did I hesitate to think that in other circumstances that instinct might have been fulfilled. What occurred to me in the apricot dining room was that a choice had all along existed in the depths of our relationship, a choice I hadn't thought about. As several people must press several keys to detonate the hydrogen bomb, I knew that Ilse had pressed one or had shown me how to press one or had accidentally knocked one. Alba reasserted his smile—this time it was a stronger, gladder smile. Of course. The choice already had been made. And it was right. And all allegations against it were wrong. He had no intention. I had no intention. I smiled back.

Ilse swept in with a large joint of veal thus causing us both to retreat. Did we retreat guiltily? I think not, yet I do think so. The meat was smothered with heavy sauce and mushrooms. She replaced the old bottle of wine with a new one. She put it to one side without corking it. It seemed likely that it would be poured out. Down the drain. "Will you carve or shall I?" she asked.

"Oh, you do. You do it better."

She sliced the perfect veal perfectly just as my father used to carve on Sundays. Rag after rag of meat fell limp under her knife. She heaped our plates with an unseemly abundance of food. To stagger through to the pudding seemed almost unthinkable.

"I wish I could cook," I said. I did not wish I could cook.

"Domesticity is not for artists," Ilse said.

"I know many who are domestic," I said. "One need only look at you."

"Oh, my career was truncated in Italy," she said. I felt Alba telescope into himself. She suddenly raked a look of terrible meaning across the table at him. I dared not breathe. Just as when a child. It was all my fault. All my fault. She recovered herself completely and turned to me. "I wonder if I might at some point stage a 'come-back' as the movie stars say." Ilse spoke as if nothing had happened.

"Why yes! I was only urging Alba . . ." Oh, God. My fault, my fault again.

They both looked at me and at each other. There was a frigid silence.

"He said he wouldn't dream of it," I added.

"We've both dreamed of it," she said. She and Alba simply looked at each other. I could not understand what was going on at all. I felt close to tears.

"Do you play the piano, Miss Eustace?" she asked suddenly.

"Why yes." How could she not know I played the piano when she had listened, as she'd said, to the lessons. I didn't like the thought that she'd listened to the lessons. Had she not heard me accompany her husband? Perhaps she couldn't even tell his sound and thought that I was playing the cello instead.

"Would you oblige me after dinner with an accompaniment to some lieder? Perhaps you could give me an opinion about whether or not I can still sing?"

I looked to Alba. Oh, maybe he was just weak. No one could fail to sense the abnormal strength of Ilse. He tensely ate his meat and gave no sign. "I am no judge of singing," I said.

"Come, come, Miss Eustace. You won't deny me." Her eyes flitted round the table. An abuse of hospitality was suggested. She paused and let that rest. "No one has heard me sing for years," she said. I looked quickly up, arrested by her tragedy of tone. She was suddenly unmasked. Her eyes glittered with unshed tears. There was no self-pity in them, only an all-consuming wistfulness. She rested her forearm on the table's edge. Her hand was clenched with anticipation.

"Of course, I'll play for you. Of course." I cannot assume she engineered my pity for her. She was too unstrung to have been deliberate.

"Thank you," she said. "Thank you." She bowed her head and I was humbled by her gratitude.

I looked quickly to Alba, but he doggedly ate, refusing to be drawn. He seemed to find it difficult to swallow.

We finished the meal in mute anxiety with chestnut pudding and ripe Camembert. Remarks from him and chat from me, an observation here and there from her only drew attention to the ice we meant to break. She sat there waiting in her *peau de soie*. I saw she had dressed for this, this recital. Although reined in by a lifetime's discipline (so that she sat erect and managed to fumble casually with the diamond bracelet on her arm), her whole being seemed to quiver with the gathering of strength, with the gathering of herself to the point of performance. From the way she almost trembled, from the clattering of her spoon absently dropped, I anticipated failure. It had not occurred to me when I'd assented. I began to see how awful it would be; I began to wonder if I'd leave the house alive. Alba sat unnaturally still.

When at last we finished dinner, she rose with the command of a duchess on the way to the scaffold. She left the table in crumbs and smears as if a score of servants waited to remove it all. I, her executioner, blundered after her. "Shall I bring the coffee?" Alba asked. She nodded. "Ilse lets me do that," he said with false jocularity.

I had neglected to notice that the drawing room contained a lovely little Blüthner upright. It was neatly tucked in a corner near the mantelpiece. My hands were stiff with the chill that hung about and nerves. Although there were a few radiators discreetly placed about the walls, none of them were on. As I later learned, Ilse was extremely thrifty about certain things and heat was surely one of them, for their house was always cold. It might have been, however, her metabolism which made her

regulate the air as she did. The heat of summer made her feel—
she once said later—sluggish, like a snake.

In her own house, Ilse carried a little petit-point bag wherever
she went. She produced a pair of spectacles from this and
perched them on her nose. She rummaged through the piano
stool for music and at length she came up with an old, bound
copy of Schubert lieder. She unlocked the piano and adjusted
the book on the rack. Then, as an afterthought, she lit two
candles which stood on the piano. The only light in the room
came from a dim lamp in the far corner and from a small spot
which illuminated the Ingres. I stroked the keys, hoping the
instrument would be out of sorts in some way so that I could
refuse to play it. It was, however, beautifully in tune.

"Will you play this for me, my dear? I used to sing it long
ago," she said. She turned the pages. "Ave Maria," she said. Her
voice clashed with a kind of challenge. She stood underneath
the Ingres.

I stalled and hoped. "I must run through it first," I said. "I've
never accompanied a singer before—certainly not one so accomplished as you." My fingers for all the cold worked on auto-
matic. "Well, shall we begin?" I cast around for some cushion to
throw under her fall. What response could there be to cracked
notes, to naked pathos? What cloak could I put round her?
What reassurance give? To shelter my blushes for her would be
worse than facing her with them. She so burnt with a sense of
failure, I was sure, sure. "Are you ready?" I thought perhaps she
would warm up with a scale or two to tune her voice.

"Perfectly," she said. There's no doubt about it—the woman
had steel. I began. She sang.

My fingers leapt to the enchantment of it. I could not believe
what I was hearing—she no more sang but soared—the purity,
the candour forced my ears open. No sentimentality came near
her execution; her phrasing was magnificent, intelligent. Her
voice had lost no jot of its integrity. But underlying skill, what
gave her mastery, was the most shining core of true, if half-
forgotten devotion that touched me and reminded me of Amy
on her mountain and Amy in her valley and Amy and me as we
fought through what grimness had been given us. Even now,

when I close my eyes, I hear what she brought forth of motiveless abundant love, disturbing and maternal from her otherwise sharp and greedy tongue.

When the song was over, I looked up and saw that Alba had come quietly in. He and Ilse stood together—curiously detached from one another—under the sloe-eyed odalisque. We said nothing, humbled as we were by the descent of peace.

"That was beautiful." I finally spoke but was barely audible. "Will you sing some more?"

She twitched her shoulder, shrugging off my praise. "The coffee will be cold," she said.

Ilse went and sat lightly on her Empire chair. She was sophisticated beyond all reasonable expectation. Although her eyes were quite transformed by what must have been (it must have been) considerable triumph, she sugared us with smiles which had no bearing on the beauty she'd unburdened. Alba looked at her with grave mistrust. I could not look at her. How she absorbed! How beautiful she was! I grabbed around in my mind for the sound of his cello. It was blurred and unclear. "You surely don't need me to tell you anything about your singing, Mme Alba," I said in awed tone. I began to see that she had not needed me to tell her anything, but had needed to tell me something. I did not know what it was, but the sense of it unnerved me. She gave me a charming smile. She held a sugar lump with tongs. Ilse was a sugar lover. There was syrup enough to sup in her but she had no wish to be dined on. "Do you think I could make it if I tried to go back?" She arranged her head in a quaint tilt. She spoke to me but looked at Alba. She seemed fully orchestrated for a Viennese waltz. She mocked him airily with her eyes—a widow on a gilt chair at a ball addressing the count with more sex than he could handle.

Alba opened his eyes wider and looked at her with an expression too tired to be described as rage.

"Well," I said, "you know what I think. I think you both should—go back, I mean."

"But, you see, we have decided against it," Ilse said. Alba seemed to crawl with nerves. She bounded on like an indefatigable dancer. "I daresay you are at an age, Maud—I may call you Maud?—when you can't get enough of it, performing I mean. Anything to stop one-night stands in filthy village halls or playing sessions for television commercials, eh?"

I let it pass that I had got beyond that. "I'm lucky that I have a private income," I said. "It's not large, but it enables me to work more or less as I please."

"In these days," Ilse said, "a private income is not considered to be a spiritual advantage."

"I earned mine in childhood," I replied.

She threw back her head and laughed. Her laugh gratified. She included me in a conspiracy with her own ironic thought. "Well, my husband and I grew tired of feeling like a pair of mountebanks," she said.

If she had not said this, I would not have wondered much. The statement fell so short of what was at the heart of their— retirement—that it produced in me the opening passages of doubt. I sat very still; doubt has the effect of nerve gas on the brain. I felt a little cold.

He sat with dignity, straight. His hands were in repose; his shoulders balanced, not tensed. He watched me. Now I think back on it, he must have known what eventually would happen. What would happen shone sadly from his eyes. It took no pre-cognitive gift to know, only a good mind for chess. What I can't understand is why he didn't stop it. What I can't understand is why he let it start in the first place.

I went home that night so full of Ilse that I could not contain her happily within my rooms. I switched on the light and could not bear the place, so switched off again. From the sodium glare of the street light, I saw in muted tones the dejected quality of my life. The nasty little oil of English countryside my father had left me wanted cleaning. I was aware of the common marble mantelpiece, the few dusty figurines from our disassembled china cabinet in Suffolk. Amy'd had half this country Staffordshire. Why, I hadn't even bothered with the scuffed emulsion since I'd moved. I'd lavished no cushions on the buttoned-up green sofa, no imagination on the walls. Even the silver wanted cleaning.

Ilse could sing: the shock of that, delayed, hit me. She could sing but chose not to. Why did she choose not to sing? It had never crossed my mind not to play the cello if I could. It was the only thing I could ever do with confidence; yet never had I made a sound drawing bow over strings that pressed so deeply on an inner nerve, nor had Alba in all his searchings of Bach come up with anything that really hunted me out like that song. I drifted to the piano in my music room, opened the lid and played a few remembered bars of the accompaniment. Then I played a snatch of the melody, hummed it—I have no voice. I slammed down the lid, stood indecisively a while, then twitching myself up, went out for a walk along the river. I then had freedom of the river and often walked beside it. Now and then some drunk would try to pick me up. I took them less seriously than blue-bottles, buzzing up and bumping, buzzing off.

That night I was aware, past Vauxhall Bridge and on, of my own body: not as I am usually aware, maniacally careful of my hands and all the muscles that go into making music, nor of any sexual hunger that I'd known. My needs had never made me aware of my being, but Ilse and her song obscurely had. She might have shone a light on something more than a sore. I was seized with the sudden pain of knowing I was infantile; that I had infantile paralysis of a certain kind.

The river was no crystal ball; it flowed, muddy, mighty, and cold, towards the sea. I did not look into it for light, but maybe depth. It was low tide; all the water seemed to do was flush up silt to be borne only to another place. I wanted it cleaned—the silt, I mean. I started to cry.

What did Alba and I mean to each other? I wasn't sure. It had to do with the sour breath of the river, whatever it was. In summer, late walkers use the light to search the mud at low tide for clay pipes tossed in from other times, gold coins, or other archaeology. They seem to stand the base smell of mud well enough, but I, I had no impulse on the windy midnight to leap the barrier and search through.

I turned and denied what I saw—or rather what I didn't see—and cast my eyes over the Tate Gallery. The thought pushed and felt through my brain anyhow like a subtle, strong anemone. Weirdly, it had to do with children: babies with lolling heads, babies with heads like bad cabbages, bad babies. I turned back to the river to face the thought out, to reconnect it with whatever sense of purpose I'd half-seen and lost of Alba, but the connection was gone, guzzled down the river. I was frightened and resistant of the idea of children and that I myself was capable of having them. It had never occurred to me before that I myself could bear them. The whole of the physical world filled me with nausea and disgust.

I walked home, having lost the song.

All night long, I slept with murderous nightmares on the brain.

But I recovered myself by morning to be hesitant about it all. To say how silly it all was. I practised long and hard. How silly it all was. It wasn't silly was it, but dangerous to ignore.

CHAPTER X

Why Maud? (This was it.)

What was Maud to her? What should Maud be to Beatrice that her mind could not be in repose without the image of Maud presenting itself to her. (This was it. Here it was. Chance? No. Opportunity? Not quite. An opportunity—oh, much more—for *what?*)

How did it present itself? Not the image, but the obsession. She wanted to go downstairs again; take goodies again. Mend? Heal? No. Inhale, perhaps. No. Yes, no, yes no.

Why did she suffer after her? What was this urgency for connection? Oh, bloody, bloody hell. Why this? Why now? She had fallen into a black hole of not knowing a thing. Was she perhaps in love?

That surely must be inspected.

She sat down and inspected it.

She was in torment.

Was this what she hungered and thirsted for in the dark? Did she want to touch her? She made herself imagine this. Something superficial in her wouldn't have minded the folds of the clothes, the hair; but balked with a repugnance—convincing in that it was mild—at final contact.

But something else was racked towards the girl, as if the girl drew and drew her out towards and beyond herself. It was cruel; it was desperate. (This was it.)

Why was this it? *What* was racked towards the girl? It was as if God had claws and bit deep; as if He clenched beyond mind some hidden aspect of her. She rocked to and fro, to and fro.

Was she due for a dreadful unveiling of motive?

She cast fretfully around for reasons she laughed at to explain—to explain. She saw herself on the playground as a small child. Actually, she hadn't been a small child at all, but had felt smaller for towering over the others with embarrassing height and early physical development. She had been smaller for that and fat. And had worn two bleak plaits—and had endured teasing for foreignness, fatness, and strangeness. Only she knew she would have been foreign, though not.

For being so good, the nuns had liked her. They'd never loved her for being so awfully good. Oh, milk monitor; oh, monitress; oh, marshal of smaller giggling girls, who obeyed Beatrice because she didn't know how to play. The smell of the school came back—the smell of children's sweat—so distinct and damp; damp girls and the damp down on Sister Felicity's upper lip. Beatrice *tried* so *hard* to like being miserable.

She saw herself scowling in the shade of the gritty brick wall with no one to play with. The central, inarticulate doubt had always been a fear of—feeling? A fear of failing? A fear of falling? A fear of all—failing, falling, feeling. She certainly had *done* lots. Hand always up first with the right answer. She had made herself useful, given sweeties to others in hopes, tears pricking at the back, never front of her eyes.

It was not an inability to feel. Oh, no.

Adolescence had been a psychic scream: a long, pressed, suppressed fury of need and guilt. She'd thrashed in agonies of love, blinked back tears at phone calls for Tatty not for her. Had stood like a stick at balls where Tatty had swanned and she'd been so awfully nice to the chaperones, bringing them ices and enduring pinches from older men.

And yet she was (no, mark this, had been) beautiful.

Beauty had been a stick in the craw. Why on earth had beauty stuck in her craw? Was she ashamed of it? Half the time she wouldn't admit it was there. Oh, *carissima* Beatrice. Mama was fat and Tatty superb and had nothing of the fragile mould of jaw, the slant of cheek, the unlikely dimple when Beatrice in fact (and wholly unbeknown to her) smiled involuntary smiles. Beatrice grown up was a swan, sailed dignified and alone down the street, down the corridor.

Conscience had bled her dry. Or was it that? What had lacerated her so? Sometimes she had the urge (had had the urge more fully in the past) to scream at it. Oh why, oh why, oh why wouldn't it let her alone!

Could have married, though not. Had she withdrawn? Not. She could not cope with the torment not conscience but consciousness had given her. It hadn't to do with whom she loved but who loved her. Jealousy cruel as the grave?

When she read the *Lancet* and pondered Freud she wasn't so sure at all; she would never have been sure except for the pain that knifed her when she wasn't with . . . God.

There had been *no* love affairs, but there had been dreadful crimes (at times) of thought and feeling. She was not made of stone (not even of finer clay). Butterflies in the stomach and the hell of watching Tatty walk off with . . . She mustn't think that way. All the same she thought that way about her brother-in-law. How she'd sat with nervous smiles on the sofa while her sister articulated bumps and grinds next to the mantelpiece.

But even in the deep thickets of her most passionate thoughts always there had been the sense that it was not for her. Did this account for a certain *froideur*? A *froideur* at the point of contact (as anyone knows, the imagination knows no bounds). She had watched Tatty's wedding dress being made with a certain fine pain. A pain as pure and sharp as the pins which stuck white bodice to satin folds. She sat as white as ice, as burnt and white and painful as dry ice: so still for fear of attempting a revenge; so still for fear of voicing the desire at all. And Tatty had actually taunted her with jealousy, because she didn't know that Beatrice was jealous.

Because:

Carissima Beatrice never minded
giving everything
away.

Because: Beatrice had held Tatty's head in her arms when she'd screamed with nightmares; when Beatrice had gone to get Tatty out of trouble at school, and once with the police; because Beatrice had tenderly loved her, had leapt into the breach, had become a bridge for Tatty's freedom.

Beatrice pulled herself right together and smiled. Wasn't her own freedom now paid for by Tatty herself who had become immaculate in motherhood and serene and happy, and now looked after Mama *because* of all those years? She had not imagined bread cast upon the waters would return, but it had.

No, she hadn't last felt in medical school with Jonathan. She'd felt a good grim deal since then.

But you couldn't put this sickness about Maud down to Tatty or desire. You had to put it down to a pain more profound which reminded her; which reminded her.

Of an incident by the river? She looked out at the river, but it wasn't the same river she'd seen that night six years ago. She wondered if she'd moved into this flat with a subconscious memory—desire—in her mind.

You couldn't put Maud down to that; but the feeling was like that. The connection locked in. (This was it. Was this it?)

Beatrice was—had always been—one for walks. *Not* given to joining the others at the pub after work, something had to be done to alleviate Guy's before Eaton Square was launched into of an evening. So she walked home, along the river, not always all the way home, but now and then she had walked all the way home, swinging arms not hips and breathing air not so much healthy as free from the suffocation of endless responsibility. Had she suffocated herself with endless responsibility? It was an evening in June that she'd seen what she'd seen—light but late light—from Lambeth Bridge—was it really six years ago?

She often crossed the river by Lambeth Bridge. She liked the view of Westminster. She sometimes stopped in the middle— exactly in the middle—she liked to be hung exact, over the exact centre, hung over water. She did not see herself as the morning star or an angel but symmetry of vision gave her satisfaction. She did not feel hung but held over the flow of water. Water gave her pleasure; oh, a stream of water soothed an ache. Ten tons of history from her native city knew that water soothed an ache. The sound of fountains was everywhere. The Tiber had flowed blood and rinsed it out and flowed again.

Even though the sun set and sometimes most spectacularly— a Turner over the Tate upstream—Beatrice preferred the down- stream flow, the lapping and slapping against the boats and even filth inexorably drawn to the sea, taken and washed and lost in the sea. For Beatrice the sea never roared; she saw it more, heard it more as eating and digesting trivia. Sometimes she liked to think of its response to the golden moon. That it responded to the moon alone pleased her and made her smile; it touched her heart and confirmed a kind of passivity she had. She struggled with the joy of fishes in the deep. Why, Leviathan even charmed her. The miracles surrounding water, such as Jonah being swal- lowed or the Lord walking, footsteps resounding on the deep, gave her a curious presence of mind before the Almighty.

She stood that June night letting the hospital wash away. She allowed the distractions of the day to run from her mind down- stream and was about to move on when suddenly she saw a police launch shoot from under the bridge. She followed its progressions with detached interest, noises from loudhailers came muffled up and lights winked from below giving an interesting impression of something quite remote like somebody else's Christmas tree flashing behind glass.

And then she saw the body floating: it was pallid and gross; it hadn't any clothes on and even from her vantage point, she could tell it was a woman, its breasts engorged with water like a mother's with milk; its hair was reddish, oddly beautiful—it floated out vivid in that it was the only thing remaining of the woman that looked the least alive. She had not seen it was a woman until the policeman turned it over. He puffed to haul it out; it was too heavy with the water. They pulled it out with some interesting tackle. Beatrice, who had sliced cadavers like so many hocks of ham, suddenly grew sick. She stood on the bridge; the corpse hailed her as a sister. She crossed herself and said a little prayer: it seemed to assert a sisterhood more profound. The features, obliterated by dusk and hair, leapt live to her imagination. Why had she not noticed before? What hadn't she noticed about death? Was violent death the difference? She hadn't dealt with violent death since Casualty and even then seldom. But it was not that. Death had had to her an orderly, contained quality. Professional expertise allowed for it. She was competent to deal with it.

She could do nothing for the woman in the water, but to pray for the woman in the water. The depth of the passivity of deadness and nakedness, the helpless immodesty before men's eyes, the complete privacy at the same time of the woman, the sudden end of whatever emergency had thrown her into the water, the spontaneity of it all. The hair fell back and Beatrice saw that something had picked out the woman's eye.

She turned in her revulsion. Something insisted itself upon her. She turned in her revulsion. Something would not let her go—insisted, insisted, insisted. What? That she face? That she face. Her own death? She faced her own death daily with serial prayers drummed like rain on the roof, drummed with the peace of rain on the roof, drummed ceaseless and never forget. The clock ticks and it encroaches like tide on the shore until swallowed up, you drift on the tide of the clock, to sea.

Where the wheel of things turned and jerked her down to the

pallid gross drowned thing who mattered—to the pallid dense flesh of a female thing—who'd . . . Who knows what she'd done? Had she jumped or been pushed or simply crumpled in? *But I lead a completely blameless life!* How blameless? Why blameless? Was she the woman in the water? Then, how was she the woman in the water? She blushed, engorged with shame that she had thought she lived a blameless life. She fingered the image of Saviour round her neck. Had given not Brompton Mixtures and advice but *self* . . . and what had that to do with the woman in the water exposed and dead possibly by her own hand. *Who* lived a blameless life? And died exposed?

What she wouldn't have done to resuscitate the woman! Her mind stood on the chest and pumped the water from her lungs. Not the answer, not the answer. Deeply drowned. It wasn't enough, not enough. How had she failed the destitute when she spent every day of her life with them?

She had hung on the bridge, now loose, not held. What had she failed to admit? She went to confession regularly and scoured out her heart. Always between herself and the priest there was a half-question, as if there were something she hadn't admitted. Not that she had failed to admit: shouting at Sister and wanting Antonio, or whatever, harbouring grudges against Mama, whatever. There was the initial satisfaction and then the little doubts crept in—something that in her was missing—but she couldn't articulate *what.* She always felt they knew but wouldn't say what it was.

And she'd wanted to throw herself in with the drowned woman, throw her lot in with the lot of the drowned woman. Why? Was she a subtle suicide? An unconventional undercurrent which tugged at her heart was not that. She had looked back into the water of the river. The launch was gone.

Her scientific eye now questioned the whole experience. How could the launch be so quickly gone? How with so little fuss had the woman been assumed from the river? She wondered whether it mattered or not, whether it had happened or not. What mattered had happened. She looked again into the now-dark water for a trace of the launch, for a trace of what had happened. There was no ridge of water, no wash—all gone. She shrugged off the idea that it might have been a vision. She'd seen the launch with its prow, the beefy police hauling and handling, the private woman; the woman dead. Again, she shrugged off the idea that she might have had a vision.

She sat down on the bench provided in the recess where she had stood, in her little buttoned-up jacket. She felt a little ill. What had come over her and why should it matter? What she had seen—or not seen? (She was not given to imagination.) *Who* was the woman? Not what but *who*? How had she seen the face so clearly in the half-light from such a distance? How seen the eye picked out?

Her consciousness had always propped up the fearful dying, had always pulled some spark of people over the border. Even to those eaten up beyond all recognition, *she* had recognized some undevourable source, a stream which might open out afterwards; often had seen healed, and rejoiced.

"I must go home to Mama," she had said firmly, and got up and swung her arms and not teetered on her sensible heels, but had placed one foot carefully in front of the other.

Well. Anyway. She turned her face from the river and made herself some lunch. She made a meal of lettuce and a piece of cheese. Having eschewed sweetmeats after the great adolescent spread, she had never been able to swallow much again, except in the doctors' canteen. She was most confident there and took a doughnut with her coffee. Did she avoid greed or what was womanly? She was never quite sure. Beatrice was thin. At any rate, she was never proud about her lack of appetite. Her eye drifted over the river again from the window. Oh, heart despised. The barges spread the water fully in a wave. Oh, heart. She swallowed a lump of Cheddar.

It had been clear enough this morning when she'd gone to the police that they weren't going to do anything about it. After all that. The agonies. The scruples about breaking her promise to Maud. What had been the morality of it? Did she tell Maud the man was out there after all and drive the wretched girl deeper into craziness just so that she could keep her promise not to call the police?

Or on the other hand, should she leave the whole thing alone as she'd been expressly bidden to?

Was there a possibility that someone could be killed if she did not go, if *someone* did not go?

Supposing Maud found out if she went. She'd hate her forever afterwards. That was the worst, and that was the struggle.

By the time she finally went, she had worked herself into this last and only possible solution; and she detested it.

She stood as clean as hospital lino in the police station and spoke to the sergeant. She held a handbag of absolute usefulness and respectability. And her mouth went dry.

"My friend and I . . ." she began. She spoke as she did when she addressed meetings and felt like Judas Iscariot. "Well, my friend, anyway, is being bothered by a man."

"Boyfriend? Husband?" The sergeant gave her a shrewd look. How could he not suspect hysteria?

"No . . . a strange man. He came to her door the other day on the pretext of some religious mission. He left her very upset, and now he's hanging around the house and won't go away."

"I'm sorry, madam, but you'll have to be a little more precise. Has he made a nuisance of himself in any way?"

"He's been watching the house from the gardens across the way, and when my friend and I went shopping, he followed us. My friend is *very* upset; she's a nervous person, and . . ."

There was a delicate pause. The sergeant looked at Beatrice as if he thought she thought babies were brought by the stork. "Did he make any explicit . . . ?" His voice hung archly over the question.

"You mean did he expose himself or anything like that?" Beatrice, who was after all grown-up, became exasperated.

The policeman was a little shocked. "Obscene phone calls?"

"Not as far as I know. Look, he's quite mad, this man. I'm a doctor and I've observed things about his behaviour which worry me."

The policeman looked at Beatrice as if it were incumbent

upon her to prove her doctorhood, and after a swift reckoning, decided to believe her. He gave an indulgent sigh. "You may be a doctor, madam, but not a lawyer." His own knowledge of the law appeared to be a great burden to him, as if he were the sole target for all ignorant enquiries in London. "Unless your man makes a definite move, there isn't much we can do. Of course, if you want to make a civil case out against him, you can contact your solicitor . . . or your friend can contact hers, which seems more to the point.

"And before that would be dealt with, your man will probably have moved on anyway."

"I see." She was accustomed to seeing official points of view. White coats, brass buttons—all had the varnish of control. All dealt out black-and-white decisions. Suddenly, she saw she wasn't necessarily on their side any more.

"If she's so bothered by this chap, why doesn't she come here herself?" he asked. God only knew what business this woman was prying into! For a doctor her hands were bloody shaky.

Especially if you were stuck for words as a rule, how did you explain to a sergeant with a blue-serge smile that Maud was irrevocably committed to her own destruction? That the police frightened her as much as Arthur? That she herself frightened Maud as much as both of them? It became clear to Beatrice that she was about to lose her temper, and there was nothing she could do to stop it.

Normally the grim goddess of hospital porters, normally the effective getter-of-things-done, normally the firm, stern friend of junior doctors, normally one never to speak above a hush redolent with command, Beatrice shouted, "She's ill! Now are you or are you not going to do anything about it!"

The sergeant floundered. Actually, he was obliged to make a note of all complaints.

"If you say so, madam." He drew his lips together primly against his own unexploded wrath.

She should never have got involved with Maud if she were to help her, *really* love her. For the second time in the last few days she'd been angry. First Celia, and now she hated the sergeant's buttons and by association the Metropolitan Police. How did you explain the sweetness of music or the loaded and afflicted heart to those to whom such things were foreign? Beatrice had always seen herself as foreign to others.

"Well, I think you ought to investigate it," she said hotly. "I shall hold you directly responsible if anything happens." She couldn't explain to herself the sense of urgency, the sudden revival of fear, not only of Arthur Marsdan, but of Maud and the sergeant too.

It was only nine o'clock, but the sergeant already felt he had had a hard day. "Listen, madam," he said, "if we picked up every nut-case in this borough and charged every nut-case in this borough there wouldn't be the hospitals or the hostels or the prisons to hold 'em. Most of 'em are pretty harmless as a rule. But, of course, if you insist, we'll have him searched and we'll pick him up—that is if we find anything—for loitering with intent."

Beatrice had made an involuntary movement of the hand. She did not like the idea of anyone searching Arthur. It had seemed simple enough to scare him off, make him vanish, give Maud to understand that someone cared, go back to Maud with the victory of Arthur's unsensational removal.

"And, of course if we do pick him up and charge him, your friend will have to give evidence against him."

Maud in the dock, ashen and shaking, giving away only her own brand of lunacy. (And why did you let him in, Miss Eustace? What did he actually do, Miss Eustace?) Beatrice knew it wouldn't hold a teaspoonful of water.

All the same. It was better that they should think what they were thinking than have anyone's throat cut. She knew what the sergeant was thinking, because that is what people as a rule thought of her. "Just go ahead and find him," she said. "Then ring me. I will decide what to do, and if it is necessary for Miss Eustace to speak with you, I will try to persuade her to do so."

She'd waited in all morning for the police to call. Tomorrow she was working and the next day and the next and so on. She got up from her half-finished meal and paced and chafed. She burst with frustration, her hands wrung with activity of mind and nothing to do. When she thought about it rationally, she saw no connection between the girl and herself, and no hope of a real connection.

"She doesn't even like me," Beatrice said to the cat and bit her knuckles. She laughed. "And what's more I'm not sure I like her."

The telephone pierced her thoughts. She leapt more startled than the cat from the sofa and snatched the receiver from its cradle. It was only Father Potter making sure of her place on the ecumenical retreat during Advent. He sawed gently on. If she could have strangled him with the cord she would have; then she repented and took careful care to listen to every word and to stimulate more words and more words still so that in the end they had a conversation neither of them wanted but felt duty bound to have. She put down the phone and let her exhausted nerves find a level somewhere at the pit of her stomach. Perhaps she could talk to him about Maud. She could never talk to him about Maud.

Was this it and did it matter why? Oh, how she wished she had *somebody* to talk to, someone who would understand the complexities of love, who had some authority and assurance on this matter of the whole self being pitched into chaos. Someone who could remarry head and heart in her. She saw now the dilemma as being extreme and not having entirely to do with Maud.

She tried to pray. The deafening silence made it worse, but she continued not to be put off by poor results. Was it a distraction? Did she hear it? She inly heard the dance and song of the cello and opened her eyes squeezed shut—to listen. The line of its meditation, the line of its simplicity, its elegance, its thick refined harmonies filled her with a kind of ecstasy.

She jumped up at her revulsion at the thing's being a—what was it?—almost an organ of desire and gripped with the dread of that she stopped and found herself shaking at the audacity of what the cello had sung to her, or what she had sung in its voice.

She resuscitated herself with a cup of tea and wondered what self-abandonment might mean. Was it her retreat from the ex-

perience or her having entertained it for a moment that left her
feeling sour?

The phone rang again. Even though this time it was the police
it didn't seem to matter as much as it had only ten minutes
before.

"We've searched the gardens, madam, and just to put your
mind at rest, I think we can safely say your chap won't be
bothering you any more."

"You found him!" Why had she thought they wouldn't? Was
she so unsure now that she saw or heard anything?

"Oh, we found him, poor devil." The sergeant's heart of gold
accused Beatrice of being dross. It gave her pain to think of
Arthur being searched, of Arthur's being scoured. Still, the insistent scent of death had lain around him.

"Have you—taken—him?" Oh, into care, not into custody,
please.

"I wouldn't worry about him, madam. He's a familiar character in these parts—getting to be sort of a friend, you might say.
He's quite harmless, I can assure you. We didn't charge him
because there wasn't anything to charge him with."

"Vagrancy?" Was it animal to pounce on anything they could
conceivably bring against the man?

The sergeant thought Beatrice most unkind. He had suspected (and indeed he had formulated his theories about social
life in the nether reaches of Victoria) her of crassness, not to say
naïveté. What did she want them to do to the poor bastard—
hang, draw, and quarter him? He'd seen enough, he'd seen more
than one lifetime could hold of the petty vengeance, of the motiveless vengeance women (particularly) were capable of.

"He has a fixed address. He lives in Hammersmith."

Beatrice paused. "I'm quite sure he's up to something," she
said. She felt sure of the policeman's disapproval, too. Weren't
doctors and policemen on the same side? Hadn't they always
been? This time they were not, which made it doubly painful . . .
to press on and on about it.

"Listen, lady" (Dashiell Hammett via Bogey had formed the
early policeman), "you say this man has made no obscene
phone calls; hasn't done anything indecent; he's carrying no

weapons; he isn't a vagrant; he's never been drunk or disorderly; he isn't even trespassing on private property. What do you expect us to do with him?"

"Officer, I am a doctor. The man is a psychotic. He ought to be dealt with—at least by the social services."

"Well, then, ring the social services. The law can't touch him. We've moved him on. All he tried to do was to convert the constable. And if you ask me it wouldn't hurt the constable to see the light."

Beatrice put the phone down in the certainty that nobody could do anything with Arthur at all—or would. She was no stranger to the social services, and in any case, the man had been moved on. She'd entered too much into the mind of Maud and now saw herself as having been rather silly. Well, anyway, he'd probably been scared off for good. At any rate, it was possible now to take a walk without worrying. She'd have a walk. She would walk and walk it all off: the idiocy of this personal concern; the folly of this personal concern. How could she have thought this was it? Whatever it was. She tidied her hair in the mirror and thought her face wizened and abhorrent. This was (arrogance) it.

Arthur's mind hailed fire, and feet skated the broad brimstone of pavement; heat seized his feet and made him walk sidewise tiptoe for the pain it gave. Maud had listened, listened, listened and now sent him away. In no grave was he but beyond and hurting too much even to feel pain. She'd sent him to where weeping and gnashing of teeth prevailed. He couldn't see so nearly got run over. He could not cry but something like tears scored his face like a ham. The constable's kindness had been a fist in his face; a fist would have been greater kindness than the kindness which was no kindness at all but a sort of British standard stamp on his ineffectual, his impotent lunacy. His thoughts were not in that thought but lay crisp and burnt all over his brain. He found himself in Maida Vale, but he did not harangue Hampstead. He began to wonder if he were floating, had died. Like a homing pigeon, at last, he crashed out in Mrs Abbott's parlour.

She was neither glad nor sorry but excited to see him—especially helpless—and diagnosed the flu. By now he had a raging temperature. But no one, least of all Mrs Abbott, knew how devils poked the needles in and sewed up his head. He saw them but was too ill to cry out.

Mrs Abbott had no time for doctors. She shunned the cold blow from the eye anyone professional was sure to give her. And when the Newsons came, she would not let them in and told a lie and said that Arthur'd disappeared.

Who had tolerated the smell of cats but Arthur? Who but Arthur had not looked at the destroyed floor nor seen her guilty longings? He'd never noticed. She'd never hoped for anything better or more than someone simply not noticing. Coexistence was all she ever dared look for and Arthur's preoccupied and involuted stare had meant to her a kind of mercy. So she doctored him with herbal tea and aspirin. She did not ask for rent, but put him to bed and while he slept, nervously kissed his fingers, and each kiss travelled along nerve ends to his brain and made it howl with needles more.

And then it stopped; as if the crust that covered canyons of the mind had finally burnt away and Arthur slept a horrible damp sleep—dank and roaring with the sound of emptiness—and typhoons hollered around corners which pitched to a shriek. Little bits of jutting mind broke off casually like bits of falling masonry and then died and a cold glassy whistle remained which whistled her name—Maud—but as the word "Maud" cannot be whistled, it was a vision of her embodied like the cold stream of air in the cavity of a drilled tooth, until he was completely possessed by the abstraction of her. She was no longer even slightly she, only the torment of what he could not have. Where her hair touched her forehead was painful beyond belief. He fell into the gap between her two front teeth. All the armoury of her underclothes he did not imagine, but was enclosed by; he strangled in her bra. She was not a nice girl, but must be saved. But Saviour, touching pity, did not touch him. How could it touch his unasking throat, his unwired mind? It was like being electrocuted over and over again.

The other one flitted in and out of his hollowed-out and gutted skull, not like a whistle but a dream. Beatrice burgeoned here and there. He had an acute vision of her but no context for her. How did she survive his dream life, his affliction? She was a form of art, which with fear and fury he studied to destroy, but weak as he was, he could not shut her out. Over and over again the eyes on the stair; over and over again he at the top of the arc plunging down was frozen like a still from a film in the moment of the eyes. She was a grey, low-loaded star, pregnant for him with light, and his broken mind refracted in crazed pattern her meaning to him.

Wherever he looked, she prevented him. For a dream, she was very solid. When he was afflicted by the vision of her, he could not come near the vision of Maud with which his famished mind was crammed. Beatrice starved him out, but did not stop the terrible lunging yearning of his appetite.

In time, he recovered, on Mrs Abbott's broth, a curious semblance of sanity. It took about a week for the eruption to subside and he was left without a trace of memory. Only untreated lesions remained. When he awoke, he was on a broad cold plain where canyons had been flattened, where lava hadn't the oxygen to live. He was weightless in the black sky.

Oddly, there arose what he had so repressed—an intellect. He sat now on his steamed sheets, his unslippered feet cold but unfelt on the tattered lino floor and produced a calculation of what he had to do. It had been, of course, what he'd intended to do all along, but now the act was justified. Maud must be destroyed. He could not now remember her name. With peculiar clarity he saw, drawing the knife of this intention from its now rotted sheath, that this was it: all that he had tended towards, consented to, merged in this, this shining, glinting, little length of steel. Didn't the hand of God kill? It was so simple. Wasn't that what Are you saved? had meant all along? It had, at any rate, meant that to him. This was what he was predestined for. He became extremely poised. Around this pure and undefiled sense of hatred, his psychic forces coalesced. He got up and shaved. He found a clean shirt in his drawer. He hesitated, then put on a tie and then his oily suit. He was iron to Mrs Abbott: she quailed before his inquisitor's stare, but he did not see her or tell her why he was going out. He just told her to burn the duffle coat. He harnessed himself in the mackintosh he'd had before and swept out. He had two distinct plans in mind.

Beatrice walked down the Embankment, her mind in deep distress. She had instinctively rebelled against talking to the police. Why had she done it and why did it leave her with such a bad taste? It had been simply that she'd felt she couldn't arrogate to herself—oh, what?—the taking of a risk with Maud's life. Just suppose he had tried to do something. But on the other hand, hadn't it been arrogance to meddle with Maud's life at all? Something was badly wrong. She knew it, but couldn't put her finger on it.

She should have talked to the man himself. She stopped and gasped, putting a gloved hand to her mouth. A passer-by or two stared. Why hadn't it occurred to her? She waved aside the thought. Oh, what could she have achieved by it anyway? Poor man.

Poor man, she'd put him through the indignity of the police. She was dragged down by an acute sense of sorrow for that. She sat still on a bench and thought "poor man, poor man," then thought, "I'm only saying that because he's safely out of the way." And then she turned again and felt he wasn't safely out of the way. She wondered if she should invite Maud to stay in her flat. Yes, that was an idea! And then felt ashamed of herself. Wasn't she just manufacturing another excuse to see her? The policeman had said there was no harm in Arthur. After all, he was known to them.

A much better plan struck her.

Oh, it had the wizardry of doing so much all at once!

The Albas! Hadn't Maud talked of them, their friendship? Oh, clearly they had fallen out, but didn't, well, people with artistic temperaments often—she was naïvely enchanted with the thought of flouncing divas.

Her mind humbled itself. To see the Albas would be—to reconnect Maud with the Albas—would be to absolve herself of the obsession. It would be a kind of gift, a selfless act, a real love of the girl to return her to her true people, to make peace. It would be an act of self-abnegation. She was shy of the idea. So much the better. It would be good for her. Why, she hadn't thought of anything so *creative* for years. If Maud went to stay with them (Beatrice had no idea the girl had anyone else) she would be out of danger, if there were any danger. And, too, she would be out of the danger of her—Beatrice's—own . . . love.

She stood and looked sadly into the river. Wistful and child-like she was: her love a danger, always a danger to others. She bit her lip and twisted round her face. She tried not to cry in public. Oh, her poverty was well deserved. She knew that, and in a wry way, it made her smile.

Beatrice reached the house in Cheyne Row without too much difficulty. She had thought to return to the flats, knock up Maud, explain about the police and wangle the address, when it struck her that it was a positive duty not to tell Maud any of this.

It was, she reflected, a situation analogous to the one she found time and time again in her work: to say too much of a diagnosis, to describe a mode of treatment to a nervous and intelligent patient so often dashed hope, a will to live. How much better it would be for Maud if she succeeded to the point of Alba's coming back with her, to the point of Alba's knowing what to do for Maud at any rate. It would be even better, she thought, if Maud never saw what part she had had to play in an eventual deliverance. To think that she might have helped with-out the girl's knowing it gave her a deep pleasure.

It was incredible to her that the Albas were in the telephone directory, but there they were, between a garage and a dry-cleaning service: Alba, T. She stood in the kiosk and quaked at the magnitude of her decision.

"I loved him so. I loved him so. I didn't think it was possible to love another human being so much."

Was that what had lifted her up? Beatrice saw the face, heard the voice—that one little set of sentences—again and again; hair fallen, fists clenched. It was as if some ventriloquist had put her own need into Maud's mouth.

Yet whom had Beatrice loved so much as that? And why was it "he"? Whom did she love so much? A blank flash of light came and went carrying no image with it, no name and no answer.

She wondered if she should phone and announce her coming, but decided not to. To be refused at this stage, while she still had her nerve, wouldn't have done.

She stood then on the polished step and rang the bell. She was appalled, really was appalled at her nerve. Why, she had never done anything impulsive in her life. Had never risked anything in her life.

The door was opened after quite a pause—when Beatrice felt it might be best to faint or run away—by a woman whom Beatrice at first took to be the maidservant, an old family retainer perhaps. Beatrice was put strongly in mind of her mother's cook, Serafina, with her heavy skin, but as her eyes became accustomed to the gloom of the hall, she saw at once that it must be Mme Alba. She was dressed in black rather like an older sort of peasant, but wore a stunning diamond bagatelle.

What could she say? How could she explain her errand? The woman looked at her shrewdly, but without malice. Beatrice thought she had a nice face and wondered what she'd thought of Maud.

She cleared her throat. "I wonder if you could help me. It's about a mutual friend of ours, Maud Eustace." She flailed her hands losing all at once the dignity she'd intended. "I know it may be impertinent of me, but I really do feel I must talk to somebody about her. I'm a doctor, Dr Pazzi," she said by way of self-justification.

"Ah," said Ilse, "what a good idea it is that Maud is seeing a doctor. Won't you come in?"

"I'd like to talk to your husband too if I may. I know he is very illustrious, and I hope he won't mind my intrusion." She knew the woman thought she was a psychiatrist, but thought to save any revelation that she was not until later.

"I'll get him," Ilse said. "You do know that she quite disappeared from our country house this summer. My husband was preparing her for her Wigmore debut, and for no reason we can think of, she vanished! Of course, we phoned and phoned, but there was no answer." Ilse shrugged and popped her lips. There wasn't a hint of criticism, only a What could one have done?—at which Beatrice instinctively frowned. But chastened herself. Indeed, indeed what *could* be done? What had she been able to accomplish on Maud's behalf this morning? In order to help, one really had to have active consent of the helpless. Hadn't one?

Ilse, with a sense of property, showed Beatrice to the drawing room, and left her there with the promise of Alba.

She stood in the centre of the floor and looked about her.

What assured her that she was in the right place? That she had come to the centre of something for her friend who was after all not really a friend but only a neighbour after all? Her nerves adjusted themselves to the nerve of having come at all, and knew where she was although mentally she was unsure of where that might be. Instinct gave her a kind of solidity on the balls of her feet, a solidity with a spring.

Beatrice disliked the room's interior for its ostentatious formality, but busied herself with looking at the Ingres above the fireplace. She tapped a foot once and was filled with a sense of the artist's irony. Now why irony, why? The ambiguity of the turned and naked back, the equivocal smile on the lady's face made her turn herself again and question the room, her sensations of it as a whole.

A bag of knitting lay on an imperial couch, its contents half-spilt as if the knitter had been too careless or hurried to put the work away. She went to the window and regarded not the street below but the swagged, dry-cleaned curtains, turned again to look at the Ingres, then subtly made a decision to go, not any longer out of timidity, but out of a curious sense of outrage. She shook her head and never-minded. At once, by some acoustical trick, she heard the faint resonance above of a cello. Alba must have his music room above: she stood suddenly enchanted by the sound of the suite she loved. There on the outer edge of thought, straining her ears to catch the tune, she heard both solemn and dear, the sound of love in the night. It sang this time with tragedy. She felt got at and sick. What a terrible noise—oh terrible—she covered her mouth but not her ears at the dreadful thing she heard. It was technically brilliant—she knew enough to know that—it was not despairing, but sought a consolation simpler than Maud sought in what she had played. It was the product of a mature and saddened mind and was rooted in a grim self-knowledge that made Beatrice feel at once naïve and faintly dishonest.

Abruptly, the music stopped, and at length she heard the tread of Alba on the stairs.

Beatrice was not entirely inoculated against the lure of fame. She flicked at her hair and quivered at the entrance of lustre. The door opened and there he was. As if she had known him all her life he smiled and in the flash of that she saw the bond revealed which was Maud.

Her first impression of him was that he was very tired. He was tall, but carried his height without conviction in it. His face was hooked, beaked, and hooded in the Spanish manner, but there was something darker in it that might suggest a Jewish connection. She got the impression that he did not want to swamp her with what he must have been through with Maud. They shook hands. "Do sit down, Dr Pazzi," he said. She found the edge of a damask-bolted chair. "My wife tells me you have news of Maud." "Maud," the way he said the word with tenderness but with an edge, as if his mouth were a pair of sharp scissors around the name which he forebore to close upon. The word jarred what had been fractured in herself by the girl and little capillaries around the wound bled.

"It's perhaps wrong of me to have come." She looked down and realized that a discreet signal had passed between them. They were both of an age and European and you didn't need a saw for this amputation. They had a context in common. Ah, she was every inch a lady and he an unembarrassed gentleman. No—more; they shared the lot of minor and depressed nobility. Not much needed explaining between them of decadence and a world war. They smiled at each other.

"Not at all. I am always glad to hear of Maud. She was a most promising pupil." He raised his brows. "It surprised me, of course, when she left me. I would have thought she might have become quite good in a few years' time. She pressed too hard to do her Wigmore. I felt she was not—how can I say?—psychologically ready for it, but was willing to help her to this end rather than to discourage her."

Beatrice was drawn into the wisdom of his smile, and more into what lay behind his eyes, things he could not state—would not state—things he felt they both must know of the young woman.

Beatrice waved a hand. "She is very depressed—I hasten to add that I am not a psychiatrist. I tried to get her to see a good one and she would have none of it." She paused. Alba made no emotional move at all, but waited.

He paused, then spoke as if plotting a course. "Of course Maud always will be depressed. She had a frightful childhood. I knew her as a child, you know—through her aunt, who was the wife of the British Cultural Attaché in Rome."

"Ah! *Sono romana.*" She had gone too far. English was clearly the language he communicated in for certain purposes—indeed, she saw him withdraw ever so slightly and she stopped in her tracks. For some reason she smelt the Via Veneto where she had harsh memories of her mother spending too much money.

"Poor Aileen," Alba said, "had a dreadful struggle with those children." His eyes achieved a faraway look for Aileen. Beatrice saw what she did not want to see.

"I had no idea she had any family, otherwise I wouldn't have come."

"They don't live very far away—in Knightsbridge—though I understand the sister's an alcoholic. Aileen is very good-hearted. She persuaded me to start Maud on her career. Maud *is* very musical."

"I know. I've heard her play." He said nothing. "She talks of you a good deal." It was like being pulled—to talk to him—up an increasingly airless slope. The closer she got to whatever relationship might have been between them, the more out of reach he was. She got the impression that Maud had behaved very badly indeed.

"She has it in her mind—I don't know whether I should tell

you, or why I'm telling you precisely—the idea that someone is
going to kill her."

He shrugged. *Quod erat demonstrandum.*

"I've seen the man whom she suspects." For some reason,
Beatrice longed to burst into her native tongue, to express more
fully, more basically, and in the language of nursery something
about what Maud really felt. "He is, to my mind, quite dangerous." She still drew nothing. "I called the police. They sent him
away, but the whole thing seems quite hopeless to me. He'll
only come back."

"Ah, she really is hell-bent now," he said; and smiled to himself. He rejoined Beatrice's eyes. He was quite relaxed against
the back of a fragile chair. "You must forgive me for saying that,
Miss Pazzi—I mean, Dr Pazzi—but one did what one could
within the bounds of possibility. Maud's fantasy life," he said,
"got very much in the way of her progress. You see, this story
you tell me of a man . . ." He didn't say it, being far too self-
controlled, but Beatrice saw, rather, heard, rather their eyes
agreed upon . . . "Isn't this what she wants? This is what she
wants." A consummation which sickened both of them in Alba's vision of it.

He let it sink in. "I daresay my wife will bring you some tea,"
he said. She was too numb to say no. He left the room and she
sat there with her friend torn up in her lap, her friend's desires
torn up in her lap: her friend's yearnings torn up in her lap like
so many bolts of cloth, like so many scraps of paper. Was that
it? Their common shame of hands? Whose hands could not
touch patients or cello for the ghastly, the pained, the unstoppable, the unutterable desire for consummation despised?

Beatrice got up, collected her bag. She slipped out of the
drawing room and crept down the stairs. She opened the front
door and closed it softly behind her. A little church was down
the road, she knew it; she fell into its baroque softness and
seeing she was alone, she cried, and cried; and cried until she
thought she'd be sick. She stopped and cried some more.

CHAPTER XI

Before I could squeak, I was pulled in and dined on.

Dinners, dinners, dinners. How can one—who after all has had concourse and conversation (deep and long and well into the night) with the Muse—be corrupted by the debauchery of so many hot dinners that Ilse gave? I was hungry, Christ knows. Oh, how hungry I was. But as I ate, the cello, the music—the purpose and intent of my whole sacrifice of life to it—receded and what came to be important were *oeufs florentine* and the pattern of china and the stems of glasses and the stems of grapes tweezed off with silver scissors and steak Tartare bloody red and eggy and peppercorns and songs nightly lifted above us from the lark's tongue of my famous soprano.

She paralysed before she sucked; she had the manners of a most delicate spider—only now and then I felt the ecstatic agony of being consumed. Oh, the soft noise of rain outside our delicate cocoon! Her odious brilliance was that she pandered to Alba and me making it seem that we were allowed. All the time I thought we were agents, we were in fact patients of those desires of hers I still can't understand.

How subtly she became our catalyst . . . that element which made feeling between us both possible. Her presence increased our love to a full aching point; her presence determined that such a love never could be consummated.

She was more than a foil to us. If she had only been that, like Dulcie Moore who lathered Maurice up with the thought of being naughty. Oh, no, not Ilse, not she. Her thrilled voice soared above the cello tones causing bottom C to be more jewelled and more resonant.

She sang, sang out her unnerving repertoire with increasing authority, almost rapture. Why was it unnerving? Unnerving for her range, her sheer weight of knowledge. One day she'd be a Cherubino. You'd close your eyes and there he was in utter freshness, an adolescent boy sick with desire: she controlled vibrato out of her voice so entirely that a flat, fluted tone came almost suggestive in its purity. Another day, she'd spit Donna Anna out like fire: outraged virtue, almost spat, but deep and womanly. There was no role she didn't make her own. She sang church music—there she was, a saint. Hey presto! Her hands dripped with martyr's wounds. She called up moments of death and love; but somehow, I think, she never got beyond the grave.

That was Alba's particular ability. I do not think she knew or recognized it. He, in playing, got quite beyond emotion. In his bowing, your hair stood up in quite a different way. Before I knew him, I never let thoughts occur when I heard music that went much beyond the basic engineering of it. But when I listened to him, his music had centrifugal force; it led your ear to a centre of gravity around which notes pitched and wheeled like stars.

But she was always there with meals and motherhood; she was always there, no more nor less sexy than a spider. She urged to do her truth and her truth it was—in metaphorical style—to reproduce, alone.

Ilse's particular gift was context and flesh. Music has always been for me abstraction; perhaps that is why I was so blind to her scenic mode of expression, her understanding of role, her ability to enhance character, aspects of character which she wished to encourage. In her presence, one became blissfully self-conscious, almost mannered, stylized. It was in her gift to confer the consciousness of self on her conquered friends. It astonished me more and more as we went on that I had known Ilse all my life through Aileen. Gesture, tone, and mode of dress: the glamour, glitter of my mother's sister were really deposits of Ilse's mind. Aileen had hitched her wagon to a star, had sacrificed her own identity and her fidelity to her husband in fealty to this queen. Just to get close to her. Just to insert her feet in those tiny shoes even if it meant the lopping off of toes. The paradox of Auntie was resolved; her doughty duty and her means of shining had seemed so utterly disparate. Now, it became clear to me that it was Ilse who had drugged my father into submission, Ilse who had slipped off her robe in Father's dressing room, Ilse who had conquered; while Aileen, simple soul that she was, had paid for cello lessons and visited Mother at the end.

I'll not forget the Sunday that came before the crash, although the crash came later by months.

Ilse kept urging me on from dinner to dinner. At last, she asked me down to country weekends at their little house on the Sussex downs. My Wigmore Hall debut had been the original excuse. I was to unleash such great things upon the public! The Bach C-major, Vivaldi, Beethoven, and Locatelli. This recital was projected to some vague time in the autumn. No concrete plans had been made with the management. Not even an accompanist had been found.

Why didn't I suspect that? I knew the drill.

I didn't suspect it because I didn't want to. All I had to do—as Alba's protégée—was whistle. Adrian Nichols—the best accompanist in the business whom I already knew, who had a lot of time for me, who'd offered in a kind of way his services one evening at the Moores'. A few phone calls. No trouble.

Wasn't this what I'd always wanted? Hadn't I seduced Maurice for this very reason and to this very end? Did Alba stop me? Far from that, he positively nagged me to get on with it. But every night when I returned to Theodoric Square it was somehow too late to ring, and every morning when I woke, it was somehow too early. Or I was practising. The days I didn't visit the Albas were days so empty of appetite, so starved of motive or imagination, so impoverished in light, ecstasy, warmth. I could do nothing but play the cello which reminded me of him. His face, hair, eyes, even smell, had to be evoked, his hands, the size of his shoes, the border of his handkerchief, the whisker he missed clipping which stuck out from his beard, had to be rested in my brain. Laid to rest. *Requiescat in pace*: peace came only from following with great exactitude every syllable of his direction to me during our sessions. I played the warmth of his smile, the light in his eyes, the love of his bosom which was me. To ring some agent seemed absurd, almost dirty, like inviting spectators to a wedding night. To play in public what he gave in private, worse.

Several times I picked up the receiver and started to dial. Each time, out of nausea, I had to put it back. Every day, my main hope was to be asked—to wine, to dine, to sit at the feet of my friends. Each successive intimacy I achieved was more to me than all the Albert Hall on its knees.

Of course, they must have seen it. How can you miss the gawp of a lover's mouth, the vulnerability of eyes? If I allow reason to rule for even a minute, I can quite see what dilemma they were in. To encourage me was wrong, to discourage me, heartless.

Ilse was the great controller of privileges. Her great kitchen with its fumes of steam, its baking fires became a goal for me. She let me do the washing up (oh, *thank* you, Ilse), she permitted me to chop onions. It was my opinion then; it is my opinion now that she felt sorry for me. Partly. She talked to me of Freud (she'd known his family in Vienna; she had been psychonalysed by one of his pupils). She hinted that I needed . . . help? She drew me out on family matters. I found I said more than I meant to say. I hid my tears with onion juice, my blushes with the steam of sudsy water. She did teach me to make *Apfel Strudel*. Ilse's pastry was light and rich. Eating it, you felt you were being stifled by balloons.

More than this, she allowed me to have that good time with them which enabled us to raise our voices in loud laughter, to tease each other and gallivant like children. There was always the feeling that it was the servants' day off even though she had no servants. Never was there a cushion out of place nor a hair on the carpet. It was the feeling one has in an environment created and maintained by somebody else. The door, I felt, had only recently been closed on a dedicated and imaginative staff who after all would have spoiled the fun by listening to our relaxed jocularity.

That Sunday I remember above all others because it showed even me, besotted as I was, just how she held the nets and just how impossible it was to betray her. She was more than amply justified in this, being as she was Alba's wife. My need, so corrosive, had no rights, only privileges. So why do I feel sinned against, not sinning?

I'd taken the coffee in after lunch. I can hear her now—she was expounding on Nietzsche. Ilse was an intellectual who read. Why did she give this impression? When she talked it seemed as if thousands listened. As if we were in a very fine play, a romance fell upon us. Alba that day leaned back in his chair looking more Spanish than ever. He seemed to emerge from a subversive light like an El Greco with those deep, smudged eyes looking in upon inward and visionary horror; those cheekbones from which gutters ran as if hollowed out by tears. When he smiled a whole nexus of thought and sensibility was shone upon. He seemed to have suffered. In her presence, he seemed to have suffered more deeply than one could have supposed. Through her? Maybe not. Supported by her in it?

I can remember, as I say—and it wasn't very long ago after all but seems aeons—pouring coffee that Sunday lunchtime. I sat bolt upright and poured, creamed, sugared demitasses embossed with gold with little ribbons of enamel in dark blue, and lifted silver teaspoons which shone with a tender suffusion of light. I stirred. She watched, having given me her job. Her mind and tongue bounded on to some other topic of conversation. What was it? Her past experience with a great couturier? Dinner with the Duke of Windsor? Memoirs of travels to Khartoum?

No, this time she settled on the purchase of a Titian which she'd later sold: a small sketch in oils of Salome with the head of St John the Baptist.

Why did she have a right to be so beautiful at fifty? Did she keep it up with asses' milk?

"Consider Salome," she said. (She really did speak like that.) "It's almost a paradigm of art against religion. Both demand perfection. When mutually exclusive, who's to judge who's right? One could say that Salome had achieved the short-term victory, but I myself have no belief—no interest in—a hereafter. Her art—the frenzy of her dance—demanded a head, demanded a sacrifice for an artistic whole. He died, but what her artistry

made of him! Would he have been anything other than an un-
wholesome fanatic eating bugs in the desert if she had not loved
him in that particular way? Now his image ravishes us. His hair
shirt, his locusts, his fastings, all come alive for us in her humiliation of him. She demanded perfection and got his martyrdom.
Both of them are necessary to each other. Without him, her
dance would never have got beyond something by Ginger Rog-
ers; as it was it reached a summit of corruption, a poetic whole."
When she spoke like this her hands fretted over the props and
scenery of her life—her pearls, the winning mole on the cusp of
her jaw.

A little lamely Alba said, "You make out a case against art."

"Oh, no, against religion more. They both pursue truth, but
art gets it right. Religion makes limitations on experience."

I could see she was getting at him. This she often did, but I
could never understand where their argument lay except somewhere in their common past. He and I never talked about art or
religion. We rarely talked at all. Alba's mouth went up in the
approximation of a smile.

"Have another fig, my dear," she said to me.

"I'm full."

Ilse used to go to the point of making Alba and me feel stupid; then she'd retract like a cat's paw the vector of her argument.

"My husband remains one of the faithful," she said. " All that
Spanish blood." She said this in more ways than one, as if Alba's convictions (which I had not known of) were faintly exas-
perating given the range of his abilities, but beneath this there
was a revulsion on her part against them. All the same, she
smiled at him kindly like a vastly able mother at a somewhat
backward child.

Somewhere she'd torn a strip off him. "I think what you say
about Salome is something that might have excited people in
the last century. It's a bit old-fashioned, my darling, and at heart
is Philistine. I sense it but I can't say why."

"Oh, Samson," she teased and flirted.

"Oh, Delilah," he said. His words penetrated more.

I know but can't tell why she'd got us into position. What

position? At any rate, she smiled now with great satisfaction.

"I'll wash up," I said.

"Maud." Ilse turned her whole attention to me. "Maud, not today. I will not think of it. I am tired, you see, and would like a rest. Maybe you and Thomas would like to take a walk. You will walk together, yes? And on your return, we will do the washing up together. You must go, because I shall be offended if you don't. If you do it behind my back I shall be murderous. The washing up, I mean."

Was there ever really anyone as awful as Ilse?

She left us at the door having kitted us out in our coats like toddlers. She put her hands above her eyes as if to veil a head-ache. She reiterated her intention to nap; in her statement, there was the mute suggestion of her body, that it might be desirable for both of us to nap with her. Such a thing with another woman had never occurred to me and never has done since. Sleep in itself I felt would have an elegant debauch in her body, in other words, that she would invite sleep down upon her like an incubus, that it would penetrate her bones with deepest plea-sure. She saw, she knew, and shrugged and gave her wisest little smile. Oh, la la.

I have no idea how far Alba and I went before the chaos of my senses started to recede. I did not dare look at him. I wanted him. I wanted her. Mostly I wanted myself. I can't explain. She'd pulled my glands like toffee into gluey, sugared strands. I felt decadent, dull, and burning. We slouched along.

"Where do you want to go?" he said at length.

(Back to my flat.) "I don't know." I'd only been aware of love and no desire as such, not that as such. How many times had I said to how many men? But not Alba, oh no, not he.

"Where do *you* want to go?" If he'd said I'd have had him right where I could've driven a stake through his heart. Oh, how his Spanish eyes darted from side to side. Oh, you universal corrupter you, him too?

"I'll take you to the zoo," he said. While Ilse slept I think she dreamed us launching out alone. I was both insulted and re-lieved and oh how I worshipped his restraint. And doubted my own power.

We looked both handsome and peculiar as we walked along. People stared at us. Stardom clung to Alba. He emitted light though long since dead. As if they knew him, passers-by looked at him. He had that quality that people want to touch for luck. He had command of his exterior self and this had nothing to do with arrogance. He neither expected nor craved applause—he assumed it. In other words, he knew his own power even though he did not publicly exercise it. His step was sure but his look was sad. Again and again I thought of him as being a deposed king.

So he went to the zoo to look at other and less ambulatory captives.

Talking was always awkward; he carried himself like a grandee. Talking had become increasingly awkward since our first meeting. It was perhaps this which made us both crave Ilse's company so. We really felt abandoned at the zoo.

How could anyone love a stick like Alba with his mannerly Spanish stiffness? He seemed etched out in brocade—stiff plaques stitched together like armour plating. No wonder she couldn't love him; she didn't hear his sound. It didn't tear her limb from limb like it tore me.

I had listened before to music—and practised it faithfully— assuming it to be either pretty or technical. I'd practised before the relationship between two quavers, between two hemi-, semi-, demi-quavers. What I'd found with Alba was the courage—courage? Freedom? No, necessity of finding the infinitesimal silence between any two given notes on the scale. I can't say it better than silence—but there is no silence in *glissando* or in any harmonic. No, I'm frustrated—can't struggle it out—what I began to find as I played at night to his hair and hands. I became aware of the notes *missing* in any harmony—I heard when we played what *wasn't* there. My assumptions about beauty challenged, there wasn't really any place to go unless I went with him. Without his protection, I could not have fallen into the hands of the force which held the music together and which begged me to tear it apart. Struggling and chaotic notes shimmered in my brain pan. Never did the line between genius and madness seem more finely drawn, never did it seem so perilous. Did he know how far I went or how much I thirsted? Did he know how much I wanted to avoid?

I can assume that he did and that is why he took me to the zoo. What a bloody afternoon! What a bloody, bloody afternoon it was. The place was filled with sticky children and fathers in anoraks photographing bears and lions eating meat unwrapped from cellophane. How he mocked and patronized me taking me there. We had a little look at crocodiles—he never spoke a word.

His silence drew me wretchedly on. "Alba, are you angry with me?"

"Why, no."

"You haven't said anything—for about an hour."

"I don't see any reason to talk."

"It's hard on your friends."

"Not as hard as talking might sometimes be."

"Then you are angry."

He shook his head. Was he weary? He was too much a masked gentleman to show, but inly I heard from him the kind of vexed sob a child or overstrung woman makes when pushed too far. Seeing him as prey had not hitherto been an admission I'd made to myself. I felt the very presence of my own flesh as an admission of guilt. It was too painful and gross to think about the flesh. I don't know who was potential lion and who potential lamb. The zoo stank of goats. Did I smell his or my avidity? Short of splintering the instrument I had no idea what else to do.

"It's too cold here," I said. "Why don't we go back to my flat and I'll make you a cup of tea. You've never seen it—I'd like you to see where I practise."

The burden of my love was intolerable. I had to put it down. Oh, I could argue that I had to give myself to him, but that won't do. It isn't honest. I knew then—I thought clearly—that the absence of touching had been like the absence of sound between two notes. To rupture that was my meaning—just as one would like to be relieved of life when standing on an unguarded height. The feet itch for the edge—one step into the air—and at least you've soared before you've died. Oh, hell!

"All right," he said slowly and after a pause. We left the stupid penguins.

I don't even have to close my eyes to see him standing in the centre of this room. It passed then for respectable. He looked around and drew off his gloves, made to throw them on the table, but then laid them gently down. I caved into this armchair where I am sitting now. I slumped like an adolescent and plunged my toes into the hearthrug next to the cold fireplace. He looked at me and smiled but only just. I shook with nervous nausea. We were conscious of each other and ourselves. I'd forgotten I had that picture of him on the table. He looked at it and then at me. "Oh, Maud," he said, cautionary and parental. He too sat but did not take off his coat. His back was to the window and his hair shone in the shallow spring light. "Maud, what shall I do with you?"

I couldn't speak. I started to cry and my hands shook with my stomach and I started to be sick, but nothing came up.

He drew in his breath. "Poor Maudie," he said. No one had ever said that.

"I love you," I said. My gorge rose again. It hadn't worked out at all, at all how I'd planned, but worse than I'd feared.

"It's all right," he said. He sat very still indeed. He might have been six miles away.

"You'll go away now I've said what I've said." I knew I was trying to hook him deeper but I couldn't stop.

He was quite quiet. "I won't do either of the things you have in mind," he said. He smiled with more warmth than a human face ought to have. He was curiously meek and full of compassion. "I couldn't hurt you if I tried."

"It wouldn't hurt me."

"Oh, yes it would," he said. He shook his head and smiled. I was suddenly quiet too. I shook now with relief.

He rose and went to the kitchen. I heard him put the kettle on. He lightly whistled Mozart and after a little while he emerged with a couple of mugs of tea, one of which he set before my feet on the hearthrug, one of which he drank himself, sipping slowly, screwing up his eyes for the steam, looking vacantly over the rim of the cup, beyond my head, but oddly enough at me. He'd put in sugar and I never have it—but somehow it tasted more delicious than a cup of tea had ever tasted. I knew a terrible thing had passed, and I was grateful to him.

"Would you like to see my music room?"

He kind of laughed. "I know what comes out of it. Why should I see what's in it?"

"It'll be all right, won't it?" I lamely hunted about for him again.

"It'll all be all right." He was completely simple. He appeared to me almost flawless like an unset gem you can hold in the palm of your hand; and somewhere in his mind I caught the deep-down innocence of things which I'd been deaf to but now heard. It was as if I'd had to try to injure him in order to find him harmless, as if I'd had to fling myself on what I imagined he might do before I found—somehow he'd known all along—his mercy.

He sat with me for a while as it grew darker, and we didn't speak and the sound of the March wind and rain dashed against the window panes, and everything seemed to thaw and there was no need to stir at all from the knowledge that I was soft and complete and vulnerable and utterly at rest.

"Ilse will wonder where we are," he said at length and again simply. He got up, took the cup from my disarmed hand and put his cup as well in the kitchen, then drew on his gloves again and softly went to the door.

"You're sure you won't despise me?"

"Yes, I'm sure," he said. "Good night. We'll see you soon." And he closed the door and walked away and I hugged my knees and let tears flow of sweet relief and dear contentment that I'd found him.

It must have been the softness on his face when he got back she saw. She saw, she saw as she woke, stretching her creamed body out—she saw, she saw in her slippery satin robe, she saw as she stretched her length at the window, as she filled her magnificent lungs with air, as she propped her exercised diaphragm between almandine fingers, smiling only to herself, running her tongue against her little teeth, splashing her little whorled ears with eau de cologne—what had not taken place between him and me. Because she had planned the wreck of his conscience, she saw it like the queen saw the heart of Snow White in the entrails of a deer. She saw what she wanted to see and she was glad.

CHAPTER XII

The Albas, for all their London façade, had a petit trianon in Sussex. I wonder how many married people take on each other's sins. At the time, I always thought it was Ilse's petit trianon, Alba's bolt-hole—an even more private place for him than the isolation he had chosen for himself in the scattered music room in town. It is extraordinary to think that they needed an escape from the escape they had already made, but behind that door— even behind the door of their secret garden with walls—there was another and behind that another still.

Ilse, having a practical nature, regarded Weir House as a nice piece of real estate. Alba did not have to think that way. Ilse did such thinking for him. What would he have done? How would he have lived without her?

The house stood near the River Ouse, and as its name suggested, there was a small waterfall, near enough to hear in the quiet of the day or in the night when casements were opened and the dew collected and absorbed in the window-seat of my bedroom. I came to think of it as mine. The house itself was a survivor. Elizabethan owners had succeeded Tudor. Although there was not a moat, there should have been. Some architect or owner had conceived more grandeur than the size of the property actually merited. There was a hall, which Ilse had turned into an exquisite drawing room. Light filtered through high, pebbled windows on to worn and valuable Oriental carpets, and plush, comfortable sofas stood about as if to receive a county crowd for drinks; they never came; she never asked them; but she was ready for them with rose bowls, cigarette boxes, and form. She'd cadged from auctions several suits of armour that stood about, and the high, dreaming reaches of the chimney-piece and upper walls bore shields, escutcheons of valour, and all the taste of an aristocratic past.

The garden, most of all, charmed. It was walled and, in the summer, unimaginably scented. The sense of smell—when I think of its lowly place among all senses—was there exalted. Roses were Ilse's chief delight. She did not grow them as old ladies or retired gentlemen do, naming names and stinking of mulch and tying back protesting branches to the walls. No, she moved miasmic through her flower beds, murmuring secrets and incantations to the plants, which seemed to come up to her fingers to be received.

She was, too, a great one for herbs. Basil, thyme, rosemary, and humble parsley unfolded. Her vegetables were engorged with fruit. Bees sang and hovered over the cracks of flagstones from which sprouted tiny alyssum and aubrietia and unnameable and desirable botanical achievements. They never stung her. She never wore old clothes for gardening, her straw hat dripped chiffon. She turned my legs to custard as I watched her. Her dark, skilfully kept beauty had more power in strong sunlight than ever. She allowed all elements. She permitted touching by the sun—responded to it—and when it rained, her skin seemed to drink the rain. Wind tousled her hair rather than mussed it. She hummed arias—not pretty nor pure ones in her garden, but unidentifiable tunes—I think they came from Donizetti. Occasionally, one would hear a snatch or two from Verdi's *Requiem* and that was very odd indeed.

She cooked more simply in the country. She cooked for Alba and me. We would sit out on protracted summer evenings. He would teach me from a stool set out on the flags, sometimes rushing in through the open doors to the piano in the drawing room to strike a note or make a point. Ilse had a chic little fringed garden swing out there full of deep cushions. They were waterproofed, stiff, and had a canvas smell and texture. Sometimes I would lie there and rock and listen to Alba playing Bach. As the sun faded, the seat retained its warmth, and the sound of the water and the music made so unselfconsciously for my ears alone from someone I so intensely loved and the smell of roast lamb and rosemary coming through the windows from the depth of the house put my spirit into something like a galactic convulsion of joy.

In the evenings, it became damp. After food and wine, Alba would light a fire in the hall. We'd sit about it and Ilse—who claimed happiness equal to ours—came to accompany herself on the piano. She'd sing Schubert for us mainly, but sometimes sad and simple songs with a runic quality which came from the depths somewhere of the Austro-Hungarian Empire. She sang them with just enough vibrato to make them throb minor and slanted into the heart.

Oh, she was a set piece. She generated Alba and me both. Soul brother and sister, she was our mother. When she'd finished singing she'd tell stories. Her family had been extremely rich. I didn't like to think about money. I never like to think about money. Money depresses me. Ilse gilded money. She was Midas with it. She turned it to gold, to emotional currency. It became romance. She might have been F. Scott Fitzgerald or Henry James for all she depicted money to its advantage. Balls in Vienna waltzed out for us; trips in her father's early Daimler to Baden; stays in grotesque rococo hotels; a friend of her father's who lost all at roulette on a dare, or was it Russian roulette he'd played for a lady? Oh, hot chocolate and whipped cream! Oh, sense! Oh, night!

How did she allow us, though? Her stories and her presence kept us, if anything, curiously apart. But the romance she engendered gave us at the same time a context for loving as we did. Did she imagine underneath the spell and shell of flesh a snail of spirit in which Alba and I could love each other purely and Platonically? It really is so hard to say, but it is most important to find out. Could it be all her fault? The fault of her rich imagination? Practical as she was about her tasks, she saw life with boots on. Or was it he who did? Is it I who do? She pushed sense beyond its normal bounds, made flesh so eerily translucent, made such artifice from nature that art occurred between her husband and myself. Each look we gave each other seemed potent—each pause pregnant. My love for him was torture so exquisite, so nearly divine—my communion with his sound so nearly complete and yet not, not quite enough to be consummated. Did I make it all up? Did he feel so?

She consistently invited me deeper into them. I was flabbergasted at the music I then made. All my sex, my curious, confused emotions locked in this one gift of sound. I sublimated, Dr Bender, yes I did. I sublimated everything incomplete in myself at the point of contact between gut and horsehair. Ilse—the lubricating rosin—freed any inhibitions I had had about it. Oddly enough, she never liked to hear me play, but the more her tongue wagged, the better I did it. And because of me (I like to think it was because of me), Alba's audience of one, he began to play like an archangel.

Does a woman like Ilse need motives? What was her motive for letting me get so far up to the sound barrier then turning me away? She was so clever. Surely she knew. Sometimes when I chopped and sliced for her in that country kitchen with its Aga and copper-bottomed pots—oh, her dolls' houses, they disgust me—she would tease me about it. "Oh, Maud, if you knew how good you've been for Maso and me!" "Maso is extraordinary now, isn't he? I've never heard him make such sound—not even when he used to be a public man. What a prince he was! His tone was so dazzling then. You have deepened it." "I sometimes think that Maso will bring you to perfection, Maud—the *Sarabande* in the D-minor—so deep, so contemplative for one your age. I felt it to be almost mystical." The *Sarabande* was my particular treasure. She knew, she knew. Alba and I had sought it out and found it together. Emotionally, I'd had to trounce lugubriousness—a morbidity in my nature—out of it in order to reach a detachment so that the following minuet didn't come out as a slow march from the grave of the previous movement but held in it the seeds of resurrection which had to be *implied* in the *Sarabande*. He played it differently from me—better because he was better. He made me take responsibility for it in my own character. He made my art proceed from my character; he'd accept nothing less and allow nothing more. Often he hurt me very much in my ambitions towards music, but I played better for this. Dr Bender, please note that Alba was better for me than you. Musically, I had the oddest knack of scuttling myself when I got above myself. When I flashed around admiring myself, when I let virtuosity get out of hand, I always ended up in a ridiculous technical muddle. It was as if all access to pride in myself was cursed by my very contact with Alba. Each mistake I made seemed worse and worse and more humiliating until I'd sort through and hear the actual music I was making, and make actual music outward from myself to him. As long as it was a gift I gave him, I received. My face in Ilse's bloody Jacobean mirror assumed a softness on such occasions and I was magically alive. The moment I tried to take from it—possess the song myself—the music was frustrated into ugliness. To receive his music from him was to give. I gave him my passive ear, I allowed him round my brain, absorbed him into me. It was heaven; it was heaven. So far from harps and angels as to be absurd. There seemed to be no bounds to joy; there seemed to be only infinite utterance and hearing, infinite hearing and utterance beyond Alba and myself, beyond myself and Alba, of which we partook, in which we moved, in which I was oddly paralysed and by which I was painfully gripped. But the pain was the loss of strip after strip of self towards something unknowable and profound. Only in the dark of it and in the way I resisted him with fear and sometimes acute rebellion in myself from him could I at all imagine what was going on.

Having failed to seduce him, I often found myself doubting him. What sort of sound were we actually making? Should I bring my tape recorder to our sessions and play back later what we had done? I'd often recorded myself practising but never him playing.

I never dared to do it. I never dared ask him. Alba had a formidable quality for me which quenched presumption.

Why did he and I go on for so long in such complete isolation? That became a more interesting question. If he thought me so good, why didn't he want to show me off? Acknowledge me? Surely he had important friends. The Albas' lives were so impeccably polished and ready to receive—someone. Who? I'd never met so much as the milkman going in or out of either of their houses.

What wove in and out of my obsession with him most of all was his own refusal to perform. Time and time again, I started to mention it, ask him, or Ilse; time and time again, I was held back. Most of the time I held the question at arm's length. They had money enough—more than enough—he did not have to perform. He had satisfaction enough—more than enough—from playing to the bees. He seemed to use the instrument to probe. It was not a thing to play for self-aggrandizement. Still.

While I was with him, I could believe all this and more about him—that he was a truly detached man, truly oblivious to ambition. He seemed to be almost a pronouncement of love, an enunciation of it which required no explanation for its existence, its ways. One might as well have asked a tree to justify itself, or a blackbird. When he closed his eyes and drew his bow across the strings, he articulated the fusion of what he was and what he heard in his inner ear. He was quite untranslatable. Who could doubt his gentleness, his lowliness? He let Ilse outshine, outdazzle him. He never snatched nor grabbed, nor took anything.

Why?

He was in love with me? That was it. That was not it. I pulled that across my mind night after night.

I was in love with him—my childhood, my life. That was it. It was not it. He hurt me in not telling me what it was; more still, in not letting me ask.

Why had he left public life? His old mono records still sold. People still referred to his "Don Quixote," his Elgar, to the masterly renditions of the Beethoven sonatas and latterly to the Bach. Shouldn't he share what he had? When I once asked him, he cut me dead. Perhaps he'd been disillusioned. Had he had a bad experience? Muffed an important engagement? Or was it Ilse? They seemed to have a pact somehow. Why didn't Ilse at least, who had no character for objecting to the limelight, go out and strike them dead again as Countess Almaviva? On this one subject, absolute silence reigned. There was no even approaching it.

And why was I his only student? Janorsky had retreated—true—but he did give the occasional concert and had a veritable dormitory of aspirants in his warm household. The Albas might have lived at the Arctic circle for all the contact they had with anyone at all but me.

I cannot separate my own gratification at this state of affairs from my inability to see their isolation in a sinister light. I myself had been so isolated as a child because of Mother's illness, so programmed by my father's retreat from eminence in London that it hardly crossed my mind until she spoke—except in grey traces of unease—that what they fled from was . . . that what they were doing was fleeing.

Why did she tell me? What can I believe? I feel I've gone through such pitch and such burning and still I don't understand why. Did I deserve it? Did he? Did I alienate his affections from Ilse? It's easy enough to believe that she was a sort of Fury avenging for no other reason than that she saw us happy and had to make the point, had to point out that life without suffering, without the knowledge of it, was somehow empty.

But Ilse wasn't a Fury—she was a flagging middle-aged opera star. Unless, of course, her unreality had reached such a pitch that it tipped itself over into—surprised itself with—something more real than she thought.

There was little enough sign of ordinary humanity in her. Now and then I surprised her in a few foibles which revealed mortality. One early morning, I found her false teeth in the bathroom in a jar; they bubbled with a preparation to remove stains. There they stood, independent of her use of them, not snapping or framed with ironic smile. It oddly grieved me to think what her face must look like without them.

Another time, I caught her weeping for no apparent reason in their London kitchen. She did not see me; she was absorbed; she gripped the table's edge and squeezed out tears—her face neither petulant nor self-pitying, nor overwhelmed with grief. She just looked tired and lost.

Now and then, her face would lose its tension of arts and smiles. In repose, she was no sexual murderess; she looked lonely and frightened, slightly wistful, impeded by her imperfections, weighted down by her own flesh aging and not too firm any more. I once saw her look angrily at her hands as if she resented the veins that stood out on them and the liver-spots which had cropped up on them like a harvest of rue.

I couldn't bear her when she made me pity her like that. Oh, more than anyone, I think, I wanted her to be adequate to the point of transcendence. I was the Albas' audience of one.

I think I shall now be able to write about the day of the betrayal. I must come to it. What is at base in all of this? What is at base?

Alba was base. How could he be so base when he was so good? Can't anybody explain that to me? There is Beatrice, in the market, good, good, good. Is she base?

Oh, I know that I am. No one can touch me for guilt or is it loss. I have lost, I have lost the only good I'll ever know. I am incomplete and I cannot complete myself with cello, with writing, or with death. I am a prisoner in the depths of my own dungeon. I know it; I confess it; but I cannot get out of it. I have pounded on the door and screamed, but there is only silence. How can I suppose that anyone has heard me or even imagine that what I feel is real? I think I shall suffocate in my own blood.

All right. All right. I will say. I will tell it.

We had a picnic one fine August day outside the garden, quite a way down the river bank and away from the weir. The Albas had established themselves in Sussex for the greater part of the week during the summer and I'd come down for a long weekend in my car. Was I innocent? I wasn't aware of guilt. Or was the crawling hope, the stomach sick with nerves I always felt when going to see them an admission of something wrong? I simply wanted to be with them day and night forever—to live in their bloodstream—to be made their own. Each encounter with them filled my need and exacerbated need. There was need for no other human being on earth but them.

Ilse had prepared a hamper full of paté, bread, and wine—

cold chicken too and globs of mayonnaise. She never served a meal of any kind without crested silver, damask napkins. There were tender fruits; peaches and squirting plums. Poor Alba had to hulk aluminium chairs down to her chosen spot. I carried the basket and she a quilted rug down to a covert place slightly away from the stream of the river which here became impassable, whose banks were gross with blackberries and thickets of rushes. Could she even order weather? The only thing English about the day and setting were the aluminium chairs which took a bit of good-hearted banging to get established under the oak. The tree was just bearing tippets of green acorns. It shed nothing but cool shade, a space to rest from the heat of the sun. And it was hot. My God, it was hot. We spread her tapestry on the grass and I adopted my customary attitude before them, as they sat more comfortably, of hunching over on my feet beneath them.

I remember looking up at them as they delicately and in unison parted chicken from bone and as wine flamed and informed my sense, and thinking they looked most ancient and archaic, almost barbaric—like a couple on some piece of funerary art exhumed from a grave—that having passed through the point of corruption, they achieved at last immortality. Their fine faces were together and yet apart in perfect balance. My happiness was so complete that speech was quite unnecessary. Ilse made a little desultory conversation. She extolled the virtues of country life and criticized the city. She wondered if they'd let the place in Chelsea go, but reminded herself of how dreadful Sussex was in winter. I found myself able to talk about Suffolk a little: about how harsh it had been in winter and in summer too for that matter. She said she'd had no idea I was a country girl, I seemed so urban; but of course, she must have known I came from the country. I'd told her. Never mind. She'd seen a family of swans at this point of the river only yesterday. We all took an interest in the swans. We all took an interest in simple natural things when we were together.

After lunch was over . . . I remember this. I remember this so well. I took off my sandals and expressed a wish to pick blackberries or at least to look at them and Ilse said she'd make jam if I picked enough and fetched up a handsome bowl for me, dumping the other fruit casually on the grass so it was gashed.

"You shouldn't take your shoes off though—you'll cut your feet and there are adders in the grass," she said.

"There aren't any adders in Sussex."

"Oh, there are."

But I was determined to go barefoot. It seemed to signify the joy I felt: the liberation from what to what? I was like a little child.

I trailed through the grasses and made for the bank where for a while I picked blackberries and then, tired by the heat and the wine, I sat for a while on a flat stone and watched the water surging purely downstream. Snatches of "The Trout" came and went; I was too happy even for "The Trout." It was shallow music next to what I felt. I was finally, finally a little child and the whole world was my mother's breast which I softly lay upon, no longer hungry, but content at last.

After quite a while, Alba came down to the bank. He saw me and I saw him—we moved freely in and out of one another's eyes and minds always. It was the last time. I can't really bear to mention him or talk about him except that both of us knew what we were to each other and that no acknowledgment of speech or touch could possibly express it. He stood a little way off and hesitated. "I'm going in now, Maud, I think I'll rest. Will you help Ilse with the other things when you come. She wants to stay here for a while."

I nodded and smiled and that was the last I ever really saw of him. He disappeared up the bank and through the grass. The water trickled on and I dozed a bit hugging my legs.

A little while later I strolled back to the rug. Ilse was still sitting under the tree in her chair. She was reading a book. Her straw hat with pink scarf tied round was freckled with the sunlight through the leaves. She held her head slightly to one side. She appeared to rest like a dancer who has executed one or two perfect pirouettes.

"You look like a Renoir, Ilse," I said.

"Oh. I didn't hear you coming. Do I? How nice."

"You do. I wish I could paint. What a lovely day you've given us." Even then I hated Ilse. I always had to flatter her. I heaved up a sigh and sat at her feet, pulling up the grass with my toes. She had packed everything neatly away. A breeze flattened the pages of her book.

"What are you reading?" I asked her so idly. All I could think of was the next meal and of how I could again drown myself in Alba.

"Ezra Pound," she said.

"The poet? I haven't read much since school."

"Yes. We knew him," she said lightly.

"I didn't know you liked poetry."

"Ah yes. Listen to this:

> *O helpless few in my country,*
> *O remnant enslaved!*
>
> *Artists broken against her,*
> *A-stray, lost in the villages,*
> *Mistrusted, spoken-against,*
>
> *Lovers of beauty, starved,*
> *Thwarted with systems,*
> *Helpless against the control;*
>
> *You who can not wear yourselves out*
> *By persisting to successes,*
> *You who can only speak,*
> *Who can not steel yourselves into reiteration;*
>
> *You of the finer sense,*
> *Broken against false knowledge,*
> *You who can know at first hand,*
> *Hated, shut in, mistrusted:*
>
> *Take thought:*
> *I have weathered the storm,*
> *I have beaten out my exile.*

I have copied this out of a book I found. She intoned rather than read it; I only half-caught the sense of it. I cannot bear to look at it, but I torture myself by looking at it.

"I don't know much abut poetry," I said. "I've never made much time for anything but music. I admire the way you read—the way you spread yourself out and know about a lot of things."

" 'I have weathered the storm/I have beaten out my exile,' " Ilse repeated as if to herself. She gave me a sharp look all the same. "It so reminds me of Thomas, that phrase—'I have beaten out my exile'—he has beaten out his. Do you think he has beaten out his?"

"His exile?" I felt there was some metaphor to grasp. Before my own exile, I never gave much thought to metaphor and so felt impressed by it and afraid of it. What couldn't slide along four strings never made much sense to me.

"Thomas was a friend of Ezra's once. They had views in common." She continued as if she'd found her own vein of thought which could touch mine or not depending on whether or not the two veins might join at some point. Just throw the old ball up and see if it bounces. There was a shade, a tone in her well-modulated voice that made me look up. Her face held a chill smile which, as she saw my look, she twisted into its familiar ironic mode.

"Views."

Neither of us spoke. I knew nothing about views and nothing about Ezra Pound. I knew I ought to move around a bit, offer to take things to the house. Was my silence consent? I knew she wanted to tell me something. I couldn't move.

"Tell me. Do you love my husband?" She asked it pleasantly enough. Somehow I wanted to talk to her—to get it all off my chest. I certainly wasn't allowed to confide in him, but maybe she . . .

"I love him. Yes. Do you mind?"

"Of course it's quite pure." I was subtly aware of her laughing at me. It was, I mean, a subtle laugh and not altogether unkind.

"Insofar as these things can be completely, it is, yes, as pure as that," I said. I manufactured the first part of this sentence to console her intellect. My love for Alba was pure; it was my pride and my health and the queer quirk of my character that felt a need for purity. I somehow hadn't seen before that moment how very odd it was that I should think in such terms about love, but I did and do, and there it is.

She yawned. "Oh, don't think I'm asking you to justify your feelings. You and Maso—both Don Quixotes—I should trust you from my grave. You can't imagine I am jealous? I've always encouraged your association, thought it good for both of you. No, I'm only inviting you to love him more—if you do love him—not less."

I couldn't quite grasp this. I barely dared to pick up a twig and peel it. I did though. I peeled it little by little.

"Ah, yes—when we are young we think we love. My darling Thomas has never grown up really. But one is in love with love—with one's own love—you see, not the object of one's affections. I mean—one does not see the whole person. One does not learn to forgive when one idolizes someone, does one?" She always liked to ape English. It amused her. She spoke now like a mother with a tender concern for the abstract. "And of course, when one is idolized, one does one's very best to conceal what is unflattering. It is only human nature, isn't it?"

"You've always seemed to know a lot about human nature," I said.

"That is what I do instead of singing," she said. "Hence the poetry. It has helped me to come to terms with him in my own heart."

Although I knew that she'd seen my love, I was very relieved that she approved of it. I was also—that day—at such a pitch, always, had been for such a time at such a pitch about him, that I would have flung myself off a cliff if someone could have told me that this would make me love him better.

She licked her lips. She seemed to invite me on deeper and deeper into them.

"You mean you don't think I'm realistic about him . . . that he has faults I don't accept?"

"Faults?" She burst out laughing. "Faults? A fault, the fault." Little tears collected at the corners of her eyes. It was as if she'd pent up secrets for years—to push her past the point of control. She calmed down, but she still seemed amused. "I have considered telling you," she said, "because you have become so close, because you have been closest to us in all these terrible years. I tell you, I look on you as almost the reincarnation of my dear, dead daughter. Ah, if she had lived, maybe things wouldn't have turned out as they did. Who knows?"

I was overwhelmed by the compliment of what she said and at the same time was at once deeply fearful of her. She looked a little mad, but not so that any doctor could confine her. She looked like Lady Macbeth. She looked like hell.

"You can never get closer to us unless you know. It is bitter fruit this thing, but if you share it with me, then maybe he will have two —he will always have two—who will stand by. If you knew the constant terror I have lived in of journalists prying . . . oh, if you knew the managements I have turned away behind his back, wanting him to make a comeback, as they say in Hollywood. He himself has had the sense not to perform. When you first came, I thought he might be tempted. I thought you might tempt him. I know you will eventually have fame. This is why I trust you now: that when you are famous, you will never never ask him to go back. Oh, night after night I have pondered it, worrying that you might try to get him to go back, but you are sensitive, Maud, and, although you haven't known a thing about this, you have been a good girl and held your peace."

"What is it? What do you have to tell me?" It was like a pinprick or a little jolt.

Ilse was so adept at strip-tease. First a glove off, then another—then back again, then off again; then a black fishnet stocking. Was anything really shocking to her? I don't think anything really ever shocked her. She hadn't even a subcutaneous morality. Or was her morality so pure it was inaccessible? Like some music to amateurs of it.

"How old were you during the war?"

"I was born in 1942. I'm twenty-six."

"Then you can't remember much except going without sugar plums." She had a quaint French smile—Mme de Sévigné enthroned.

As Ilse was always rhetorical, she did not give me time for thought or an inept answer, but now gathered up more control into her hands like cloth. "Does the word '*collaborateur*' mean anything to you?"

"I've never thought about politics." Why did I say such an asinine thing as that? Like squirting water down a volcano. Did my magic mountain secrete fire? Like Alba? And brimstone? Everlasting?

"How comfortable for you," she said. "But you do know what that word means?"

I was extremely calm and distant as if I saw everything through the wrong end of a telescope. "Collaborators helped the Gestapo in France during the war," I said. I had the strangest vision of holding a dead child on my lap. I knew what she was going to say and what was odder still is that I knew she had said it already. From the moment I'd laid eyes on her she'd said it and it was implicit in all my dealings with them. Her body, her houses, her smiles were all statements of it. Like an ancient vine round an older tree, it had been almost inseparably entwined with him and had little or nothing to do with the war. Like a ventriloquist, my voice appeared to come from somewhere else. "What did he do?"

And she told me.

It was so easy, like having an operation under an anaesthetic. It was so easy. She was like my gynaecologist, my own, my father removing wombs. It was so silly; she made me giggle a bit to myself. It was like having locutions with the damned. It made me yawn and giggle a bit to hear what he had done.

You will never believe what he did. What he did. I cannot tell what he did.

If I flicked through every film made and every story written about the war.

It had nothing to do with books written about the subject. You wouldn't believe it if I told you.

Some things are locked beyond the capacity for speech. She locked me in; if tortured I could not tell because struck dumb. She sat there under the tree and she went on and on and on and on and on. There was a child. There was a child. There was a child involved in—that was one aspect of it—only one. She produced quite a dossier of his activities—more than that—more than that, his state of mind. It had nothing to do with self-interest—oh, no. He was protecting nothing. He even used his cello for his ends—like the Pied Piper of Hamelin—to get what was irresistible in evil.

Oh, no, it can't be so. He couldn't have. He *couldn't* have.

She mapped the dates and places out well enough. I was seven in 1949. The Nuremberg Trials were in 1949. He was here in 1949. Then he and she disappeared. I know this is all disjointed. That the infliction of pain was a major source of . . . That they lived in Vichy, France. And that Ilse—what was Ilse after all to do? When she'd begged and begged and pleaded with him and now at last had got him better.

It wasn't true. He *couldn't* have. I know he couldn't have.

It had nothing to do with the war. It really had nothing to do with the war. All the time you think you are worshipping and it turns out to be Dagon or Baal? No. It's nonsense and I never worshipped him, but loved and he led to . . . it couldn't be so. It really couldn't be so. "It can't be true," I kept on babbling over and over again in the midst of her auto-da-fé. She shrugged and shrugged, without a movement of shoulders she shrugged her face, her face was a vast shrug. At my suspicion of her story, she took no obvious offence. Before her set face I quailed. She told it all—all as if we had taken it all out of a modern history as a subject for ladylike debate.

I am not really able to remember most of it.

"He must have been ill," I do remember saying at one point.

"Oh, ill? Not unless the same Don Quixote whom you love is ill. It is part of his character—his greatness if you like—that he has such capacity for evil. Making excuses for him only prolongs the agony and evades the central issue of life. The truth, you see, is more important than a childish faith in him. I thought you were capable of truth, but I may have been mistaken. I've told you all of this so you can love him more truthfully—so that you can endure what I have endured."

"And you've forgiven him."

"Ah," she said. "I never blamed him in the first place—nor condoned. My interest has been to get him through. My interest has been to love him." And suddenly she smiled an almost triumphant smile; and suddenly, she, Ilse, advised me hooded and swaying above me of how and in what way she personally had taken him on board. How did she inform me? With a look? I saw how he'd sunk himself into her like a piranha into flesh—hers which renewed itself every night like a salamander—oh, she drank pearls in tea and suckled adders every night, every night. That she was able to contain him, that she had grown to be adequate to his needs was clear: her expert lap had held him and there was nothing left of me but frost.

I couldn't understand it or believe it.

She understood everything and was finished. As suddenly as she had begun, she stopped. Quite without warning, truncating her story almost in the middle of it, it seemed, it seemed, she rose from the chair and closed the book. She was as realistic as anything you could name. She was far, far more realistic than reality itself. The essentials of life like birth and sex and death now all seemed a little quaint in relation to Ilse, her flatness, her earthiness, her vision of practical truth. She had had that one last look at me—the one last look that had had nothing to do with the war or her story—that one last look which not only suggested but proclaimed that she and Alba, that Alba and she much more than cooperated, that they were à deux—but much, much more—that they shared not only one and the same weakness of the flesh but a similar and ineffable turpitude of spirit.

She folded the chair up with little difficulty and slung it over her arm. She grasped the picnic hamper in her free hand. "I think my husband has always thought of you as his possible redemption," she said and laughed. "You see, he feels so guilty and you're young." She paused. "Do bring the rug in when you come." She walked back to the house with no apparent sign of strain. She walked away as if she had not fixed me with malignity, as if she had not stabbed me over and over again with malice and aforethought, with premeditation and every desire to wound with the total thrust of her power to destroy. Her eyes held so firmly the awareness of what she had done and the pleasure of the doing it—oh, there can be no mistake in that—and never, never have I ever, ever met anyone who was fundamentally incapable of mercy. Never. She held her book of poetry in one hand and balanced it against the hamper in the other. Poetry. Ilse. My God.

I sat on my knees on my heels under the tree, my hands folded in my lap. There seemed to be no way to take it. The sun still shone and the breeze still hissed through the grasses. The tree still held itself together as if the universe were still intact. As if it were still held in place by its casing as a corpse for a while sustains flesh. I was oddly struck by the mute vision of slamming doors, each one slammed methodically and silently around a circle of which I was the centre and sat as mute as mute as mute—my tongue unstrung, cut for what I tasted. From that time to this there has been no music and life has fallen silent: not a note, not a quaver, not a hint, not one reverberation past a natural echo gone out to the farthest ripple of it has sounded. Only the mechanical gramophone reminds me . . . there was sound once—but was there? If a tree falls in a forest does it make a noise? Did I hear it? I'm not sure I ever heard it.

Jesus! How could she have done it? How could anyone deliberately do it? At random almost. Without true motive. There was no motive for it, only a resulting feeling of triumph for the action in her. Jealousy, pride, these are only insubstantial labels one can pin. It was as if she'd started on high C and gone atonally on without context or harmony. I felt I had touched toads, eaten toads, practised arts alien to the warm-blooded, done things unmammalian or had concourse and parley with a goat. It was her anti-gift of doing it that has most silenced me; not him—so curiously—not him at all. What she did was a non-doing: like a negative number or dwarf star, she cancelled out and sucked in, gashed the fairly agreeable picture of observable reality to make, to reveal a vacuum which removed you airless to another area actively sterile and beyond the moon. I am fixed and numb, engulfed in silence that neither heart nor head can of themselves . . . move.

At length, I returned to the stone by the river. There seemed as much point in being there as elsewhere. It occurred to me to drown myself, but the pain in my chest—the true, asphyxiating quality of it—was somehow more effective. From a long way off, high and to the right of my consciousness, I saw my mother dangling and was oddly amused that she'd bothered. Why had she bothered? Why taken the trouble? Pain is infinite and cannot be repealed by death. But Alba drowned. I disconnected him and let him float down the river. I went back to the tree, picked up the rug, and started for the house.

Alba had got up from his rest and was coming down the path to meet me. He saw me coming from a long way off and his face transformed at the sight of me coming up, at the sight of me there. My heart slouched away from him and hid from him. Disgust filled me and I was far away from him. There was no decision to be made about him, only a pose to be adopted so that I could conceal myself from him. No accusations crammed my mouth. There was nothing left to do.

"Hello," he said. I heard how ordinary his voice.

"Did you have a nice nap?" I printed this out.

"Yes. Fine." He slowed down to stopping. We stood together amid the leaves. "You've put your shoes on." He had nothing better to say and I said nothing. I no longer knew his face. I felt that anything he had to say about my feet was a possible impertinence. He caught my eye, tried to delve and dive in it, but his sight bounced off mine. He abused me; he abused me; like Arthur Marsdan, he abused me. The embrace of a python—he crushed with . . . the eyes of a basilisk. Never mind, never mind. I gave him a knowing little smile of times remembered with other men. I don't know whether it hurt him or not. At least it made him admit the truth. He should have admitted the truth. Why didn't he admit the truth?

"I've been talking to Ilse about the war," I said.

"Oh?" he seemed puzzled.

I couldn't even look at him without guilt.

What could I do? I couldn't stand there with him.

The flight was terrible. I really don't remember much about it except that I wound up somewhere like Lewes or Brighton—it must have been Lewes. I don't remember seeing the pavilion, but a jail and a castle; it must have been Lewes. I know water was somehow involved. There was the curious lapping noise of water in the dark and I was sick on a cheese omelette. I don't remember eating the omelette, but I still taste the smell of being sick on it and chips and a room I rented for the night, not even counting the money I had, whether I had enough to pay for the room or not. It is very strange that under the circumstances of grief people are often kind. There was a coarse-looking land-lady—the sort of woman I've never looked at twice—the sort of woman who looks as if she'd like to be a whore but hasn't quite the impetus. How pitiful we both were in her kitchen where she said, "You look done in, dear," and gave me tea. I reached across and took her married hand and thanked her. She didn't know about music but was playing Radio Wonderful from which the rocking sound of the Rolling Stones gathered no moss and the sound of water came rocking through the window. I left my cello in the car with the windows open, but nobody stole it because after all nobody is really interested in the cello and it isn't important anyway.

It did require superhuman strength to stay alive. That is quite clear. On driving back to London the next day there was the question of whamming into lorries and brick walls which would have been effortless.

And then I forgot. There was a long period which I forget entirely and know I forgot both Ilse and Alba, but had a kind of brain fever in which I understood that I could hear the grass growing if I listened and in which I dreamed chamber music starting in quite the normal way then becoming quite peculiar and atonal and very loud.

I am not quite sure whether the telephone rang a lot or not. I had the impression that it did. It pleased my fancy to think that

Alba was ringing me again and again, trying to get me to come back, but I had no solace in that and could not answer it; that is if it rang at all.

CHAPTER XIII

Self-doubt was an inner milieu for Benjamin Rose: outwardly, he covered its traces as carefully as a tracked tracker, filling in prints with snow.

He was a good-looking man—though slight—and not without charm for women. He did not consider this an attribute, rather as part of the whole nexus of defences he threw up against what he mistrusted. Further attributes joined forces with his appearance. He was a good heart surgeon; his reputation grew; the idea of him had begun to stick in the minds of his colleagues and superiors. Glamour attached itself to him, and of all defences he had found, this was the most powerful.

He was utterly friendless: his isolation had nothing whatever to do with lack of opportunity for friendship. He was considered likeable, but enigmatic, and this heightened rather than depressed everyone's good opinion of him.

He had not become a doctor out of any impulse to serve mankind, nor out of a desire for prestige or money. He had had to be a very bright little boy. Doctors had seemed to him, when as a child he had been nipped away from death (he'd had meningitis), not benevolent, but Byzantine with their flat, white, scientific shapes, their hierarchical, expressionless, mysterious power to divide life from death. Like Jehovah dividing dark from light in the Torah, so had the doctors divided him from death in a way to make his mother seem to sink and pant with gratitude like a saint in ecstasy. He was all she had.

Benjamin was fundamentally a religious man, though he shunned orthodoxy. So he became a doctor in order to be in

touch with light and dark; with what he sensed as a Being outside his control who divided, gathered up, or cast down; with a
beauty beyond human reason. He did not arrogate power to
himself: he was more in the way of a passionate observer; one
who cooperated in what he felt was a universal will to life.

Ulteriorly, his career was a blessed mask.

Before he fell in love with Beatrice Pazzi, he'd been in love
with another devoted servant of the Lord, that time a Quaker.
The inner life Benjamin so rigorously defended was love. How
he loved! It was gruesome; it was terrible. Post-adolescent en-
counters with women had sickened him, quite literally. He remembered vomiting once after an episode in a parked car. But
Sybil, with her white-hot fervour, her dedicated plainness, her
ruthless virginity, had pitched him past all bounds of what he
thought it possible to feel. When she deserted him, it was hardly
a surprise. He saw, in the course of time, that he'd set it up to
happen that way. She'd inflicted a torture so fine upon his sen-
sibilities that his most private and most inward keep was
broached and broken open. He began to write poetry, reams of
it and good. He published it under a pseudonym. He kept its
existence from everyone and most particularly his mother with
whom he lived, at thirty-five—a fractured, ironic, but not a bitter man.

Benjamin knew, for instance, that he was an impossible romantic. It cheered him up to know that he was a romantic: as
long as he knew he was one, it cheered him. He laughed at
himself for being a glamorous surgeon; he laughed at himself
for communing with himself as he, solitary, and with a deliberate style, walked across Hampstead Heath in the rain. He
amused himself with his own strong attachment to his mother:
his poetry mocked himself. In turn, he knew that self-mockery
was only another form of self-dramatization. He also knew he
had never come to grips with early experience. Early bad experience was completely unmentionable to him. It sat at the base
of his brain like a buried mine.

Sometimes when the pain became bad, he considered having
it removed by psychoanalysis. What it was could not be removed by psychoanalysis. Instead, he adopted an attitude of

patience under suffering and opted for the leading of a constructive life.

When he first saw Beatrice, he was stunned into mental silence. A break in his perpetual circuit of conscious thought occurred. He'd seen her before, often enough, as they passed in corridors. He knew about her. It was bruited about that she had been offered a consultancy which she'd turned down. She had, it was said, an excellent mind. A thoroughgoing competence, a conscientious exactitude; these were her qualities. She carried the work-load of two and had never, ever once let anybody down. In other respects, she rather blended with the walls and polished vinyl flooring.

Why? he thought when he had seen her. He had *seen* her. *Why* wasn't she made a queen?

All he'd seen was Beatrice waiting at the bus stop, sitting in her tweed coat, legs crossed at the ankles, hands gloved and folded in her lap round a small handbag. He could not interpret to himself the experience of vision. Why did he have such vision? Such a vision? It had been years and years since Sybil. Years. He couldn't get over it. What was she? Benjamin had a kind of superstition about Cupid which arose from having been shot. The arrow sunk and Sybil-in-his-heart dropped dead. He staggered home in a delirium.

It wasn't possible; his knees went. What was this? Who could she be? Why hadn't he seen her before? He pressed his mind to make sure he was intact. He told his mother he thought he was coming down with a cold and this elicited from her a threnody of cautions and I-told-you-sos, nostrums and home cures he subtly desired. He did in fact think himself ill. He hideously suspected that at thirty-five a man shouldn't be open to such an event.

He went to bed early with a toddy and decided it would be over in the morning. In the morning it was worse. His mother tried to persuade him to stay indoors (she was quite blind to his utter lack of symptoms); this is what he thought, but she was fond of him and sensed something wrong.

Nothing could keep Benjamin from the hospital the day after he'd fallen ill with Beatrice. As it happened, it was her day off. It was hard for him to know what to do with himself. He would have strapped himself to one of the beds and raised the sides of it to keep himself from damage. In the course of the day, he did a lot, performed unusually well. Ever since he'd collapsed over the departure of Sybil, anguish of mind had served him well. It heightened his responses, quickened his reflexes. Suffering became a fuel—when it came. He did not actively seek it.

Without the detachment to overbalance nightmares, Benjamin would have sunk beneath the waves. He wondered as he sipped watery coffee if he had enough detachment to offset good dreams. He himself knew she was a dream—or what she had appeared to be had the nature of a dream. Why did she particularly on that particular October day lift him up? His liftings-up and castings-down were what he so strongly wanted to keep from prying eyes. Usually, they were bearable. Usually they were perceptions on a lower level. This, he felt to be insane. He'd never seen beauty of that order. She was his femme fatale. He had never had the experience of sensing another so fully and that in a flash. He felt, under the tightness with which she held herself, a flawless physical grace. Her awkwardness, her angularity only underscored a softness. Her cheeks, the mould of her head, her hair made Duccio seem like a poor child with crayons: but most of all, it was her eyes that fulminated, as if she were a mother of sorrows, pitiful beyond the point of his endurance. He felt a need to comfort whatever it was; to be comforted by it.

All the time, he cursed himself for letting himself get away with it. He had the modern conviction that there was no such thing as love at first sight, and even if there were, it didn't count as love. His poems about Sybil had the flavour of black coffee: Beatrice was all myrrh. He racked his brains to think why. With a fine-toothed comb he went over the events of the day in which he saw her at the bus stop. Recalled every conversation he'd had with her or about her. He encouraged discussion on her with his colleagues. "Poor old Beatrice," they said. He made a mental note never to speak to them again. He found out where she lived.

As things progressed, he went from one day to the next in a daze. His feelings for her did not lessen; she became only more refulgent, and he all the more tormented because he suspected the vision of her wasn't true. His commonsense told him she was a sad and overdedicated old-maid.

By happy chance, they met in consultation over Mrs Bounds who had heart trouble on top of cancer. Benjamin had enormous black eyes. He tried beaming them at Beatrice from every conceivable angle. She smiled at him kindly, with patronage. Not with patronage. He saw at once she hadn't the skill with men to patronize them. He saw the outlines of a crucifix under her jumper. She fingered it from time to time, during their conversation.

She threw him into a chaos of creativity with her shy smile. He went berserk, writing a poem a night. As if he were a painter, he studied and chronicled the shapes of her movements. The lean of her head in contrast to an upright pillar she sat next to, the finished polished way she walked from bedside to bedside were like a glass-and-velvet case for sweetly given compassion to the sick. At the same time, he hated her for being so tritely heroic; seethed at her chaste little habits, the unconscious primness of her mouth. All the time she asserted perfection to him, she gave herself away as being less than perfect. She was less than she could be; he knew this. Yet he was disgusted by what he wanted her to be.

Was she smug? He wanted to kick her. Was she ordinary? He knew she wasn't ordinary, but she kept trying to pretend she was. Or was it the other way around? He wanted to shock her; give her a surprise. He wanted a depth of contact with her he felt her too unimaginative to allow. He had the urgency of mission to show her how beautiful she was. He wanted to holler to her through a mental megaphone to stop trying so hard.

Hampstead Heath became an exercise ground where he prowled. He was no longer in love with his own vision of his vision, no longer enamoured of himself as a latter-day Keats. As he walked, he hunted. He was aware of the crackling of twigs under his feet; he avoided piles of leaves and went with stealth. Inwardly, he tracked and explored for the source of his experience. There was no such thing as love at first sight. Why then had he fallen in love at first sight?

As days went by, he became more restless and impatient with himself. He was Hamlet with himself. Had it been a trick of light, seeing Beatrice the way he'd seen her? Did his inability to declare himself to her, even modestly, come from doubt of the truth of this unwelcome happening? Or did he finally lack courage? If he really spoke to her, wouldn't the dream vanish? It was odious to him to think of reality installing itself in her eyes, her smile. Was that it?

He refused to comb Dante. He combed Dante. He hadn't known her name was Beatrice until after, until Anno Bus Stop. Or had he heard it by the by? Had the notion penetrated his unconscious mind? The whole thing was utterly absurd.

Yet, every day, he intended to present himself to her, engage her in conversation, ask her out to dinner; and every day, he could not. The seams of his mind burst with longing to touch and prove the mystery that love might come like an annunciation. He feared a phantom pregnancy.

Why had he become available to the experience of Beatrice? Had writing deepened the end into which he fell? Had he so opened his mind to imagery that images took actual life or did they haunt, merely, because of their insubstantial nature?

He knew no one else saw Beatrice as he saw her, yet in seeing her this way, he knew he possessed a reality about her she didn't herself own. To give her the self that she didn't possess became his passionate desire. Her buried treasure lured him into words which dug. His poetry now dug—to an end. His poetry dug, mined, polished. A publisher suggested a slim volume. Ordinarily, this would have pleased him more than he would have wanted to admit: he forgot to answer the letter for a fortnight, then came upon it in his monastic little study and panicked. Yes, indeed, he'd like to do a collection. He wondered if he were losing his mind.

He was so continually aware of her, so continually observant of her every fluctuation of expression, that he could not believe she did not notice. But she didn't and this sent him into short paroxysms of fury. Sometimes she represented to him the whole punishing fist of Christendom upon his people; the whole sneering, rejecting race who'd been responsible for his own mutilation. In her essence, however, he caught the scent of kindness: more than that, he caught more than that. She was not so much kind but in touch with something embedded in his own deepest mind which was also in touch with something his conscious self dug to understand.

He did become so closely united to her in his mind that he instantly saw the change. One day, she changed. How? It was evanescent, but he was overjoyed. As she sat with their colleagues, he noticed her eyes dart round; lively now, they lit on this and that, once on him: she smiled *at* him in the corridor. Her hands shed their schoolmistress tightness like gloves. She touched things with them; then withdrew as if burnt. She became nervous and jumped at noises. She blushed when he stood close to her. Did she sense how he inhaled her? She had a profound personal scent. He felt that she had sensed—him—but not admitted it. He lived on the blush for days.

On the fourth or fifth day of the change so subtle only he could have seen it, he took his life in his hands.

He always sat alone in the canteen; she always with others. Although it was quite clear to him that she derived not an iota of pleasure from their company, he saw she did it out of a desire for camouflage. When, on this day of his, she sat by herself three tables from him, he could not believe his luck.

Benjamin's self-confident manner did not derive from any good opinion he had of himself. He was a thoroughgoing architect who'd built his house on sand. The real rock of his character lay elsewhere cloven by events of pain. It was the deepest necessity of his being to become whole in this respect. At any rate, after nearly fainting, he got himself together with an air of debonair assurance and sauntered over to Beatrice, who stirred and stirred and stirred her coffee and then stirred it again.

Beatrice wished the coffee not so foul, the doughnut not so stale. Still, the high steamy room gave her comfort. She really rather sank into its familiarity. The sight of Edna, with her white-netted hair and crêpey arms, doling a nameless stew out of stainless-steel containers, did not erase, but put into some perspective the memory of Alba. Alba. She shuddered as if bitten at the centre by something cold.

How did they fit, Alba and Mme Alba, into a world like this, quotidian, inhabited by herself? She couldn't fit them anywhere to her past experience. The feeling of having had Continental Europe and a certain type of breeding in common vanished into thin air as soon as it was touched.

She realized that she blamed them horribly, but why? She shut her eyes and let the coffee steam her eyelids to give her, perhaps, further vision on the matter. She couldn't fault them—at any rate, not Alba. She remembered little of Mme Alba but a scent, a trace. She had the vague impression she felt sorry for her for some reason. Why did Alba leave such a bad taste in her mouth? Her mouth really did taste bad.

She had assumed that Alba and Maud had been lovers. Alba and Maud had not been lovers. Somehow she knew this with her whole being and for some reason, the knowledge filled her with an obscure and unorthodox rage. No, it wasn't *that* which made her angry. Oh, it was all Maud's fault, surely, clearly. Surely, clearly it was wrong to want a married man, or rather to deliberate to want one. Oh, Alba was flawless, all right.

"My own experience of rejection," thought Beatrice, "has led me to sympathize with the wrong party. Wrong party. Wronged party." She had an inner picture of a party on a barge carelessly floating down the wrong tributary of a river.

Oddly enough, she had not been tempted to tell Maud anything of what she had seen. She had returned to the flat and sat with the cat in a stiff attitude of grief. She had been terrified that Maud would come up. She knew her eyes would have given away pity; that her expression would give away what Maud already really knew but could not face. Should she make her face it? Could she? She would not.

All Sunday there had been no jumpiness, no dialogue with the cat. She sat still with the knowledge of unrequited love. There was something unendurable about unrequited love. How could you plead for Maud against reason, even against morality? One couldn't. One shouldn't. One wouldn't. Silently, she did.

She propped her elbows, Monday morning, on the disinfected surface of the table and drank what she now wished were tea.

She became aware of someone standing beside her and

looked up. In a tantalizing moment, as if one life continued from another without break or interruption, she felt as if she saw her own mental state, cast of thought—whatever—reflected in the eyes of the man who stood edgily above her. It seemed so perfectly natural that this should be so, that she was surprised only when she gathered her wits about her and recognized Ben Rose whom she'd spoken with from time to time and always subtly liked.

"May I join you?"

She had chosen to sit apart from her colleagues because she wanted to be alone. As a rule, they sat together, a group of them, and she felt safe in this undeveloped camaraderie. A few put her through an enervating dance of ritual flirtation which she privately sucked for being starved. Her first instinct was to refuse Benjamin, but instead, she hesitated.

He quickly sat down. "You looked very worried," he said.

He sat quite close to her; he was overbearing from nerves. She retracted. He made to stand. "I don't want to interrupt you," he said.

She had a full second to decide. Why did she decide what she decided? "No, do sit down. I am sorry. I *was* worried."

It was his face when she retracted. Had she done this before to people? Had she failed to notice it? She'd cut him to the quick, but he was quick to mask the cut.

He sat again, but moved a little farther away, pushed the chair back imperceptibly. What was she going to do with him? She feared him.

"Alone at last," he said. His eyes were large and round, somehow independent of his face. He played this remark coolly, with a faint, back-handed irony.

Beatrice had never been at home with sarcasm; even wit rattled her a little. She did not know why she was physically aware of the man, but because she was, she assumed that he was mocking her. She flushed and bent the paper cup, spilling a little coffee. Benjamin whipped out his handkerchief and mopped the coffee up. Beatrice looked from side to side for an escape route.

"The coffee's awful," he said.

"It is." As he mopped, she noticed that his hands were taut, almost trembling. They reminded her of Maud's hands. She looked at her own hands and noticed that they too were shaky. She and Benjamin looked at each other now in cold blood. At once, his eyes softened and brightened. It she'd been a little off-balance first thing, she now was completely thrown. She suddenly had a complete sense of having been aware of him before on several occasions. She had ducked his glance coming at her.

"What are you worried about, then?" he asked.

"Oh, it's silly."

"That's the sort of remark people make when they want help but don't like to ask for it."

She thought it sensitive of him to think she needed help. No one ever thought she needed help. At the same time, she did not like to think she'd given herself away.

Benjamin felt the need to become more and more drastic as the conversation lurched on. She was hamfisted and butterfingered with him. He knew that he was making her so, but he could not stop. He felt it necessary to dare an icy shower from her.

"You're very shy, aren't you?" He waited for the destruction of his dream with crouched shoulders. She was going to rise and find that really she must go back to work. In fact, she did nothing of the sort.

"Yes, I am. You are too, I think." His system of attack brought her out in a way which surprised her.

He settled back against the chair, jolted. "I'm not," he said. He was a little distressed that she hadn't utterly disappointed him. He smiled to himself.

They both retreated. Beatrice felt she had been extremely stupid. She thought she'd better dig up some shop to talk in order to cover decently the failure of what had been tentatively tried between them. But despite herself, she drew a breath and said, "I suppose it's because I live alone with my cat." There! She'd given him the portrait of an old-maid. Why had she gone and done that?

"I live alone with my mother." Only his eyes put an editorial slant on this remark. He did not think Beatrice an old-maid. Did he?

She was obscurely relieved he wasn't married. "You're not married either?" Had he been? Just as bad.

"No. I've never married."

In one way, things were going too fast for Beatrice. In another way, they weren't going fast enough. "I looked after my mother for *years*," she said. Her own wrath startled her, but not Benjamin. She looked at him with new respect.

"We play dominoes," he said. For its refusal of sarcasm, his voice was all the more withering.

"I used to read Dante aloud. Every night."

They exchanged glances. The subtleties of feeling already expressed in looks and little gestures of face and hand had taken them both farther into each other than either had meant to go.

"Are you doing anything tonight?" he asked.

"I'm off at six." They looked at each other with deepest mistrust. Beatrice suddenly found herself capable of a wry smile which Benjamin returned.

"What a coincidence," he said. "So am I." He had already checked when she was off duty. He quickly calculated who would take his place as he, in reality, was on till nine. "Will you have dinner with me?"

Was Maud a real excuse or was it a retreat against what she knew from experience might be painful? Little episodes of embarrassed silences in restaurants with likely gentlemen came to mind.

"I don't know if I can," she said and felt failed.

She could not believe that she was capable of causing pain. Why did he look so wounded? She didn't even know him. He bit the tip of his thumb. His eyes looked elsewhere.

"I mean, I . . ." She almost gave up. "What I mean is that I would very much like to come. You asked me earlier if I was worried—you see, it's so hard to describe." She floundered deeper and deeper on to his hook. If she told him, then there would have to be, for her at any rate, an intimacy with him which gave him the power to wound her. Suddenly, she had to tell someone. It was like a blitz attack of vomiting. "It's my neighbour. I've been in the most terrible state. For days." Tears sprang to her eyes. She shuddered with violent and inexplicable emotion. She had to get away from Maud and the thought of Maud. She had to.

Benjamin was lost in wonder. He resisted an impulse to catch the tears in his palm and with them bathe his own face. Had he expected this? He was tipsy with a weird joy that his love for her—love? Love. Was justified. He quickened towards her as she cried. He no longer had to touch her to see if she were real. His experience of love at first sight was ratified in his desire to be of some real use to her.

"I'm sorry. I'm sorry, it's most unlike me. I've been under a dreadful strain." She absently blew her nose on his coffee-stained handkerchief. "The thing is, I don't know why it is so upsetting to me. This girl was attacked by a stranger—a religious fanatic—and I went to her flat to see what was the matter—you see, I heard screams. She's the oddest girl, a musician. She'd wrecked all of her things. You should see that place. It's terrible." Beatrice shuddered and realized she was being disjointed. "I used to hear her play the cello at night. It was very beautiful. Beautiful. She won't play any more. This man is lurking outside our house and she won't do anything to get him to go away. I've *tried*. I got the police and they said they'd 'moved him on,' but I . . . oh, it must seem so incoherent to you."

"You've become all involved."

"I had to sometime, at some point. Or maybe not. Maybe not." She surprised herself with that.

Detachment was Benjamin's favourite anaesthetic, but with the years, it had worn off. They looked at each other with astonishing mutual understanding.

"I don't know why I'm talking to you like this."

He looked and looked at her. His look overrode all that she had said. She felt that she, not he, had missed the point. She stopped crying more because it made her look ugly rather than undignified.

"It is strange," he said. "You don't even know me, do you?"

She felt she did know him, but dismissed it as an illusion. "I'm worried about this girl, you see. I feel a kind of responsibility for her. She might be in danger, she might want to talk. It could be crucial. That's why I don't know whether or not I should come out with you tonight."

"If you were on duty, you would stay here, presumably." Benjamin had little interest in Maud. The Mauds of this world were to him like Sybil's starving Africans. Benjamin rejected need-in-abstract. Love, he felt, should involve the particular. Subtly, he knew that the particular in Maud was the source of Beatrice's torment. He did not, however, recognize a bleak suspicion that his own need would again (and again and again) go unrecognized, but the fear crushed his face into a frown. "Anyway," he said, "I think you look exhausted. We'd be out for only a few hours and it would be a change for you."

She had to go with him. Was it love? It wasn't. She *had* to. Was it duty? It wasn't duty. It was inner compulsion. Having thrown caution to the winds for Maud, further cautions went for Benjamin. Why? Why this? Why him? Why now? She'd seen Maud and now Benjamin as being really there. The man sitting across from her was there. Somehow she was struck by the enormity of her former evasions. How could one fail to work out the equation of self and others once it had been presented? He had been completely unpredicted, but he sought her and she knew it. "You're quite right," she said. "Shall I meet you at six?"

"At the gates." They shared a sudden sense of common satisfaction.

As he rose to go, he hesitated. "Why?" she asked. It was hardly a formed word; she felt ashamed for having asked it.

He shook his head. "I don't know." This time he didn't smile.

CHAPTER XIV

Beatrice's day, though well spent, spent her. She had no time to think of her distractions: still, the heavy thud—the tread, tread of Alba—his face, his coldness, his betrayal, by the barest shrug of Maud, emptied out her heart like a pump. So that was it. Was that it? And could one finally know? Oh, he was good, surely, yes, and always on the side of goodness she.

She thought of Mr Rose—cleared her throat and practised calling him Benjamin to herself. The prevision of the evening came freshly out to her like a clear tune of Beethoven. She found she wanted to see him *so much*.

They met at the hospital gates at six. She had arrived first. Oh, he wasn't coming. He wasn't going to come. It had been a joke the nurses had put him up to. He had had an emergency. He'd simply made it up about his mother. The contact she thought they'd had was fictional: a case of wishful thinking on her part. Anyway she should be at home, manning the fortress. She had scanned the damp pavement. It was dark and the air full of traffic fumes, but autumn was not quite obliterated. An elderly cripple lurched down to the zebra crossing and stood waiting for the rush hour to stop for him. Without premeditation, Beatrice saw a patience in him. His hips were slung out at a cruel angle. Suddenly she felt for him that every step must be like walking on a fracture. Pain stop pain stop pain stop. The Belisha beacon flashed on-off on-off over his bent, capped head. At once, she saw that even a week before she would have marched forth, policed the traffic for him. Now it was enough to watch with drawn-in breath the remarkable achievement of his waiting, how he'd come down to stop everybody's hurry. At last the cars relented and he crossed—pain stop pain stop—he laboured like Hercules to the other side. Beatrice was proud of him and felt it was enough for any man to do in one day: to cross the road like that.

When she looked around, Mr Rose was at her elbow. She was dazzled by his watching of her. Never had she been so watched. A sense of herself was suggested to herself. It was as if she'd always been at one remove to herself, had addressed herself politely and formally as "*Lei.*"

"You like to walk," he said. "I've only once seen you go home by bus. *Never* in a taxi. Would you like to go in a taxi tonight?"

They agreed to walk. They walked for miles as the autumn

evening gathered in. Their elbows barely touched; each time
they did, Beatrice felt the ache of loneliness bite deeper in her
chest and stomach. Like coming round from sodium pentathol
she hurt the more for the curious man who walked beside her
and woke her up. A drugged life of penal servitude *he* understood; though he didn't say so, she felt so.

Their conversation, eased by the knowledge that silence
might be just as good, covered more territory than their feet.
Why this? Why now? Why such immediate liking?

"I hope you don't think me strange—approaching you today."

"I find it strange to be approached at all." Only being outright
would do. That—she felt—was key (committee-meeting word—
she used so many of them—an irritating habit she must break).

"Patients find you approachable. Everyone speaks of it. You
have a reputation for goodness."

"All that means is that people won't swear in front of me."
Still, she had an anarchic feeling of pride.

"All right then. Bugger." He laughed, then paused. "You see
you don't like it really."

She didn't.

She felt not only impelled but able to say, "Are you taking
me out as a curiosity?"

He hesitated. "That's a coarse motive I probably have. What I
really like is that you are introspective like myself. Actually, I
used to dislike you (she was cut to the quick). I thought you
condescending, pleased with your own beauty like women I
used to know; like *the* woman I used to know who was assumed
into a heaven of her own making."

"Where was that?" The area of Beatrice's soul was clearly
defined to her as a block of ice somewhere behind her pineal
gland. Why was he talking to her like this, as if they were
intimate friends?

"Oh, she's very happy now being admired by an African village on its uppers. She went to Biafra and it stuck."

"You're unfair," she thought, but said, "What made you
change your mind about me?"

His bitterness receded. "Don't think me bad about Sybil," he said. She didn't have to look. His voice held in it a refined sort of tenderness. She sensed he had been accurate about the woman. He drew breath and continued. "I saw you sitting."

She expected him to go on, but he didn't. "Sitting?"

"Sitting at the bus stop across from the hospital. The bus came and went; you didn't notice."

"How did you know it was my bus?" She realized there was something caustic about her that hadn't been tempted out by the simple virtue of her not knowing anybody well enough to hurt.

"I know which bus you would take because you fascinate me. I have looked up your address."

"What quality did I have when I missed the bus then?" Saint Beatrice was testy for the impertinence. Beatrice longed to know.

Benjamin cast a hand into the air as if he were throwing something away. "I've written some poems about it. I am a poet."

Beatrice was intensely pleased. "I don't associate poetry with medicine," she said, however.

"I take as my precedent Keats, Chekhov, and William Carlos Williams."

"Chekhov was a playwright."

"You're so *plonking*. Plonking is Stephen Potter. I expect you don't know who he is. I can see you don't. Ah, well. Yes, I *know* Chekhov was a playwright." He paused. "I've published my poems about you. So there."

She said nothing. To have had poems published about her; to have been sung: it made her wretched. It made her feel fictional. Poems devised for her sole benefit would have deepened her sense of contact with him.

"Do you think yourself—well named?"

"No!" She felt she'd like to pull pillars together in one last effort to bring the Divine Comedy down on her own head— never mind the Philistines.

He shrugged and laughed. "The association sticks. Beatrice takes the fiery car all the way to Pimlico."

"Oh, death!"

"The beatific vision on the bus."

"Why are you making fun of me? I thought . . ." Her earlier yearning for romance was admitted in her outrage.

"I've admired you from afar." He almost sneered. "I'm fed up with that. I'm too old for that. Anyway, there isn't time. *There isn't any time.*"

"*What do you mean?*" She went rigid and put her hands on her mouth. Somewhere he'd undone the catch of a trigger. "*What do you mean there isn't any time?*"

He put his arm around her and sheltered her head in the nest of his neck. "I don't know what I meant. I'm as puzzled as you are that I said it. I guess I meant I'm getting older and I'm lonely."

She pushed away, but had inhaled his scent—a scent of his flesh which was mingled with Phisohex. The smell threw her into chaos. Memories of events which had never happened to her—lost capabilities—wheeled about her mind. Why was it so easy to let him touch her?

They had reached Trafalgar Square. Beatrice felt flat and ashamed—a bit, but not too much. Why not? What was different about him? Still, she inspected Benjamin's face for animal tracks or evidence of disease. No, love; maybe his capacity was for emotion.

They walked on in silence. She tried not to discount Benjamin. To retreat from him would be easy enough; she less than hardly knew him. It would be hard to retreat from what she now saw she wanted to know of herself. Ah, it was cruel to have to face the inferences that glinted round the events of the past few days. Was it the good God's meaning that she should see herself locked and bolted? Withdrawn into barrenness and not virginity at all? She did not know what He meant any more except that she had taken Him for granted and at face value all her life treating Him in some senses like a fool of a bureaucrat with a rule book. She cowardly supposed for half a moment that this was due to the flawed teaching of others. *Rex tremendae maiestatis*—she trembled at half the cusp of the knowledge that she'd never acknowledged His creativity. Herself—unaided and alone.

She did not seek Benjamin's hand, but as they wandered—

pole-axed—down St Martin's Lane, she allowed it to be taken. Her mind beat against the discipline of being held like an animal in certain despair of asphyxiation. If she had been younger she would have torn loose; as it was, she had the sense to feel and to appreciate her luck.

"I'm taking you to Bianchi's for dinner. You'll like it," he said after a pause.

She said nothing, but she liked the thought of a place called Bianchi's.

"From my observation of you," he said (he always seemed to speak as if there was little between exterior and interior thought so that words were a mere continuing process of what he assumed his listener understood), "you make moral judgments too quickly. I wonder if you confuse your deep sense of propriety with the truth."

"Maud," she said. She was confused by him into the unexpected. How long had she muddled Maud in her mind with what she now saw in the Charing Cross Road of skinflicks and massage parlours, windows dangling with contraptions the use of which she did not know but made a stab at in the imagination which she herself had limited? She had bound imagination. Was she dwarfed?

"Is Maud a whore?" he asked with considerable interest. There was no getting round Benjamin's fundamental stance of curiosity. Whether it was good or bad she decided not to guess. She was propelled by necessity into accepting him as he was. The impoverished part of her which had always been like the dark side of the moon—that, that was what had miraculously revolved; he shone on it and warmed it. Something in her released and she relaxed.

"No, of course not." She laughed. "At least, I have no real idea what a whore really is. She doesn't take money for her favours although she's been generous with them, I suppose."

"A whore with a heart of gold. How ghastly!"

For a poet, she decided, he did not choose words carefully. Maud was ghastly. Beatrice was aghast at her. Her skin had a ghastly hue: but she was not ghastly in the affected English diction which Benjamin had used. Yet he had chosen the word carefully she saw when she looked at him. He had resumed backhandedness out of a sharp desire to bring her further out.

"She hasn't been generous with her favours at all." Beatrice now accused herself of imprecision. "She's used them to obtain things for herself."

"Such as love? She's undefiled inside and probably suicidal. I know the type."

Loyalty for Maud against this accuracy streaked from her like a bullet. "She isn't a type. She's Maud!"

There was something dashing about Benjamin. He would have leapt up and caught this bullet in his teeth. "You see!" As they walked, he waved arms passionately around. "You see! None of them are types. You see! They're all Mauds or Doreens trapped in various stages, as we are, of the net. Your Christ had pity on them!"

"He did not condone immorality." Inwardly, she stuffed her mouth with ashes at this remark. Its outward truth had nothing to do with her own disposition.

"He had a knack for persons, far from or near to truth!" His voice had reached the pitch of outrage. Fairly ordinary persons, milling towards the theatre or onward home from jobs, stared at the choked doctor.

"Are you a Christian?" She was startled into a genuine desire to know.

"If you have to put a label on me—I'm Jewish. Perhaps it gives me an access that you lack." He was huffy.

"Perhaps it does." So that was the minor key in him she danced to. His identity as also being chosen sung with the bitter force of psalms down a tunnel of wind. She saw them both (in varying degrees) expectant in the night desert. She was recollected to the thought of stars. As if he'd been a compass, she now knew where she was. She rocked back to the seat of herself like a dancer who—uncertain of the force of gravity—now felt what she might and might not do with its principle.

"*I'm* a person," he said, "and if you'll stop regarding me as a wolf, we'll have a pleasant evening."

"A wolf is the emblem of my city," she said vaguely. "I like wolves."

"Rome or Wolverhampton?" He was facetious, even a little fatuous. Their teeth chattered in the common, mute understanding that they'd got out on to a limb, and that the limb was invisible.

"Rome," she said in her mother's Schiaparelli tone. Like any hand-me-down it didn't fit, but it relieved Benjamin, she could see. The British spirit of compromise had never afflicted either of them, but they now both sought it as wise.

Penitential visits to the White Tower with Mama were Beatrice's only brush with eating out. Mama with her beaded bag; Mama with mink cape. Mama like a Rolls-Royce consumed, necessarily, a lot of fuel. Mama's idea of a fast was grilled sole. Oh, Mama! A shriek of love shocked her mind. Mama's wrinkles were gorges in her face where powder caked. Mama's little elegances, her fictional cosiness with Caesars made Beatrice ache. She had endured the contempt of waiters for her Mama. Mama as she pretended to know wines, as she assumed a knowledge of art, as she dragged young men at neighbouring tables into conversation when they regarded instead Beatrice's beauty and she'd curled in anguished guilt. Mama'd always liked Tatty better. They had not only lasciviousness in common, but pathos. Beatrice had always stiffened against the wind. She sat back in Bianchi's and let it blow.

"Orvieto doesn't travel well—or does it?" Benjamin said.

She shook her head. "No it doesn't," she said. She'd learnt the rules of gluttony to protect Mama.

"So what?"

"So what." She couldn't resist the yellowed walls and the faint scent of basil, the unpretentious waiters and the sight of other diners actually having a good time.

"*Buona sera,*" she found herself saying to the waiter who circled the table which was clothed white, and starched as a wimple. Both Benjamin and he were pleased. If a flood of love for her Mama had inexplicably hit her earlier, so now did she find another tributary for country. The waiter was a Florentine: she could tell by his accent. As they made the banal but ineffable contact of countrymen abroad, she found another vein she'd cauterized; not so much walks in the Borghese Gardens on Roman holidays or times when she'd been taken off to Venice and stood encased and small in the Bridge of Sighs, but other and profounder memories of fluid words she'd first learned—eased Latin—which flowed like oil flicking and gushing from her child's tongue to which English seemed a blunt instrument by comparison, and even though she had the law of her adopted language letter perfect, so that not a trace of accent remained, her ability to express was—had been—always cloven, so that everything always was and had been a translation quick to the point of being simultaneous. As she sought the tongue of the waiter, he revived within her a kind of volubility like song.

She saw herself in her mind's eye, shopping in the market in Victoria eschewing her native speech to the Italian greengrocer; eschewing the language at the delicatessen where she was too ashamed to buy tagliatelle, Dolcelatte, and hefty blocks of Parmesan her appetite longed for. She saw that she was not after all ridden by the fear of allegorical Luxury (a demon she particularly despised) but by mere childish horror of identifying with those who like herself were different. Her difference from others had always hung round her neck like an iron cross. Then, after the war, her mother had been stranded in England (a long story that); she had said—she now remembered—had often said, "Mama, don't use that language." "That language" was how she saw it, something bordering on obscenity. Any English word which ended with "a" or "o" had embarrassed her as if it had had a sexual connotation. She remembered being unable to write about the "frozen tundra" in a geography test. She now thawed into her ravioli. She was absolutely starving.

Benjamin tilted his head and watched her eat with appreciative pride. "Oh, it's so good!" she exclaimed. "Just like home."

"I expect you don't cook for yourself," he said. She shook her head. "You'll have your own dietary laws. It often amazes me that if they don't exist, people have to invent them either in fastidious habits or in some other way. There's a feeling about food that it's unclean."

Beatrice plunged her nose into the goblet of wine and drank.

"You amuse me," she said. "You seem to want to make a running commentary on life."

"Yes, but my poetry's alive."

"Are you famous?"

"I shall be," he said. She saw at once that it was true.

"You shall be." She glittered at him over the edge of the glass.

"Do you know, you're essentially a passive woman. That's an awkward way of putting what I saw at the bus stop. You're receptive, you call out creativity in people."

Her white-coated, good-works life fell round her ankles. She stood glistening in her chemise. She covered herself modestly with words. "I'm forty, you know."

"Age cannot wither nor custom stale your infinite variety. I'm being silly, I must be drunk."

"That's good. Did you write that?"

"It's Shakespeare, you ignorant woman."

She was now quite sure she didn't want second-hand words. She veiled her eyes again. They ate calves' liver in silence. Again she felt she'd snubbed him. The last thing in her mind for the hour they had been sitting had been her will to the spiritual. But, as the unseen had seemed to cut her moorings and dunk her unceremoniously in prayer—a state she never understood nor even wanted (she saw for the first time she'd never wanted it)—so did she apprise Benjamin, only partly and through lashes. She was seized by an intention to love him. So many areas of her didn't want him. Nothing in her understood him and that was only in part because she didn't know him; what she saw was that she would never know him and that it was not required of her to understand him and that was why, if such a question could be answered, he had fallen in love with her. Had he? He had. That she would not measure him according to his adequacy or inadequacy to her needs became certain; that she would not prop up his needs with various tricks and lies, lies she saw she'd told and told and told to all her poor-sick she'd pretended were her friends, she was also certain. She was consumed with gratitude for the bread she broke with him, for the ease he made her feel, for the love he thought he had for her, for his comparative youth; but more importantly for the ability he gave her to bestow herself in return for what she saw the immeasurable gift of himself: immeasurable because it wasn't adequate, immeasurable because she wasn't either. She was wrapt in a quiet she'd sought, a quiet that she had tried to impose upon herself like an iron maiden. She looked at him and for a moment, she thought he was going to cry.

"Eat up your nice spinach," he said instead. "You'll want an ice."

Their conversation dawdled over hospital gossip and over a series of disparate interests they had made common by the unity of newly conceived love. He liked yachting; she told him about her fondness for the English countryside. She was pleased he liked Turner and he was pleased she liked Blake. They hit upon a meeting at the Tate on Saturday. And so on. Interests did not come from them as attitudes or weapons of defence, they rather showed each other their collections and agreed to swap in areas. When they got to music, he turned to Maud.

"Do you think now you could explain to me why this girl throws you into such an uproar?" Having made their meal, he approached her with every confidence that something could now be solved.

Beatrice came to a sudden halt and every thought they'd shared piled up behind her almost as dangerously as cars on a motorway which meet a patch of fog.

"I don't understand." Every thought of Maud went blank. She could not even see her in her mind's eye. Why to a halt? Why screech to a halt? She had not been so relaxed or understood in years. She had not been relaxed or understood *ever*. Now here she was. Why this? Why now? Feeding on lilies and why this, why Maud now?

She watched him watch her inward motion. How explain this now? The importance of the dinner seemed to recede. They had consumed and he had brought her round to the inconsumable.

"I have a feeling of necessity about her," she said at last. Language to her was never a satisfactory instrument.

He showed he gripped this word but had not grasped it. He

knocked his spoon rapidly against his teeth. "Do you mean she is necessary to you?" He had mind, had Benjamin. Things interested him and she liked that.

"No. No. She was never necessary." She hoped she was right about that.

"I think it lacking in wisdom," he said, "to define too crudely how a person is necessary to one. If you see her as a necessity . . ."

"I don't see *her* as a necessity. I long to see her—I want to be with her . . ."

"You're afraid you're in love with her." He spoke with gentlest understanding.

Was it or wasn't it wonderful that she now felt her mind melt to speech? "I've been afraid all my life of loving anyone," she said. She was shamed into tears forcing themselves to the front of her eyes: it wasn't shame she largely felt but a deep relief at finally suffering. Pain satisfied her chest.

"I don't know that love was meant to be either comfortable or orthodox," he said, "but then, according to you I'm a heretic."

Once relieved, she blurted. "Oh, are you? I don't know. I really don't know why anything. I've lived the safest life imaginable. I suppose it was bound to hit me some time. I'm thrown into a state where I couldn't blame anyone for being in love with a cat. Sometimes I think everyone in the whole world is starving—starving. I gave my life to medicine hoping *that* would feed. I give no end of my salary to the poor—you don't know. Are you shocked? I am slammed up against a sort of hunger in this girl—in myself, even, perhaps, in you, Benjamin (the word was lovely in her mouth)—that can't be fed with money or pills or even roast turkey: *that* is the necessity! If sex could fill it, well, then why doesn't it? Casual observation proves it doesn't. Or if it does, it does so on a fairly short-term basis." Her voice had risen to a fine whispered shriek. Several of the other diners looked around. Her eyes took fire; she was almost irresistible to look at; at the arc of her passion, she fulfilled her beauty. "Love seeks to fill insatiable need, the heart craves to be fed with something more than you can touch. I *myself* need what I crave to give. I never knew it or saw it before I met that girl and it's put me in a stinking dilemma I can't solve. How can I give her or anyone else or myself anything more than I've given!"

He sat back and received the tirade with closed eyes and a gratified smile. "Because you haven't given it before," he said. "Because before it's cost you nothing and you've done it intravenously so there'll be no mistake, no error in the balance of saline and glucose, and the one thing I can say for your God, if you'll permit me to say it, is that he managed to part with his life at what appears to be considerable cost to himself. I suppose that's right but I'm not sure and I don't know. All I do know is that I couldn't have approached or come near you some weeks ago and here we are having a dinner beyond my wildest dreams." He paused. "Do I matter?"

She sat and almost shook, her chest still heaving with the outburst of emotion it had taken forty years to achieve. She saw him; he was there, had called out stifled drawers of self to be spilled over the cloth, the crumbs of bread that lay on it, the drained wine glasses and the remaining spoons they had not used. "I cannot conceive of why this has happened to me," she said, "but it has. Yes, you matter—of course you do. But you should have mattered in the first place—I should have noticed you before."

He was at ease and shrugged. "Could you?"

She shook her head.

"Well, then."

A party at the next table was drinking a lot and making cheerful noise. Beatrice was inconsequently struck by their innocence.

"Come along, I'll take you home," he said. Deus ex machina, he paid the handsome bill and swept her into a taxi-cab. Ah, at last sweet hero and listener to a voice. She let it happen, let herself be cared for. When they reached the tall, narrow house, it was effortless to ask him up.

They stood on the pavement. Beatrice searched for keys. She became aware that Benjamin paced with some agitation about. Nervous? Was he nervous?

"Where did you see that man last?" he asked. She now felt silly about Arthur. Was he killing time?

"There," she said. She waved her hand at the fence around the garden. "In there. Underneath the tree."

Benjamin crossed the road with the confident trepidation of a poised cat. In a leap and a scramble, he cleared the fence and disappeared into the dark thicket of leaves. Beatrice stood tensed and still for quite a while. It was gallantry or was it? Should she or shouldn't she have asked him up? Did it compromise? Would he take advantage of? Having shoved out from shore she realized she'd forgotten the oars—or really never had them. She did not know what to do or how to cope with a man at midnight. She looked at her watch. Well, ten-thirty anyway. Of course it would be all right, how stupid.

He was such a long time that she crossed the road herself and put her hand on the fence. "Benjamin? Are you all right?" she called softly. Suppose that man *was* there, had surprised and overpowered Benjamin.

A few more moments passed. She heard another scrambling, then Benjamin reappeared, his coat covered with leaf mould. He stood breathless beside her and brushed himself off. "You'll be glad to hear that he isn't there," he said. "There isn't anything there. The police must have scared him off.'"

She closed her eyes. She was sure he had been there day and night. She was sure if he wasn't there, he was somewhere.

"I looked everywhere. You saw what a time I took."

She saw he needed to be thanked. In a funny little jolt, she saw that meant more than on the surface it appeared to mean. She thanked him and he smiled proudly like a little boy.

Beatrice let him into the hall. It smelt dank, but its darkness was welcome. Her scruple about entertaining gentlemen late at night prevented her from turning on the hall light. She explained to him, however, that it might disturb the neighbours; so, they stumbled up the stairs drawing more attention to themselves with the resultant clatter than they would have done had they been able to see. She'd give him coffee, or some of the Christmas brandy she'd received last year from grateful Mr Holmes, old Mr Holmes, old, grateful Mr Holmes. She hadn't touched it. As they passed Maud's landing, they heard the muted strains of—a Schubert quintet? Yes, a Schubert quintet, coming from behind the door. She craned her ears. "That's where Maud lives," she said. "Sounds as if all's well." "Some people manage quite well on despair," he said. "It teaches a kind of thrift."

She couldn't see his face. She flared loyally for Maud. "I think she had a dreadful, *dreadful* childhood and I know she's had the most appalling rejection from a man she loved." She still saw Alba, but he was translated into something different. It had been the solo cello in the dark. Beatrice was at a loss to describe what this meant so she gave way to puffing up the next flight.

She felt something tentative and shaky about Benjamin behind her. Why did it cross her mind that he was about to kill her? Oh, Freud, Freud, Freud would know. No. Not kill. Teach her how to die? Die. No. Her released mind caught something from his that had a connection with the cello song: it had the deeper noise of an organ in the dreadful registers.

"Things like that teach people to survive," he said. "My mother and I survived the Holocaust," he said. He threw it away lightly there on the dark landing. "My earliest memory is of crossing Poland in a cattle truck. My father and sister were killed. Do you want to know how? And only my mother and I survived. It seems awful that we did."

She switched on the light of her flat having been struck cold at the door by what he said. His face was sad in the weak overhead light, but when he saw her look at him, he made a comic little smile. "It was my fault, you see," he said. "She did what she had to do for me."

Arthur crouched in the black crook of the stairwell. He had gained entrance quite niftily that afternoon in the wake of Mrs Burns and Mrs Yates who came to scrub out some of the flats, the stairs, and the hall.

After they had finished, they had left Arthur—whom they hadn't seen—alone in command of the hall.

It had been a neat trick, not being seen: it added to the fun. Most of the time, he had sat, clenched by the armour of his thoughts, snail-wise and along under the lift of the first flight of stairs. By the time the working population of the flats returned with chops and evening papers and longing for a drink and feet propped before the telly, Arthur had dozed off into that swoon which always stood for sleep in him.

He awoke in the dark to the sound of the voice of Beatrice. At first, he thought, "I am dead and buried." But the lilt in the woman's voice scaled him back into life, and the man's response—more murmured, but nonetheless as happy—revealed to him where he was. "Don't turn on the light, don't turn on the light, don't turn on the light" screamed in his head. Even the thought of light hurt his eyes. He wasn't concerned or in any doubt that he'd actually screamed it. That he'd thought it meant that it was real and that he remained in darkness made it powerful. He listened for the trudge upstairs and the receding voices. When he was sure that he was once more alone, he unlocked his bones and stretched. Three days of sleeping rough had matted every muscle together and every movement distinguished new areas of pain for him in his now-purposeful mind.

He stood and felt round for the Plasticine. He had bought it yesterday—after the plan had arrived—at a toy shop in the market where tricycles and dolls' prams hung outside swept by rain.

He stood now and undid the cellophane wrapper from around his purchase. His fingers worked in nursery pleasure round one ridged stick. He moulded it and squeezed it soft, then with stealth he ascended the stairs and stood there before Maud's door.

What was the noise? Was he in heaven already, had he really died after all? The rolling jump of viols played by angels—oh—seemed to surround. Was it music? It trickled like molten silver through a sieve, burning shining, shining burning, hurting. He fell on his knees by the door and with all the senses of a lover took the Plasticine and tenderly, tenderly pressed it like a mouth on the lock—deep into the lock—then pulled it tenderly away. Tomorrow, he would possess incarnate music, Maud. She would be dead, transfigured past harm. He wrapped his treasure up in the torn bits of cellophane and stole away. He'd get the impression of the street-door lock now, and early tomorrow,

when the mist had risen, he would take the bus to Hammersmith. The Gas Board job had come in handy after all, though
he now despised it. The occasional desperate woman had jem-
mied metres, but the more sophisticated had had recourse to
keys. His workmates whom he shrank from knew and talked
about—of course—Jinty the bent locksmith. Arthur had
wheeled his bike often enough past Jinty's shop. The man had
little darts for eyes and a nose like a weasel's. When Arthur had
been a mere sinner, he had been shocked by Jinty's very existence. Arthur metamorphosed into the ranks of the saved and
was liberated to use whom he chose for his ends. In the wilderness of the fever Jinty had come to Arthur in a dream: a foxy
face inscribed on a golden Yale key. Arthur had taken his
thumb and forefinger and squeezed the key, pinching Jinty's
eyes out. A hollow echoing yell had awoken him with the plan
firmly fixed in mind.

Once he had taken the impression of the front-door lock,
Arthur was filled with weightlessness. He no longer needed to
rebury himself in leaves outside the house. He roamed London
fitfully till dawn.

CHAPTER XV

I was very ill for a long time after Ilse told me what she did, so
ill that I remember very little of what happened. Did he ring
me? I still can't make out whether I imagine he did not or
whether he actually did not. It was a terrible effort to go out to
the shops in case he rang, in case he came. I slumbered as if
drugged; dragged hours out at the window. It was as if all reality
had been chemically changed into Alba. Trees, books, stones
became Alba and Alba himself ceased to be real for me, having
turned into trees, books, and stones. Every word beginning with

"a" became Alba and every word ending with "a" was also Alba.

I became terrified but I do not know of what; and guilty, guiltier, guiltiest when I did not know what I had done.

Why didn't he ring me? He must have known what I had done. But what had I done? What had he done? Had he done it? Did I do what he'd done? Had he done what I'd done? Did it matter that we had done nothing?

Had we or had we not done nothing?

What can Bach forgive me—him? Muscles would not obey my commands. I slurred and fudged notes. My music room had been broached and contaminated. It was as if I sat there in the eye of God, Who watched my suffering with cold contempt. Had I or he done or not done—what? I could not play at all. The gift of my playing was no longer acceptable. There was no rest or peace anywhere.

All the time I thought of the eye of God—the eye of pure God on me. I never believed in Him until He peeled the skin off my heart with the look of His eye, until He saw me, caught me in the act of—*What?* If there was pity in Him, I did not find it, but He, *He* was inexhaustible. He is inexhaustible. The beauty I'd loved in the depth of my meditation on it was as trivial to Him, as valueless as a bangle in His sight, as the squeaking of a penny whistle.

Was I ill or was He there? Who, what entered my veins with the stealth of an embalmer? Did death grip? Surely death cannot be so bad as the silent watching of God?

I am frightened to touch Him or mention Him.

Beatrice wonders why I haven't driven away the man who came. Do you drive the accuser? Over and over and over again—my sin—he kept talking of my sin. My fault. What was my fault and where is the foot of the Cross?

There is one interesting corollary to my story. Indeed, it is really the only interesting thing about it. My reaction to this event is more profoundly confusing than anything else that has happened.

At the end of this time I cannot remember nor forget, I went to see Aileen. I am not sure why I did this. Perhaps she's the only one I know who's left intact. She grows low; the winds don't blow her down and maybe there is something to be said for that.

Like the Mad Hatter and the March Hare, Aileen and Horace always seem to be having tea. The Dormouse in the person of my sister sat on a low stool contemplating the fire. Amy did not rise to greet me. She resisted my eyes, my instinctive lunge of sisterhood, with a faintly contemptuous smile. Amy has Mother's eyes, those brown and saturated irises. She has Mother's quaint grace around the temples; her sensitive, moulded mouth.

Aileen had let me in; she dithered about at seeing me. She always smelt of dry-cleaning fluid and cologne. She and Horace pranced and kissed the air beside me.

I want to kiss someone radically. I want to kiss someone— anyone—to a depth of being. Who has done that for me? Someone, somewhere at base. I cannot understand who has given me such, who has loved me so. Now I know it wasn't Alba, who was it?

Whoever it was, I know that no one should kiss the air beside you. I yearned towards Amy and longed to hold her. "Amy?" She looked at me with a conviction about me which had developed since our last meeting. "You've changed your hair," I said.

I got the vague impression they were frightened of me, all of them.

Oh, Amy, Amy! She wouldn't be pulled by my eyes. Amy?

I used to have fantasies of playing to Amy. I used to imagine that when I did my Wigmore, Amy would be there. She would wait until the houselights were down, and she'd pick her way down the aisle, look furtively at Apollo rising in the niche above my head; then sit, folding her skirts beneath her.

When she had settled, I would begin to play. I wouldn't play to move her, but to knit her together in one whole cloth. She would participate in the music, make it happen, will it to happen, and then it would and I would be beside myself at last, released and lost at last but for the track of her eyes riveting me back to base.

But Amy doesn't even like classical music. Amy doesn't even like me. So who is it? Have I distorted myself so far that I have lost everyone to whom I cannot play? Is it the case that now I can't play I have lost everyone?

"Amy!" I went over to the fire and kissed her. Please.

"Hullo, Maudie, would you like a muffin?"

Why did she look at me like that? What have I done to her? Why should she have mattered to me then?

"I won't have a muffin," I said, but I sat down beside her.

"You look cold," Amy said, disagreeably.

It was then the tremors started in earnest.

"I am cold."

My sister stirred slightly. She didn't move the toasting fork. She was attentive to me. She leaned against one fireside chair and I against the other. Our legs formed a basket round the fire, a fender. They almost touched.

Amy was frightened of me when we were children. Amy? Because Father never hit me, only her? Of the cello? Of my hands that must never be touched or wounded? Of my gift that made me independent of the whole lot of them? That I saw Mother die. (She never knew I saw it. Did she?) That I got more "A"-levels than she? That I pinched her in her pram?

"Can I toast it?"

She gave me the fork. She had the habit of obedience. (Can I have your sweets? Let me play with your doll. I did her sums for her. She was rotten at sums. All this in return for protection. I took her protection money. Ah, yes.) I took the toasting fork from her and dropped her muffin on the fire. It curled and burnt. "I'm sorry," I said. She stared at the muffin as if it were an omen and then at me. I put the fork down and held my knees. She took the fork up again. "Are you on the waggon, Maudie? I am, at the moment, on the waggon. But you don't drink much, do you? It would have interfered with your career."

Aileen gave me a cup of tea. "How are Thomas and Ilse?"

"Oh, fine. Just fine."

Horace is inclined to reminisce. He wears a tweed jacket with leather edges and he smokes a pipe. "I must say, Alba has changed a lot since the war," he said.

Amy watched me with fine interest while my teacup rattled

and splashed tea. I gave her the cup and saucer and she took it from me after a slight hesitation.

"I didn't realize you knew him during the war, darling," Aileen said.

"Oh, yes. Surely I must have told you. We met in Paris, under the most dramatic circumstances, you know." I was hidden from Horace completely. I cannot believe that Amy took pleasure in what she saw. "Seeing Maud's put me in mind of it, but he's probably told you, Maud."

"I don't know anything."

"Well, you know it did give me quite a turn, seeing him at your dinner party, Aileen. It makes one wonder what heroism can do to a man, how it might change and sadden a man. He was in the Resistance, you know. The courage, quite remarkable. Used the music as a front. He played Beethoven to the Gestapo and at one point got old Göring so drunk he gave away the plans for an attack."

"What?"

There was an uneasy silence.

"What did you say? Did you say Alba was in the Resistance?"

"What's so amazing about that? Everyone knew about it. He got the Croix de Guerre."

"Well, I didn't know," Aileen said.

"Modest chap," said Horace.

All she said under the tree. Why? All she said. So easily checked. Why hadn't I checked it? How can you fault the Croix de Guerre?

Why did I keep pressing on? Did I want to believe evil of him? To have believed evil of him would have been—easier? More concrete. Something here or there. Like two plus two is always four and the key of C is relative to the key of G.

"Was Alba a particular friend of Ezra Pound?" I asked. I turned round and faced Horace and Aileen. They pried into my face.

"Oh, Alba was the friend of everybody in those days. Picasso, Gertrude Stein, Casals. I think he mentioned Pound, but he didn't like his politics." Was it true? If it were true, did it matter?

"You know, I've never quite got to the bottom of it why Alba had to give up his public life. There's so much I don't understand."

Aileen leaned on her hand in a musing fashion. "I would have thought you would have understood him, Maud. God knows, I can't tell why he changed. People do."

"Maybe he got tired," Horace said. "Older people often do."

My aunt slanted her eyes towards the fire. She suddenly looked pained and lonely. I wouldn't let her alone. "You never saw him after Uncle George died. He didn't even send you a letter. You were hurt. Don't you remember?"

Aileen looked at her hands. "There was nothing between us, you understand."

Horace drew in his breath. "Everyone was a little in love with Alba," he said.

"Oh, it was Ilse, really," Aileen said.

"Ilse," I said.

A sadness overcame my aunt. She sat and looked far off down into years and I acutely saw her past as being past and real, not a Past as she'd made it up for two unhappy children. In a touching little gesture, Horace took her hand and let it fall again. He smiled a little ruefully; shook his head, and drank some tea.

There was a photograph of my uncle on the mantelpiece. I looked at it, then looked again at Horace and Aileen. "I can't see them ever again, you know."

Aileen said nothing. Then she spoke with some hesitation in her voice. "That's happened to a lot of their friends, Maudie. I wouldn't let it worry you."

I picked up my handbag from the hearth. "Amy, will you come home with me and have some dinner?"

Amy pulled herself back into the recesses of the shadow of the chair; she pulled herself back, her eyes and mind like a catapult, then very quietly, so no one else could hear, she said from back between her teeth, her mouth curling and withering like the burnt muffin; she said from the back of her brain; from years and years and years of bitter experience of me—it *must* have been—she said: "Go to hell, Maud." It seemed to relieve her greatly. Without another look, she prodded the fire. She'll never speak to me again.

I've gone over and over it. If Alba were innocent, then why wasn't I comforted? Why didn't it matter that he did or did not do what she said he did do? I wholly believe Horace. There is no reason at all to doubt him.

Alba would not have sullied his purity with such filth as she said he had sullied himself with.

But why doesn't it matter any more whether he sullied his purity or not?

Surely it is something I have done. It is my fault.

Surely, oh, surely, it is all my fault.

CHAPTER XVI

Beatrice sat on her bed and rolled on stockings. She'd never got the hang of tights. She carefully did suspenders, stood up, then sat down again. There could be no moral uncertainty about this. Moral uncertainty was the uncertainty she was used to. Should she or shouldn't she, will or will not this or that? Should she or shouldn't she choose this or that horn of any given dilemma? Oh, she had been gored enough by mistakes. She saw her life now most accurately depicted as a series of moves, which, when having been completed, resulted in a crown at the last square, and ultimate queendom.

What were you to do with people then?

What were you to do with the grieving head you held in your lap last night whose hair in tendrils you comforted, whose eyes pulled you by gravity through space into the atmosphere? What were you to do when it was no longer a question of mistakes; when it became a question of how much you were prepared to give to an embrace?

Was that a moral or a psychological uncertainty? Was it a spiritual uncertainty?

She craved an objective replay of last night.

She made her bed which was as chaste as it had ever been. She was an early riser; the dawn dawned, inveigling rosy light into the white tufts of candlewick bedspread, into the pockmarks and wormholes of her bureau drawers, into the black filaments of her hair. Light slid over her hands and touched her slip, her feet, her cheeks.

Just how much had she given? Had it been prudent? Had it been wise? She'd weighed, measured, sifted nothing.

He'd been careful enough with her and she with him at first. Her spare living room had seen to that. All that simplicity had drained any Orvieto from their veins. They had sat on either side of the sofa with chilled stomachs and had given nerves away to each other in the tremors of hands and the shifting of eyes. Somehow her airy flat dictated the impersonal, insisted correct behaviour upon them. "Please" and "Thank you" and clearing of throats took place; and yet that embarassment had also insisted, the formality of it all had also insisted upon them a seriousness in their intent to each other. A phalanx of angels could not have been more effective chaperones than the shut, starched folds of curtains, than the polished, bare floor, the steel image of Saviour, the rectilinear sofa, and the cat who meandered betwixt and between their legs, the one soft utterance of life, independent and inscrutably stupid.

What had happened to his importunate ardour? He stammered out dribs and drabs of life story. So she wasn't safe after all to assume he would consume her.

She gave them brandy, but its fire met asbestos in them both. She began to be anxious that he'd leave, bored, or worse than that, put off. She tried to inject a note of casual intimacy into their halted conversation, but eyes and smiles were worthless. She only weighed down, complicated, and made worse the sudden ton of shyness they already felt.

They both fell silent and looked wildly around for help. He tickled the cat; she jiggled her glass.

How many times had Benjamin imagined her flat? It had always had in his inner mind an Oriental splendour. Why had he supposed cushions and rugs? Musk? Was Beatrice a secret voluptuary? He was not put off by the flat, but rather stunned by it. Its severity cut off one line of thought he'd had about her and opened up another. There was something—a vision? a sensation?—about the place that insisted itself upon his mind. Was it peace? Where she lived was deeper than a haven, but it left him wordless and he half-sought escape. Had he wanted to make love to her? He looked at her carefully. He could not bear it; it would be like trampling snow. He knew she didn't know this. She was too breathtaking to touch, yet she attempted to make herself available to him in various little ways that he, but not she herself, understood.

Or did he just want her to be that way?

Suddenly, he was too tired to care. He was both disappointed and relieved that she was out of his reach, and knowing this became suddenly too exhausting a burden to bear.

"Will I see you tomorrow?" he asked. He simply lost the grasp of how he could go with her. In a way, she was like having a work of art you could hang on the wall. You could benefit from a contemplation of it, but there it was—on the wall. What could it do for you but cheer you up with the knowledge that spiritual beauty did exist. Once you took it down and mauled it, you spoiled it and it could no longer enunciate to you a principle.

He's giving up, he's giving up, ohmygod, he's giving up.

"You're seeing me now!" She'd meant to say it quietly, but it ripped out and clutched after him. Immediately, she realized how she had spoken. She put her hands in her lap and blushed scarlet.

He felt her need with a sense of emergency. What was he going to do? Had it been wicked, arrogant to regard her as even a priceless painting?

Beatrice could not understand why her lip trembled and her eyes burst with tears. She looked into the abyss of her own inadequacy and somehow couldn't take it any longer.

Benjamin had produced a number of reactions in a number of women, but somehow never this one. Why was she so vulnerable? What could he do? He hadn't thought her vulnerable. It frightened him to the pitch of near disgust. The ordered room reeled round him as if from an attack by poltergeists. "I can't touch you," he cried. "Can't you see? I can't touch you."

The emotion in his voice might have been the short fuse to her own bomb. "Nor can I you!"

They sat on the sofa looking at each other, both shaking with shock and mutual astonishment. She shook and shook. "I can't touch anyone. No one. No one at all. I'm like you, you see. I understand." The grief behind her words gave edge to them. It pitched and bucketed around her mind, then ebbed into a curious pool of peace.

They were even more startled by the evenness they'd achieved between them. "It doesn't matter, does it?" he said.

"It doesn't matter to you?" She put her head on one side. "Does it to you?"

She shook her head and watched him; she began to get a stride to take him into. It was odd and she didn't know where it came from, but all at once, she saw she had a warmth. It seeped through her. Was it femininity? She relaxed back into the sofa arm and let the sensation of warmth permeate herself. Its abundance spilled out towards Benjamin. Without knowing it, she did have the most wonderful smile.

Could he bear to tell her that he had always been capable of touching others but not her? At any rate, this was only partly true.

What was the real truth?

What was the real?

What. It came. Coldly, sluggishly, spreading and numbing, not the memories he'd already recounted, but their meaning. The little ice-thorn pinched, the splinter of death drove its meaning home where you lived in the splinter and not it in you, foetal, ungrown, sucking and unsatisfied—eternally unloved, unwanted you. Something shrivelled you so you could only love in two dimensions that made interesting patterns in your pale grey frozen sac. And sex was relevant to it only in that it's something that should be done with your whole self which you've never before possessed enough to give.

Benjamin looked at Beatrice with two equal impulses in mind as if his mind had been cut in half. In a most atypical way, he had the instinct to strangle her for knowing. He watched her knowing. He watched her loving him in knowing. And he knew it was true of her too. In rather a different way. Instead of throttling her, he laid his head in her lap. She stroked the hair at the back of his neck while he plunged his grief into her like hot nails.

They shared a physical anguish while they talked and talked and talked and talked and pulled out of each other all sorts of burning shames, crushings, and mutilations. It really did hurt Beatrice so much to hear what they'd done to him that she thought she'd be sick. She told him things she didn't even know she knew. They were bound like twins in a hatching egg.

What sort of bond was it? At about three they had achieved a deep friendship without brandy. Was it a communion? What was it? Their arms tangled about each other awkwardly. They rather rocked each other. They both felt amused at the anarchy in this: that they were doing something, sneaking away from nature somehow in a way both of them knew might be called perverse.

Really, Beatrice couldn't have cared less. It was the first time in her life she couldn't have cared less about what she thought she ought to feel. She couldn't get over knowing him and being known. Why this? Why now? Why hadn't she known that such a person existed? Was it possible that she had lived in the dark and hadn't known that people could love each other?

But she talked about love *all the time*. Was this love? If it hadn't hurt so much, she might have thought it mere delight. Had she known that this was love when she talked about it? It was nothing short of a miracle. Why did it hurt so much? When he left, they only squeezed hands. Was that what hurt so much? That really, really they'd only suppressed nature?

But now, in the early morning, she made tea and thought that her nature, at any rate, was released as far as it could, at the moment, go. Far from suppressing her nature, she thought, she had for the first time in her life understood it—and accepted it. She inhaled steam through her nose and flung back the weight of hair she hadn't yet put up. She drew her ghastly dressing-gown around her. Her flesh felt curiously supple and at ease, though unfulfilled.

Would they ever marry? She wasn't at all sure either of them wanted to. It was enough to know they had time to find out.

She wasn't at all the same as she had been yesterday. Why had . . . ? She decided to stop asking questions. Was Maud all right? Surely she had to ask *that* question. She had the afternoon off. She'd pop down for a moment. It suddenly occurred to her that Maud might just as well pop up. She had never quite left it up to the Mauds of this world to do that. Why? Maud was a person too and had legs. Beatrice was not personally responsible for the sins of the whole world. Why had she thought she had been?

Beatrice thought she surely would see Ben today. She began to panic and draw mental blanks.

He wouldn't. She wouldn't. They didn't.

And she shut herself up.

She switched on the radio. There was a torrent of Brahms. She switched it off again. She scuffed her slippers on the lino and admired her pretty toes. She stopped admiring, out of force of habit, and went to get the post, which was bumf from the BMA. Having played back Ben, she played him back again—this time, whirring him on, stopping, cutting, speeding up, and slowing down.

It was really very sensational—she had to admit that—her year, this year. She had more unconscious fun with her toes. She switched the radio back on, then noticed a letter from Mama in the pile.

"Darling Beatrice, I had no idea Antonio could be so brutal—he made poor darling Tatty cry last night because he was so savage to me over quite a little thing." (Beatrice knew too well the enormity of Mama's little things.) "I know when I'm not wanted. I am *not* wanted Beatrice. I think I'm coming home to you, *cara*, where my real home always was . . ."

"Oh, hell!" Beatrice cried, then stopped her mouth, then started to giggle, then laughed loud and uproariously. Wait till Mama and Ben get a good look at each other—and Maud—if Maud—*and* Maud! Jews and louche women gave Mama the jumps. ("They crucified the *Saviour, cara,* that is what I can't forgive.") Oh, bloody, bloody hell how absolutely funny. How many times a day every day do we crucify the . . . who was after all Himself . . . She stopped quite short and her mind and body—even with her hair down and even in the dressing-gown; even before she'd said her prayers—quaked at the point of contact: the solemn image froze her scalp and pitched her into pangs of love. She dropped the onion-skin air letter to admit what ravaged at her inner ear like the noise that Maud's cello song had made at midnight, only deeper—again an organ sound. But it stopped. She knew better than to try to recapture it. She knelt and there was the sound of silence. It drifted round and importuned to enter, but she was afraid of it. Inasmuch as she could let it in, and with her heart and soul she tried, she was touched with little slashes of joy. Why joyful? She knew none of them would give her anything but pain. Masochistic was she? "I'm healthy enough," she said aloud. She realized it was true. It struck her intelligence with the clarity of a note in perfect tune that Ben had somehow proved that this was true. Didn't she just function normally? She was suddenly red to the roots of her hair. Whether or not he could manage her, it was safe to say that she could manage him in her famished appetite.

It became clearer still that she would not.

Could not betray him.

To himself.

Or

Would and could and wanted

When he could and would want

Her.

They would have to see.

What *mattered* after all to *her* (if she would think of her) was the knowledge she could cope with being all there.

Avoiding pain had been her practised art, her science. How many times had she thrown Molotov cocktails—of opiate—into veins? She could not bear, could not stand the sight of pain. It still, after years of practise, made her nearly vomit to see it.

As if from a long way off and still detached, she saw her own—existential—pain. Or fault? Was it fault? What was the cause? Where did it come from? Was it morbid? What was its meaning? It seemed to track across the desert in a black cloak. It shuffled itself sideways like Cancer the crab, scuttling and alien and only too familiar. Oh, sinister, oh, heart. She deeply looked into her own well and shuddered at the leeches there. Oh, heart, oh, heart, was this temptation or the burning out of—the black night of—? Jesus, God! The voltage of it threw her up and out past stars into the cold pit of the turning of things. No beauty in what is—only is is is. The Love God cold as Cupid in the dark— and she could light a lamp to see? What had she done? Had she come out to see?

Curiously, beneath the pain which mind could only just endure occurred the man with tracts: as when in illness, people babble on, her mind with fixed delirium saw his hunched bedevilled form. Better, I'm no better, I'm no better she horror-stricken saw. Oh, black! Oh, black death-night took her and shook her like Cerberus as terrier to the bone—but worse. I'm worse. And oddly, oddly it was true. Oh, her arrogance, her perky little presumption in face of the awe of the awe of God. Oh, awe, oh, terror through and through had riven prophets? Or was it the jerked meat of sinners? She very nearly expired, torn hair cascading down like tears.

All along it had been this refusal. But what had she refused? She had refuted nothing. Nothing! Nothing of which she could be outright accused. And yet she, bleeding, felt it so.

She shook, she shook, she shook off the experience and went to work. Still, the image persisted. She knew in some uneasy way she was at fault. Surely, it was only guilt at love.

She knew in her heart it was more than that. Her fault. What was her fault?

Yet all the time there was this core of pain she resisted, this insistent sense of contrition she pushed off. She moved down corridors with the assurance of a ship in full sail. The shame of hands, at any rate, was gone. She did not find herself touching patients. She touched them. She did not feel herself smiling. She smiled. All the while, her heart bled and insisted a magnitude on her greater than she'd experienced the night before. It was in a similar area but of a different order.

She looked all day for Ben, but couldn't find him. Suppose she'd said something to upset him. She resisted the temptation to hunt him out, find what he was doing. She was a little crushed he hadn't met her at the gates with bunches of flowers, but she was firm with herself. The peg she hung their future on was the mutual understanding of each other. Of course, he had to have time to work out what last night had meant without the pressure of her presence. The good deal she had to do sapped her of anxiety.

Why did she feel she wanted to be forgiven? Forgiven what? She was so tired she could hardly repiece their conversation of last night, but somewhere inherent in it was the secret of what she'd shut her eyes to.

Something pulled at her harder now than it had done last night. The pain was of the deepest grip she knew. She stood slightly out of breath, by the bed of Mr Newbold, who asked for more and more morphia and knew. Oh, you. Oh, poor you! She felt for him and wondered if he could tell. He did smile. She took his hand.

At about a quarter to three, she had to go. She was drawn, pulled, pushed, impelled to slake her need. For God. She had. To talk. To Him. She was frantic to fill the hole that had been dug with Him. She ought to go to confession first. It really wouldn't work if she didn't do that first. But what to say?

For the first time in her life, she didn't rehearse on the bus. She knew what to say.

If Beatrice had put off going to confession, it had been because she hadn't been entirely sure what to say.

She was now entirely sure of what to say.

What could she say to no face in the dark behind a grille? She said to no face in the dark what she had to say. What she had to say was not bailing blood from the wound. She had bailed and bailed and bailed and the boat hadn't sunk but had been always grounded with the hole of the wound in her heart: always on the gravel she had sat, cleaned then with new freshlets of blood welling and welling again through the hole of what she hadn't said of how she couldn't? wouldn't? didn't love. How she'd accepted no gifts from gentlemen or ladies, no gifts from children; how she'd accepted nothing from anyone; how she'd refused everybody everything always, she'd put nothing of herself in nothing of anyone.

Oh, the wound had been sterile; there had been nothing unclean about it.

However, cleanliness had not been godliness after all.

She apprised herself as sinner for the first time in her life. It gave her one hell of a shock. She apprised herself as sinner not because she had but because she hadn't. It really was quite painful to see in her precious purity a prudery, a pride; in her well-connected spiritual life a cowardice; in her much-vaunted inner life a kind of presumption; in what she called detachment a remoteness from the human race—the human race—why, after all, God had died for what she chose to snub. Had she snubbed it? More gently she saw that she was frightened of it, but had put her fear to use in such a way as to make a greater not a lesser distance between herself and others. Like a quaking, guilty tourist in a Calcutta slum, she had thrown money to the ravening poor to keep them at bay. Oh, God, she'd wanted her conscience left alone! I'll give you anything, oh, God, only leave me alone. Touch me and I'll scream.

The priest was ruthlessly silent in the dark; in the dark. She saw how much she'd wanted commendation for the smartness of her soul; how much she wanted him to say she wasn't quite so wounded as she thought. He'd only sewn her up and left her dry.

Afterwards, she sat in the dark, interior vastness of the church and tried to assemble her mind; then disassemble it. A few wanderers, blown like birds from the rain outside, walked on hushed feet around. Beatrice was vividly present to them. She produced a vital image in the mind of which she was hardly aware: because . . . she sat so still. How effortlessly recollected. She sat so still and meek, how effortlessly still. She sat so still, so stilled in thought, so still, stilled, distilled in calm thought—not thought. She sat so still—stiller than ever, stilled in calm thought.

She sat so still still still—still steeped—stopped between one heart-beat and the next heart-beat. She sat so still without thought out of healed veins' clamour or rushing arteries—so still between one breath drawn and another and another breath barely drawn. She sat so still she communicated stillness.

She sat so still and empty like a cup awaiting wine. Only the rush from sky's caverns sounded on the church roof bountiful around her stillness.

Her stillness was not the gush of feeling better—even for having nailed all faults to the Cross—but that was in part it. All faults nailed to the Cross—made neutral, made tranquil in this outrage of pain—had moved her earth. The earth moved for her into its real axis. She was a lame lamb absolved, directed down into the saddle of her being no more forlorn forgotten. She was well met; she met a smile, not frozen or imagined. Oh, the whole earth shook with the smile. Oh, the whole heaven and earth quaked with the smile not forced or plastered on. Smile not sincere or insincere. Smile not smiled at all but deeply is I am for her, oh, her, for him for Maud for all I am.

She was plunged into shock and deep surprise. It was almost shocking so close—so much closer than the head on her lap, closer than brother-sister-mother-lover ever could be close— even more shocking than kinship or begetting. Why hadn't she known this? Beyond endurance tender—beyond assurance or need for reassurance there—sure—wholesome beyond any means of expression—tender and explicit.

Her heart was eaten alive by love. How often had she eaten love herself with reverent *froideur*. It shamed her to see how He ate—with what courtesy and with no greed or impulse to possession, only a steeped deep love unendurable in its passion for, compassion on, her.

The pain was unendurable—could only be endured by the strength He gave to endure it!

All those sacrifices

All that silence

All that time
All that way.

He'd met her when she'd least allowed Him to be there; when most aloof; when blinded in the worst possible way by self—had been there dark because so humble. She couldn't look.

What had she done to deserve? Nothing. Nothing! She shrugged inwardly in wide-eyed amazement. Had she known it was coming? No. Had she known, wouldn't she just have done her best to stop it? Had humbled her in the worst possible way so she could look. Her clean heart pierced was bloodied by love as if pearls bled. Why me? Why me? Why me? Of all people why me? The union was intolerable and more than flesh could bear. She was dashed to pieces in the shock of His purity; His unstintingness—the flow of tender, of infinite generosity—could not stop giving, could not stop humbling itself to the feet of His wretched beloved who must permit self to be washed with the tragic lovesick tears of God. His yearning for His creatures pulped her heart. So *this* is His agony! So this is His agony! My, their, our unresponse to our flatness, our despising of His desire.

The weight of the jewel joy made heavily gravid her heart. Hadn't He said wait? Hadn't asked watch? Why hadn't she listened? Why didn't everyone? Listen. To this this: in disguise as a poor man; this in disguise as a rule book; this in disguise as a frightener; this in disguise in disguise in disguise as Benjamin or Maud; in disguise as a monolithic set of buildings to be heated, as lectures to be heard and duty to be done whose value permeated all. Disguised because of His creatures' shock and horror and disgust at His wounded, personal, passionate love.

The shock of the jewel love; the outrage of it all. How had she defended herself against it? How He had protected her from the perfection of His intimacy. What couldn't she now *not* give away? Life itself was less than a straw. And what she'd seen was nothing compared to what really was.

She took the bus back to Pimlico. She rather forgot where she was and enjoyed the ride. There seemed to be a lot to see of children chewing gum and sweaty old men. They seemed no less soiled for her vision, but much more solid. She no longer wondered how little she could have for dinner. She rather forgot about dinner at all. On an impulse, she bought some flowers for Maud and couldn't have cared less whether or not Maud would be pleased with the gift or doubting of its emotional provenance. She wondered if it would be at all possible to waltz with the cat and giggled slightly at the notion.

She wondered if Ben would turn up probably late, possibly never; it didn't seem to matter, yet it did. Was he clean and at peace? That was what she wanted to know. She understood now that having confided so in her the night before he must feel ashamed. Why feel ashamed? She remembered all too well why feel ashamed for self. She hoped he did not feel ashamed. He had been in such extremity, it had been almost unendurable to bear with him what he had had to bear. Had she borne? She was no mother but felt delivered. That he had told her had been handsome. It had made them kin under the skin. There was neither rejecting nor being rejected. She was pleased to wait. She bought a pound of steak in case and a bottle of wine but thought he wouldn't come.

What connection with Maudy, stuck in her crevasse without light for life, only endurable in the unendurable God?

Was she touched and healed by the confidence given her the night before and latterly an hour ago? Oh, dear, people do talk best in the night. Do give themselves best at night.

When Beatrice was sure he wasn't coming, she gathered up the bunch of flowers she had bought for Maud and went downstairs. In the florist's they had looked beautiful surrounded as they had been by the grand refrigerated display of roses, mignonettes, and other things forced to blooming out of season. On their own, the flowers seemed paltry—a bunch of white chrysanthemums with little or no beauty. They were cut; one was slightly brown around the edges. Beatrice fished it out and stuck it in her lined trash bin.

The hall, as she descended, seemed to her to be almost unbearably dark and narrow. People's cooking smells leaked out from behind doors. Frying onions and the smoke from sausages were mingled with the faintest smell of stew with too much thyme. Dried thyme and packaged food—she remembered sitting under her grandmother's arbour despising (in her most strict and particular days) *osso buco*. Why had she despised it?

She banged on the light as she came down: her habit had been to save electricity and come down by touch. The sound of televisions tuned to different programmes came faintly through doors. The other occupants of the building were discreet; the volume of their lives was decently controlled. No one trailed garbage through the hall or played a thing too loud. No one spoke on the stairs beyond good morning, noon, or night—a curt nod did.

Maud answered the door. She had a stained and sticky look as if she had been sleeping. She barely smiled, then smiled.

"Did I wake you?" Beatrice asked.

"No—not at all. I haven't been sleeping. Would you like to come in?"

"Yes," she said after a moment, "I would like to." They were a moment hesitating on the threshold. "Are you better now?" was an instinctive question Beatrice forebore to ask.

Maud appeared to have moved from her station next to the fire. There was a pile of papers on the coffee table, thumbed as if read and reread. In the lamplight, Maud looked more subdued than she had looked. Beatrice noticed her handwriting was thick and energetic; she wondered what Maud might have acknowledged in the manuscript.

"I brought you these," she said, handing Maud the flowers.

"Am I ill, then?" She did not quite repel the gift; in fact, after a pause of habitual mistrust, she took the flowers from Beatrice in a gesture which resembled a snatch and sank her face into them. "They're lovely," she said. "I'll put them in water."

Beatrice laughed. "I don't bring ill people flowers," she said. "Doctors never do. I hadn't thought of it before. In fact, I never bring people flowers or buy them for myself although I like them. Silly, really, when they give pleasure."

Maud looked at her without much understanding; her eyes kept returning to the gift. "I'll put them in water," she repeated. Beatrice found it suddenly touching that she wanted to hoard them. Maud went into the kitchen. Beatrice stood in the centre of the room, but not any longer without a thing to do. She looked around. Somehow the trauma of the room was ended for her. It seemed enough to be there: it seemed enough to leave soon. She couldn't think why the room was better; it was not a great deal more tidy.

Maud came back with the flowers stuck in a dingy cut-glass vase. She had taken no trouble to arrange them, but still she kept on looking at them. "I haven't had flowers for years," she said.

They both looked at the chrysanthemums. They did seem nice. They had spikes; their leaves folded over velvety and with charm, they stuck straight up in the water. They smelt of woodliness, almost of Christmas. Maud put them on the table and sat on the floor beside them. The flowers added something to the tone of her skin. Beatrice was conscious that she herself could not sit down on the floor without doing it awkwardly. She sat in a chair and her back did not object to its comfort. She could not resist the notion that Maud was now perfectly well and happy and adjusted and that it was her doing, but that thought had a nasty metallic quality which irritated her conscience. Maud's hands were more still. She looked a good deal at Beatrice, but her eyes' real continuing absorption was with the manuscript on the table. There was something surreptitious about this regard. Maud smoked and peeled a fingernail; her eyes slanting off Beatrice's new clarity of sight. A little moan almost escaped into Beatrice's throat; she did not know but felt a fundamental dishonesty—in Maud?—rather in what Maud had said of herself than in what lay on the table. Was she a woman thronged about with enemies? Had she justified herself to self? Had she failed a final facing out to self? Beatrice closed her eyes unconsciously. What was humanly possible somehow lay before her as being very little. That didn't matter; really it didn't matter.

"I opened up the music room tonight," Maud said.

An inability was not precisely crime. Why think of this anyway when so probably inaccurate? "What did you say?"

"I opened up my music room."

"*Did* you?" Beatrice was not quite sure why she exalted in

this. The reason the room had seemed better she saw at once was for an extra sense of space and light which came from the other door being opened. "Why did you do that?" Oh, if glue held and pots of soup sustained; oh, if cures worked against disease! Had always hoped in that—had she not—in the plain vain hope in the order of mere solutions. Which now she sought, thought as not being so. Oh, not so.

To place your hopes in things going merely better for Maud was not true about her: the depth of human confusion was more appalling than she had surmised or wished to face.

"I thought I might have worked out Alba—myself—what went wrong, what continues to go wrong and has gone wrong by following your advice and writing it all down. My hands failing me made nonsense of my life. My life's failure makes nonsense of my hands. I'm not so sure now whether it's important to understand either. What I can do is to play the cello—at least I always could. I opened the room in obedience to what I can do. It isn't much when you think how much I had pretensions, ambitions towards ultimate . . . truth? It embarrasses me now to say that. I must confess my own emptiness was nothing I'd expected to see."

Beatrice laughed. Maud smiled. Suddenly, they liked each other.

"Would you like to see my cello?"

"I'd like to hear it again." She could hardly bear to remember what chaos it had pitched her into.

"I nearly broke it. Did I tell you that?"

Beatrice went cold with revulsion.

Maud seemed to want her to accompany her to the music room. Beatrice was surprised to see how clear a mental map she had had of where Maud worked. There was only furniture in it: chair, music stand, and cello case—an upright piano and a stool. The floor was carpeted in sisal and the room was painted white. Had she expected tapestries? She was altogether glad there were no tapestries. The room was still an intimate place. Maud stood quite still, but her face worked with mental strain.

"I thought you were going to show me the cello," Beatrice

said. "Come along. Show it to me. It's all right."

Oh, grown-up, oh, sensible in the living room was not enough
here. The girl stood paralysed in a crisis of movement. Deep, hot
tears flowed from her closed eyes. "I can't. I can't."

"Please." She laid her hand gently on Maud's shoulder. She
had not expected this at all. It did not throw her nor did she try
to meet it. She tried to get a purchase on it somewhere below it.
"I can't."

She led Maud back into the living room, but left the light on
in the music room. Maud did not precisely allow herself to be
led; it was more a matter of being got down from an impossible
position. She was still quite rigid and wouldn't sit. "What happened to me? I don't understand it. I don't understand why I
can't understand."

Oddly, Beatrice let go of Maud in some area of herself. She
ceased to control her or want to at any rate. She stood and
watched the horrible cracking sliding tears and accepted them as
being enough. Enough for what no longer seemed to matter.

"What's happened to me? You do know, don't you?"

Beatrice was seized and flushed by having been to see Alba.
How could she have, could she have intruded on privacy in such
a way? Oh, she knew all right, she knew. She pressed the tip of
her tongue to the roof of her mouth.

As if by a link of thought they had, Maud said, "I wish I
understood why I loved Alba and what happened so that I lost
him. You see he was accused of a crime . . ."

Beatrice thought of Alba's crime. She knew she knew. She
thought of Alba's face. She knew she knew what crime. Was it
a crime? It wasn't a crime. But what she'd seen of him was
cold—cold. Should she tell? Would she? Should she, could she,
would she tell? How could she tell the deepest hell of his indif-
ference? Make Maud accept rejection?

She shook her head mutely. It hardly could be borne that the
Albas didn't care. It was in her own flesh it could hardly be
borne that they didn't care. She did not approve or disapprove.
She simply saw no way out beyond telling and that she could
not inflict. A fundamental arrogance would have made her tell

before. Sort out, tidy up, iron, and cure did not make true obeisance to a pain.

Maud stood, hands out, arms out, like something she had seen before. It was an attitude of poverty. It was surely, surely an attitude of helplessness against inner circumstances. She saw Maud, saw there was nothing either of them could do.

That was all right.

There was nothing that either of them could do and still that was all right. She saw that Maud must be left alone; that she must work it out for herself. That she *was* being worked out in some sense for herself Beatrice obscurely trusted.

"Will you stay and have a drink with me?"

Only last weekend had been the hell of being snubbed. "I was hoping my friend would come tonight. It sounds silly to call him a friend. Imagine that at my age." She laughed lightly. It mattered and it didn't matter that Ben might or might not come. She gave Maud a spontaneous little hug. "Really you'll play again. You really will, you know." Maud neither gave in to the hug nor did she push it away. Couldn't she? Wouldn't she? She didn't receive it, but as Beatrice left the room, she startled and reached out after it.

Arthur had found that the key could not be copied from Plasticine stuck into the lock. Arthur had stood in waiting for Jinty's straight customers to vacate the shop—veins jumping and pumping—only to find that locks did not give away keys, but that keys gave away locks. He had got out bank notes to bribe Jinty, who laughed. How to be informed this way with laughter—he had careened round and round all corners both familiar and unfamiliar of Hammersmith and Baron's Court. But the vision had said had said had said. It was more than his trampled mind could bear; he found himself beating his head against a wall in an effort to walk through it. He had to he had to he had to get *in*. Had to—like thirst—had to had to had to. Wilderness was really absolute except the sharp intention; only intention was sharp so that he saw sharp things in the depths of his head. And then from a long way off, scuttling sideways like a crab, he saw the point coming to him on jointed legs. First gripped with deep excitement by the legs, he hardly saw the nose and then he did—it humped and jerked along on legs, crawling sideways: it was a very large screwdriver with a red plastic handle on long humping anthropoid legs. It (the legs and all) was articulated like a scorpion and Arthur felt a squalid desire to grasp it even though it stung. It had rather a dense point and a long shaft. It couldn't stop crawling towards him.

How did he do it, random as he was? As crashing blindly from one side of the road to another, head hammering? But he did— he managed this final practical detail.

An amiable ironmonger sold him the largest in the shop. He rejected the one with the yellow handle. It had to be red to do. He was surprised it didn't have legs, but he forgave it. It was very, very large and that gave him a trickle of pain down his neck. It gave him a sort of straight line to follow down the pavement. He hadn't eaten all day. His skin roughly drank the rain. The more he felt the screwdriver the more it calmed him down. Like a radio thing, it seemed to receive his thoughts. He bought a cup of coffee at Victoria Station, having arrived there at about seven in the evening. He had come on foot. He also had a ham sandwich, then a little walk up and down the platform. He found the trains very absorbing and for quite a while he watched them as if he had nothing else to do. However, from time to time, he remembered what he was going to do and it gave him little shivers of delight that crawled, not really pleasurable, up and down his spine, but like silverfish. He really was waiting for a very deep dark to fall. A foreign lot they were waiting to go to Ostend or Dieppe or Calais—the passengers for the train, that was. He could not see them as people; he jutted his chin up against their being people; but he really did like the mechanism of the trains. Waiting and reading the twenty-four-hour clock with its importance to travellers, its important look of purpose, snapping over minute after minute after minute made the thrill almost unbearably lovely. In his own terms, what he planned to do had extreme beauty.

At last he was an angel, at last detached from body and from human kind: utterly mechanical and masked he was, death-wings well oiled, so engineered and with such fine precision for flight. At 10:00 P.M. he flew, swimming the streets of Pimlico, altogether skeletal for all considerations of anyone's frail flesh dropped off. By the time he reached the square, the patrol car had made its round and swept off to a false alarm downriver. His own hand looked awesome to him as he touched the highest bell. He did not look to see whose bell it was—he only knew it wasn't Maud's.

After a while, the intercom spoke. "Ben?"

"Yes." Once laws of gravity had been breached there could be no surprise at luck.

"I'll let you in." Beatrice pushed the buzzer which released the lock of the big front door. Arthur was surprised at its weight, but pushed it open and made his way directly and by touch alone, fearing light as he did, to the hollow beneath the stairwell. The possibility of being caught did not occur; he was at last invulnerable. He waited there for all to sigh in sleep, for radiators to knock with cooling, and for boards to crack with the contraction of the cold, for final moans and scuffles to subside; for Radio One, Two, Three, and Four to close down and for the "Epilogue." He was alert as a bat and wholly on his radar; he sat quite still, stroking his screwdriver and at one with the dark.

Beatrice was overwhelmed that he had come. She'd so accepted that he wouldn't; it hadn't been a death but a cutting off of something that he hadn't at least rung—after what had gone on the night before. But having accepted, his coming was more bonus than she had looked for. She waited for his hand upon the door of her flat, but when quite a time had elapsed and there wasn't any knock, she rose, opened the door and went out on to the landing. "Ben?" she softly called him in the dark. She banged on the light and went down the stairs to Maud's landing. "Ben?" From behind Maud's door she heard again the sound of Schubert chamber music and that indeed was something.

She banged the light again and proceeded to the lower landing and then to the front door which she opened. She looked out into the night, the dripping trees in the sodium glare. There wasn't any Ben. She went upstairs slowly, not so much puzzled as aching. She wondered who it could have been. As she passed the flat not under hers, but between hers and Maud's on the other side of the staircase, she heard the restrained thud of pop music and a number of raised voices straining at a good time. Of course—a party and how many Bens in London would there be? It had often happened, to her suppressed irritation, the wrong bell pushed. Of course.

She could not help but wonder how he was; however, she drew her bath and as she washed she realized how tired she was. She shook her head and laughed to herself when she remembered she'd forgotten she'd had only four hours' sleep in the last two days and sank profoundly in the tub and smiled.

After she had put her nightdress on, she played for a while with the cat on the rug; its slippered paws caught her hand, she rubbed its stomach and it purred. Alice-wise, she told it about her day. Told it about her friends.

"Oh, my mother!" she cried. She realized she hadn't answered her. She fished a letter form from her desk, groaned at the sight of undone paperwork, wrote an affectionate, peace-making, understanding, kind, loving, and tactful letter to Mama and put it on the mantelpiece. Was it the girl, the man, the church, the bath? Her nerves and muscles both were penetrated with a deep serenity, a drowsiness that bordered on a doze.

She woke up to the telephone.

"Beatrice?"

"Ben?"

"Is it too late?"

"Oh, no. I wasn't in bed."

"Tonight," he said, "we had a change, Mother and I. We played Mah-Jongg."

"Mah-Jongg?" She shook her head and laughed. She allowed her hair to fall over the receiver of the phone in a heap of beauty. She'd forgotten his mother.

"Were you very busy today?" she asked.

"I had two nasty emergencies in addition to what else I had to get through. I felt guilty operating on no sleep, but actually I felt tremendously alert."

They both paused. Neither spoke for not knowing what to say.

"After what I said last night I . . ."

"I didn't want to make you feel . . ."

"I wondered where you were all day. I thought you might be avoiding me. The real reason I rang so late was that I couldn't bear the suspense any longer."

"Oh, Ben!"

"You thought I thought—oh, dear." They laughed.

"In fact," she said, "I so hoped you would come to see me tonight that I bought the makings of a meal for you—and then you didn't—and then a curious thing—the doorbell went and I thought it was you and I said, 'Ben' and the voice answered 'Yes,' but it must have been another Ben. There was a party going on downstairs. It must have been for them."

"*Beatrice!*"

"Whatever's the matter?"

"Beatrice, for God's sake! That man you told me about . . ."

She put her hand to her mouth. "But it couldn't be." She knew it was. "I checked. I went downstairs and *checked.*"

"It's the way burglars get in all the time. My mother is obsessed with burglars and we have the place practically wired up to Scotland Yard."

"It couldn't be. I passed Maud's door and she was playing Schubert again."

"Look, Beatrice, just don't move. I shall be with you as soon as I can get there. For God's sake, don't move. Just wait."

"But . . ."

"Don't let anyone in. Don't—don't open the door to anyone but me. I'll say my *full* name when I arrive, do you understand?"

"I'm sure it wasn't anything." She faintly hoped he wasn't going to be hysterical and possessive.

"I'll be there in twenty minutes." He put down the phone.

She knew he was going to be hysterical and possessive, but she wasn't sure she . . .

She loved the man. His flaws were as charming as cracks in an ancient statue.

They weren't flaws: she was pleased to be protected.

They weren't flaws but flashes of love she couldn't help but gather to herself, even if she could not touch; they were like light.

She looked at her watch. It was twenty past midnight. He'd be with her soon.

Why did she know that Arthur was in the building? Suddenly she knew Arthur was in the building. She sat on the edge of the sofa—it was like being winded with a punch. How did she know? Did she hear? What did she hear? She wasn't sure she heard. She fell into a sluggish terror; her limbs refused to move. Maud? He'd said twenty minutes. Maud?

All she'd do was listen, chain on door at the landing. It was quite hard to move for the torpor. Oh, it was silly. Surely he wasn't there. It seemed to take a long time to get to the door. She opened very quietly and listened. She looked at her watch again. Ben?

Oh, wildest nightmares do come true, they do they do. She thought she heard a muffled stumble float up the freezing shaft of stairwell—no, not—late home. And then the cracking noise of wood. There was the noise of cracking and of splintered wood.

Oh, my God, oh, my God, Maud.

Twenty minutes would be, surely be . . .

Oh, coldest logic told her ten would never do.

A deep revulsion sank her heart and numbed her heart. She fumbled with the chain. It took every strength to open the door; inertia of the flesh reeled her tightly back as the cracking went on. Revulsion pulled and pulled her paralytic limbs to halt—but could not would not leave Maud to die like that. With something like a deep rage (but not) she saw she could not leave the girl to die like that. Not that death, any other one, but that one not.

She banged the light and walked down stairs and there he was. It all seemed so simple. Of course he had been there all along. There he was worming and working away at the lock of Maud's door with a long utensil prising, prying it in, oblivious to light or sound.

Beatrice stood on the stair in an eternal moment of shock. Shock clicked and moved her fluid parts into place. She knew with that absolute clarity emergency gives that she could not go back. She opened her mouth to scream but no scream came. She tried again to scream but she could not. There was only one thing and with a final impulse, with the most complete impulse she had ever had in which there were no questions, she finished the journey down the stairs and dumbly clapped a hand on Arthur's shoulder and thought of Ben and wished that he had come.

Arthur didn't feel the clasp at first. He worked away. He did not feel the clasp. She could not speak. It was all she could do to move hand to his shoulder. Then with curious thaw, he felt her hand's touch. Who clapped him on the shoulder? Wasn't really happening—but all the same, he looked from side to side like a very strange animal with a bone, bone, bone. Looked from side to side to side.

And saw her. There she was. Her black hair flooded down her back and little nightdress open at the throat with maiden touch of *broderie anglaise,* and the throat opened and the face and the hair now opened, and fear in the eyes open and the heart open and all open without any sense of defence, she was.

Curiously, as he saw her, he was never so moved by beauty, never so touched by beauty in his life, never so touched or moved by anything so beautiful in his life. Never was there a creature like this one who was like violets; never was there anyone like this one clothed in white, her eyes wide open and afraid and grave.

Why did he do it? Why did he? How could he do such a thing to her? She almost seemed to love him. Why did he do such a thing? She loved him he was sure. But he removed the screwdriver from the door and in an arc of triumph, a curious glee of absolute pitch, in an arc, in which he was stifled first and struggling, he plunged it upwards through her breastbone.

It didn't go in like a piece of cheese. She didn't cut like butter.

He really had to push it in through rib and muscle case and wall of body to the heart. And it felt so good to do it and it was almost over, but again, he drew it out and again he plunged it in in several different places.

Her face, oh, my God, her face as it did at last release a scream at the wound and flung hands upwards to beat him off, but she fell and as she died, she had the faint sensation of being stabbed again and again and again. The light snapped off.

She did not hear the terrible, terrible pounding of Ben at the big front door or the sound of sirens. She did not hear much but distantly the scream and the scream and the scream and the scream of Maud and the running of neighbours wakened and she faintly felt, oh, faintly felt, her murderer being prised away from her because—

She was rested as after birth and reached the depth down past any deep—the depth of death and drowned—in the deep depth of death, so deep so deep beyond depth, depth beyond all mystery and heart to tell of it . . . dear and deep dear deep death. Deeper dead beyond the cello noise, beyond the depth of river, beyond the depth of ocean deep. Beyond and deeper than the depth of ocean sounding down deeper than whale could ever go: deeper and dearer, deeper and dearer than wounds of love or pain could go, down through the shallows, feet walking down— long and naked into Jordan—down, long naked feet past Jordan's shallows into depth of death to the depth of the depth of the depth of death, past any accusation, past any grave mistrust, past any doubt or depth imagined or imaginable—deep past silence, death past darkness, deep depth deep death past all darkness and all silence—through all darkness and silence joy and all sleep deep joy death dead.

They gathered round her, some crying and some measuring and some holding dazed Arthur, so steeped in blood and wondering what he'd done. And Maud and Ben stood stunned as there were measurements and measurements and photographs with flashbulbs, and sirens, footsteps, questionings, and a silence in all.

CHAPTER XVII

I wasn't sure about marrying, but I married.

For a long time after the murder, it seemed I had to deal with Ben Rose. If ever there was a punishment for her death, it was Ben Rose. I didn't think there could be such grief. I didn't think it was possible for such grief to inhabit one human skull.

There was solace in his not going mad with it.

The time it took to heal! All the time he supposed how important she must have been to me, assumed how much I'd loved her too, when I hadn't. The sacrifice. He kept talking about her sacrifice, but that was only after the funeral when he'd calmed down and started accusing.

He did support me through the funeral. There was no way of avoiding the funeral. He and I were a pair of mourners. I'd never seen a man cry. I didn't know they could. I suppose I was fairly dishevelled. Her family was *not*. I was interested (through the wool of shock) to note her soft, stupid mother, a tragic sister who reminded me of Amy, in formal and expensive black, and an extraordinary number of people quite unrelated to her—people you never knew she knew. I always thought of her as being so alone.

I must say this; her coffin never looked absurd; it was draped in gilt-edged purple as though she'd been a queen, and so many flowers. An odious little woman called Celia something-or-other nosed through the crowd afterwards. She looked so proud of herself. She gathered I was Beatrice's "friend." A kind of crawling tolerance for what sort of "friends" she thought we were crept in. She reassured me (as if she had a private line) of God's mercy. I merely stepped aside to show her Benjamin. "He was her friend," I said. Even she could see a face chopped in half. He just laughed. Not much, not aloud, but it sent the woman packing.

At any rate, he and I didn't march along together for very long. I don't think he'll ever be able to bear another woman but Beatrice. Because she loved me—and this I never knew until he told me—he thought I might do. Because she'd drawn out of me what had had to be drawn; because she loved him, I thought he might do. But we didn't do—anything.

Of course, I had to sell the flat. The scandal of the trial was dreadful, the police absurd and accusatory as if *I* had personally wielded the screwdriver. I got letters from strangers.

All the while, I felt serene. That is the oddest thing about it. I feel I understood her, as if she'd been my mother, a mother, built-on somehow, almost like an artificial limb with nerves, some connecting, some not, but a limb nevertheless and serviceable. She did what she did for me, for herself—because it was the thing she had to do. There's no more guilt attached to that than there is to the scale of C major. It simply *is* a progression of tones. Beatrice simply was—or is—a mathematical fact.

I know this because I have children myself now. I gave birth to them because they needed to be born. It hurt; I cursed, but I didn't begrudge them the pain. It's odd to think of my mother's head being turned for that reason; but then that's what Aileen said, and I really no longer believe what Aileen says. She's old now and Amy's pulled herself right together and looks after her.

Is normality a place for me to be? I touch the sore of Beatrice's Catholicism through my husband and our children. He's a pianist. Sometimes I love him and sometimes I don't. His name is Joseph and his mother is French. They understand distance and regulations. But he has that sore Beatrice had and every time I touch it, I wonder if it's the place I ought to be, away from this metronome normality of mine, away from the merciful dark in which I live where nothing can be transcendent or too great a pain is felt.

I write again because of what happened the day before yesterday.

The day before yesterday, abnormality broke out again.

Let me see, how did the day begin? Joseph was teaching and I sent him off with a packed lunch. There was talk at the breakfast table of an engagement he might get somewhere in the North. Clare went to school with the beginnings of a cold. After they'd gone, I did the dishes and put Stephen out in the garden in his pram. I never did this for Clare when she was little; for years after the murder, I was convinced that Arthur Marsdan would escape from Bradmoor. I had fantasies all the time that he would come and kill my baby. Nobody ever bothered to tell us he'd committed suicide. Joseph, who is continually concerned about my mental health (as well he should be), discovered for himself the man was dead.

At any rate, I had started to put Stephen out in the front while I practised, because the music woke him. Joseph has been so emphatic about my playing again, and somehow, after two babies, I've found that I am able. My sound is winded and broken, but now I've got a husband and children to live for, it doesn't seem to matter so much that it isn't perfect. Joseph and I play together in the evenings, and sometimes with friends. The last seven years of my life I have found severed nerves reconnecting themselves slowly. Gentle people and soft babies have surrounded the gash; I shut the door to the house and call it home. It's in a cul-de-sac near the common. Clare rides her bike there; it has seemed so safe.

Why did I look out the window when I did? Of course, I often checked the pram—put it where I could see—but the day before yesterday I stopped right in the middle of a phrase when all at once my blood ran cold. I stood up, without regard to the cello or the bow, and ran to the window. One may say I heard the gate click or Stephen cry; perhaps, subliminally, I did.

A woman in black was leaning over the pram attempting to lift up . . . The fainting sickness swam—how many nightmare moments did it take to get out there?

As I stood on the step, I saw it was Ilse.

I couldn't speak. Stephen was screaming "Mama!" He clutched his rabbit. "Mama!" I moved very slowly, I very slowly moved out towards him and she turned her head. "Why, Maud," she said. The child stopped crying all at once from all the sense of terror in the air. Why did she have to touch him? I didn't want to touch him after she had touched him. She straightened up, leaving him alone.

All I could think of was Joseph. Where was Joseph? The dishes fell down in the sink; the house broke down and all was razed by her hard heels on the path, her little business black amongst the butterflies and flowers, her hair hooded by a black cloche—I saw at once that Arthur Marsdan had had nothing on her; I rather wished he were alive.

I was transfixed by her. I couldn't move. To see her was to slide six feet into my own grave. There was nothing I could do, nowhere I could go, no way I could move. There was no rescuer at hand. The road was quiet and the common empty. There was only the sound of bees.

"What do you want with me, Ilse?" I finally asked.

She stepped rather daintily up the path, as if she might soil her shoes. Her face had aged, but it looked more weathered than old. She smiled, but not openly.

I thought of Beatrice. I usually try not to think of Beatrice. I thought of Beatrice and touched the sore in my mind. What sore? Where was it? It was so important to think where and what it was. It wasn't the wound in her chest that bled so much, that the coroner described so bloodlessly. Something grasped and touched me. No, it didn't. How could it?

"What do you want with me, Ilse?" I asked again.

Beatrice was good. Why do I cling on to that? Why did I never make the effort before to think whether or not she was good? Why didn't I try to *know* her? She loved me. Why did I suddenly know she was good?

I fled to the pram and snatched up the child. Imagine an eighteen-month-old baby with a look of relief on his face, a look of relief such as an adult would have. He didn't cry, though. He clung to my neck and looked hotly at Ilse. I propped him on my hip and thought suddenly that he and I were in this together.

"What a pretty little boy," Ilse said. "It took me some time to find out that you were married. I had no idea you had children. It is hard to imagine you with children," she said.

I wasn't going to tell her about Clare.

"Did my aunt give you my address?"

"I didn't ask your aunt. Your sister told me."

Of course, Amy couldn't have known.

Amy knew.

"May I come in?" she asked. "I have something to tell you."

"You can tell me here." I didn't want her to look at my things.

She looked at me, lightly despising. "It's a warm day. I've come a long way. I'm not a young woman and I would like to sit down. In fact, I would like a cup of tea."

"Would you?"

"I would."

She did not look old or in need of a cup of tea.

"You can tell me what you have to tell me here."

She looked for a moment at Stephen. "I'd put him down if I were you."

"You mean I might faint."

She shrugged.

"Alba's dead. That must be it. You wouldn't come for anything else."

She made a little noise in her throat and smiled too widely for pleasure. It was a cosmetic smile; it masked a slanted pain I felt come from her.

It risked a lot to ask her in, but I did. Her eyes made no motion around the living room. She sat on the horsehair sofa and took nothing in. She crossed her stylish legs. Stephen lay motionless in my lap. She desecrated my house with her shod, gloved, hooded neatness. All I'd made of it looked poor and absurd next to her.

"Is he dead?"

Her voice was muffled, as if covered with felt.

"Dying."

"Why do you wear black?"

"I've worn black since the death of my child," she said and looked sharply at Stephen. "I always wore black, except in the evenings. I've always worn it."

This was not literally true, it did not suffice. It was not sufficient. I kept fobbing her off round the central point; that Alba was dying.

"What's he dying of?" I kept thinking of a wedding feast. I don't know why or what suggested this. Lots of white flowers and a white dress kept on insisting themselves in my nether consciousness.

"Cancer of the throat," she said. "It's very unpleasant."

"Does he want to see me?"

She laughed. "Goodness, no."

"Then, why are you here?"

"To see what you made of what I told you the last time we met."

"*What?*" I couldn't believe it. "What do you *mean?*"

"I would like a cup of tea," she said again.

"Ilse, I do not understand what you mean." I began to suspect that she wasn't real. It began to occur to me that she was not and never could have been real. I rose with guarded horror, taking Stephen with me, and went to the kitchen where I made a cup of tea. "If she drinks it, she's real," I said again and again to myself. I understood how ridiculous I was being, but I kept on saying it.

She took the cup from me with the command of a gentle-woman and drank. I have saved the dregs to prove to myself that she was there and that she drank. The cup is still standing by the kitchen sink, a relic to her existence.

"Ilse," I said, "are you aware of what you did when you told me that story about—your husband?"

"Aware?" A movement in her subtle face made me see that what she meant by "aware"—what she saw as "awareness"—was different from what I saw of it. She was aware of attitudes, of herself, of the colour of her fingernails, of the night. She was aware of wallpaper and the singular behaviour of people. She was aware of the steam of tea, of how her pores responded to the steam of tea. She had been aware of what she'd done. What she'd done had made a pattern. She had wanted to know; she really did want to know what I'd made of what she'd told me. She had, if you like, a scientific interest in the outcome.

"You told me a lie," I said.

"You believed it," said she.

"I found out soon enough from Aileen that it wasn't true."

"But that didn't matter to you." Ilse put the cup down. Indeed, the tea had refreshed her. She now seemed corrupt beyond bounds. "I thought this had happened, but was unsure. How interesting. I always thought you were interesting. It occurs to me, however, that you might have fled because you felt I'd driven you away, because you thought I was jealous of you or something like that." She flicked a hand; her rings clicked. "I came here today because I wanted to establish with you once and for all that this was not the case. My husband found you tiresome and often told me so."

One can accomplish only a little truth. At length and at last I understood that she did tell the truth and that I was liberated to hear it. For some reason, it came as an enormous relief.

Without knowing it, so deep was I in my relief, I said, "You're the sadistic one, aren't you, Ilse? You were—are the sadist—not Alba. You invented a story of his sadism, but all the time, you were being, and are being now, sadistic to me. That's the truth, isn't it?"

She flushed and gave an unnatural little smile.

"You've come all the way out here for the pure enjoyment of watching me suffer, haven't you? Alba, I suppose, is in hospital. You have no one left on whom to inflict suffering, have you? What would you have done to your daughter if she'd lived— hmnn? It's unimaginable."

Suddenly, her whole face collapsed. It was like a landslide—I knew I had hit—"scored," as Joseph might say. Joseph, who watches people and cricket on the green with interest, might have told me I had struck her for six.

Where did she go? Into herself. She collapsed into herself and vanished—not like the dwarf star I had always thought she was, negatively capable of infinite density—yet not unlike that either. Hand clawed hand on her lap and her mouth twitched convulsively as if on the verge of confession or attack, but her tongue, agile and dancerlike, remained numb and sodden in her mouth. What other wound was she going to inflict and how was she going to inflict it?

She looked at me and she looked at Stephen, who was too frightened to cry.

I became aware, as if a deep gorge had shifted its tactics from its roots, of what had happened to me when I nearly killed my cello, whose face it had been behind cot bars and why I had wanted to expose my own little children to the cold hillside when they were born. And Joseph had been compassionate and had said never mind, and had understood and it had been all right. All right. I became aware of whose wing had brushed me and who had saved me from its ultimate embrace.

I became aware that Ilse's misfortune was mine.

Did she do what I thought she had done to the child over thirty years ago? Why did it suddenly alarm me and why did I suddenly see that she had? Had they gone into hiding? They had. Had they been blackmailed? Thirty years in hiding and both so talented. Except for me, they had seen no one. Only me—the everlasting daughter of everyone. Good Alba. Bad Ilse. How had she survived his goodness? His cold, inhuman, inflexible forgiveness for years and years and years.

Of course, it was nonsense. Utter nonsense. Only my imagination. Except I knew that the black angel passed me over but not Ilse; yet our affliction was the same.

Poor Ilse. I'd given her a cup of tea at least. She'd come all that way in the heat and her shoes were dusty.

Poor Ilse. I put Stephen down and reached out my hand to her.

But either she would not or could not take it, and it never was—not all of it anyway—all my fault.